A Waken

AWAKEN

A Divine Hunter Novel

L.J. Sealey

www.ljsealey.com

AWAKEN
Copyright © 2013 L.J. Sealey
ISBN: 1490552413
ISBN-13: 978-1490552415

Second edition published in 2014

The moral right of the author has been asserted

This is a work of fiction. Names, characters, businesses, places, events and incidents are either the products of the author's imagination or used in a fictitious manner. Any resemblance to actual persons, living or dead, business establishments or actual events is purely coincidental.

All rights reserved.
The reproduction or utilization of this work in whole or in part in any form by any electronic, mechanical or other means is forbidden without the express permission of the author. Your support of the author's rights is appreciated.

Cover designed by: L.J. Sealey

ACKNOWLEDGEMENTS

Firstly, I'd like to thank my family: to my mum who encouraged me to write this book every step of the way and had to put up with me pushing it under her nose every five minutes; to my sister and brother and everyone else for their support. And to my husband who has, on times, had to fend for himself and often hasn't seen me for long periods of time while I've been hidden away writing, I love you.

I'd like to thank my friends for their encouragement and enthusiasm. You really have helped me on this journey. To my 'Breezies' street team, you girls are awesome and Lisa, you've been such a big help with everything. I'd also like to thank my editor Catherine. I really do appreciate what you've done and am grateful for your time.

And lastly, to Michael Warden. You were persistent, I'll give you that. You were determined to get out of my head and finally you did. Now here you are, about to tell your story. Thank you.

"A man plans his course, but
The Lord determines his steps. . ."
- Proverbs 16:9

CHAPTER ONE

October 4th, 2011.
Cambridge, Ohio.

Michael sat alone at the bar with a double whiskey, though he wasn't drinking so much as staring into it trying to establish what it was that had brought him on this journey from Columbus.

Yesterday's newspaper article had read that four teenagers over the space of seven days had thrown themselves from their dorm windows at State Park University. Although the authorities were treating it as some sort of suicide pact, Michael suspected otherwise. People don't just throw themselves from buildings for the sake of it and, knowing what he knew now, he wasn't about to ignore it.

Michael Warden is an investigator.

Not your usual, ordinary type of investigator—like the ones who track down criminals or follow people suspected of having affairs and such—but an investigator of the paranormal kind. Some might say a *Demon Hunter*, a *Ghost Buster*. If only it was as simple as that.

He read the page that he'd printed out from the Daily Tribune's website again to make sure he hadn't missed anything. Then he folded it up and placed it back into his worn, black, double breasted coat pocket. He knocked back his whiskey and made his way out of the bar. It was early evening in Baltimore, MD, and a slight mist had started to settle in. Michael still had a little over three hours' drive ahead of him to get to where his reservation was: a small place called The Sunshine Motel a couple of miles outside of Garrett Co. He'd planned on having an early night so he could make a start on his new investigation early the next morning, but he'd made an unscheduled stop for some food on the way.

He crossed the rush hour traffic and headed towards his car. The dusty, beige, 96 Chevy Cavalier (which had seen much better days) was parked up on the other side of the street. He reached for his keys and was about to unlock the driver's side door when he heard a female voice cry for help behind him. He looked back to see a young woman struggling to hold on to her purse as one of three hooded youths attempted to prize it from her hands.

"Hey!" Michael shouted over the noise of the traffic, loud enough for the youths to notice him as he immediately ran back to help. Two of the hoods ran off, leaving one—who had succeeded in his goal—fumbling with the woman's purse. He looked up at Michael, dropped it in a panic onto the sidewalk, and ran like hell.

"Are you okay?" Michael asked as he passed the young woman her purse from the floor. She nodded, clearly shaken by her ordeal, but instead of staying with her and waiting while the cops were called, he decided to do something about it himself. After he'd visually checked her over, he turned and ran after her attackers.

The group of youths made a right turn down a dimly lit alleyway between two tall office blocks. Michael followed them. A few faint street lights highlighted a row of dumpsters down one side; the heavy stench of their rotting contents filling the air. They reached the end of the alley, and faced with nothing but a high fence which split the dark space in two, they began to get visibly agitated.

"You might as well give it up boys," Michael shouted to them after he realized they were trapped. One of them began to climb up the fence and easily managed to pull himself to the top. Then he jumped down the other side. "Come on!" He gestured for his buddies but they were bigger and heavier than he was and were having some trouble executing the climb with the same ease as their friend.

Michael caught up to them and grabbed hold of one of the boys—now half way up the fence—by his waist and pulled him down to the floor. "Get off me!" The boy shouted as Michael grappled with him before managing to pin him to the ground. Too busy batting the youth's hands away as he tried desperately to lay one on him, Michael hadn't noticed that the other boy—the largest of the group—had jumped back down from the fence. Suddenly a thick arm wrapped around Michael's neck, dragging him to his feet and holding him back long enough for the other boy to jump up, grazed and bloodied. As he did, he pulled a blade from his inside pocket and held it out in front of him pointing the dangerous end right at Michael.

Michael managed to break free from the large boy's surprisingly strong grip after elbowing him right in his diaphragm. He paused for a second and looked at the knife: nothing special, just your everyday Smith and Wesson pocket knife with a three inch blade, but Michael started to back away. There was no point getting into something he wouldn't be able to explain to the authorities, especially as he still had a long journey ahead of him. The boy had obviously seen it as a weakness and lunged straight for him, causing Michael to jump back out of his reach until his back hit a wall, which stopped him from going any further. "Son of a. . . "

The youth never stopped and at the last minute he lost his footing. Falling forward, his knife plunged straight into Michael's stomach, causing him to gasp. His eyes widened with surprise.

The boy looked down at what he'd done and his face instantly paled. Michael saw a moment of panic as he stared straight into the boy's deep indigo eyes. He couldn't have been more than seventeen years old if he was that. After a moment, the boy let go of the knife to leave it sticking out from Michael's flesh. He stood frozen to the spot, his mouth working like a goldfish with no sound escaping.

"Come on dude, let's go!" the boy's friend urged as he grabbed him by the arm. "We gotta split before anyone sees us. Leave him, come on!" That was enough to snap the boy into action and they both ran back down the alley to the street, leaving Michael standing there looking at the knife as blood soaked through his gray T-shirt spreading outwards from the wound. There was no pain, though. In fact, he'd hardly felt a thing which hadn't surprised him too much.

Now all alone in the alley, with nothing but the sound of dripping water from a leaky gutter nearby and the distant traffic noise, Michael placed his hand around the black handle, held his breath and pulled the blade out slowly. It felt strange, not like he'd expected at all. It was almost numb with a slight scratchy, pulling sensation as the cold steel exited his flesh. He dropped it to the floor and lifted his T-shirt to assess the damage. There was now a deep slit right under his ribs on the left-hand side, but he felt okay. There was no panic because he knew he'd be perfectly fine.

Under different circumstances, though, he knew that right about now he would be dropping to the ground and waiting to die from such a lethal wound. He'd already lost a lot of blood and was pretty sure that the knife had punctured his kidney.

That wasn't about to happen to him though. You see. . . Michael was no longer human. The body he walked in wasn't his. Neither was the name he now used. Both used to belong to someone else—a young man. Someone who'd been down on his luck, who'd had no family to care about him, and his misfortunes had led him to choose a dark path. Fortunately for Michael, who now inhabited it after discovering he could *borrow* a body. Which he had many times. This one, however, was more of a permanent thing. After discovering that using someone's body could ultimately lead to their deaths, Michael had managed to find someone close to death, who wouldn't need theirs anymore. So, that man was the reason he was standing in the alleyway at that moment instead of being hauled off in a body bag.

He assessed the damage to his shirt. "Shit!" he said, poking his finger through the tear. "This was my last decent goddamn T-shirt."

* * *

Forced to change his plans and find a motel room for the night—aptly named Comfort Motel—just on the edge of the city, Michael had cleaned himself up in the shower and was standing facing the bathroom mirror, naked, staring at the slice in his stomach. He already knew he felt no physical pain and was stronger than he should be, but this was the first time he'd ever been stabbed. He'd had punch-ups and clashes, of course, that had been almost an everyday situation for him since becoming what he was, but this was the first time anyone had gotten that close to killing him—or trying to, anyway. He hadn't thought about what would actually happen when they did. It was ironic that a human would deliver his first, *fatal* blow given how many monsters he'd fought in the past ten months.

He was quite used to his new, thirty-one year old body by now—even though it was still strange seeing himself with dirty blond, choppy hair and not his own black, sleek style—but he still found it hard to accept that it was indeed him that stared back from the reflection as he stood before it.

The wound had finally stopped bleeding as he examined it in the mirror. His lean, athletic body had been in quite good order anyway for someone who'd abused it in such a way, but was now bigger, more muscular due to his regular steam releasing sessions at the gym. Now, though, he was going to have a pretty decent sized scar which would join the faded needle marks on the insides of his arms from his body's previous host's drug habit.

As he ran his fingers over the small, white scars, he couldn't help his mind wandering back to the darkest period of his life so far: the day he'd woken up dead.

After making a success of his life—good career, lots of good friends and family around him—it was hard to adjust to being so alone now. His success had taken him to places far and wide and it was something he never took for granted. He'd finally been in a place where he'd stopped hating his life, and then one day, someone took it all away from him.

He'd been murdered. That much he knew, though the reason, and his killer, still remained a mystery. With no recollection of what happened, Michael had awoken in a place he thought only existed in nightmares. A place he'd never believed existed at all until now.

Hell.

He leaned his hands on the sink and dropped his head, hating that his mind would throw the sordid memories up to him whenever possible. He hated remembering how much of a tortured soul he'd been down there in the pit—a demon along with the rest of the damned, even though he hadn't been worthy of the punishment, given the honest life he'd led. He had no memory of how he'd died, and no justifiable reason as to why he'd ended up being punished in the worst ways imaginable. But he was also glad that he couldn't remember much of what went on while he was in Hell. All he was left with were flashes of memories of what he could only describe as an excruciating inferno of pain that he'd endured right up until the point when he'd lost himself, as though the burning fire and the torture had finally become too much for his body and soul to bear and he'd simply passed out.

Afterwards, he'd awoken to a different kind of nightmare. The visions of which were playing out right now as he stood in the dingy motel bathroom.

He was back on earth, no longer a prisoner, but not as he once was. He looked down at his body which wasn't real anymore. There was no flesh or bone, just a spectral image that was lost in a parallel world where he had no more human interaction, just ghostly beings who were as lost as he was. Spirits of the afterlife who—for whatever reason—hadn't managed to find their peace either. He was lost, afraid, broken. How could this have happened to him?

He shook himself, determined to push the unwanted memories away. But even when he wasn't seeing them plain as day, they were there, always.

Ghosts and entities weren't the only beings that Michael had had to deal with during his time in that in-between world. He quickly learned that other creatures existed alongside the spirits, creatures he'd already encountered, who knew he was there but would ignore his spiritual form like he was nothing but dust blowing on the wind. But it was only then that they'd taken no notice of him. He'd had no such luck since being corporeal.

The memories of the torture and suffering he'd endured were all that he was left with. He'd tried and tried to forget, but there was no way of blocking them out; so much so that they'd become the reason he hardly slept anymore, not that he needed to, but when he did those memories would become vivid enough for him to mistake the nightmares for a reality that he just couldn't endure again.

His existence was now haunted by vengeance; had been that way every day since he'd been back on earth and the only reason he'd kept his sanity through all of it, was the determination to find out what had happened to him and the hope of catching his own killer someday.

Hopefully soon.

He wrapped a towel around his waist, grabbed his laptop and powered it up at the small dresser by the window. He had quite a bit of work to do, including faking some papers for himself. The best thing about acquiring a dying man's body, and nobody knowing that the poor guy had died, was the fact that Michael had inherited the man's whole life not just his physical form. He now existed, which meant he was in the system. If he was going to find out who or what was causing the students to make like lemmings and jump to their deaths, he would need to get inside the university. He'd decided the easiest way would be to work there. That way he'd be on campus for most of the time and could have a good look around without question.

In his life, he'd been a qualified computer programmer with his own successful business and now having so much time on his hands allowed him to improve on his skills which came in very handy for situations like this. He successfully hacked into the university's database and struck lucky. There was already a transfer in place for a substitute to fill in for someone who was due for maternity leave in three days, so he changed the name and then set about faking some documentation. All he had to do after that was reach one of his contacts—who just happened to be in Kent, OH—send him to find a Mr George Cole, and persuade the guy to take a little vacation.

When he was done, he leaned back in his chair, placed both hands behind his head, and smiled with smug satisfaction that he'd just created a new career for himself in a matter of minutes without a glitch.

After finishing his research, Michael glanced at the digital clock on the bedside table. It was almost midnight. He figured he'd leave for Garrett County at around six that morning so he decided to get some sleep. Not that it was necessary for him to sleep; he needed it about as much as he needed food, which was never, but it passed the time and he'd inherited a lot of that since he'd died. And as for the food thing, well, not needing it didn't mean he didn't want it. He could still taste food just as well as before, so that was a bonus if ever there was to be one in this arcane situation. Truth was, he needed to hold on to as much of his humanity as possible if there was any chance of him remaining sane.

He climbed into the bed and pulled the musty blankets up to his waist, switched off the lamp and lay on his back staring at the ceiling.

The darkness wasn't as dark for him anymore—another thing he'd acquired: night vision. Although the world was more insipid, almost colorless to him, when the lights went out he could still see quite clearly. Great when he needed it, but now, in this quiet motel room, he'd give anything to have that darkness back. Sleep didn't come as easy to him as it used to. His body or mind never tired, so it was now something he had to will.

He thought back to his life and how much simpler things like sleep had been to him back then. Closing his eyes, he thought about how he'd get home late in the evening after a long shift at the office, switch on his computer and work some more, often accompanied by a large glass of whiskey. Then he'd fall into bed and sleep without even trying—another one of the many things he yearned for: to feel tired again.

Wondering what tomorrow would bring, he lay quietly and hoped that sleep would soon take him.

Eventually, it did.

CHAPTER TWO

It was a frosty morning in Oakland, Maryland. The first crack of dawn was peering over the distant mountains, sending bursts of golden red light streaking across the sky to fight away the dark. After Lacy Holloway pulled her front door closed, she paused for a moment to take in the view which was particularly breathtaking on this brisk fall morning; one of the reasons why she loved living so close to the mountains.

Thursdays were usually pretty busy at SPU, where Lacy worked as an assistant professor in the Department of Psychology, and today would be no exception which was why she was leaving the house at the crack of dawn. She had plenty to do before classes started and always preferred to go into work an hour earlier than needed to make sure she had everything prepared for the day.

Weighed down with briefcase and files, she walked to her car and clicked the fob on her keychain to deactivate the alarm and unlock the doors.

Great. The windscreen was frozen solid.

After getting home as late as she had last night from work she'd forgotten to put the antifreeze cover on. She cursed quietly. Avoiding this was the reason she'd bought one in the first place. She went to get the antifreeze spray from the trunk only to find it empty. She huffed, her cold breath creating a cloud in front of her face. Not a good start to the day. She'd have to pop into Jim's Hardware store on the way home this evening to pick up some more and maybe a new brain while she was at it.

Admitting defeat, she grabbed the plastic scraper from the inside of the driver's side door and began attacking the window. A few minutes and two soggy wet gloves later and she was in the car, heater full blast, on her way to work.

One of the good things about heading out so early was the lack of traffic on the roads at that time of the morning which made the seven mile trip a pleasant one.

A ground mist covered the woodland on either side of the road, like a translucent blanket rising from the earth's bed. As Lacy looked out at the long, straight road ahead, the mist-laden forest stretched out as far as she could see. The sky was now a rich, golden backdrop to the tall trees in the distance, its sun ready to peer over their canopy at any moment.

By now the birds would be singing their morning chorus' but Lacy couldn't hear them as she was too busy singing along to Charm, her favorite band at the moment, which blasted through the stereo. It was her usual morning ritual and the best way to wake herself up at such an early hour.

She had worked at SPU for almost three years now, the only reason she'd moved to Maryland in the first place. It was the happiest she'd been in a long time being in the small picturesque town of Oakland, Garrett Co. Even though she was away from all of her old friends she'd settled in well, finally feeling comfortable enough to call the place home.

It had been almost three and a half years since her grandma had died, leaving her house and all her other belongings to Lacy who was her only living grandchild. It was hard for her to continue to live in the house after that because there were far too many reminders of her past. The house had seemed too strange with only her in it so, after battling with her conscience because she knew how much her grandma had adored the place, she put it up for sale. In the meantime a vacancy had popped up at SPU. Lacy applied, got an interview and sailed through it. They offered her the job just after she'd accepted an offer on the house.

For once in her life things had fallen into place perfectly.

She still really didn't know that many people in town aside from work colleagues and only had a couple of friends—none she knew well enough to really rely on—but she was happy with the way things were. Since moving to the states when she was fourteen, she'd always been a bit of a loner. In fact, even before then. She'd moved away from her only parent leaving her life and her troubled mother behind in England to start afresh with her grandparents in Ohio.

Her grandfather had died when she was twenty-two, leaving another gaping hole in Lacy's life. After that it had just been her and her grandma who never got over the loss of her beloved husband and, Lacy suspected, eventually died of a broken heart.

It's as if Lacy was meant to be alone.

She was fine with that now though. Besides, her work kept her busy so she had no time for a social life anyway, even if she wanted one—been there, done that and found it hard juggling the two.

Destined to be on my own. . .

As she ironically sang about there being "*nobody who can comfort me*", she glanced down at the clock above the stereo to check the time and just as she looked back out of the windscreen she gasped and swerved to avoid a dark figure standing in the road. The Ford Focus came to a screeching halt just before the grass banking. Before Lacy could gather herself, she looked back through the rear window, eyes wide, frantically scanning the area.

Nothing there.

She glanced over her shoulder, her heart pounding in her chest so much that it felt like it would burst through her rib cage at any second.

Nothing there either.

"*Shit!*"

She slammed the off button on the stereo and sat for a moment in silence, her heartbeat drummed loudly in her ears as she forced herself to breathe steadily—in and out, in and out—in a bid to calm herself down. She double checked the area to make sure there was definitely no one there. What the hell was that? Had she imagined it? Her stomach suddenly felt heavy and a wave of nausea washed over her. Oh no! Not that. Please. Not those damn hallucinations again. She thought as she reached for the door handle with a shaky hand.

She got out and, after another quick glance around, her eyes checked the car over: everything okay. So far so good until she reached the passenger side where...

Dammit!

Her front tire was shredded.

So much for getting into work early, now she'd have to call AAA and wait God knows how long for a truck to get to her. She had one last glance behind her before she got back in the car and reached over the passenger seat for her purse. She fished around for her cell, called a report in and was told they'd be there within the hour.

She sat quietly playing what had just happened over in her mind. It had happened so fast she'd barely had time to register what it was that was in the road. Could it have been an animal? No. The only animal that could be that big would be a bear or something, but there's no way it could have disappeared that quickly into the forest.

There one minute, gone the next.

A person?

Lacy let out a long sigh. Yes, she thought, a person that was probably only ever there in her mind.

She cursed.

All those therapy sessions were supposed to have worked. *Post Traumatic Stress* her therapist had put the hallucinations down to after many hours of delving into Lacy's past. You'd think she'd have been able to diagnose herself given her profession, but that had never happened, which is the reason she'd hoped that someone else could. Well, it had all been a complete waste of money now. Oh well, nothing that another few sessions couldn't fix, she supposed, then she could look forward to another five years without them.

She rested her head on the back of her seat and waited for the recovery truck.

CHAPTER THREE

Michael had been in Oakland for three days, had checked out the area and done some research on the town's history, but nothing unusual had come up. Getting close to the student's friends around campus and seeing if there was any connection between the victims was the only plan he had right now.

He walked along the quiet corridor of the administration building at SPU. His footsteps echoed lightly as he passed a long row of gray doors that ran uniformly down one side. The sound of muted voices reached him from time to time from a couple of the rooms as he walked by but none of those were what he was looking for.

Towards the end of the corridor, there stood a small wooden table against the wall. Framed pictures of each of the dead students were placed upon it along with various other objects. A pegboard hung right above on the wall with more pictures pinned to it; a memorial of happier times before each of their friends had met their demise. There were also messages of condolence from those who knew them.

Michael read one of the notes:

Dear Emily...
I wish we'd known the hurt you must have been feeling to make you do something so desperate. At least you are now at peace. Forever in our hearts.
Your Friends
Jo and Sandra x

A young woman approached the table and stopped beside him. Her dark, backcombed hair almost covered her whole face, but Michael got a glimpse of her pale complexion and thick dark eye makeup as she threw him a sideward glance before placing a small glass next to one of the framed pictures: a young man who looked to be wearing almost as much makeup as she was. He watched as she pulled a lighter from her pocket and used it to light a small candle which she then placed inside the glass.

She stood staring silently at the picture.

Michael thought he heard her sniffling and decided to step back from the table feeling that this was a moment he shouldn't be intruding on.

He was about to continue down the hall when a tall, middle aged, bearded man approached quickly. "Nina!" he snapped. "I'm sorry, you can't do that in here." His harried expression suggested he was a faculty member.

"Do what?" the student replied in a brash tone.

"The candle. . . It's against university safety rules. You'll have to put it out I'm afraid," he ordered as he peered at her over the top of his narrow rimmed glasses.

The female's shoulders slumped. "Fine!" she said quickly, and blew the flame out. She gave him a sarcastic smile and walked off down the corridor in the opposite direction.

As Michael turned away, he noticed that the man had caught sight of him. Hoping to avoid him, Michael continued down the hall.

No such luck.

"Excuse me," the man called after him. By the time Michael had turned around to answer, he was standing right in front of him. *Jeez! This guy's keen.*

"Can I help you, sir," the man asked, again over his glasses which he seemed to do a lot making Michael wonder why he wore them at all.

"Maybe. . . " Michael replied, taking a step back so he didn't feel so crowded by him. "I'm looking for the Dean's office. I have an appointment."

The man's features relaxed. "Ah, I see. Well, you're heading in the right direction. If you come with me, I'll take you there myself Mr. . . " He waited for a response while holding out his hand.

"Warden." Michael shook it firmly.

"Mr Warden. Ed Wilkinson." He continued to shake Michael's hand while he spoke. "It's right this way."

After eventually letting go, he led Michael down another short corridor to a room with several windows overlooking the outside. "Miss Taylor, the Dean's secretary, will assist you now," he said as he opened the door and walked straight in.

Michael followed.

"Morning Ed," said a young blond haired woman sat behind a desk opposite the doorway. She was well presented, wearing a cream blouse and her hair neatly tied up in a bun on top of her head. To one side of her were two tall, metal filing cabinets and to her right, the wall was covered from floor to ceiling with shelves full of books.

Mr Wilkinson gave her an affectionate smile. "Morning Sarah." He gave her a little wave on his way out and nodded to Michael before closing the door.

Sarah gave Michael a friendly smile as he approached her desk. "What can I help you with?" she asked as she left whatever she was typing on her computer.

Michael noticed her large, brown eyes behind her glasses, the kind of eyes that smiled with her. "I have an appointment with the Dean," he explained. "I've been sent from KSU for the substitute position." He'd never actually been to Kent in his life, let alone the university there, but no one needed to know that.

She tapped a couple of keys on the computer in front of her. "Name please?" she asked.

"It's Michael Warden."

She typed some more. "Ah, yes. Here we are. Please take a seat, Mr Warden." She pointed to two plastic chairs, under the window which overlooked the corridor, and picked up the telephone receiver from her desk. "Mr Raynor, your nine o'clock is here." She paused for a second. "Yes, sir." She then placed the receiver back in its cradle and looked back over at Michael. "He'll be with you in a moment."

"Thanks." He sat down, placing the envelope which contained his papers on his knee. While he waited, he read through some of the book titles on the shelf next to him: *The Hidden Curriculum; The Concise Dictionary of Literary Terms.* The usual stuff you would see in a university. He scanned some more until he stopped on a title that made him pause for breath: *The Remembrance of Death and the Afterlife.* It was hard not to find it amusing, not that his situation was funny in any way. Maybe he should write a book; after all, having experienced it first hand, he should be able to sell a few copies.

The phone made a beeping sound and Miss Taylor picked up the receiver and paused. "Yes, sir." She looked over at Michael after hanging up. "You can go in now," she said, gesturing towards a wooden door on the opposite side of the room. "Mr Raynor is ready for you."

"Thanks," Michael said, then headed towards the door which had a gold plaque on it that read *Dean's Office - Professor Joseph Raynor* in black letters.

He entered the large room which was brightly lit due to a large arched window overlooking the front grounds of the university. In front of it, dressed in a gray suit, Mr Raynor sat behind a dark wooden desk flicking through some paperwork. He glanced up at Michael. "Ah, Mr Warden. Please, come in and take a seat." His office was full of books on shelves that covered the walls from floor to ceiling, except for one wall which had a large oil painting of the main university building surrounded by a heavy, gilded frame.

"Thank you, sir," Michael said as he sat down in the chair in front of the desk.

"You're here for the substitute position?" Mr. Raynor asked, spotting Michael's file containing his *homemade* papers and holding out his hand for it. His voice was stern but polite all the same. It couldn't be easy running a university department, which was evident in his well lined face. He was almost bald apart from a little patch of stubble either side of his head; probably also the result of his work load.

Michael handed the envelope over. "Yes, sir. That's correct," he replied.

"And you're aware it's only a two month position?" Mr. Raynor began to flick through the paperwork which made Michael a little anxious as he silently prayed he hadn't missed anything. He really didn't want to have to re-plan everything.

He nodded. "Yes, I am." It was much longer than he'd planned to stay, but at least it gave him plenty of time should he need it.

"And it's a live-in position?" Raynor confirmed.

"Yes." Michael replied. The university had accommodation for adjunct instructors and lecturers filling a temporary position as they would usually be from out of town. So, Michael would be on campus for most of the time; right where he needed to be.

There was a long silence as Mr. Raynor continued to read through Michael's papers. This was the part where—if he could—he would be sweating as he waited to see if he'd manage to fool the Dean or not, but he'd realized that sweating was another thing that wasn't a problem for him anymore.

After an anxious wait, Mr Raynor raised an eyebrow and looked straight at Michael. "There appears to be something missing." He looked a little put out and flicked back through the papers again as though he were checking he hadn't missed whatever it was.

Michael's shoulders slumped a little. He felt sure he'd done everything required. He'd checked everything over three or four times. Dammit. This was his only way into the university. He didn't have a plan B so if this didn't work he didn't really know what else he could do.

"I'm sorry, sir?" He said with a relatively calm voice, wondering how he was going to get out of it. What could he have missed?

"The form containing your bank information isn't here. . . " Mr Raynor looked up at him. "For your salary? You'll be paid into your bank monthly and our accounts department won't be able to process the payment without it," he explained.

Michael relaxed and had to fight back his laugh. Relieved, he smiled at Mr Raynor. "I'm sorry. I don't know how I've missed that, sir."

"It's no problem. Just ask Miss Taylor for a form on your way out and pop it back into her before the end of the day." He picked up a pen from a leather bound holder and began signing a few of the papers.

"Sure. No problem." He smiled.

"Right!" Raynor slammed the folder closed and placed it down on the desk in front of him. "That seems to be everything. I'll get someone to show you around the department and then take you to your accommodation building as soon as possible." He buzzed through to reception. "Sarah, could you page Miss Holloway from Psychology and ask her if she's free to show Mr Warden around please."

"Of course, sir." Miss Taylor replied politely through the loud speaker followed by faint tapping noises that sounded like a computer keyboard. "Her first class isn't until ten o'clock so she should be available."

"Thank you."

Mr Raynor stood up and held his hand out to Michael, who did the same. They shook hands. "Welcome to State Park. I hope you settle in well. Take a seat back out in reception and someone will be with you shortly." He politely showed Michael to the door.

"Thank you again, Mr Raynor." He said before leaving the office.

Miss Taylor smiled at him as he sat down. The chair was still warm from before.

"Can I get you a coffee or something?" she asked him as she picked up her cup from the desk and headed over to the coffee machine.

"Please. Coffee would be great."

"Sugar? Milk?" He barely heard her ask over the noise of the machine.

"Yeah, Milk. One sugar," he replied. Exactly how he'd drunk it before he'd died.

The slight aroma of ground coffee beans, the same smell he'd noticed when he'd first walked in, had now intensified and he couldn't help but inhale it deep into his lungs. It was a normal, familiar smell that comforted him a little.

After the sound of hot steaming liquid dissipated, the petite blonde female brought him over a steaming hot mug which had the SPU logo on it. "Be careful, it's extra hot." But he'd already wrapped his hand around it and taken a sip of the hot liquid by the time she'd finished speaking the warning. Michael noticed her eyes widen a little, probably surprised that it hadn't burned him.

"Thanks," he said, and then blew over the top of it, only for effect, before attempting to drink more.

After watching her walk back to her desk where she quietly returned to her work, Michael reached for a community magazine from the coffee table in front of him and began to flick through the pages even though he wasn't really taking anything in.

He was pleased that he'd managed to get through the meeting with Mr Raynor, and that he'd done everything he was supposed to, but he had no idea what to do next. He assumed the rest of the day would be spent being shown around, learning the ropes and other things, so was pretty certain he wouldn't be teaching any classes until tomorrow which was probably for the best considering he knew nothing about psychology. Not needing any sleep was going to be pretty handy tonight as he had a feeling he wasn't going to get any. Instead, he'd be spending the night studying for tomorrow's classes.

It will be a miracle if I manage to pull this off.

It wasn't long until the reception door opened and in walked a tall, attractive woman with sleek, long, blond hair. She was tidily dressed in a navy colored pencil skirt which stopped just below her knees and a casual, maroon V-neck sweater. The scent of her perfume followed her into the room, filling the air with a sweet, floral fragrance and. . . apple?

Miss Taylor pointed over to Michael as she spoke to the woman. "Morning, Lacy. This is Mr Warden. He's the new sub filling in for Joanne Hart while she's on maternity leave."

Michael stood to greet her as she approached him with her hand extended. "Pleased to meet you, Mr Warden," she said with a soft British accent.

Michael realized he was still holding his nearly empty mug in one hand and the magazine, he hadn't really been reading in the other. "Uh. . . " He fumbled and then quickly shoved the mag under his arm, freeing his hand to shake hers. "It's Michael," he said politely. "Please, call me Michael." As he looked at her, he couldn't help noticing that she had the palest green eyes he'd ever seen.

"It's nice to meet you, Michael. I'm Lacy." She smiled at him, revealing a perfectly straight set of teeth, except for one of her bottom ones which bent inwards. "If you come with me, I'll show you around."

* * *

After a long day spent mostly sitting in on classes and getting a feel for how things worked around the department, Michael was finally at his apartment building. Lacy had been kind enough to show him around the lecture halls, meeting rooms, and the two counselling clinics that were regularly used by members of the community as well as students; the latter being the main focus in light of recent events. They'd finished up having coffee in the staff room before she'd asked one of her students to walk him to the building where he would be living for at least the next couple of weeks.

Benjamin Hall was one of many colonial type buildings that he'd seen on the university grounds, this one being quite small compared to the others. As he walked through one of the large oak doors, he was faced with yet another reception that was on the left. This time, an older lady with short gray hair stood behind the counter, barely tall enough to see over it. She looked up at him.

"Can I help you?"

"Yeah, hi. I'm the new sub from the psychology department. I understand there's a room available for me." Michael towered above the woman who had to stretch her neck to look at him.

"Name?" she asked as she lifted the glasses that were hanging on a cord around her neck. She put them on and then pulled out a drawer from underneath the counter. Her voice was quite stern considering the size of her. And she wasn't at all polite.

Michael gave her his details and she began sifting through some cards and pulled one out. "Here we are. You're in room B-7." She pointed across the way towards a wide staircase that was framed by a chunky oak handrail and wooden panelling which also ran around the bottom half of the walls. "It's the first floor towards the end of the hall." She passed him a small key ring, which had the SPU logo on it and two brass keys attached. One of the keys had blue around the ring. "The blue one is the key to this building. The door will be locked from nine every evening so that key is the only way to get in. There will be a guard on duty from then, but he's off patrolling the grounds most of the time. The other key is for your room."

"Thanks," Michael said.

"Can I help you with anything else?" She placed the card back in its holder amongst the others.

"No. Thanks. That's everything."

"Very well," she said and carried on with her business.

The large reception area was more like a common room. It was brightly lit and the walls were painted in the university colors: some white, some navy blue. There were a few soft, brown, leather chairs and a couple of sofas to match which had low coffee tables in front of them and there were two vending machines tucked away in the far corner: one for hot drinks and the other contained snacks and sodas.

Up the stairs, Michael walked along the narrow hallway, where the decor matched the lobby, watching the small brass numbers counting upwards on the navy doors on the left-hand side until he got to his, which was the very last one opposite a floor length window that overlooked the university grounds.

Inside, the room was bigger than he'd expected. It had a spacious living area with a black leather sofa and one chair, and a TV which sat on a wooden unit in the corner by a small window. The decor was cream throughout with dark wooden floors. In the corner of the room to the left was a small kitchen area which looked to have everything a person would need: kettle, stove, microwave and an under-counter fridge.

Just next to the kitchen were two doors which, after investigating further, turned out to be a small bathroom with a mirror above the sink and a very petite bedroom with just about enough room for the single bed, which was dressed, and a small closet against the far wall. It was as big as a small apartment which wasn't what Michael expected at all. He thought he'd have a room like the dorm rooms the students usually have, but this was much bigger than those.

Michael noticed some paperwork on the kitchen counter and picked up an information sheet which explained about the fire drill, where the exits were and other general safety information. There was also a list of codes for the telephone, most of which were to dial through to different areas of the campus and a code to dial out which was 09. At the bottom of the list was a Wi-Fi key and instructions on how to set up an account—*faculty only*. In fact the whole building had Wi-Fi which was perfect for Michael's research and would also come in handy for the teaching he had to do. He had no idea how to teach even one class of psychology, let alone a whole term.

After fetching what little belongings he had from his car, Michael had begun to settle in. It was dark outside. Most classes had finished for the day, except for a few evening courses, which meant that the university was quieting down slowly. He decided to take a look around the grounds to familiarize himself with the place and thought he'd start with some food. He still loved his food almost as much as when he was alive and not having a single thing in his new apartment meant that he'd have to eat out tonight.

The fall night air was crisp. The moon bright in the sky with a hazy glow around it and one or two stars had managed to glisten through the light mist that was now creeping over. It was a perfect night for a stroll around the grounds.

He walked across the green and past the football field which was brightly lit with flood lights in all four corners. Training was over and what remained of the team—a couple of players and a coach—were walking across the grass to the exit.

He reached the food complex on the other side of the campus. It was certainly the busiest part of the campus where, he would guess, that most of the live-in students spent their early evenings socializing. There was everything they needed: several food outlets including a burger joint, a restaurant, and one bar— Lucky Seven's, which looked quite large—situated at the end of the block. On the opposite side of the complex was an entertainment building called The Hub. It had a ten lane bowling alley, electronic video games, pool tables, computers with internet access and a shop for school sports equipment.

After familiarizing himself with it all, Michael grabbed a burger from the takeout window at Denny's Ranch: a half pounder with extra cheese and bacon, topped with Denny's Special Barbeque Sauce—no good for the prevention of heart disease. Not like he had to worry about those kinds of health problems anymore.

He sat on a secluded bench on the grass out of the way of the busy complex and watched the students—illuminated by the tall, ornate street lamps that lit up the campus—enjoying their down time now that most classes were out.

He finished off his burger and was thinking about heading back to his room when he spotted a familiar face coming out of the bar. It was the young Goth girl from this morning. The one he'd seen at the memorial table. She was followed out by a boy who seemed to be annoyed with her. While he was still saying something to her, she stomped away from him with her head down. She cut across the grass and headed in the direction that Michael was sitting. Her long black skirt dragged on the floor and now and again revealed her purple Doc Marten boots. Her hair was backcombed into a black, shoulder-length mass, much like how it had been earlier, and her skin looked paler under the false lighting.

Michael remembered her looking at a photo of a young man, one of the dead students, and wondered how she knew him. He stood up and walked towards her. "Excuse me, Miss." She clearly hadn't seen him because she looked up at him with a startled gasp. Her face was glum and he noticed runs in her thick black eye makeup. She'd definitely been crying.

"Is everything okay?" he asked.

"Fine," she said solemnly. "Did you want something?"

"I saw you this morning. You knew one of the boys that died didn't you?"

The girl frowned even more than she was already. "Yeah. Why?"

"I was just wondering how you knew him."

"Why?" she repeated. "Who are you anyway? I haven't seen you here before."

"Michael Warden. I'm new here. . . Psychology sub," he explained. "Someone was talking to me this afternoon about what happened here over the last couple of weeks. It's terrible." He didn't see the harm in lying to her in this situation. After all, he couldn't exactly be honest could he? *"Oh, I'm really a dead person and I believe that an evil spirit may be responsible for your friend's death."* Somehow, he didn't see that going down too well.

"He's my. . . "—she lowered her head—"*was* my boyfriend, Danny." The hard edge had suddenly disappeared from her voice.

"I'm sorry." He tried his best to be sensitive as he could hear the pain in her voice. "I don't want to trouble you. I can see it's hard for you to talk about."

She shook her head and her sullen tone quickly returned as she tried to hide her sadness. "No, it's fine. I mean. . . there's nothing I can do about it now is there? He's gone and that's it." Michael saw straight through it.

"I hope you don't mind me asking, but can you think of any reason why he would have done what he did? Did you know he was so unhappy?"

Nina sat down on the bench thumping her black denim bag down on the floor. Michael joined her.

"No, in fact, he was the opposite." Her voice softened again this time and Michael was surprised when she continued. "We'd both just decided to get a place together as soon as term ended. So, no one was more shocked than me when he killed himself." A tear ran from her eye down her cheek following the trail that was already there. "He didn't even leave a note."

Michael pulled a napkin from his pocket that he'd got from at the takeout stand, and handed it to her.

"Thanks." She sniffed as she wiped her eyes.

"The police are treating it as some kind of suicide pact aren't they?"

"They're wrong," she snapped. "Danny only knew one of the others. Jason Miller. He was in his Chem lab, but Danny didn't even like him very much. He never had that many friends. We don't exactly fit in here."

"And there was no other connection with any of them? Maybe he was involved in something you didn't know about."

She shot him a funny look. "He never kept anything from me." Then shook her head and sighed. "Look, I was the only person who *really* knew him. I would have known if there was something wrong."

"When was the last time you saw him before. . . you know?"

She hesitated. "Two days before it happened. We'd had an argument. I tried to speak to him, but he wasn't answering my texts. I figured he needed some time to calm down so I didn't think anything of it." Her face was blank and there were more tears balancing on the edges of her eyes ready to drop any minute.

Michael felt a little uncomfortable hitting her with so many questions, but it was vital for him to get as much information as possible. "What was the argument about?"

"It wasn't even anything serious. A guy from my English class, Jake..." She waved her hand in the direction of the bar,

"He'd asked if I'd help him out a little after lessons. He was struggling with the course and wanted my help that's all. So a couple of times we went to The Hub after class and I helped him study. It really made a difference, so I continued to help him and have been for the last couple of weeks."

"That guy you were just with?"

"Yes. Danny was fine with it to begin with but he became really unhappy about it all of a sudden. He'd always been a little insecure, but it was never a real problem before. He seemed desperate about it; asked me to stop helping Jake, but I told him I didn't see any harm in it. We argued about it and I told him he was being ridiculous." She dropped her head again and said quietly, "I never thought it would be the last time I saw him."

Michael felt for her. On the outside, Nina seemed cocky and thick skinned with an I-don't-care-about-the-world attitude, but that really wasn't who she was. Inside, she was as vulnerable as everybody else. She just dressed differently.

She reached down for her bag and stood up to leave. "I have to get back and study." Which was just as well as Michael didn't feel the need to upset her any more than he already had.

"Again, I'm sorry for what happened to your boyfriend." He stood and turned to her before leaving. "Will you be okay?" he asked with genuine concern.

She wiped her eyes, which smeared her thick make up even more. "Yeah," she nodded.

"Well, if you remember anything else, or just need to talk, I'm always on campus."

"Thank you, sir," she replied and gave him a strained smile before walking away.

Back in his room, Michael had thrown on some sweat pants, made himself a mug of coffee and was now sitting on the sofa with his bare feet propped up on the coffee table and his laptop on his knee. He had quite a lot to do to prepare for tomorrow's lessons, but, honestly, had no clue where to start.

He flicked through Mrs Hart's notes, which had been given to him earlier that day, trying to make some sort of sense of them but, honestly, they might as well have been written in Chinese for all he could understand of them.

Michael was pleased to read that she was teaching Statistical Methods in Brain and Cognitive Science at the moment, which was also something he knew absolutely nothing about. By some miracle of mammoth proportions he had to know enough to teach a class about it in the morning. He had approximately eight hours.

It was going to be a very long night.

A few hours passed and, after several cups of coffee and a bacon sandwich, Michael was well on his way to constructing his first assignment at SPU. He was surprised, and relieved, at how much information was out there on the internet. The clock in the bottom corner of his laptop screen read 02:14 so he thought he deserved a break and decided to make yet another cup of coffee. Not that he had anything else in his kitchen to make. He made a mental note to go to the store after work and get some groceries. Having nothing to snack on was not helping with his all night study session.

The sound from the boiling kettle was just beginning to die down when Michael heard a noise coming from outside his building. It sounded like distant sirens. He walked over to the window, opened the curtains and peered out. He saw a flashing blue glow rising up from behind one of the student dorm buildings across the green and opened the window which increased the volume of the emergency vehicles. He saw scattered lights being switched on around the rest of the building and the one next to it. It looked like the whole campus was waking up from the commotion. He threw on a hooded sweatshirt, pulled on his Nikes and headed out to see what was happening.

By the time he reached the student dorm building a crowd had begun to gather in the parking lot trying to see what was happening. Some of the students were crying, some seemed to be in shock and one or two were even videoing the scene on their cell phones.

Unbelievable.

Michael squeezed his way through to the front. There were two police cars, lights still flashing, and an ambulance was just pulling up beside them. Officers were ushering the onlookers to stand back including Michael now. He stretched his head to glance around the officer that was standing in front of him and could see a gray blanket covering every inch of what appeared to be a body on the ground. Whoever it was, was dead. Another *jumper* he presumed.

He watched as one of the medical crew pulled back the blanket. A young girl with blond hair lay still and lifeless with her eyes wide open. She was dressed in her night clothes—light blue pyjamas from what he could see—and there was a pool of blood by her head. One of the ambulance crew checked her over only to confirm the obvious and placed the blanket back over her face. He heard sobs in the crowd and one girl fainted across the way from where he was standing. An officer went to assist her followed by a medic. This was the fifth suicide in just over a week and Michael knew that if he didn't find out what was going on pretty quickly it wasn't going to be the last.

* * *

The ambulance had taken the body away and, after taping off the area where the body had been with yellow tape, most of the police had gone. Students had begun to return to their rooms. Most were still shocked and upset by what they had just seen. A few of the officers had stayed behind to get statements and any other information they needed from witnesses.

Michael made his way back to his building.

Before going back to his room, he bought a hot cup of coffee from the vending machine and decided to hang around downstairs for a little while. There was a security guard, a large man with graying hair and mustache, now sat behind the desk watching a small portable TV.

Michael noticed the guard watching him as he sat on one of the sofas near the door.

"Have you just come from the drama?" the guard asked with a deep gravelly voice. He had a strong accent. Michael guessed from the south somewhere—Texas maybe?

"Yes. Were you there?" Michael replied.

"I was the one who called it in."

"*You* found her?" He sipped on his coffee.

"I sure did. I was out doin' my rounds. By then there was nothin' could be done for her, poor soul." He had no idea how right he was about that. Committing suicide definitely wasn't the best thing for her soul. "Cops just took my statement. Makes you wonder what's goin' through these kids' minds. It's gettin' crazy 'round here lately."

He reached over and turned the sound down on his TV. "Haven't seen you before. You new here?"

"Yeah. Just got here today. I'm filling in for someone. I'm only here for a couple of months." That was only partly true. He hoped his investigation wouldn't take anywhere near that long.

"Well. You couldn't have come at a stranger time," the guard said. Then he turned the sound back up on the TV, leaned back in his chair and propped his feet up on the counter.

Michael finished his coffee, which was just as well as the guard was clearly done with the chit-chat. He needed to wait until the heat died down a little over the new *jumper* before asking any questions so he figured he might as well go up to his room and get back to what he was doing before he completely gave up on the idea of studying for the next four or five hours. His first class was at nine and, although he couldn't care less about his teaching skills (or lack thereof), he had to make a good impression on his first day so he needed to make sure he was ready for it; putting it off wasn't going to help. *Why couldn't the position have been for something more interesting like a football coach?* Well. . . he wouldn't be much good at that either.

CHAPTER FOUR

Time had passed quite quickly once Michael had managed to get his head back into his research. By the time he'd finished piecing his class together and gathering up his notes on Statistical Methods and Social Cognitive Theory, his laptop clock read 07:15. He powered down and after a quick shower, rummaged through his only bag of clothes—which was actually a canvas sack, like the ones you got in the army—and pulled out a navy blue shirt and a gray pair of trousers. They were crumpled but clean. Still, he wasn't going to look good turning up for his first day of work looking like he'd just stepped out of a tumble dryer. He looked through the kitchen cupboards and thankfully found an iron and did his best to iron the clothes on the countertop which wasn't easy but he somehow managed. They weren't perfect, but it was a big improvement.

He quickly ran his fingers through his deep blond hair in the bathroom mirror until he had some kind of style before heading out early for some breakfast.

It was already busy in the large dining room situated in the main building to the front of the campus. Michael stood in line at the food counter with mostly other members of staff. There were one or two students about, but not many due to the fact that most classes—for them anyway—didn't start until nine. He helped himself to the various hot breakfast buffet items on offer, piling his plate high with bacon, scrambled egg and hash browns, before grabbing a cup of coffee from the machine and paying the rather grumpy looking cashier. She was an old, gray haired lady who clearly looked like she'd had enough of the job because she'd probably worked there for far too long. He was beginning to think that all the staff were miserable in this place. Well. . . all except one. Lacy Holloway couldn't be included in that thought because she'd been pleasant to him yesterday.

He sat at a vacant table by the far window overlooking the main parking lot and placed his bag—which was full of his research and notes—down on an empty chair next to him and tucked into his food.

It wasn't long before he was interrupted and a pleasant scent of rose mixed with a hint of apple filled his nose.

"Michael? Hi," a pleasant female voice said. He recognized the soft British accent of Miss Holloway straight away and when he looked up, she was standing across the table, smiling at him, her large, pale green eyes smiling with her. Her blond hair was tied back in a ponytail except for a few wispy strands that fell either side of her face. She was dressed in a beige pencil skirt that stopped just below her knees and a black short sleeved blouse, holding a blue file in one hand and a breakfast bar and juice bottle in the other. "May I join you?"

She'd been kind enough to spend the time explaining things and showing him around the place just after he'd arrived yesterday which made him grateful for that and the fact that he felt like he actually knew someone now.

"Hi, Lacy. Yeah. Sure,"

She sat down at the opposite side of the table, freeing up her hands and pulling the straw from her juice box. "So, are you ready for your first day?" she asked as she pierced the little round hole on the top with it and took a sip.

"Yes. I am actually. A little apprehensive, maybe, but I'm looking forward to it." Was he hell! He had no idea what he was doing, but it was hardly the worst thing he'd ever had to do so he'd get through it somehow.

He threw a convincing smile at her.

"You'll be fine. They're really not a bad bunch. I've taught Joanne's class a couple of times when she'd had doctor's appointments."

Michael liked her. She was easy to talk to—friendly, and her perfume made the air around them fresh and comforting. He decided to casually ask about what happened last night to see what she knew about it all, if anything. "Terrible what happened last night wasn't it? That's five all together, isn't it?"

"Yes. I was filled in when I arrived here this morning. I've heard that there are going to be police patrolling the campus for a while." She sighed heavily. "I can't believe what's happening. They're saying it's a suicide pact. Even though we know that these kinds of pacts are usually made because suicide to an individual is so daunting that they can't face it alone, there's also a chance that the victims have no connection to each other. Apparently the local media have been asked by the authorities to hold off printing their article about this latest one. They fear the more media exposure, the more copycat deaths. It's just so awful. "

Michael took another sip of his coffee and then swilled what little was left around the bottom of his cup. He nodded. "Did you know any of them?"

"No. None of them were in psychology. I'm glad I didn't. It saddens me enough as it is and I daren't think of their poor families." She took another sip of her drink.

"She looked young," he said before drinking the last of his coffee.

"You saw her?" Lacy looked surprised.

"Yeah. I heard the sirens from my room and went to see what was happening." He shook his head. "Such a waste of life."

"Indeed," she said, and for a moment it looked like her mind had wandered somewhere else. Then she blinked and looked at him again. "I'm sure they'll get to the bottom of it."

Michael wasn't convinced.

After a short silence, Lacy looked at her small black leather strapped watch. "I better get going." She grabbed her stuff. "I have to finish preparing an assignment. Good luck today."

He laughed. "I think I'll need it."

She smiled at him. "You'll be fine. If you need anything at all just come and see me. I'm in room M103 for most of the day."

"Thanks."

"Bye, Michael."

"Bye." He watched her walk away happy to know at least one person.

He finished up and decided to head for his first class. No use trying to put it off. He had no choice but to get on with it and hope that the day wouldn't be a complete disaster.

He walked along the old, dark corridor of the psychology department. The building on the west side of the campus was the oldest on site and the many wooden classroom doors all looked the same, each with small plastic plaques on them containing white class numbers. He finally reached his room—CS101—and hesitated for a moment with his hand on the handle. He felt nervous, which was strange. He hadn't felt that in a long time. *Get a grip, Michael!* He told himself, clutching his file under his arm. He took in a deep breath, turned the handle and walked in to face a large room full of faces that looked up at him all at once. *Damn!* He thought, feeling like a rat in a cage. *Here goes.*

* * *

Michael was back in his apartment by three.

He sat in blissful silence. He'd done it.

Relief washed over him quickly as he sat leaning on the dining table with his head in his hands. He'd managed to get through it. There were no hiccups, no one had questioned his work and he hadn't made a fool of himself like he thought he would. He'd survived it. No more classes or lectures for today. *Thank God.*

He'd grabbed a coffee from the machine downstairs on his way back and was about to enjoy it when the phone rang. He reached over and grabbed the handset from its cradle on the kitchen counter and answered, "Hello."

"Hello, Mr Warden?" a male voice said at the other end.

"Yes, speaking."

"I'm from Oakley Laundry services. Your suit is ready, sir."

Michael had dropped it into them yesterday afternoon, but had forgotten all about it with everything that had happened. "Oh. Great. I'll come collect it. What time do you close up?"

"Five-thirty, sir."

"I'll be there before then. Thanks very much."

"You're welcome." The voice said before hanging up.

Michael didn't have much but there were a few things he always made sure he did have: a computer, for research purposes; a heap of fake IDs, for when he needed to be someone else; a gun, which he'd stored away under a loosened floorboard by his bed; and a good suit.

He had the rest of the day off so he figured it was a good time to go into town and pick up his suit and get some groceries and a few other things he needed.

Oakland was a small town. There seemed to be plenty of stores, though they were all pretty small: thrift stores, grocery stores, coffee bars, the odd second hand book store and a sports store which sold mostly college stuff.

After picking up his suit and grabbing some groceries from the store across the street from the cleaners, Michael began to head back to his car. He noticed a young man leaning against a wall by the bus shelter up ahead, hood up, smoking a cigarette. As he got closer, the man looked up at him and as soon as he saw Michael he pushed himself from the wall and began to walk away. It was Jake, the guy he'd seen Nina leaving the bar with last night.

Michael called out to him as he upped his pace. "Hey!"

The young man stopped and slowly turned around. His black, hooded top was torn on the arm and his scruffy indigo jeans didn't fare much better. The guy lifted his head and as he stood and stared, as if Michael had inconvenienced him, he played with the piercing in his bottom lip with his tongue. Michael saw another stud in his left eyebrow.

"You go to SPU right?" Michael asked.

Jake flicked away what was left of his cigarette; sparks flickered from it when it hit the ground a few feet away. "Yeah. I've got no classes this afternoon, though."

"That's okay. I just saw you last night with Nina. You were leaving the bar with her, right?" Michael tried to sound as casual as possible.

His eyes narrowed. "Yeah. Why?"

"Well, it looked like you were arguing. Is everything all right? I'm a little concerned about her that's all." Michael explained. He was just clutching at straws, but he had a feeling that something was going on between the two of them and found it a little strange given how upset Nina was last night about her boyfriend dying. It was probably nothing, but it was an avenue he felt he had to explore before he could move on.

"She was just in a weird kind of mood. She's like that. She stormed off back to her dorm or something, I guess," he replied. His voice was almost as blank as his expression. His eyes were framed by dark circles and his skin was pale. He looked like he needed a good sleep, and a long soak in the bath.

There was his first lie. Michael thought. Jake had definitely been the aggressor outside the bar and Nina had been visibly upset by it. Not realizing that Michael had spoken to her straight after, Jake was trying to pull a fast one and he wasn't buying it.

He had to find out if there was a connection between Nina's dead boyfriend and Jake. "You're her friend right?"

Jake was beginning to fidget, pulling the zipper on his sweater up and down. "Yeah."

"So, how well did you know her boyfriend? Danny, wasn't it?"

"I didn't. Look. . . I gotta go." He pulled another cigarette from his pocket, then turned and walked away.

Michael raised his voice after him. "You'll let me know if she needs anything won't you." No answer.

He needed to have another conversation with Nina.

* * *

Later that evening, after Michael had eaten some frozen pizza that he'd burned for himself, he'd decided to take a walk over to Lucky Seven's figuring if he was going to bump into Nina that would probably be the place. It was a modern looking bar: lots of dark wood beams across the ceiling, a dark wood floor, and a large round bar in the center which was lit with color changing panels all across the bottom. Apart from some more of the same panels around the edge of the ceiling, there wasn't much light to speak of. His eyes scanned the place, but there was no sign of Nina or Jake. It was busy, mostly students, and yeah, he felt a little out of place so he ordered a beer and found a corner where he could keep his eye on the entrance and still hide away quite easily.

Or so he thought. . .

"Hi, Mr Warden," one of three girls said, all were smiling, as they passed his table. Students he recognized from one of his classes earlier. He acknowledged them with a smile and carried on with his beer.

About an hour passed and there was still no sign of either of them. Michael was on his third beer and was still sitting alone, even though another one of his students had asked if he'd wanted to join him and his friends for a game of pool over in the other corner. He'd politely declined.

He was about to give up and try somewhere else when he caught sight of Jake amongst a crowd who came walking through the door. He was on his own. Michael sat back in his seat and watched as Jake scanned his eyes around the room, then ordered a drink at the bar. He seemed anxious, looking over at the door every time it opened. There was no doubt he was waiting for someone; could be Nina. Hopefully, he'd find out soon enough.

Another hour soon passed and Michael was beginning to get a headache from the Indie music that was blaring through the sound system: At the moment, some guy was singing about a girl out of her head and staring at the ceiling. It was no wonder half the campus was suicidal. He watched as Jake threw back the last of his Corona and headed for the exit. Looked like whoever he was meeting had stood him up and he was clearly pissed off about it. Michael got up to follow him out and got collared by the girl who'd smiled at him earlier. "Mr Warden, I was wondering if—"

"Not now. I have to go. Sorry." He dismissed her quickly, but by the time he'd gotten outside Jake had gone. "Shit!" He looked around, but there was no sign of him.

CHAPTER FIVE

Days had passed and Michael had seen nothing of Jake or Nina; in fact, things were quiet, a little too quiet. Apart from working, he'd spent most of his time doing research on the internet and finding out who the friends of the dead students were. He'd gathered a list of those who he wanted to speak to so he could see if he could find out if there was any connection whatsoever between those who had died. There had to be something. Even though the cops had asked all the questions they could and had concluded that none of them even knew each other, there still had to be something they were missing.

His research into what kind of creature could be responsible for the deaths hadn't really pulled up anything solid either. A couple of passages he'd read had caught his eye. The website had written about a spirit who causes un-natural death to those who perform disrespectful acts, cause harm, have affairs etc—known as a *Sowin*—but he had to look into it further and unless he could come up with something solid on the students there was little evidence to support the theory.

Damn, he was hitting nothing but dead ends.

He'd had no luck locating Nina either. He'd found out that some of her classes were in the Micro Biology building which was right next to the Psychology department. He'd asked around, but no one had seen her. She hadn't shown for classes for the last two days. He had a bad feeling.

Sitting down at his table in the dining hall at the south end of the campus, he read some papers on *Humans in Biological Perspective*, which he'd printed out from last night in prep for today's classes, while he finished off his breakfast omelette. He had another half hour until his first lecture and figured he needed the extra run through before then. It was funny how he'd settled into his latest role. It was boring subject matter but he was actually quite enjoying being Prof. Michael Warden. It made him feel like he had a bit of purpose for once; like he was still relevant in a world that was very different to him now.

He was about to take a sip of his coffee when he looked up to see Nina walking over to the line for the buffet cart. She looked so different that he wasn't sure if it was her at first. Her hair was pulled back neatly into a slick ponytail, she was still dressed in all black, but gone were the heavy boots and long skirt, replaced by skinny jeans, gray converse pumps and a loose woolen sweater that hung off one shoulder. She had half the makeup that he'd seen on her before and no longer looked like the brooding Goth girl with the heavily backcombed hair that he'd met only a few nights ago.

She looked happy.

Michael watched as she carried her full tray over to a small table on the other side of the dining room and sat down. He contemplated going over to her, but quickly changed his mind when someone else approached her table.

Jake.

He spoke to her and when she looked up at him, her whole face lit up with an adoring smile. Jake sat down on a chair beside her, they shared a laugh and a joke and then he leaned in and kissed her on the lips.

Only a few days ago Michael had seen how distraught she'd been over her boyfriend's death and now she was cozying up to some other guy? The same guy who she'd seemed to have problems with not too long ago. Something wasn't right.

A female voice interrupted his thoughts. "Hey. Penny for them." Lacy stood beside him looking elegant in black leggings with black knee high boots and a royal blue long-length sweater that hugged her slim figure. She was holding a juice box and a granola bar—her breakfast of choice, it seemed; although, how she could function on that little amount of food was anyone's guess. Hell, he didn't even need to eat anymore, but still wouldn't be able to manage on that.

"Hey, Lacy." He blinked, realizing he'd taken too long to answer.

"May I join you?" she asked politely.

"Of course. Please, sit down." As she did her fresh, rose tinted perfume filled the air around them as it always did when she was near. He couldn't help himself as he inhaled deeply. She smelt like spring flowers. Her hair was loose today, neatly ironed into place.

"How are you settling in?" she asked, smiling up at him as she stabbed her straw into her apple juice.

"Good, thanks." He nodded, glancing back over at the two unlikely lovebirds that were now holding hands on top of the table.

Lacy must have sensed he was preoccupied. "Is everything okay? You look a little distracted."

Michael turned his attention back to her. "Yeah, I'm fine. I just didn't get much sleep last night." At least it wasn't a lie.

Her expression changed to one of understanding, like she could relate to it. She gave a small sigh. "Well, this job can do that to you."

Michael nodded. "Has there been any word on the *jumper*?"

"Nothing, as far as I know. They've sealed off the area around her dorm and are still interviewing students. That's about all I've heard."

"Yeah, it can't be easy for the cops. I mean, She's the fifth one now, I'm sure people are feeling pretty anxious." He noticed Nina and Jake getting up to leave. The guy had his arm flung over Nina's shoulder as they headed for the door, both still laughing and joking. Michael's brows lowered as he watched them.

Lacy followed his gaze and turned around to see what he was looking at. "You know those two?" she asked.

Michael shook his head. "No. Not really. The girl, Nina, her boyfriend was one of the *jumpers*."

"Oh!" Lacy turned back and raised an eyebrow. "Clearly she got over that quickly."

"I know, right? Strange thing is, I spoke to her a few nights back, my first night on campus, and she seemed distraught as though her whole world had ended. And she looked completely different too." He finished off his coffee.

"Different? How?"

"Her whole style has changed in the space of a couple of days and she's acting differently. If I didn't know any better I would swear she wasn't the same person I spoke to the other night. And now she's all loved up with that guy, Jake." The more he thought about it, the weirder it felt.

"I'm sure it's nothing. You know what it's like being young. These things happen all the time. You'll never understand it, so why try?" She laughed a little and Michael couldn't help but smile at her. Perhaps she was right. Maybe he was just looking for something that wasn't really there. He would keep an eye on them regardless.

"So, how are you finding it here?" Lacy asked. He was glad of the change of subject. He'd had his head in nothing but this stupid case since he'd gotten here, well that and studying for his fake job.

"Classes are good. It's been a little easier than I thought. I have a couple of lectures today that I'm not quite sure I'm fully prepared for but apart from that, things are going okay." He watched as Lacy bit into her granola bar then wiped away a crumb from the corner of her mouth. She was certainly attractive. Well groomed with striking features which he guessed would turn any man's head as she walked into a room. But it was her smile that he liked the most: it was genuine. He could see it in her eyes and he felt comfortable in her company. He had a sudden need to know more about her.

"What about you, how long have you worked here?"

"This is my third year," she replied, her mouth still half full.

"And I'm guessing with that accent you're not from around here." He popped an eyebrow up at her.

She laughed softly. "Good work," she mocked. "No. I was born in a place called Chelmsford in England."

"So how did you wind up here? If it's okay to ask, I mean." Michael was surprised how eager he was to know more about her. It was nice to be focusing on something other than suicidal students and spirits and all things supernatural. Besides, she seemed comfortable enough to answer.

"I moved over here from England when I was fifteen to live with my grandmother because. . . Well, let's just say me and my mother had a turbulent relationship. It was work that brought me to Maryland; been here ever since," she explained.

Michael picked up his cup, forgetting that he'd finished his coffee already until he glanced into the bottom to see it was empty. "Do you have to be in class yet?"

She glanced at her watch. "Not for another half hour."

"Great," he said as he rose up from his seat. "I'm going to grab another coffee, would you like one?"

She smiled up at him. "Yes. Thanks; white, one sugar."

As he walked away, Michael smiled to himself. He didn't know why it pleased him that she took her coffee the same way as him, but it did.

He returned with the drinks and they chatted easily for the next half an hour after which he realized one good thing: he'd found a friend here.

* * *

Michael sailed through his first half of the morning's lectures and everything had gone well—all but the last one anyway—which he'd had to cut short before anyone realized he had no clue what he was talking about. It was a little after two thirty in the afternoon and he had a spare hour to kill before a scheduled faculty meeting which he was *really* looking forward to.

He decided to see if he could find Nina. She had to be at her classes this afternoon after showing up this morning so, ducking his head down in an attempt to shield his face from the heavy rain, he made his way down the street to the Micro Biology building and headed down the hall. When he reached Nina's class, he glanced through the small square window in the door and noticed her sitting at her desk in the far corner of the room. Everything seemed to be normal as she sat with her head down writing out her work, so Michael decided to wait it out in the corridor until class was out.

Fifteen minutes later, and after reading the same poster over and over again on the notice board, something about a Carbon Sequestration Seminar at eleven in the morning, Michael headed back down the corridor just in time to see Nina walk out of the room.

"Nina? Hi," he said nonchalantly, acting like it was a coincidence that he'd bumped into her. She looked surprised to see him.

"Mr Warden, right? Hi."

Her behavior was the polar opposite of what it had been just days ago: She wasn't hunched over with her chin almost on the floor but the exact opposite. She seemed to have more life in her, a spring in her step. Either she'd had a personality transplant or she was just really good at dealing with grief.

"How are things?" He already knew the answer.

"Good. I'm feeling much better about things. Thanks."

"That's good. . . good to hear," he said. "I saw you this morning at breakfast in the dining room; you were with your friend. . . Uh, Jake isn't it?"

"Yeah."

"Are you two okay now?" She knew he was referring to their little altercation the other night. He waited for some kind of tell in her expression, but if she had something to hide, it didn't show at all.

"It was a little misunderstanding that's all," she explained.

"Good. You two seemed pretty close this morning." He was pushing it with that one and expected some sort of attitude back from her but it never happened.

"Yeah, we kind of are. He's been so good to me through all of this. I don't know what I would have done without him." Her smile looked genuine, and even though it seemed strange for her to have adjusted so well so soon after Danny's death, he guessed it could have been. Like Lacy said: it was probably nothing. "Sorry sir, I gotta run." She began to walk past him.

"Sure. Take care."

* * *

After his last class of the day, and after all the students had left, Michael sat quietly thinking about the dead end he'd walked smack-bang into earlier. He was going to have to start from fresh. He had the list he'd gathered of all the students' friends and associates and would start there, then he'd have to look into the investigation, see what the cops were saying. The authorities weren't treating the deaths as suspicious, but there might be something they'd missed, something that they wouldn't necessarily be looking for that Michael would.

He opened the top drawer of his desk with a small key and pulled out a file, opened it and pulled out the newspaper clippings that he'd gathered since he'd arrived in Oakland.

Each of the victims' names were highlighted in each article: Claire Miller, aged 19; Kevin Mitchell, aged 20; Ryan Willis, aged 20; Danny Wheeler, aged 20; and the latest was Marissa Jacobson, also aged 20. Like the authorities, he'd established that none of the victims knew each other, hadn't shared any classes together and there was nothing similar in their appearance. No connection; just random suicides.

Michael wasn't accepting that. There was definitely something not right. He could feel it.

He leaned his elbows on the desk and pinched the top of his nose with his fingers, heaving a sigh. A knock on the open door caught him off guard and he swung his head around to see Lacy leaning against the jam with a thick pile of folders in her arms.

"Hey. You look like you could use a drink too," she said as she walked into the room.

Michael slowly closed the file in front of him, making sure all his clippings were tucked away inside. "It's that obvious, huh?" He grinned up at her, glad to see her smiling face behind a slender pair of black rimmed reading glasses that he hadn't seen her wear before. "You wear glasses?" Not really a question, more an observation. They made her features even more striking.

"Ah. . . yes, but usually only in class." She removed them as though she felt a little embarrassed. "Tough day?"

"Not the best." And not for any reasons he could talk to her about.

"I was thinking of grabbing a coffee and a bite to eat before I head home, care to join me?" She fidgeted with her glasses before sliding them into her purse.

Michael smiled as he watched a shyness in her that just positively melted him—which wasn't good. The last thing he needed right now was any complications, so beginning to like a colleague a little more than he should was really not an option. But he did like Lacy. And besides that, it *was* just coffee and a bite, and he was in the mood for some food. What harm could it do?

"Sure. That'd be great." He noticed her shoulders relax in that instant.

* * *

Lacy had insisted on driving them out to a small Italian cafe bar called Carlito's on the other side of town, a small place set back from the road. Inside, the welcoming cream and red décor felt warm, and the heavy scent of roast coffee and Italian cuisine made Michael's stomach groan with anticipation.

They were seated at a small table in the corner by the window. The lighting was dim and there was a tea-light in a red colored glass holder flickering in the middle of the table.

This is not a date. He thought as he reassured himself that everything about this was okay. *It's just dinner with a colleague.* He looked up at Lacy, who smiled back at him, the glow of the candle light on her face enhancing her features and creating shadows that made her eyelashes appear twice as long. She was. . . beautiful.

Oh, Hell.

They ordered food and while they waited, the waitress brought their drinks over: cappuccino for Lacy and a whiskey for Michael. He only wished that the alcohol would affect him in some way so he could relax a bit. Even just a little fuzzy would be great right now. One day he was going to drink and drink as much as he could to see if he could actually get drunk at all. But for now, he'd have to make do with sober-as-a-judge no matter how much of the brown stuff he drank.

Realizing they were both sitting quietly, Michael pulled himself away from his thoughts and tried to look a little more relaxed about the whole situation. "Nice place," he said, breaking the awkward silence.

"It is, isn't it? I come here once in a while, nice atmosphere and no students. It's nice to relax here after work." She took a sip of her coffee. "How's life for you on campus then? I don't envy you having to live as well as work there. I think I'd go insane."

"It's not so bad, but I haven't really been there long. I'm not sure I'd be happy with a permanent situation." And it did beat some of the musty motel rooms he was so used to. "My place is bigger than I expected actually. I have my own kitchen, albeit small, and the living area is plenty for me. I'm in a quiet part of the building which is good. There's just me and another sub on our floor and the other rooms are empty. So you see, I can't complain."

Lacy cocked an eyebrow "I didn't realize it was so luxurious over there."

"Oh, it is. You should see the size of the bedroom." *Shit!* He held his breath and shook his head slightly as he realized what he'd said. Thankfully, when he looked at Lacy she was grinning right at him. They both laughed. "I'm so sorry, I never meant for—"

"It's fine. I know you didn't," she interrupted. After that, there was no more awkwardness or silence. The ice had been broken and they both began to feel much more relaxed as the night went on.

An hour passed easily. Michael was feeling well fed after polishing off a large Penne Arrabiata and a tomato and onion salad. He watched Lacy intently as she finished off the last of her tiramisu. "I enjoyed that so much," she said after swallowing her last mouthful and dabbing at her mouth with her napkin.

To his chagrin, he'd enjoyed it too, watching her eat the little slice of coffee flavored, cream dessert. He had to stop it. He grabbed the attention of a passing waitress and called her over. "Another coffee?" he asked Lacy, who hesitated for a moment before turning to the young girl waiting with her order pad at the ready.

"Hey. Sarah. Would it be okay if I left my car in the parking lot tonight? I just really fancy a beer."

Michael spoke before the waitress had time to answer. "I can drive back."

"Are you sure you don't mind?"

"Of course not." He turned to the waitress, "A beer for the lady and," he smiled back at Lacy, "a coke for me, please." Lacy mouthed the word thank you so he waved his hand in dismissal, "I was fed up of the whiskey anyway."

The rest of the evening consisted of more drinks and plenty of conversation. Michael had done a good job of keeping it mostly about Lacy, wanting to know more about her and her life and figuring now was as good a time as any. Luckily she didn't mind and, to his surprise, she was actually quite open about things. How her life had been since moving to Maryland, even past relationships. She spoke more about her mother and how they'd never really seen eye to eye, which is why she'd come to live with her Grandmother in the first place. She told him how her mother cared more about her job than anything else and she couldn't stand it anymore. He was quite content to leave her to do all the talking and was sitting back in his chair, pleased that he'd managed to avoid her asking any questions about him.

Until. . .

"So, how about you?" Lacy said, catching him off guard for a second. "You must miss your family when you work away like this."

He should have expected it, been more prepared for it, but the truth was, he was so fixed on listening to the soft tone of Lacy's voice that he hadn't really been paying attention to everything she'd said. He cleared his throat, buying himself time to prepare his answer which shouldn't have been a problem. Lying was a big part of his existence now and it usually came naturally to him. But somehow, now that he was sitting in front of her, it didn't feel right.

"I'm actually kind of a loner." Wasn't a lie. So far, so good.

Lacy's eyebrows lowered. "Oh. . . I don't believe that."

"It's true, honestly. I don't have any family around and I'm an only child. So. . . yeah, just me." He said it matter-of-factly as though it didn't bother him and the truth was it didn't anymore, not really. Perhaps it was just because he'd been so wrapped up in his quest to find whoever had killed him that loneliness no longer played a part in his existence. Or maybe he just hadn't allowed it to.

"Okay then. . . Girlfriend?"

He grinned and shook his head. "No."

"Um. . . Boyfriend?"

His eyes widened and so did hers. "No! Definitely not my thing." He could have sworn she looked relieved for a moment. She took another swig from her bottle of beer.

"What about friends then? You must know someone."

Michael inhaled deeply, pleased that the four beers she'd drunk had given her more courage and that it had somehow made her think that she was hosting an episode of *Twenty Questions*. He was strangely amused by it nonetheless. "Just work colleagues mainly."

Her shoulders slumped and her tone of voice changed to something slightly more dejected than before. "I'm sorry to hear that. It must be bloody miserable being on your own."

He smiled. "It's really okay," he said reassuringly, wanting the silly, relaxed, slightly drunk Lacy back even if it did mean more questions. "I have plenty of work to do to keep me occupied. I don't have time to feel alone." Thank God that seemed to lighten the atmosphere again.

Lacy sat upright, her mouth curling up into a warm smile. "Well, Michael, in Oakland you have a friend." She held her hand out to him over the table. He shook it and hesitated before letting go.

"I think I can live with that."

As the evening went on, and the place filled with diners at the tables and drinkers at the bar, Michael had managed to switch the subject back to Lacy. She was pretty tipsy and he didn't even need to ask questions anymore; information was just pouring out of her and he found it hard to keep a straight face. He sat listening to her talk about her ex fiancé, Simon, who'd had an affair for over a year with a colleague from his work. She'd only found out about it because she'd become friends with a woman at her weekly spinning class; neither of them knowing that they were seeing the same guy until they went for coffee one afternoon, and her friend had pulled a picture of Lacy's fiancé from her wallet claiming him to be her long term boyfriend.

"I seem to be as unlucky with men as my wonderful mother is. . . " She went on, getting more and more animated much to Michael's amusement. In fact, he wasn't even sure what she was saying anymore. He was lost in his thoughts. What was it about the tone of her voice that warmed him so much? He felt like he could listen to her talk forever. She was fascinating to him and he couldn't help feeling a connection between them that maybe they both shared. They seemed to have at least one significant thing in common: they were both alone.

Instead of listening to her talk, he studied her face, noticing how smooth her skin was. Her large green eyes looked darker in the soft hue of the candle light. Then he realized what he was doing and snapped himself back to a reality he needed to make damn sure he clung on to.

". . . and thinks it's acceptable for a forty seven year old woman to date a man who's four years younger than her own daughter—"

Michael leant his mouth on his hand and tried to stifle his laugh.

Lacy blinked and focused her eyes on him. "Oh dear, I'm waffling aren't I?" Her words were beginning to slur a little. "And you haven't spoken for a very long time."

"I'm enjoying listening," he said before asking for the bill from the passing waiter, "but I do think I should get you home."

"I think you're right." Lacy began to rummage through her purse as though she'd lost something. Michael stood and reached for her jacket from the back of the chair and retrieved her car keys from one of the pockets.

"Are these what you're looking for?" He grinned, dangling them from is finger.

She reached for them. "Yes. Thank you—"

Michael snapped them away. "I'm driving remember?"

"Yes. Of course you are."

Michael helped her into her coat.

* * *

Luckily, Lacy was just about sober enough to remember how to get to her house. With only a couple of wrong turns along the way—and plenty of laughs about it—Michael eventually pulled into the driveway of her quaint, one story home in a small suburb just on the edge of town. He got out and hurried to the other side of the car to help her.

She giggled as he took hold of her arm to steady her. "Quite the gentlemen aren't you?"

"Just don't want you falling on my watch," he replied as he guided her from the car to the front door. She rooted through her purse for her house keys under the glow of the porch light, cursing under her breath until she finally pulled them out and attempted to unlock the door. Michael assisted.

"Are you going to be okay?" he asked as she stepped inside and turned to face him.

"Yes, I'll be fine. I'm feeling a little dizzy, that's all." She brushed a stray hair from in front of her eye and tucked it behind her ear. "I had fun tonight." She smiled.

"Me too. Good night Lacy." He began to walk away down the narrow garden path which cut across the grass. The crisp fall air left his mouth on a cloudy exhale as he prepared for his brisk walk back to campus; the walk that would clear his head and bring him crashing back down to reality as he berated himself for nearly letting his feelings rule him for the very first time since he'd been Michael Warden. He was about to unhook the small gate when Lacy shouted from behind him.

"Wait!"

He turned back to see her still standing in the open doorway, the glow from the hall light silhouetting her slim frame.

"How will you get back?" she asked as she took a couple of steps towards him.

He held his hands out and looked up at the clear night sky. "It's a great evening. I'll walk."

"But it's right across town."

"I'll hail a cab or something. Don't worry about me, I'll be fine." Again, he went to open the gate.

"Why don't you stay here?" His hand froze on the catch at the same time his breath caught. *No. Definitely not a good idea.* He turned back to face her as she started to walk towards him. "Look. . . I have a spare comforter. You can sleep on the sof—" She stumbled, but Michael hurried and managed to catch her by her arm.

"Are you okay?" He couldn't help laughing.

"Whoa! I may need coffee." She held her hand to her head as if that would stop it spinning. "I'm okay, really. So, what do you say? It's the least I can do after leaving you stranded."

It would *be much easier.* And they could both travel to work together in the morning. But he really shouldn't, not after the way his mind had been working back at Carlito's. He should be spending less time around her now not spending the night. "I, ah. . . I really should go."

Lacy tilted her head to the side and smiled. "It's just a sofa."

He exhaled sharply. Yes. She was right. It *was* just a sofa. What was he thinking? "Okay. But only if you're sure."

Lacy linked her arm through his and pulled him back towards the house. "Of course I am."

* * *

"Michael."

A soft voice pulled him out of his slumber and caused him to bolt upright. He rubbed at his eyes and as he did, he heard a sudden gasp.

"I'm sorry I didn't mean to startle you." That same voice said. He looked up to see Lacy with a plate in one hand and the other covering her eyes.

"What..?" He looked down. "Oh. *Shit!* Sorry." He cursed again as he realized his boxers weren't quite doing their job properly. He quickly pulled the comforter over his lap. He must have kicked it off in his confusion. "Panic over," he assured Lacy, who looked through a little gap in her fingers before removing her hand. Michael smiled coyly. "Sorry about that."

She shook her head quickly; cheeks lightly flushed and, thankfully, carried on as though nothing had happened. "I made breakfast; my lame attempt at an apology for last night."

She handed him the plate of freshly cooked pancakes smothered with syrup. Her cheeks were still a little pink and she looked fresh like she'd been awake for hours. Her hair was tied back from her face and she was wearing gray colored trousers and a slim purple turtleneck top. She always presented herself well.

"Thanks. But you don't have to apologize." He tucked into his pancakes. Man, they tasted good. He noticed her eyes flick down to his naked chest and she quickly blinked and turned away. He smiled.

"Yes. I really do. I have no idea what came over me." She walked over to the ornately carved wooden fireplace and leant her arm on the top. "I hardly ever drink, but I think I drank more last night than I have in a whole year. I don't do that. It was rude, and I'm sorry." She paced across the room, towards the window this time, squeezing her fingers together. "I can't begin to tell you how embarr —"

"Lacy," he interrupted. She turned and looked at him. "Quit apologizing. And would you keep still?" It was more an order than a request but she was about to wear a path in the carpet.

She plunked herself in the chair opposite him and sat quietly.

"I actually really enjoyed myself last night," he told her and he meant it too. He was so used to being on his own—and if he wasn't, he was hanging with mostly dead people—that he hadn't realized he could still be sociable. Last night, for those few hours with Lacy, he hadn't thought about what he was or what he was really doing here in Oakland. It was a welcome relief.

She raised an eyebrow. "Really?"

"Are you kidding me? Great food, great company. . . Why wouldn't I?" He stuffed the last fork full of pancakes into his mouth after making sure he used it to scoop all the rest of the syrup off the plate first.

Lacy laughed a little. "Yeah. I enjoyed it too." She smiled at him then, "Oh no," she groaned, her face disappearing behind her hands. Michael looked down at himself again just to be sure. Yes, comforter still in place. "I told you about Simon, didn't I?" She looked over at him, her face full of apology.

He couldn't hold back his laugh. "Yeah, you did. And for the record. . . He's a complete jerk!"

CHAPTER SIX

"**O**kay, don't forget your assignments need to be in by the end of this week."

Lacy raised her voice to her hurried students as they left the class. She packed up her files from her desk, relieved that she had a couple of hours before the next lecture. It was a little after one in the afternoon and her stomach grumbled loudly, reminding her that she'd hardly eaten a thing since leaving the house with Michael that morning. A piece of fruit wasn't sufficient enough for a day's work, especially with the day she'd had so far. But truthfully, she hadn't even been able to think of food let alone eat any. Her stomach was just too sensitive today. Add to that the shame of her near emotional breakdown in front of a work colleague, she barely knew and her day could only get better. *Right?*

She grabbed her purse and threw it over her shoulder, picked up a large stack of files and made her way to her car. As she walked through the double doors to the outside, she winced at the bright sunshine, squinting as a blast of pain shot through her temple; the effects of last night's highly embarrassing, drunken stupor refusing to wane. *Why did I allow myself to drink that much?* She huffed. She'd actually enjoyed herself up until that point. Michael had turned out to be good company which was a pleasant surprise. She'd always thought he seemed a little serious, but she'd seen another side trying to creep through last night, even if she had sensed him holding it back.

And then there was this morning. She flushed as she recalled seeing him almost naked on her sofa. His body was pale, but surprisingly well defined with tight muscle in all the right places. He clearly looked after himself, and she'd found it hard to look away from him as he fumbled for the blanket to cover himself. *Oh, God! I hope he hadn't noticed me gawking at him.* She berated herself. She couldn't have embarrassed herself any more than what she had last night. Thankfully, he'd been very polite and a lot more relaxed as they'd spoken about nothing but work in the car on the way to campus.

Out in the parking lot she reached her silver Ford Focus, clicked the lock to open the trunk, and placed the files inside finally freeing her arms from the week's heavy work load. It was going to take her all night to get through that much work and she wasn't feeling in the best of moods.

Just as she reached up to close the trunk she paused at the sound of a distressed female voice. Slowly peering around her car she saw Nina, the dark-haired girl who Michael had been concerned about, with the same young man whom she'd been with yesterday morning in the canteen. They were arguing about something.

"Just stay away from me!" Nina demanded as she began to walk ahead of the man.

Lacy watched discreetly, staying behind her car and hoping they wouldn't notice her.

He caught up with Nina, grabbed her arm and swung her around so she was facing him. Lacy didn't like how rough he was being.

"Let go of me!" Nina cried.

The young man's expression changed to something Lacy couldn't decipher: a look of anger? No. . . Hate. Lacy gasped and quickly put her hand to her mouth. She continued to watch as he bent down towards Nina so his face was inches away from hers and appeared to growl something at her through clenched teeth, his eyes were fierce but he spoke too quietly for Lacy to hear. She watched as Nina's expression changed in an instant. Strangely, she seemed to relax and nodded at him without saying a word. He turned her around and began to walk with her; his hand gripped tightly around her arm. Her face was blank, almost trance-like as they disappeared around the corner out of view.

What the hell. . . ? She remembered what Michael had said to her yesterday. He'd been worried about the young woman's change in personality and the fact that she was hanging around with that young man. She'd told him not to worry, that it was probably nothing. But after witnessing what she just had, she knew Michael was right to be worried. Okay. It's not like she'd never seen young couples argue and fight before, but this was something more than that. That look in his eyes was frightening—so full of anger like nothing she'd ever seen before. For a moment she thought about following them, but stopped herself. She had to tell Michael straight away.

She reached Michael's classroom moments later. The door was open. She was just about to knock when she saw him leaning on his desk, his fingers pinching the skin between his brows similar to how he'd been yesterday. "Oh, sorry. I don't mean to disturb you," she said, unsure if she should trouble him right now as he already looked strung out.

Michael looked up at her. "Hey. No. It's fine. Come in. Just feeling a little tired I guess." He smiled at her from his seat and she felt a little guilty for persuading him to sleep on her sofa last night.

She closed the door behind her and walked over to him knowing that his day was maybe just about to get a little worse. "There's something I need to tell you."

He looked at her, brows drawn tight, and she could tell he'd sensed that something was wrong. "What is it? You look a little pale."

"I've just seen Nina, out by the parking lot. She seemed to be in some kind of altercation with that guy she was with yesterday, the one you were concerned about." She explained how the boy was acting towards Nina and how he'd practically dragged her with him. "Michael. There was something wrong with his eyes. I know it's probably nothing but. . . I'm really worried for her."

Michael shot to his feet and began clearing his desk, shoving everything inside the top drawer and locking it. "Where was this? How long ago?"

"Five minutes at the most, over by the admin building. I came straight here."

He threw his jacket on and shoved his keys into his pocket. "I need to find them. Where were they headed?"

"Towards the quad. I'll go with you."

They reached the quad and both stopped to scan through the busy lunchtime crowds. Even though there was a biting chill in the air, the sun was shining which meant half the campus was outside enjoying the sunshine while they grabbed some down time between classes. The quad and the green were both busy, making it harder to spot them.

There was no sign of either of them as Michael and Lacy rushed towards the student accommodation buildings. They'd rounded the corner, passed the admin building when they heard a loud scream up ahead. Lacy began to run towards John Blake House, the last building on the edge of the parking lot. "I think it came from over here," she shouted back to Michael as she sprinted towards the main entrance, following the many other people that were now running over to see what had happened. Lacy became more anxious as she approached the crowd that had gathered in front of the building, preparing herself for what she feared she was going to see. She pushed through the crowd, Michael right behind her, and choked back a sob, bringing both her hands to her mouth.

* * *

Michael pushed passed Lacy only to have his suspicions confirmed as things came into view. He immediately pulled

Lacy into his arms, holding her head against his chest as she sobbed. Mr Grace from the football coaching staff was attending to a body lying on the ground.

Nina.

She was lying on her stomach, her body splayed out and her eyes closed.

He looked on as Mr Grace placed his fingers to her neck, feeling for a sign of life. "Someone call for an ambulance! She's still alive," he urged.

Lacy turned around, keeping hold of Michael's arm, which she squeezed as she looked on with tears rolling down her face. She let go and joined Mr Grace at Nina's side. She placed her hand on the young woman's head and began to stroke her hair gently. "Hold on Nina. Help will be here soon honey." Her voice trembled.

Michael looked up at the dorm building and spotted the wide-open window from where Nina must have jumped. He scanned the crowd of onlookers to see if he could see Jake, but there was no sign of him. This was too much of a coincidence. Jake was, in some way, connected to this and there was no doubt in Michael's mind that he would find out how.

He looked back at Nina's body lying limp on the asphalt and just then saw something unexpected.

What the. . . ?

A mist began to rise up out of her before hovering inches over her body like a cloud of black smoke. Michael's eyes scanned the crowd and as he suspected, he was the only one who could see it. Being dead had its advantages. The smoke became darker, more visible, and began to transform. The cloud shifted at one end and a face began to emerge right above Nina's head. Its face was distorted, like nothing he'd seen before: demonic, with pained, twisted features that grew more solid with each passing second. All Michael could do was watch as the form began to lift higher.

Lacy and Mr Grace were still by Nina's side, thankfully unaware of what was in front of them.

Moving slowly, the non-corporeal being gradually pulled itself further away from her. It twisted around to face Nina's unconscious body and seemed to glance at her before drifting towards the crowd who were also oblivious to what was happening.

After all of this time trying to find something—anything that would lead to who or what was causing the students to jump to their deaths—there it was right in front of him. Now all he had to do was find out why. One thing was for sure: it hadn't noticed him, which made things a whole lot easier. There was no way Michael was going to let it out of his sight.

While the creature passed through the unknowing crowd, Michael approached Lacy and placed his hand on her shoulder. "Stay with her. I'll be right back." His voice was almost a whisper.

She nodded to him, tears still falling down her cheeks, leaving watery streaks in her makeup.

Michael kept his distance as he followed the black form which had now floated around the corner of the dorm building and towards the football field. Before it reached the edge of the building it suddenly changed direction, sweeping down an alleyway and disappearing from sight. Michael rushed over. Keeping his back pressed up against the wall at the side of the alley, he leant his head and peered around an open metal gate which, he assumed, would normally be locked because he noticed a piece of chain which had been cut.

He watched patiently as the haze passed through the wall of a prefabricated utility shed that stood next to a couple of green dumpsters at the other end of the alley. Michael hung back waiting to see what would happen next.

In the year since Michael had returned to this world he had seen many things. Although the memories of what had happened to him were just flashes of jumbled images in his nightmares, he knew he wasn't the only one to walk the earth in the afterlife (or whatever it was). He'd witnessed many things so was well aware that there were demons and spirits everywhere—hell, he'd encountered enough of them—but this *thing*, however, was new; to his eyes anyway.

He was about to give up the ghost (pun intended) and head down the alley when the utility shed door began to open. He watched intently, not paying much attention to the sound of sirens that grew louder in the background, as a figure walked out from behind the door.

Son of a bitch!

It was Jake. At least, it was his body, but he very much doubted that Jake was aware of much in there. He was in a trancelike state as he paused and stared ahead. Then his whole body began to shake coming to an abrupt stop before his eyes closed and he stood stock-still. Then the young man's head quickly turned and his eyes opened and fixed on Michael.

"Shit!" he gasped as he pulled back behind the wall.

There was no doubt that Jake was possessed by that thing—a demon of some sort, he guessed—which meant things just got a whole lot more complicated.

Michael quickly headed back towards the scene where Nina was now strapped to a gurney which was being lifted into the ambulance. The medics still worked on her once they were inside, placing needles in her arm, attaching wires to machines, and one placed an oxygen mask over her face. She was still gripping on to her life, but only just, by the looks of things.

He walked up to Lacy, who was standing watching in distress. He placed his hand on her shoulder and she turned to look at him. "How's she doing?" he asked.

"She's holding on." She sniffed as she wiped her tears away with the back of her hand. "I'm going to go with her to the hospital."

"Sure. I'll let the department know."

Lacy's lip curled as she attempted a smile. "Thank you," she said as she climbed inside the ambulance and sat on the bench seat next to Nina. The doors were pushed closed and Michael inhaled deeply as he watched the ambulance pull away, its sirens blaring then fading off into the distance.

He had work to do, and it wasn't going to be easy.

As the crowd of onlookers dispersed, he reached into his jacket pocket and grabbed his cell phone while he headed back to his room. He flipped it open and scrolled through his small list of contacts until he reached the name he was looking for: Evo, His one and only friend. He hadn't spoken to him in a while, but he sure as hell needed to now.

"Mike." A familiar voice said through the phone.

"Hey buddy. I have a situation here that I'm gonna need your help with."

CHAPTER SEVEN

Lacy paced up and down the empty corridor praying for some news. She was still shaking from the ride in the ambulance. Seeing the medical staff fighting for Nina's life in the back of that vehicle was pretty harrowing to say the least. She'd sat stone-still watching as they cut Nina's clothes open then stuck needles into her skin as one of them used an air bag to pump oxygen into her lungs. She was sure she'd nearly passed out on more than one occasion, but managed to stay conscious for the rest of the journey.

Nina had been in the OR for nearly two hours. There was no doubt she was in a bad way. The fact that she was still alive was a miracle in itself, after the distance she'd fallen. *Jumped? Oh, God.* Lacy struggled to push the image of her lying on the ground from her mind as she choked back a sob. The fact that Nina had no one there for her made things worse. Lacy had tried to find someone to contact—family member or a friend, but according to Miss Taylor, who she'd spoken to when she'd called the Dean's office, there was only one name listed as her next of kin and the number on file was unreachable. That poor girl whom she'd sat next to in the ambulance—her life slipping away from her with every second—had no one.

Lacy leaned against the cold cream wall opposite the double doors that Nina had been rushed through. Her arms were folded around her chest as she waited anxiously. The sparse corridor was quiet for the most part, except for the occasional nurse who would come through the doors and rush down the long empty space, each time making Lacy stand to attention in the hope that they were bringing Nina back through with good news.

But it was a lot better than sitting around in the waiting

area like she had to begin with. The harsh memory from her past back in England had already started to rear its ugly head so she'd left the stark room pretty quickly, not wanting to relive the last time she'd spent hours waiting for news in a room that looked so similar.

But it was too late.

Memories she'd locked away for such a long time had already begun to creep back into her head, reigniting feelings of dread similar to that day, back when she was just a young girl. Sitting in that room on her own, waiting for news, had made her remember that day as though it were yesterday; only then, the patient had been her sister.

Her beautiful younger sister had been taken through similar looking doors nearly sixteen years ago, but she hadn't lived for long after she'd been wheeled back out of them. Lacy took a deep breath and closed her eyes. The anniversary of her sister's death was approaching; a time that she more than dreaded every year.

November 2nd, 1996.

She pictured her sister's face. Her long wavy brown hair had run half way down her back and her squeaky laugh had always made Lacy smile. They'd run around in the patch of wasteland at the back of their small town house in Chelmsford where they'd lived with their mother Sheila. There had been just the two of them at home the day the accident happened which was nothing unusual. Their mother thought nothing of leaving a twelve year old and a nine year old at home alone while she went to work. Of course, Lacy discovered much later that *work* actually meant working on some gentleman in his fancy apartment across town, but at the time she thought Sheila worked shifts at a local pub. Lacy found out a couple of years after her sister's death that, in actual fact, her mother was nothing but a high class hooker who pleasured lonely businessmen.

Although Sheila was always in and out of the house, she

would always make sure that there was food prepared for them, mostly sandwiches and stuff to reheat in the microwave, and that the cupboards were well stocked. She was out of the house a lot and if anything, it made Lacy and her sister Beth's relationship stronger. They were close and Lacy would always do whatever she needed to do to look after her.

Their house had been small: a two up, two down affair that had the bare minimum as far as furniture was concerned. Lacy and Beth had shared a bedroom which had been painted lilac when they were much younger. Their mother had painted a rainbow on the wall between their beds which made the room feel a little brighter and cheerier than it actually was. Lacy remembered the small lamp, that had sat on the bedside table in between their beds, that she'd put stickers all over. The bulb inside it was dim and she'd always made sure it was on when they were in bed until Beth fell asleep because Beth was afraid of the dark. There was no garden to speak of, just a small concrete yard with a tall gate leading to an alley, across which was their playground: an empty plot of land that had a chain link fence around it. There was a part of the fence that had been cut and even though they weren't supposed to leave the back yard, whenever Sheila went out to work the pair of them would go in there to play, but they knew never to leave the alley, not with the busy road at the end of it.

Lacy desperately wished that she could go back in time and not let Beth out of her sight that day like she had done. But there was no changing the past no matter how hard you wished for it.

The hardest part of remembering was the pain that she'd gotten so good at hiding away. She never let herself think about it which was the only way she stayed sane and how she'd managed to get through every day, even sixteen years later. But today, here in this hospital, she was failing miserably. It was too familiar, too tragic, and was triggering every memory she'd ever shut out.

She squeezed her eyes shut as she thought back to that day.

Lacy wanted some tinned custard. Beth was in the yard outside playing catch with a tennis ball so Lacy had gone into the kitchen, straight into the cupboard and grabbed a tin of ready-made custard. Remembering how her mother had done it, she reached for the tin opener, placed it in position at the edge of the tin and squeezed the two handles shut. The metal point pierced the tin and she twisted the handle around over and over until the lid snapped off. She got a small pan from the bottom cupboard, poured the contents of the tin into it and placed it on top of one of the rings on the electric cooker. She turned the dial to half way. As she waited for the custard to heat up, she looked through the small kitchen window and saw Beth crouched down stroking the tabby cat from two doors down. She watched as the cat arched its back to her and walked around in circles enjoying Beth's affection. She reached into the cupboard by the sink and grabbed two small bowls.

As she looked up from what she was doing, she noticed that the back gate was now open. Immediately she went to the back door and saw that Beth had followed the cat out into the alley. She went straight out and yelled at her to come back into the yard. Beth protested and continued to stroke the cat.

"You're not allowed out of the yard without me, now come back in before. . ." Lacy remembered she'd left the custard on the heat and ran back in the kitchen, just catching it before the whole contents had boiled over the side. It was a mess. She poured what was left in the two bowls and put the pan into the sink. She took two spoons from the drawer and put one in each bowl, pleased at how grown up she felt.

She went to the back door and shouted to Beth. She couldn't see her anywhere. The gate was still open, but Beth was out of sight. She stepped into the alley and when she realized how far Beth had gone, she gasped and then called out to her sister, as all she saw was Beth running towards the main road after that stupid cat. . .

Lacy's hand went to her mouth, holding back her sobs, as

what happened next played out in slow motion in her mind: running down the alley after Beth, her shouts for her sister to stay where she was falling on deaf ears as Beth followed the cat between some parked cars and straight out into the road.

What happened after that was still quite blurry except for the vision of little Beth lying in the road with people rushing around her. Lacy remembered that far too clearly. Her memories flicked through her mind like a movie on fast forward, only picking out the bits that she'd hung on to: the driver of the car who was in shock with his hands in his hair, who had a look of sheer horror on his face; the ambulance crew running to her sister's side, the panic, her mother in hysterics in the hospital waiting room as some stranger—she still didn't know to this day who he was. . . probably one of her mother's clients—tried to calm her down. Then came the worst memory of all: the doctor coming into the room and telling her mother that Beth was gone.

The sensation of a wet tear travelling down her cheek brought her back to the present. It had been a while since she'd thought of that day. No matter how distant it now was, it didn't get any easier. The pain was still very much the same. Only now, she was much better at locking it away.

Her head fell back against the wall.

She closed her eyes and thought about Nina, who had been in a similar position on the ground as her sister had all those years ago. She wasn't religious—who could blame her? Her faith had been taken away that day in the hospital when she'd told herself there couldn't possibly be a god. Not if someone so precious to her could be snatched away so cruelly. Despite this, she silently prayed. *Please God, if you* are *there, let Nina survive this.*

As if by coincidence—because that's all it could have been—the double doors in front of her burst open. She stood up rigid as the gurney that Nina was lying on was wheeled out and into the corridor by a tall man dressed all in white and a nurse walking by his side. A man in green scrubs followed soon after and walked straight over to Lacy. His name tag was pinned to his breast pocket and he was removing a paper face mask that dangled from one ear.

"Miss Holloway?" he asked as he held out a hand to her. She nodded. "Hi. I'm Doctor Green, Nina's surgeon."

She was surprised how young he was. His short, salt and pepper hair was out of place atop his young features "Hi," was about all she could manage to say as she shook his warm hand.

"We've managed to stabilize her but her condition is still critical. The impact of the fall had caused some internal bleeding in her abdomen, which we've managed to stop. She has a couple of broken bones: a break in her left tibia and another in her left femur. But we're more worried about the swelling in her frontal lobe. We've managed to release some of the pressure from around the area, and the swelling seems to have reduced slightly, but we will need to keep a very close eye on her."

Lacy exhaled a long breath she hadn't realized she'd been holding, remembering that she did still need to breathe if she wanted to remain vertical. The situation was too similar to her sister's all those years ago and she realized she wasn't handling things very well. "I want to stay with her."

"Of course. They're just about to take her up to ICU. Go and get yourself a coffee and some fresh air and give them time to get her settled." The doctor placed his hand on her arm and in a kind voice said, "She'll be well looked after here."

Lacy smiled as best she could.

CHAPTER EIGHT

Since waking up dead, Michael had spent most of his days alone. For that he'd been grateful: no distractions. Giving him plenty of time to do what he'd become very good at: seeking out and fighting evil supernatural beings in the hope that they'd be of use to him during his search for the truth. Not that he was ever into company all that much, even before his death. He'd had lots of friends and acquaintances due to the nature of his career and had been fortunate enough to enjoy many of life's luxuries. But his success had attracted many people. He'd had enough of all the fake friends who'd admired his status more than anything else.

There was none of that now.

Being who or what he was now, the only human interaction he'd had was when he'd needed something from them. He'd used people, taken advantage of kindness that was offered to him on many occasions, and tried his hardest to remain alone. He'd even dated the odd female to get information; of course, that never lead to anything more than a movie, dinner or a midnight stroll. There had never been so much as a kiss between him and the few females he'd interacted with. They, on the other hand, had been more than willing, but for him it was just business and nothing more. As soon as he was satisfied that they were of no more help to him, those people were quickly forgotten about, never seeing or hearing from him again.

Well, that is, except for one person: Evo. His go-to man whenever he needed a little back up. A human whom he now considered a friend and a person he could trust with his life, or. . . death. Whatever.

The last he'd seen of him was about three months ago

when he'd been in Colorado on the hunt. He'd needed a little help with a *Djin* that had been sapping the life out of some of the clients of a small bar on the outskirts of the city. Michael had never encountered one before and hadn't liked the look of it either. He'd needed as much information as possible about the son of a bitch before he'd dare attempt to take him on.

His friend knew a lot about the supernatural world and the *things* that shared the earth with them now. Evo was a living, breathing, demon encyclopedia, but he hadn't always been that way. His life had been on a downward spiral until one day, in Ohio nearly nine months ago, Michael saved his life.

His mind went back to that rainy night in January.

Michael had only been in his new body for a little over a month and was still adjusting to it. It was a whole new experience for him after being ethereal for the first part of his new existence and he was still finding it hard to accept the way things were for him now. The why, however, was still yet to be discovered and Michael had made it his sole purpose to find out who, or what, had killed him.

He'd hunted high and low, crossed many states and cities, searched through the dregs of the underworld for the kind of creatures he was hoping to get information from but all he'd encountered were a handful of wraiths which were, quite frankly, useless at giving information. And then there were the endless lost spirits that wandered the streets and buildings trapped in a world that was neither life nor death; some for all eternity, others, until they found peace with whatever was keeping them there.

After a few days in Cleveland, Michael had become restless. He'd spent his days scouring the local papers and internet news sites for signs of unusual activity—all to no avail—until one night after he'd re-acquainted himself with Mr Daniels in a small, dingy bar on the corner of 9th Street and Sumner.

He'd propped up the bar feeling sorry for himself for the past hour, unsure what to do next, until his ears pricked at a conversation between two men who were sitting at the opposite side. A thin, red-haired man was talking about something that had gone down last night at one of the clubs downtown. Michael wasn't really paying much attention, but from what he gathered, it was your usual, city nightlife stuff: police cornering a man in an alleyway after some sort of altercation. The guy was found crouched over a stiff—*nothing unusual about that.*

As redhead went on, Michael ordered another JD without the coke this time. One thing he'd discovered about his new self was that he could drink and drink and it hardly affected him, much to his annoyance. Well, he was determined to keep going tonight until it did.

The female behind the bar placed a napkin in front of him, followed by his order. As he looked up at her, she winked and a flirtatious smile graced her lips. "There you go handsome." Her hand lingered on his glass, then she stroked her finger up the side seductively. Michael just about managed to raise the side of his mouth, then went back to ignoring her, supping back the frosty contents in one.

"Apparently the guy was all kinds of crazy," *he heard redhead saying to his overweight buddy sat beside him. They reminded him of a couple of characters from* Cheers.

"Yep. They usually are," *his buddy said.*

"This guy more so. Jock was there when they hauled him off. He said the guy was protesting his innocence, and then he shouted something about a big guy with red eyes, dressed in black, who'd just disappeared in front of him."

Michael looked over at the men.

Plump-guy laughed. "It takes all sorts."

Well, now their conversation just got interesting. "Hey!" *Michael shouted over to* Norm *and* Cliff *over the bar.* "Did they take him downtown?"

"What d'ya say man?" *redhead grunted, clearly wondering why their private conversation had just been interrupted.*

"The crazy guy? Did they take him downtown?"

"Uh. Yeah," *he scoffed. His buddy looked equally annoyed.*

Michael took no notice. He held up a twenty to Blondie behind the bar, slammed it down next to his empty glass and left without saying another word.

Standing in the doorway of an unused building, Michael watched the doors to the precinct across the street through a thick blanket of rain. A few hours outside the police department and there was still no sign of the man he'd heard about at the bar, so he could only assume they were holding him overnight which would make things way more complicated. Michael could hardly walk in and ask to have a private conversation with the guy. He was going to have to think about breaking him out of there.

Just as he was about to head over there, he hung back as a young male, around 6ft, with scruffy, brown hair came through the double doors and walked down the steps from the building. He hadn't seen the guy enter the precinct and as he was dressed in a scruffy denim jacket with a hooded sweatshirt underneath and dark colored cargo pants, he assumed he wasn't an employee. He had to be the guy he'd been waiting for.

Michael pulled his hood over his head, crossed the heavy traffic, and followed him making sure he kept his distance. The man took a left at the end of the street. He was clearly on edge; jumping with every noise. His head darted around in all directions, no doubt making sure he wasn't being followed. Fortunately, he hadn't spotted Michael. He turned right, heading down an alleyway up ahead between a couple of rundown apartment blocks. Michael picked up his pace a little so he didn't lose him.

He followed the man into the alleyway still staying well back so as not to startle the guy. A foul smell of human garbage filled the air as Michael passed a row of dilapidated dumpsters on the left side. Just then, he felt a strange shiver run up his spine, which stopped him in his tracks. He watched as the man he'd been tailing also halted.

The man's head crept around. Michael hurried to a dumpster and crouched down beside it, peering over the top where he could see the man scanning the darkness like he'd sensed that someone was watching him.

"Hello! Is someone there?" He heard the stranger say.

The sensation that Michael had felt just then began to get stronger, a coldness creeping up his spine and heightening his senses. It was familiar to him. He'd felt it before just before fighting one of the many creatures he'd battled over the last few months. But what was causing it this time?

Michael stayed in his position and continued to watch the man walk further down the alley, taking tentative steps this time. Michael stayed back, sensing his trepidation.

There was something else in this alleyway with them and it wasn't human, that, *Michael was sure of.*

Soft lights that hung over the two fire doors from the apartment block began to flicker, causing the man to stop walking again. He looked back, but didn't notice Michael. "Who's there?" His voice was broken. He was scared.

It took a moment for Michael to register what he saw next. A dark figure jumped down from a metal fire escape that clung to the side of a building up ahead, landing in front of the man who yelled out in shock and stumbled backwards. Gaining his footing, the man walked backwards as the dark figure walked towards him, eyes as red as crimson, closing the gap between them.

Demon. Michael was certain. He'd seen eyes like those before.

The young man spoke, "Who are you?" he asked. His voice trembled.

The demon lunged forward and gripped the frightened male by his throat, lifting him into the air like he was nothing. The man he'd followed was tall, but there was barely anything of him. He didn't stand a chance

"Someone you shouldn't have seen," was the demons reply as it began to squeeze the poor guy's throat, abruptly cutting off his cry for help.

Shit!

Michael stepped out from behind the dumpster. "Let him go," he ordered as he walked towards them. He heard the strained chokes coming from the frightened man as he struggled to breathe under the demon's grip. As Michael got closer to them, he noticed the demon's eyes were more illuminated and the crimson glow was now fixed on him.

"Of course." It mocked as he flung the man away like he was flicking a fly. There was a thud as the man hit the wall on the other side of the alley. *"But you're just delaying his fate."*

The demon's voice was deep and angry, with all its focus now only on Michael. A black buzz-cut revealed deep scars upon its head. Its all-black attire dishevelled, floor length leather jacket worn and faded and there were black binds wrapped around its wrists. Its skin was pale and its fingernails dark and jagged.

Shit! He was a mean looking SOB. It looked like it had used the body it was in for a long time. Some demons preferred to use only one vessel.

"Leave him alone. What could you possibly want with him?" Michael asked as they circled each other in the dimly lit space.

"He's seen too much." The demon snarled back at him.

"And who's he going to tell? Besides, who would believe him?" Michael had positioned himself in front of the man who was now slumped against the wall and coughing in pain.

"I'm not about to take that risk. Why should it concern you? He's human. He's nothing."

The demon knew Michael wasn't human. He tried a different approach. *"Exactly, so why waste your strength on a weak human like him?"*

"Enough of this!" The demon ordered as he made a charge for the man. Michael jumped and grabbed hold of the demon's neck, but his strength was no match for it and it threw him off with no effort at all. As Michael hit the floor the creature stuck a boot into Michael's side, sending him skidding across the wet concrete. He quickly managed to get to his feet and before the demon got to deliver another kick, Michael swung a right hook into the side of its skull which momentarily knocked it off balance.

In the short time it took for the SOB to shake the hit off, Michael had managed to grab his blade from out of the strap inside his coat and slashed at the demon that laughed as it jumped back out of the way. Michael knew from the demon's strength that it was playing with him and that at any moment the bastard would strike to kill.

He felt a familiar feeling of rage building inside of him. It seemed to be happening more often lately when fighting and each time it got stronger. It was that rage that had helped him defeat the many demons and other creatures he had battled with in the few months he'd been a part of the underworld.

Just as the demon was gearing up for his next strike, Michael braced himself. Taking a deep breath, he crouched over ready to pounce. But the demon halted suddenly.

"Your eyes! It's not possible." Then the demon growled a word Michael didn't recognize. "Gazriel!"

Michael had no clue what the demon was talking about, but remained still. It whispered something in another language and then suddenly vanished into thin air, leaving Michael panting and looking at nothing but the depths of the alleyway in front of him and distant traffic speeding past at the end.

What the fuck just happened?

A groan came from his left. The man had pulled himself up and was sitting against the wall in between two dumpsters. "What the hell was that?" he asked as he wiped his forehead and examined the blood that was now covering his hand from a small gash above his left eyebrow.

Michael went to his aid, holding his hand out to him. "You okay, buddy?"

He took Michael's hand and pulled himself up to his feet. "Yeah man. You saved my life. I owe you one." He dusted down his trousers. "What was that thing?"

"I have no idea but—"

"And what the hell are you?" the man interrupted; his eyes wide as he looked at Michael waiting for an answer.

Michael was confused. "I. . . What do you mean?"

"I saw your eyes just now, when you were fighting that thing.*"*

"What the hell are you talking about? I think that bump on your head has affected you."

"There's no human I know whose eyes glow white like that. What the hell are you man?" He wiped at his head again.

Ignoring his question, Michael gestured towards the guy's forehead.

"You need to get that gash checked out. You're gonna need some stitches."

The stranger looked frustrated. "Come on. Are you kiddin' me man? A guy with bright red eyes just flew down from the sky and tried to kill me. I think we can safely assume that I'm all shocked out right now. You can tell me what the hell it is that you are 'cause you're certainly not normal."

Michael shook his head. Granted, he was still discovering things about himself but. . . his eyes glowing white? "I didn't know that happened." He couldn't understand it.

His confusion must have surprised the stranger as he was now looking at him with a bemused expression.

"Damn, I could use a drink!" Michael scoffed. "No doubt we both could. Come on. I'm buying."

From that day on, and after never seeing that demon again, Michael and Evo had been best friends.

It was good to hear his voice after so long. Evo was due to arrive in the next half hour or so and Michael had insisted that he stay with him on campus. He didn't have much room in his apartment but he had a sofa which was quite comfortable and in truth, he would quite enjoy the company right now.

After work Michael had returned to his dorm. He'd powered up his laptop before heading out to meet Evo in front of the admin building and was just about to sit down with his freshly made mug of coffee when the phone rang. He walked to the counter top and grabbed the handset from its cradle. "Hello?"

A familiar British accent sounded on the other end of the line. "Michael? Hi. It's Lacy. I'm calling from the hospital."

CHAPTER NINE

The constant, familiar beep of the EKG machine was enough to keep Lacy on edge as she sat in the bucket chair that she'd pulled over to Nina's bedside. She looked at the many tubes and wires connected to Nina, whose gaunt face was hidden behind an oxygen mask that clouded over with each exhale that she made. The fact that she was breathing on her own was a small relief, but Lacy still felt a knot in the pit of her stomach as she sat and stroked Nina's hand. She'd only left her side once since she'd been brought into ICU a couple of hours ago, which had been to call Michael to inform him of Nina's condition but there had been no answer on his cell.

A deep groan came from the pit of her stomach. The hunger was too intense to ignore now and she knew she'd have no choice but to eat something soon, if only to keep her own strength up.

The door swung open and a brown haired nurse came in giving Lacy a warm smile as she walked over to the bed. She picked up the clipboard from the end of the bed and walked over to the EKG machine, pressed a few buttons and wrote something down on the sheet of paper.

"How are you holding up?" she asked Lacy over her small black rimmed glasses.

"Good. Thanks. How's she doing?"

The nurse finished up with the clipboard placing it back on its hook and walked over to an IV drip that hung on a metal stand next to the bed. She reached up and turned the small clamp on the tubing.

"No change as of yet," she replied, her voice soft. "With trauma like this I'm afraid it's a waiting game, but she's comfortable. She's being kept sedated so there is less stress on her brain." The nurse put her hand on Lacy's shoulder. "I know she's been through a lot, but she's in good hands here. Listen, you've been here for quite some time. Have you eaten?"

"Not since lunch. But I'm fine, really."

"You need to eat something. It won't help anyone if you neglect yourself. Why don't you pop to the canteen and get something? I'm sure Nina won't mind."

Lacy glanced over at the young girl who looked so peaceful in her induced slumber. The nurse was right; no sense in starving herself and her stomach had begun to shout for food a while ago. It would be good to stretch her legs, she supposed, and she could also try calling Michael again. "Okay." She got to her feet and placed her jacket on the chair. "I won't be too long."

She swung her purse over her shoulder and gave the nurse a smile.

"I'm on duty all evening so take your time. I'll keep checking in on her for you." The nurse's smile was kind and sympathetic, reassuring Lacy that it was fine to leave Nina which, for some reason, she found extremely hard to do. Still racked with guilt over her sister, she worried about something happening to Nina while she was alone. She couldn't bear the thought.

After sitting in the canteen for half an hour, pushing some berries from a slice of cherry pie around her plate instead of eating them, Lacy had given up on food. She couldn't conjure up any kind of appetite, which was no surprise. She knew when she'd ordered at the counter that she wouldn't eat it, but had ordered anyway in the hope that she'd change her mind when it was in front of her. Not the case. All she'd managed was one measly fork full and a few sips of her coffee. Her stomach wasn't cooperating and it was pointless trying to make it, so she decided to head downstairs.

She reached a bank of pay phones down at reception, put

a few quarters in and dialled Michael's number. At seven thirty p.m, he should be home from work by now. After a few rings, Lacy was relieved to hear his voice on the other end of the line.

"Hi. It's Lacy. I'm calling from the hospital."

"Hey. How's she doing?"

She let out a heavy sigh. "It's pretty bad." She repeated what the surgeon had told her earlier about Nina's condition as best she could; surprised she'd even remembered what he'd said. Even more surprising was how badly the whole thing was affecting her. She hardly knew Nina; had spoken to her, maybe once before, so why had it hit her so hard? Deep down, she knew the answer: she'd replaced her sister with Nina thinking that if she looked after her, it would take away some of the guilt she felt over not looking after Beth. Her previously buried emotions about her sister's death were now a high speed train she wasn't ready to board yet. The guilt that had buried itself right down to her marrow was now raging like a hot furnace. She thought she'd dealt with it after all these years, that she'd finally put it to rest when really all she'd managed to do was push it further back, all the while fighting hard not to let it rise to the surface.

"Are you okay?" Michael's voice snapped her away from her inner struggle and she inhaled so deeply her lungs burned. "Lacy?"

"Yes. Yeah, I'm fine. Just a little tired, that's all." It wasn't a complete lie. Somehow Michael's voice soothed her. It was nice to speak to someone she classed as a friend even though they hadn't known each other all that long.

"You don't need to stay with her all the time," he told her, his voice sympathetic. "I'm sure the hospital will let you know if there's any change. You're going to wear yourself out."

He was right, of course. There was nothing she could do for her right now so exhausting herself was just silly. Besides, she needed to stop by her office to get some of her things so she thought it best to leave now before it got any later.

"Okay. I'll just pop back up to see her before I leave and make sure they have my number."

"Then go home and get some rest. I'll speak to you tomorrow, okay?"

"Yeah, okay."

On her way back up to the room she stopped at the nurse's station to leave her home and cell number then went back to Nina's room. Still lost in her inner turmoil, it wasn't until she was through the door that she saw a familiar figure at Nina's bedside, leaning right over her. Lacy froze. Her breath caught and her eyes fixed on Jake's as his head snapped towards her and he stood up straight.

What the hell was he doing leaning over her like that?

"How did you get in here?" she managed to ask him through her alarm. "Visiting is over."

He was silent for a moment and just when Lacy was about to repeat her question he spoke in a quiet mumble that she barely heard. "I needed to see her," he said.

She felt annoyed at him for avoiding her question. She slowly walked towards him, keeping her eyes fixed on his. When she got closer to him she noticed how pale he was. His face was gaunt; his deep blue eyes weighed down with dark, heavy circles. She happened to glance down and saw that his hands were thick with dirt. As she stood near him, his empty stare seemed to burn through her like he wasn't really seeing her even though he was looking straight at her. Lacy felt a chill creep down her spine, but shook it off. She had to find out what had happened between him and Nina. "Do you know what happened to her?"

She watched his face intently for any kind of sign, but he looked away from her. "No."

"I saw you earlier today. You and Nina. . . You were arguing about something."

He didn't respond. Didn't even move, just continued to stare at her; his eyes still devoid of any emotion. She backed away from him, walking around the foot of the hospital bed to the other side. His gaze followed her. The chill came back, telling her she should get out of there, but she wouldn't leave Nina, and she had to know if he was responsible for what had happened to her.

"What was it about, Jake?"

Finally, his eyes dropped to look at Nina, a wrinkle appearing between his brows. "It was nothing." He sounded strangely despondent.

"It didn't look like nothing to me." Her voice was stern as she stared at him over the bed, willing him to look at her so that she could gauge his expression. She remembered his face, as he'd grabbed Nina back at the campus, and the way it had made her feel in that moment—the dread that had hit the bottom of her stomach as she looked on from across the car park—and now, deep down to her marrow, her instincts were telling her that this boy was dangerous. She felt certain that he was the reason Nina was lying in a hospital bed fighting for her life.

"What happened to her? What did you do?"

He took off towards the door without saying a word.

"Jake!" She was angry now. How dare he just ignore her? "I *will* find out what happened," she promised as he left the hospital room without as much as a backwards glance.

After her anger had begun to subside, Lacy sat watching Nina, contemplating staying with her. She was even more worried about leaving her on her own now. Seeing Jake standing at her bedside had freaked her out. What if he came back when she'd gone? Lacy didn't trust him at all.

She tried fighting back a yawn, but it beat her. She had to get some rest, there was no doubt. She figured if she spoke to the nurse on duty and explained about Jake they'd keep an extra eye on Nina's room. She'd stop by her office on the way home like she'd planned. Then when she got home, she'd have a quick shower then bed. She could call the hospital in the morning to see if everything was okay, then visit Nina tomorrow afternoon.

It was a good plan. Little did she know that her plans were about to change.

* * *

The drive to her office had been a quiet one. She was glad to be away from all the beeps and drones of the hospital machinery that was currently helping to keep Nina alive, even though she still felt uneasy about leaving her. She couldn't help but think of what happened all those years ago when she'd left her sister. The fact that she hadn't been with her sister when she'd taken her final breath still affected her greatly and she couldn't bear the thought of poor Nina being alone if the time came. She wiped a stray tear from her cheek and parked the car as near as she could to the psychology department building.

The night had brought along a slight ground mist which had covered the whole campus. There was a cold bite in the air; a sign that fall was in full swing. Lacy pulled her jacket tighter around her as she walked towards the brownstone building where her office was. It was always pretty quiet around this part of the campus at nine o'clock at night. Most of the students hung out around the bars and leisure areas when they weren't in their dorms.

Most of the evening classes had finished by now so the hallways were empty as she walked towards her office. Far away footsteps echoed down the other end of the building as she unlocked the door. She paused, waiting to see who it was—maybe a colleague—but the footsteps stopped abruptly before they rounded the corner. She thought nothing of it and went inside her office, gathered up some files from her desk, turned out the lights and locked the door behind her.

As soon as Lacy was outside the building her skin prickled with a sense of foreboding. Something inside was telling her she was being watched. That *something* wasn't wrong.

She looked around and saw the figure of a man, shadowed by the large tree he was leaning against. She could feel his eyes on her as she began to walk swiftly, but calmly, towards her car.

Just stay calm, she told herself even though her hands had already begun to tremble.

She walked a little faster, cutting across the grass as she reached into her coat pocket for her car keys. A quick glance behind her caused her to panic as she saw that the man was now following her. She walked as fast as she could without breaking into a run; her heart pounding as her car came into view. She pointed her keys at it, hand shaking, and unlocked the doors.

Quickly, she climbed inside and pulled the door shut. The man, who was still heading towards her, lifted his head and as he walked into the light of the nearby street lamp she gasped.

Jake! He must have waited at the hospital and followed her.

As she fumbled to put the key in the ignition, she dropped the whole bunch on the floor. "Shit!" She bent down to grab them and when she sat back up again, she screamed when she saw Jake right outside her window. Frozen for a moment by his vacant stare, Lacy fixed on Jake's eerily dead expression which sent a feeling of dread to the pit of her stomach.

Jesus Christ! What's wrong with this guy?

Desperately trying to calm herself enough to stop her hand from shaking, she attempted to put the key in the ignition again. She managed it this time, and inhaled a deep breath when she heard the roar of the engine. Jake reached out for the door handle, but she managed to slam the car into reverse and maneuver out of his reach and out of the parking lot. She didn't dare look back as she sped towards the gates at the front of campus.

CHAPTER TEN

A brisk wind blew through the campus as Michael walked out of the doorway of his apartment building. His black, wool trench coat was more for effect than actual need for warmth, and it also hid his weapons nicely.

Evo had called twenty minutes earlier to explain that there'd been a delay with his flight and he was now in a rental on his way from the airport. Michael had arranged to meet him by the main gates as the campus was fairly large, so it was easier than explaining where his apartment was.

No sooner had he arrived by the brass monument of Charles Benedict Calvert, the founder of SPU that stood proud on a grassy island just inside the gates, than a large black MERCEDES GLK350 SUV pulled into the grounds and Michael knew straight away who was driving it. A familiar face greeted him with a big smile from behind the wheel of the large 4x4 as it pulled up to the sidewalk. The passenger side window slid down automatically. "Hey buddy!" his best friend said from the comfort of his plush leather seat.

Michael leaned in the passenger window and shook his head. "Flash enough for yer?" he laughed.

"Hey, you know I like to travel in style," Evo answered, then he jumped out of the driver's side door and headed around to greet Michael with a big hug. "It's good to see you man."

"You too buddy."

Evo hadn't changed much since the last time Michael had seen him. Apart from the fact that he now looked about fifty pounds heavier, his hair was still the same short, brown, chopped style he always wore and he was simply clad in his choice uniform of black fatigues, tucked into a pair of combat military boots; a plain, deep gray T-shirt; and a black wool overcoat, collars turned up. He looked like a mix between SWAT and someone from the front cover of GQ magazine.

"Jesus, Evo. You been juicin' up since I last saw you?" Michael raised his eyebrows, looking his muscular frame up and down.

Evo laughed. "Nah. Wouldn't put that shit in my veins. I spend most of my spare time training in the gym now. It keeps me stimulated."

Since he was nearly killed in an alleyway last December, Evo had dedicated his life to finding and logging information on every supernatural being in existence. He was a hunter like Michael now, but much more ruthless. It was more like a sport to him and he enjoyed it way too much for Michael's liking. The guy couldn't get enough of killing monsters. But his obsession had taken him to places even Michael knew nothing about. Realizing how good he was at hunting, Evo had also become a bounty hunter; his clients being mainly of the dead variety. He was lethal and had carved out quite a reputation for himself amongst the underworld.

Michael didn't always approve of the clients he sometimes worked for—after all, who can trust a demon, right?—but it was Evo's business. It certainly was a far cry from the dodgy dealings he used to do when he was a no-good conman who often ended up in all kinds of trouble.

Besides, his best friend working for the creatures of the underworld had its advantages: Evo had plenty of contacts; he was trusted. He'd tried to use those contacts to his advantage over the last few months to try and get information that could help Michael. But even though he'd come across a few names that he thought could have been leads, they'd led to nothing.

"Come on. My place is on the other side of the campus." Michael said as he jumped in the passenger's side of the SUV. When Evo had gotten back behind the wheel Michael paused. He might as well just come out with it. "Hey, while you're here. . . can you please try to remember that, right now, this is my place of work? If you could behave yourself. . . that would be great."

He could see by Evo's smug expression that he knew damn well what he was referring to. His friend's sexual habits weren't a problem usually—and Jesus, he made Michael envious sometimes. He was a good looking guy so why not?—but not here. Michael knew it wasn't ideal having an experienced philanderer staying on a university campus that was full of the opposite sex, but he would just have to keep it in his pants for the duration of his stay which, hopefully, would only be for a couple of nights until they'd checked out the campus. After that, Michael would help him find a motel.

"Evo?" Michael pushed for an answer after his friend had remained silent for too long.

"Okay. Okay. I'll be a good boy," the smirk that followed made Michael raise an eyebrow to let Evo know he wasn't satisfied with his response. "What? I promise." Evo held his hands up in the air in mock surrender before turning the key in the ignition.

Shit! Remind me why I thought this was a good idea.

A car screeching around the corner made both men sit bolt upright. As it got closer Michael thought it looked familiar. Yes, he knew the car alright. "What's she doing?" he whispered as Lacy's Ford Focus sped right past them and out of the main gates.

"Who was that?" Evo asked.

"A colleague of mine." Michael buckled his seat belt. "Something's wrong. Quick! Get after her." No sooner had he said the words than Evo had spun the car around and was now heading out of the college gates after her.

After Lacy had somehow managed to get away from them, they pulled the SUV up to her home: a modest, single story house set back from the road. The suburban neighborhood was quiet, as it would be at that time of night, and the only thing that didn't seem right was that Lacy's place was in darkness, with the exception of a dim porch light over the front door. She had to be home as her car was now parked in the driveway.

Michael knocked on the door.

No answer.

He knocked again, harder this time. "Lacy. It's Michael."

They waited silently. He heard movement, then the sound of deadbolts opening. The door opened slowly and Lacy peered out from behind it. As soon as her eyes met his she visibly relaxed.

"Michael, thank God," she exhaled. "What are you doing here?" She opened the door and gestured them inside.

"You practically wheel-spun past us back at the campus. I was meeting my friend at the front gates. What the hell's going on? Are you okay? You look pretty shaken up."

They both walked into the dark hallway and Lacy quickly shut the door after them.

She turned on the light. "I'm fine now. Can I get you both a drink?" They followed her to the kitchen.

"I'm good thanks." Michael watched her fill up a large glass with white wine. Her hands were shaking.

"Got anything stronger?" Evo asked, looking at the bottle of wine with distaste.

Michael rolled his eyes. "Lacy, this is my good friend Evo."

Evo gave her a wink. "Good to meet you, Miss."

Lacy raised an eyebrow as she poured some wine. She looked unsure of him as she eyed his clothes. "You too. . . Evo? Unusual name?"

Michael smirked, keeping his gaze on his friend. "It's short for Evan. . . Evan O'Reilly."

Evo looked a little disgruntled as he dragged his eyes away from Michael's and turned to Lacy. "But don't ever let me hear them words leave those beautifully pink lips of yours." He warned her playfully. "Evo's just fine."

Lacy gave him a half smile. "Whiskey?" she asked, pulling out a bottle of Jack Daniels from the cupboard.

Evo's eyes lit up in an instant. "That's more like it." He rubbed his hands together and took the glass that she offered to him. He glanced at Michael. "I like her already."

Michael ignored him. "What's going on Lacy?"

After she'd taken a large gulp of wine, she sat down at her small wooden table over by a set of French Doors. Michael followed. She inhaled a long breath. "After I called you earlier, I went back to Nina's room and Jake was there—"

"Jake? Jesus Christ." Michael snorted. "Jake is the guy I told you about on the phone," he explained to Evo. Jake being at the hospital only meant one thing and it wasn't that he was worried about Nina. That bastard demon had more than likely gone to finish her off. And what if he'd hurt Lacy? Michael felt his stomach clench. "Did you talk to him?"

"Yes, briefly. I told him that I saw the two of them arguing this afternoon and asked him if he knew what had happened. He didn't want to answer me. So, I got angry with him and he left. He was acting pretty strange."

"How so?" Evo asked as he leaned against the kitchen counter.

She finished the last of her wine. "When I first saw him in the room, he was bent right over her, like he was whispering something or. . . I don't know."

Michael hadn't had a chance to explain everything to Evo yet, so Evo didn't know that Jake wasn't actually Jake, and there was no way he could tell him in front of Lacy. He'd have to wait until they were back at his place before bringing him up to speed.

"But that's not why you were driving off campus like Ayrton Senna, is it?" Michael observed.

"No. It was what happened when I called in to my office on the way home that caused that." She poured herself more wine as she went on to explain how Jake must have followed her from the hospital and how he'd come after her across the parking lot. "Michael, his eyes. . . I could swear he wanted to kill me."

And so could he. In fact, he was damn certain of it, which was a huge problem. Lacy was now a target which meant she would need protecting. There was no way he could leave her here in this house alone, but how the hell would he explain it to her? And he needed to tell Evo what was going on. He leaned on the table and rubbed his brow. Damn, this was a problem he didn't need. He shifted uncomfortably before he turned to Lacy. "I don't think you should be left alone right now. Not until I deal with Jake."

Lacy looked confused. "*You* deal with Jake? Shouldn't we call the police?"

"Not yet. I'll have a word with him first." The cops were the last thing he needed. "But you can't stay on your own."

"I'm fine. Look, I don't know what's gotten into him, but I'm sure everything will be fine."

Michael stood up from the table. "Evo. Can I talk to you for a minute?" He caught Lacy's frown out of the corner of his eye before Evo pushed himself from the counter and followed him out of the room.

"Sure."

Outside on the porch, Michael explained to Evo what had happened with Nina and the strange looking demon that had left her body that was now possessing Jake. Evo nodded his head, understanding the predicament that Michael was now facing.

"I need you to go to my apartment. Use my laptop to find out anything you can about this thing, but be as quick as you can because I'm gonna need you to watch the hospital. If

Jake's been there once, it's only a matter of time until he returns."

Evo nodded. "What about you?"

"I'm going to stay here. She's not safe right now."

After Michael had given him directions, Evo started down the path towards his SUV. "I'll call you as soon as I have any info," he shouted over his shoulder.

No sooner had he gone than Lacy opened the front door. "Hey. What's going on? Where's your friend going?"

Michael checked the street, walked back into the house and shut the door. Lacy watched as he clicked her dead bolts into place.

"Evo's headed back to my place. He'll be staying with me until he's found somewhere more suitable. Listen, I think I should stay here tonight. I can crash on the sofa again, it's no problem. You shouldn't be alone, at least. . . not until we know what's going on with that guy, Jake."

* * *

She didn't know what to say for a moment. She stood in her narrow hallway contemplating telling him to leave as politely as she could. Lacy hadn't had a man in her house since Simon, who was the only man she'd allowed to stay over until last night, so it felt strange. She winced as she thought of that disaster of a relationship, if she could have called it that. Thankfully, she'd escaped that one unharmed. Well, except for her pride.

She hesitated; never one to need babysitting, especially from someone she hardly knew. But as she looked into his kind blue eyes she saw nothing but genuine concern and the truth was, she trusted him. Even though they'd only known each other a short time, she felt comfortable with him; a little too comfortable if she was honest. She thought about what he'd said. She was still shaken after what had happened, Jake had really scared her. Would it really be that bad having some company? "Okay," she finally said, "but just for tonight."

He nodded.

They ordered takeout: Italian. After the day Lacy'd had, she wasn't in the mood to cook. She'd enjoyed her chicken Caesar salad, washed down with some leftover wine, while Michael had eaten his lobster linguine. Afterwards, he'd even helped clean up, then made coffee insisting that Lacy had a cup, but she'd refused in favor of another large glass of wine from an unopened bottle of Pinot she'd found in the fridge. She knew it was probably best to go for the coffee, but she'd had a crappy day and had convinced herself that she deserved a little drink.

After food, they'd sat in front of the TV and watched TERMINATOR 2, which she'd already seen but Michael had insisted. She'd nearly nodded off a few times only to remind herself that she wasn't at home alone and wine induced slumber wasn't at all pretty. She was glad she'd agreed for Michael to stay. He'd proven to be good company and just what she'd needed to take her mind of everything that'd happened.

After the movie had finished, they'd talked. Michael had cleverly avoided a lot of Lacy's questions about family and where he'd lived before and she'd begun to wonder if maybe he was running from something. Either that or he was just very private. She didn't feel it necessary to keep pressing him so again, the conversation had mostly been about her. It couldn't have been interesting to him at all, especially as she'd left out a lot of the personal stuff about her mother and her sister so her life must have sounded really bland.

She managed to change the subject of how boring her life was by asking about Evo. It was interesting hearing Michael talk about his friend. He clearly had a lot of affection for the guy as it was the most she'd seen him smile all night. Michael had told her how they'd met: Evo had been attacked in an alley and Michael had been passing by when he'd heard the guy yelling. He told her how he'd managed to scare off the attacker and how it had sparked a real friendship between the two of them.

She watched him intently as he spoke, noticing things she hadn't before like how straight his nose was, the little creases that appeared at the sides of his eyes when he smiled, and how his deep blond hair looked a little sun-kissed towards the front. She suddenly felt an urge to run her fingers along his strong jaw to see how soft his stubble was.

She inhaled deeply and mentally slapped herself for letting her mind wander like it had, thankful that he was completely unaware that she was totally checking him out while he spoke.

Michael continued to explain how Evo had become a hit with the ladies during their time together and there were numerous stories about when the two of them would go out for drinks to let off steam. Michael would end up leaving Evo at the club after the guy's many trips to the *private* bathroom facilities—*Jesus. What types of clubs were those*—with a different woman on his arm every time, which, apparently, didn't interest Michael. His friend sounded like a first class whore to her, but Michael seemed very fond of him and who was she to judge, just because *she* may as well have taken a vow of celibacy?

"And what about you? Hasn't there been a special someone in your life?" Lacy asked, wondering why she felt a little nervous about his answer.

She saw that her question was unexpected. "No. No one special." He answered quickly, but she wondered if that were completely true.

She narrowed her eyes and cocked her head to the side. "Oh, come on. You're a fairly handsome guy. You must have had women in your life."

He smiled at that. "Only fairly?"

She laughed and suddenly felt a little shy. He was more than *fairly*, but she decided to keep that to herself right now.

"There was someone I was with a while back; a colleague at my previous job—Jessica, her name was. It was just casual, nothing serious, although, I think she wanted it to be. We dated for a short time, but I didn't see it going anywhere. He shrugged. "That's it really."

Lacy could see he wasn't comfortable talking about it and suspected there was more to it than what he'd told her, but she knew it was time to drop the subject.

She was yawning just about every two minutes now. She tried to focus on the clock on the mantle, only then realizing she'd overdone it with the wine, again. *Shit!* Surely she was on her way to convincing Michael she had a drink problem. She squinted and managed to make out the small black hands on the clock face. It looked like it was just after midnight.

"I think I'm going to go to bed." Thank God she'd managed to speak. She swung her legs off the sofa and stood up all too quickly. After a little wobble she moved forward and went straight down to the floor after stepping on the wine bottle—which was now empty—and losing her balance, landing in a heap on the carpet. *Oh, God. Kill me now!*

"Whoa! Lacy, are you okay?" She felt Michael's hand on her arm as she tried to right herself. Jeez, could her day get any worse? "Here, come on. Let me help you." She could hear the amusement in his voice as he hooked his arms under her shoulders.

"I'm such a. . . I'm so sorry," she said as Michael helped her to her feet. She knew when she'd opened the second bottle that she was making a mistake but couldn't seem to stop; another sign that she was feeling way too comfortable in Michael's company.

"Where's your room?"

"It's just down the end of the hall on the right." She started to giggle and stumbled again but Michael held on to her. Her head was cloudy and as she walked towards her bedroom, she tried her best to walk straight but it was no use. She was well and truly drunk.

They got to her room and Michael was about to open the door when she stopped him. She wasn't ready to let a man in there yet, even if he was just helping her stand up straight. "I'm fine now. Honestly, I can manage from here."

Michael faced her. "Are you sure? 'Cause you're still wobbling all over the place you know." He was clearly amused by her poor effort to remain upright. As she looked up at him, his face came into focus all of a sudden. His pale blue eyes were so clear to her that even through her drunken haze she felt drawn to them. Her eyes shifted to his full lips and she frowned as she was suddenly filled with an urge to have her own mouth on them.

What was she thinking?

Whether it was the wine or just the fact that she was feeling so emotional right now she wasn't sure. But she knew that in the morning she was going to regret what she was about to do.

She placed her hand on the side of his face. "Has anyone ever told you how good looking you are?"

"Okaaay. I think we should get you to—"

She cut him off as she leaned up and quickly pressed her lips to his. She closed her eyes, feeling the softness of him, and then suddenly they were gone.

"Whoa!" Michael's voice had her snapping her eyes back open as he held her away from him by her shoulders. He didn't look angry, in fact, it was hard to tell what his expression was saying, but regret hit Lacy as quickly as the urge to kiss him had.

"I'm so sorry. I didn't mean. . . " *Oh, God.* There it was: the sharp sting of humiliation. There was no going back now. She'd made a complete fool of herself and probably ruined any friendship she'd started to have with him. Her head began to pound and she reached up and placed her hand over her eyes with a groan. How could she ever look at him again? She felt his thumbs stroking her shoulders.

"Hey. It's okay," he said, and she thought she heard him sigh. She forced herself to look at him with an innocent forgive-me smile. He looked serious for a moment, but then he smiled back at her. "You need to sleep."

She felt him place his hand on the small of her back then he guided her into her room. She didn't stop him this time. If her room was untidy, then so what. Nothing could make her feel more ashamed than what just happened. Yes, she was still wobbly, but she tried with great determination to get over to her bed without embarrassing herself any further.

She managed it, thank God. By which point her eyes felt heavy. She climbed on her bed, lay back on her pillows and closed her eyes. She felt her shoes being removed and realized through her foggy, drunken state that Michael was talking to her. ". . . bad head in the morning."

"Hmm. . . " was all she could manage while she snuggled into the comforter that had been placed over her. Then she remembered who was in the room with her. "Michael."

There was nothing but silence. *Was he still there?* Her head was too heavy to look for him so she said it anyway just in case. "Thank you for staying with me."

The bedroom door closing quietly was the last thing she remembered before passing out.

* * *

Lacy came awake to voices down the hall. . .

". . . just wondering how your night went that's all." *Evo.* She recognized his deep voice straight away.

"Well, don't bother. I slept on the sofa which, as you knew damn well, was always my intention. So you can get anything else out of your head. And keep it down. She's still sleeping..." Michael's voice trailed off into the living room.

She groaned and turned onto her side, eyeing the digital alarm clock on the sideboard next to her bed that read 07:12. It wasn't the time she wanted to be awake on a Saturday morning, especially after throwing back nearly two bottles of wine. She managed to sit up and she swung her legs off the side of the bed.

Whoa! Too fast...

An almighty pain shot through her left temple as she sat up. The effects of last night were definitely in full swing: her mouth was bone dry, her teeth fuzzy and her limbs were refusing to cooperate. *Groan!* And then there was the realization of what had happened when Michael had helped her to her bedroom last night. Dear God, she'd actually kissed him.

"*Shit!*" she cursed out loud. How could she? The guy was clearly concerned for her safety, and kind enough to look out for her, and she goes and pulls something like that. Well, at least she'd probably solved the problem of him staying another night. She felt sure he wouldn't offer again through fear of a repeat performance. The last thing he'd want is to be jumped on again by a sad, lonely woman with no self respect and, apparently, now a drink problem.

She heard the muted sounds of laughter coming from the kitchen. The thought of facing Michael made her stomach lurch, or was it her monster hangover? Whatever, she wasn't going anywhere until she'd gotten out of last night's clothes and showered.

Dressed in a pair of navy sweat pants and a baggy, white Pearl Jam '98' tour T-Shirt, Lacy towel dried her hair in front of the vanity mirror. At least she looked more alive now. She knew she couldn't put off seeing Michael any longer. Hiding away, as much as that thought appealed to her, was not an option. She stepped into her slippers, heaved a sigh and forced herself to leave the safety of her bedroom.

Michael and Evo's conversation cut off the moment she walked into the kitchen which didn't make her feel awkward at all. She looked over at the dining table where Michael was looking straight at her. He smiled and she instantly felt the blood rush to her cheeks. She mentally cursed herself for being so pathetic. *Get a grip, woman.* She berated herself as she smiled back at him acting like there was nothing wrong, even though she wanted to bolt straight back out of the door. What was making the situation worse was the fact that while she'd showered, she'd surprised herself by thinking about their kiss last night and how much she'd enjoyed it, however brief. It wasn't helping at all.

"How're you feeling?" Michael asked, snapping her out of her inner turmoil.

"You mean aside from the fact that I feel like I've slept with a sponge in my mouth? Pretty awful, if I'm honest." She heard Evo snigger and threw him a look that told him it wasn't appreciated.

Michael frowned at him too. "There's fresh coffee in the pot, and I found some bacon in the fridge so there's some left in the pan. Hope you don't mind."

"No. Of course not. Thanks." She poured herself some coffee and passed on the bacon, not willing to risk eating anything just yet, then joined the men at the table and sat quietly.

She noticed that Evo was wearing the same clothes as he'd had on last night and wondered if perhaps he'd had one of his busy nights like the ones Michael had told her about. He'd obviously been out all night.

She hadn't realized she'd been staring until he looked up at her and his mouth curled up on one side.

Oh no. Had Michael told him about last night?

Michael broke the awkward silence, thank God. "What are your plans for today Lacy?"

She thought for a moment. Usually, Saturdays were what she classed as *lazy days*. She normally had a pile of assignments to mark over the weekend, and this one was certainly no different, but she always left them till Sunday in favor of trash TV and PJs. Not today. Present company had put a stop to that happening. She thought about the marking, but couldn't face it.

"I'm not sure," she said, at a loss. She hadn't really thought about doing anything except visiting Nina later on. She was glad, in a way, that she had company as the thought of spending time alone with just her thoughts, the ones that had been so unexpectedly dragged back to the surface again, made her palms sweaty. "How about you two?"

She watched Evo's brow lift as he turned to look at his friend. Michael heaved a sigh. "I still don't think it's a good idea for you to be alone until we figure this thing out."

"I'll be fine," she quickly protested. She wasn't fully on board with the babysitting. "He was probably just high or something."

"We can't know for sure so whatever you decide to do today, you'll have me and Evo for company." His smile looked almost apologetic.

She was about to object when her phone rang. She shot up from the table, forgetting what happened when she'd done that earlier in the bedroom, and winced at the pain in her head as she grabbed the handset from its cradle. "Hello." she said, before a female voice spoke on the other end of the line.

"Hello. Miss Holloway?"

"Yes, speaking." She opened a drawer in front of her and retrieved some Advil.

"Hi. My name is Claire Roper, I'm calling from Union Memorial Hospital about Nina Murphy." In an instant, Lacy's stomach sank. She'd asked for them to call her if there was any news, but at this very moment she didn't know if she wanted to hear it. She braced herself for bad news.

"Hello. Are you still there?" the woman asked after Lacy had momentarily gone silent.

"Uh... Yes. I'm here."

"We thought you'd like to know that the doctors will be bringing Nina out of her coma this afternoon. She's had a good night and the swelling has reduced significantly, although she's still not out of the woods yet. We'll have to monitor her closely and see how she responds. The next twenty four hours are going to be critical and we won't know the full extent of the damage to her brain, if any, until she comes around from the sedation."

Lacy's vision went blurry as her eyes filled up with tears. She knew there was a long way to go and not to expect too much given the extent of Nina's injuries but still... there was new hope.

"Would you like me to keep you informed of her progress? You seem to be the only person we can contact," the kind female voice asked.

"Yes, please. Could I see her?"

"I'm afraid you won't be able to visit until this evening. That's if all goes well. We want to monitor her very closely this afternoon. Like I said I'll keep you informed."

"Thank you." Lacy had planned on going to the hospital sooner, after what Michael had just said, this morning in fact. It would have been her excuse for avoiding being cooped up in her house with him and his slightly irritating friend, but, while that didn't look like it would happen now, knowing they were bringing Nina around from the sedation today had lifted her mood.

After hanging up the phone, she saw that Michael and Evo were looking at her, eagerly awaiting the news. "Hospital? How is she?" Michael asked.

Lacy nodded. "They're bringing her out of her coma today." She turned the faucet on and filled a glass of water, then went on to explain what the nurse had told her before popping the pills in her mouth.

"That's good news." Evo said after taking a sip from his mug of coffee. "They were just taking her down for assessment when I left earlier."

Lacy looked up at him, confused. What did he mean? *Maybe he'd popped into the hospital before he'd come here.* Yeah, that must be it. Michael must have asked him to check on her because he didn't want to leave Lacy on her own.

As if reading her mind, Michael explained. "I asked Evo to watch the hospital through the night. To make sure Jake didn't show up again."

Lacy felt a twinge of guilt over assuming Evo had been whoring himself all night. That's why he was in the same clothes. He'd been making sure Nina was safe just like Michael had with her and yet she'd mentally scorned him. She looked at him with a grateful smile and a silent apology. "Thank you." He looked surprised for a second before his expression changed into a cocky smile and he winked at her. Jeez, he was annoying.

She saw him look at Michael and then his face went serious. His eyes darted back to Lacy and between them again before he let out a sigh and got up from the table. "Damn, there's too much tension in here right now. I'm popping out for a smoke," he said as he strolled out of the kitchen door leaving it to slam shut behind him.

"You get used to him." Michael said, as if sensing her annoyance.

She rinsed out her glass and placed it on the drainer. "He's okay, really. I'm just a little sensitive today." She grabbed a small plate and contemplated eating some of the left over bacon, but still couldn't, so she put the plate back.

"More coffee?" she asked as she topped up her own mug.

"Not for me. I'm good thanks."

She felt him watching her as she stood at the sink staring through the small window that overlooked her back garden. The silence between them was uncomfortable and just as she spoke, so did Michael.

"About last—"

"I was—" They both paused.

"You go." Michael smiled.

She took in a deep breath and tried to dampen down the glow she could feel creeping back into her cheeks. "About last night. . . I wanted to apologize for what happened."

Michael's lips curled up. "You already did," he said, reminding her of her slurred words after he'd pushed her off him.

"Yes, well, I wanted to repeat it now I'm sober. I'm just. . . it's a bad time for me right now and I'm having trouble keeping my mind off something. I don't normally behave like that. I was out of line. I'm sorry." She stared into her coffee; too much of a coward to look at him, then heard the shuffle of his chair and the sound of his heavy boots approaching her.

Michael placed his hands on her shoulders. "Hey." He moved his head to her line of sight so she had no choice but to look at him. "It's okay. We're all entitled to get a little drunk once in a while." His smile was genuine, and she liked the way it lit up his whole face.

She relaxed a little and smiled back at him, the feeling of comfort creeping back over her. It was nice, but at the same time strange, to feel so close to him. It was like she'd known him a lot longer than she actually had.

He shook his head and laughed a little.

"What is it?" she asked, wondering what had tickled him.

"Nothing. . . it's just, well, maybe next time we should ban the alcohol."

"Oh. . . God," she groaned. This was the second time she'd been alone with him and both times she'd drunk too much. "You must think I'm a total wreck," she said covering her eyes with her hand and shaking her head in shame. She knew she had to get a grip on her emotions, but it was still hard for her at this time of year.

She opened her mouth to say something, but hesitated.

Michael's brow furrowed. "What?"

"Next Tuesday will be the anniversary of my sister's death," she explained, surprised to find herself opening up to him so easily.

Michael inhaled deeply. "I'm so sorry. How long ago did it happen?" He led her back to the table and gestured for her to sit down and sat in the chair beside her. Just then Evo pushed the door open and she saw Michael glance up at him and give a subtle shake of his head. Then there was the sound of the door closing and a mumble as Evo walked away.

"It was a long time ago. Sixteen years. I still have a hard time with it." She was surprised when Michael's warm hand covered hers on the table. It felt nice, comforting.

"How old was she? If you don't mind me asking."

"No, not at all. She was nine, three years younger than me." Lacy couldn't believe how much was coming out of her mouth. She never really spoke about it to anyone—her friends from work, not even her Grandmother when she was alive—so why did she feel she could tell him? All of a sudden it was pouring out of her. Michael sat quietly as she explained what happened all those years ago, including the truth about her mother's so called career choice and how they were often left on their own. Michael sat quietly, his impassive expression welcome. If he'd shown her any sign of pity she was pretty sure she'd lose it, but he just listened.

She hesitated as she got to the part of the accident. Michael must have sensed her anguish because he squeezed her hand gently, reassuring her that it was okay to go on. A tear broke free and rolled down her left cheek as she told him what had happened, reliving it all over again for the second time in less than twenty-four hours.

Michael moved his chair closer until their knees touched. Then he reached up to wipe her cheek with his thumb. Quietly he said, "It wasn't your fault."

She closed her eyes and inhaled deeply, her breath shook as she heard his words. She wished she could feel that way—that it was just an accident, but ever since that day her mother's words, the first words that had come from her mouth when the doctors had told them that Beth had died, had played over and over in her mind: *"It's your fault she's dead! You were supposed to look after her. How could you let this happen to my baby?"* Then Sheila had broken down, sobbing into the strange man's chest as he'd looked down at Lacy with what she knew now as contempt

Michael's brow lowered even further and his mouth tightened. "She had no right to say those words to you. You were a child left to fend for yourself and your sister. That should never have been your responsibility. It should have been her job. She's the one responsible for what happened because she left two young children all on their own."

Lacy was taken aback at the anger in Michael's voice. He shook his head and then reached up placing both his hands on her face. "It was bad enough that you had to witness what happened to her, but all of these years you've carried that unnecessary guilt around with you when it should have been your mother's burden."

Lacy could barely speak and she slowly moved his hands away from her face. It was hard for her to accept what he was saying. Nobody had said anything like that to her before. She had just always accepted that it was her fault that her sister had run down that alleyway straight into the busy morning traffic. But something about his words hit her hard.

"That should have been her job." "It should have been your mother's burden."

He was right. She thought back to how she used to envy her friend's parents. The few times her mother had let her go to Sophie's for dinner, she would sit at the dining room table and watch as her friend's mother prepared dinner for them. It was much different to anything she'd seen at home and she used to imagine her and Beth sat at a table in their own house with their mother placing a plate full of home cooked food down in front of them both with a loving smile. Afterwards, Lacy's mother would kiss their imaginary father on the cheek and join them at the table.

That's how it should have been.

She looked at Michael as a familiar feeling began to rise from the pit of her stomach. *Oh No! Not again.* This was something that hadn't happened to her for a long time. *Just breathe,* she told herself as what little air she seemed to be taking in began to feel thick in her lungs.

Breathe, dammit!

She began to tremble as the panic attack began to rise from her feet all the way up her legs, reaching her stomach and rising up further until it hit her chest, washing over her as quickly as it used to. She tried to breathe slowly in an attempt to get it under control, trying desperately to remember the exercises her therapist had taught her years ago to calm herself down. But her mind refused to work; she couldn't remember what to do.

She spoke to Michael, hardly noticing him now as she stood up from the table. "I. . . I have to get some air." She croaked as she reached for the lock on the French doors that led to her back garden. Her hands were shaking too much to turn the key.

Michael shot up from his chair and rushed to help her. "Jesus! Lacy. You're trembling. Are you okay?" He unlocked the door and opened it wide.

"Can't. . . breathe!" she struggled to say as she placed her hand over her throat. Her breaths were getting shorter and shorter now and her vision began to swim. She felt Michael's arm around her waist as he helped guide her out into the frosty morning sunshine.

"It's okay. I've got you," Michael said, his voice was gentle, soothing, and as she bent forward and leant her hands on her knees, she felt him gently stroking her back. "Just try to relax. Deep, slow breaths." She copied his rhythm as he continued to breathe with her.

The feeling of dread that consumed her whole body from head to toe began to slowly subside, washing away from her like a retreating tide. Her heart rate was returning to normal and the dizziness was fading. Breathing in through her nose and out through her mouth slowly, she began to feel herself again. She continued the pattern for a minute longer as the trembling subsided.

"Better now?" Michael asked while he continued to stroke her back.

She managed to nod her head. She felt relieved, ashamed, and scared that it might not be just a one off—that the panic attacks she'd spent years getting under control had just returned in an instant.

"I'm sorry," she managed to say before she walked back inside the house.

Michael followed her. "You don't have to be." He closed the doors. "Here, sit down and relax, okay?"

* * *

Lacy was still clearly shaken from what Michael assumed was some sort of anxiety attack. Talking about her past was understandably difficult and to think that she'd suffered all of this time. . . It must have weighed her down. He didn't know why he should feel so angry towards her mother but he did. He wanted to somehow take Lacy's anguish away, to talk to her, tell her everything was going to be okay. It worried him that the thought of someone hurting her plagued him so deeply. But for whatever reason, it did.

"I'm feeling better now. Thanks," she said to him as he sat down across the table from her, allowing her some space to pull herself together.

"Does that happen often?"

"It used to, at least once a day until I finally got a grip on it. Well, I thought I had until now. I haven't had one for nearly three years. My therapist taught me to control my breathing and not let them consume me and it was hard at first, but I persevered and finally learned to control them. Eventually they went away completely. I don't know what happened."

"Well, you've had a lot to deal with over the past few days. It's probably all just become too much for you." He noticed her hands were still a little shaky. "Are you sure you're okay?"

"Yes, honestly. I'm fine. This thing with Nina, It's just brought some bad memories to the surface."

The kitchen door opened and Evo strolled in looking pretty grim. "No. Before you say it, I'm not going back outside. I've gone through nearly half a pack of smokes since I've been out there leaving you two to talk. I don't think you're very good for my health." He joined them at the table. "Now, who the hell do I have to screw to get a cup of coffee in here?"

Michael rolled his eyes. Leave it to Evo and his inappropriate behavior to kick a fragile moment right in the ass. As Evo sat down next to Lacy, Michael was pleased to see her mouth quirk at the corner as she looked back at him. Evo gave him a friendly wink while she wasn't looking.

Smart bastard.

"Hey, I'm going to make some more breakfast." Evo was on fire with his manners this morning, jumping up and going straight to the refrigerator and grabbing some eggs, more bacon and what looked like cheese in a can.

"God help us." Michael said.

"Not much *he* could do to stop me filling my stomach right now." Evo threw some bacon in the pan, then cracked two eggs in there as well and began to fry it all up together.

"I'm sure he could teach you some manners, though." Michael looked at Lacy and mouthed, "Sorry." She gave him a half smile but looked like her mind was somewhere else. "Penny for them. . . " he said, using the phrase she'd used on him the other day.

"I wish he was real. . . then maybe he could help her," she said as she stared down at the table, ignoring all the clatter coming from Evo.

"You don't believe in God, Lacy?" Michael hadn't been that convinced himself at one point, but given his current situation, and what he'd seen over the short time he'd been dead, he couldn't be more convinced about God's existence. It was hard to ignore when you'd been plunged into a world where fighting demons and vengeful spirits had become a regular part of your day to day routine. He had to be real. Although, where he was and why he'd let this happen to him he had no idea.

"How could I? After what happened to my sister? My mother never really spoke about God, so what little I knew of him I'd learned in school. It was enough to make me believe he was real. But after"—she hesitated—"the accident all my beliefs were gone."

Michael noticed Evo had gone quiet and looked up to find him watching them from across the room. Evo raised an eyebrow at him, he too had seen the things that Michael had; fought with them in the same way, but right now he looked to have the same understanding as Michael did for Lacy feeling the way that she did.

"I don't know why these things happen. I can't give you the answer to that. But I know God exists even though I can't explain to you how. Not right now anyway—"

"It wouldn't matter what you said," Lacy interrupted, "I don't think I'll ever be able to believe that."

Michael inhaled a deep breath. He truly understood her reasons, but he tried a different approach anyway.

"Have you never had anything happen to you, I mean, any time in your life which has made you think that, just maybe, someone was looking out for you? Could've been something as simple as seeing something that's made you cross the street right before that cab drove straight through a puddle that would have drenched you otherwise?

"Or, for example, I remember an employee of mine many years ago—Joseph I think his name was—had left his house one morning to come to work as he always did, and had headed to the subway station to get the seven forty-five train into the city, the same one he always travelled on. This particular day, he was late getting in the office, when I asked why, he explained to me that he'd left an important file at home and had to go back to get it. He missed his train and had to get another one which took him on a different route. Later that morning, reports came in that a train heading from Granville into the city had de-railed, causing the front carriage to burst into flames."

Lacy sat upright, "I remember that. It was all over the news. Forty-eight people died and a load more badly injured. It was tragic."

"Yeah. Didn't they put a memorial plaque outside the station to remember the dead?" Evo mumbled; mouth half full.

"Yes, that's right." Lacy replied.

Michael just nodded. "It was the train Joseph would have been on had he not left his file at home."

Lacy gasped and held her hand to her mouth.

"Someone was looking out for him. Call it fate, divine intervention. . . whatever. But he wasn't meant to die that day. Needless to say, after the news, I gave him the rest of the day off."

Lacy looked stunned for a moment and sat quietly as if she didn't know what to say.

"I'll make some fresh coffee." Michael said as he picked up her used mug from the table in front of her.

"Okay," she whispered.

He walked over to the kitchen and gave Evo a look of disbelief as he watched him place his dishes in the sink and begin to wash them. "You feeling okay, buddy?" Michael asked, placing his hand on his shoulder. It wasn't every day he got to witness his friend being all domesticated.

Evo shrugged. "Just doing my bit."

"Hey. Actually, there may be something." Lacy said, swinging herself around on her chair to face them as Michael filled the coffee machine with fresh ground beans from the jar on the counter.

"Go on," he urged.

"There was this group of girls who I'd had a bit of trouble with in high school, you know the type: perfect hair, designer clothes. The popular girls who treated everyone else like crap? Anyway, it was mostly jarring words and occasionally one of them would shoulder bump me as they walked passed me in the hall, making sure I dropped my books. Anyway, I remember this one time they followed me home taunting me. When they caught up with me down a small alleyway that I always had to walk through to get to my street, one of them dragged me back by my arm."

Michael listened as he shoved Evo so he could get to the sink to rinse their cups. "Only cowards behave that way." he told her.

Evo shoved him back. "I would have punched the bitch."

"Well, it was because I tried to do that very thing—and missed—that I ended up on the floor with two of them kicking hell out of me."

"Damn." Evo said.

"Yeah. I was lucky when a boy from school, a senior, came down the alley and thankfully intervened. He managed to stop them and threatened to call the police. Needless to say, the girls said some choice words, but then left pretty quickly. It was something that the boy said to me that I've just remembered. He said that the only reason he was passing that way was because he'd left a term paper in class, and going back to get it had made him late for work so he'd taken a shortcut."

Michael stopped pouring the coffee for a minute, struck by a familiar memory. *It can't be. . . No. No, there's no way.* He shrugged the strange feeling away and filled up the two other mugs as Lacy went on.

"If it hadn't been for him, who knows how badly I could have been hurt. My only regret was that one of the girl's older brothers beat him up after school one night. I felt terrible because I knew it was because of what he'd done for me."

"Shit. Remind me never to get involved in a bitch fight," Evo said as he dried his hands on a towel hanging from the cupboard door.

Michael continued to ignore the tight feeling that had now grown more intense in the pit of his stomach as he sugared the coffees.

"The worst part about it was that the boy ended up in hospital, all because he stopped *me* from ending up there, or worse. I wish I could remember his name?"

Michael placed both his hands on the counter and tried to clear his head for a second. She couldn't have been talking about the same day. It had to be a coincidence, a very *large* coincidence. He picked up two of the mugs to take over to the table and as he walked away from the kitchen counter, the next words that Lacy spoke almost floored him.

"Jack! That was his name. Jack Pearson"

The coffee mugs that hit the floor smashed into pieces.

CHAPTER ELEVEN

"**S**hit, my man. Watch what you're doing next time."

Evo began to wipe spilled coffee from the bottom of his trousers with the dish towel.

Michael bent down to pick up the broken pieces. "Sorry, buddy." He was still feeling a bit numb after hearing Lacy say his name—his real name—from when he was still human. The name he hadn't heard for over a year since he'd died. Or, whatever the hell he was. *Fucking hell!* He couldn't believe that she was the girl he'd been beaten up over in his last year of high school.

"What high school did you say you went to?" He sounded apathetic even though he was barely able to speak as he tried to comprehend what he'd just heard.

"Clearview High. Lawrence Co. Do you want some help with that?"

"No, it's fine. I've got it. You never mentioned you lived in Ohio."

"Well, I was only there for a few years and then I got accepted into UMD so I came to Maryland to study." Lacy began to squeeze her hands together on her lap looking quite sullen all of a sudden. "I desperately wanted to say sorry to him, but when I went to visit him his parents were there and wouldn't let me see him. They told me it was my fault and to never try and contact him again. I never saw him after that. I wonder what happened to him."

Michael placed the broken pieces of coffee cup in the bin. *She'd come to the hospital?* "I never knew," he whispered.

"Sorry. What was that?" Lacy asked as Michael realized he'd said that out loud.

"Uh. . . *They*"—he cleared his throat—"never knew. His parents I mean. If they'd known what had happened, they probably wouldn't have blamed you." Though, he wasn't entirely sure about that.

"Maybe," she replied. "It upset me for a long time not being able to see him; even if it was just to say how sorry I was."

Michael finished dusting up the last of the mess he'd made on the kitchen floor and swept it into the bin. "I'm pretty sure he wouldn't have expected an apology from you." That was the truth. He never did blame her for what happened.

Soon after, Michael's parents had moved them out of the area; said they didn't want him getting into any more trouble, as if what had happened was his entire fault or something. After the Johnson's fostered him from the Heritage Boarding Academy when he was seven years old, they were never really very fond of him. He knew from an early age that they'd never liked him, but he'd accepted it, staying out of their way as much as he could by working as soon as he was old enough to. That way, he would get home from school just in time to change for work, eat, and then he'd go straight back out again until late. It was what it was. And it beat living at the children's home that he'd spent most of his miserable childhood in.

He never got to finish high school either. After leaving Clearview High, there was no point enrolling into a new school where he lived as there was only four months left of the term.

It never stopped him though. If anything, his relationship with The Johnsons had made him more determined to achieve something much higher than their expectations of him. He saved what money he earned, put himself through college, graduated and got himself a good job as soon as he'd left, working as a programmer for a software development company. After working as part of a development team for nearly a year, Michael himself went on to develop a web portal designed for investment companies to access global market data, and went on to have huge global success with many large corporations buying his software. After which he built up his own software development company and was a multi-millionaire by the time he was twenty-six.

It was a very different life from the one he'd led for the past ten months. He'd had no shortage of friends, colleagues who admired him and a busy social life. Being CEO of a large company was a big deal. He was very well respected, rich, he could have anything he wanted, any woman he wanted—and he did—but the money, the status, it never changed him. He made sure he gave back too. He cared about people, was always passionate about helping as many as he could, a "true philanthropist" they'd called him.

Why he was now dead, he had no idea.

"Michael?" Lacy's voice hauled him away from his memories, pulling him back to the present, back to the kitchen with her and Evo, and he noticed they were both looking at him. "Is everything okay?"

"I'm going for a walk."

* * *

The SUV pulled into the hospital parking lot.

It'd been a long day of waiting around and Michael had hardly seen Lacy after what had happened this morning. He'd avoided her as best he could. Not knowing how to handle the fact that she wasn't a complete stranger to him anymore.

She'd certainly surprised the shit out of him when she'd said his real name and he didn't know how to handle it. It wasn't as if he could tell her. To take his mind off things he'd headed over to the college in the hope that, if he'd found the demon that was possessing Jake, he could have taken some of his frustration out on its ass. No such luck. Jake had disappeared since going after Lacy.

Michael had left Evo alone with her for half the day. She hadn't been happy about it, but in fairness—in between catching some sleep on the sofa—his friend had behaved, keeping his eye on her for the right reasons and even making sure she'd eaten. Michael hadn't mentioned the panic attack to him, but he'd made sure Evo understood that she was still shaken from what had happened with Jake and had told him to go easy on her. His egotistical buddy may be a shit sometimes, but he knew when things were serious.

They pulled into a free space by the main entrance of the building. Michael was sitting up front with Evo, with Lacy in the back. She hadn't said a word the whole time, which was fine. Michael wasn't in the mood for talking either.

"You go ahead, I'll hang here." Evo said as he killed the engine. "No point in us all going in."

Michael flicked his seat belt. "Thanks, man."

He saw Lacy hesitate. "Actually, Michael, I was wondering if I could go in alone for a while. Just until I know how she is." He understood. And as much as he didn't want her to be on her own at all, he had to give her this.

He glanced at Evo who shrugged his shoulder like he could care less.

"Fine, but if you see Jake, you get straight out of there, okay?" Lacy nodded to him. "Just take as long as you need. We'll be right here."

"Thanks," she said as she left the vehicle.

Michael watched quietly as she walked away towards the slow rotating doors at the hospital's main entrance. He knew she was in serious danger and it was unsettling him. It wasn't fair to her that she knew nothing of the danger she was in, and not being able to tell her was eating at him in a big way. So much so, that it surprised him how much he did care. Deep down, he knew he was getting too emotionally involved in this particular case and it wasn't because of Nina, the girl lying in the hospital bed.

To his chagrin, Lacy had been on his mind all day. It wasn't so much about how amusing he found her when she was drunk, or that he'd enjoyed spending time in her company—again—but about how he'd felt when she'd kissed him. *damn!* He couldn't believe he'd actually contemplated kissing her back. Of course, not only would it have been a selfish thing to do on his part given the state she'd been in, but it would have also seriously complicated things. The last thing he needed was to get involved with someone while in his current... *state*. He'd forced himself to push her away last night, but for some reason, he was having real trouble pushing her from his mind.

This is a big problem.

"So, what's the deal with the chick?" Evo asked, his eagle-eyed friend never one to miss a trick.

Michael shifted uncomfortably in his seat. "What do you mean?"

"Come on, I've seen the way you look at her. You're into her aren't you? Don't blame you though; she's a nice piece of ass." It was all Michael could do to stop himself wiping the smirk of Evo's face. He sooo wasn't in the mood for his buddy's clever quips right now.

"Forget it Evo, we're not going there, okay? She's a work colleague who's, regrettably, already too deep into this shit that's going on." He tried to sound convincing but knew his friend wasn't stupid. Thankfully, and to Michael's surprise, Evo didn't press. Good, they had more important things to deal with at this present moment in time. Like what the hell had decided to use Jake as a suit and why?

"I think there needs to be someone watching the hospital at all times. Jake's bound to show up again at some point. That demon's gonna try and finish the job and I want to make sure one of us is here when he does."

Evo nodded his head. "Agreed. I rang the college earlier and managed to speak to Jake's roommate. He hadn't seen him since early last night. I'm not surprised he's gone AWOL though. It's a little hard to act like a model student when you're full of *demon*." He exhaled.

"I know. I went over there this afternoon. No sign of the son of a bitch. It's like he's just vanished. So what do we do now?"

Evo picked up his Lucky strike cigarettes from the dash, shook one out and stuck it between his lips before lighting it. He inhaled deeply, then blew the smoke towards his open window. "We wait. Sooner or later the bastards going to show and we'll be here when he does."

Michael felt anxious as he thought about how Lacy could have ended up like Nina, wired up to machines in a hospital room, or even worse. That bastard could've killed her. How he felt when he thought about someone hurting her bothered him. It felt foreign to him. Those kinds of feelings hadn't existed in him before, even when he'd still been alive, and it was seriously unsettling. And now, whether he liked it or not, she was his responsibility.

Sure, they'd spent a little time together over the short time they'd known each other, but how had she gotten so under his skin? It made no sense. He'd had plenty of opportunities to be with women since he'd been in his new body. He knew that some of the women he'd helped had been attracted to him but he hadn't been interested. Not even in anything casual, with any of them. So what was so special about Lacy?

After an hour or so Michael couldn't stand sitting in the SUV any longer. His anxiety had only gotten worse, so he needed to get out.

"I'm going to check out the grounds. I need some fresh air," he said to Evo who was sitting as still as a statue looking straight ahead out of the windscreen. With Evo's work, this whole stakeout thing would be something he was well used to but Michael couldn't stand it. Not tonight anyway. Sitting around doing nothing was driving him insane.

"Okay, man, no worries."

"Call me if anything changes." He got out of the SUV and inhaled the crisp fall air deep into his lungs as though he'd been trapped in a confined space for a decade and had just managed to break free.

He walked through the parking lot, straight past the main entrance of the hospital, through a small crowd of smokers and towards the edge of the building. Eyes scanned the area while one hand was in his woolen trench wrapped around the Glock that was strapped to his chest. Still no sign of Jake. He walked past the old, original brownstone building that was hidden away behind the new modern build which now took pride of place at the front of the grounds. He continued on past the ambulance service yard, which was situated at the back of the building, and carried on walking until he'd come full circle, ending up right in front of the revolving doors which led to the main reception entrance.

Unsurprisingly, he found the urge to go inside and check on Lacy too strong to fight. Before he knew it, he was in the elevator travelling up to the third floor where ICU was. The walk down the corridor was a long one. The trauma ward was alive with the many nurses and doctoring staff that were on duty, rushing in and out of rooms that spread all the way down to a set of double doors at the end of the cream hallway. Some were open and as Michael walked past, he glanced in and saw families sitting by their loved ones' beds. Some were laughing and joking; some sat quietly, their anguish clear on their faces. A female voice came over the Tannoy system requesting the presence of a *Doctor Henley* to treatment room 4.10.

Visiting was until nine p.m and would soon be over. With no sign of Jake yet, hopefully Michael could get Lacy home quickly and safely while Evo watched over the hospital for the second night running.

He pushed through the double doors and into a smaller corridor which was much quieter. The decor looked the same, but the strip lights overhead seemed a little dimmer. The information sign on the wall in front of him had an arrow pointing left for the nurses' station. He headed straight there where a nurse with brown, shoulder length hair was just coming out of a small room behind the desk with a file in her hand. She was laughing and spoke to someone over her shoulder before smiling at him. "How can I help?" she asked in a soft voice.

"I'm looking for my colleague. She's visiting a patient here."

"What's the patient's name?" She sat down on a chair and placed the file on the desk in front of her.

"Nina. Nina Murphy." He fastened a couple of the buttons on his trench just to make sure his weapon was hidden.

"Ah yes, you're with Miss Holloway?"

"Yes. She asked me to pick her up."

"No problem. She's in room 3.08 just down the hall on the left."

"Thanks." He smiled, and headed in that direction.

When he approached Nina's room, he stopped at the large window, looking through to the cream room with its navy blue linoleum floor. The lighting was dim and the bed was in the middle of the room with a boom arm—which was attached to the ceiling—that housed the EKG machine which was monitoring the student's vitals. Lacy had fallen asleep in the chair next to Nina's bed, her hand resting on Nina's arm.

Michael couldn't help but watch as Lacy slept. Some of her blond hair had fallen loosely over part of her face and she looked so peaceful. He couldn't understand why she'd become so emotionally attached to Nina. She'd never met her, never even knew who she was until he'd pointed her out in the dining room a few days before, but she was acting like a family member would. Maybe it was just her nature. He hadn't known Lacy long, but he knew her enough to know she had a kind heart. She was there for Nina purely out of kindness when the girl had no one else. That knowledge, and the way she looked as she slept in that chair, was what made Michael realize how much she'd captivated him. He suddenly realized how beautiful she was and not just on the outside.

He frowned as his conscience spoke up and told him to get a grip. This wasn't going to happen. He couldn't let it.

He noticed a hot drinks machine down the far end of the hall so he left Lacy to sleep for a little longer while he went to get them both a coffee. He felt around in his jeans pocket for change and managed to scrape together the three dollars fifty he needed for two cups. The swishing noise from the machine was a stark contrast to the quiet of the ward so it was good that it was right out of the way of the bedrooms. All that was by it was a linen cupboard and the family waiting room—to which the door was open. He heard sniffling coming from inside, but ignored it as he sugared the coffees and stirred them with a lollipop stirrer. *Useless things.*

He was heading back to Nina's room when he glanced into the waiting room and saw who the sniffling was coming from. A woman sat by herself with her head in her hands. He walked inside, approaching her slowly so he wouldn't startle her. "Are you okay?" He kept his voice low.

The woman looked up at him and began to wipe her face with a tissue. "Uh. . . Yes." As she looked up and her eyes met his, her brow furrowed. At first she seemed weary of him, but then she looked surprised by something. A strange calm then settled over her face and she sat unmoving, staring at him from the small gray sofa across the room. Her tears had stopped falling and her hiccuping breath calmed. Her mouth curled up slowly into an unsure smile and she spoke in almost a whisper, "Are you here for him?" She looked down at her fidgeting hands then back to him. "My son. . . Are you here to take him?" Her hand snapped to her mouth as she choked back a sob.

Clearly she was going through some kind of emotional breakdown resulting from somebody close to her being on the ward. He approached her, slowly, placing the two coffee cups on a sideboard as he passed. "Would you like me to get a nurse?"

The woman, who looked to be in her sixties, brushed her shoulder length gray hair from her face, stood up from the sofa and began to walk towards him, reaching out for him and stopping him in his tracks. She didn't seem to register that he'd spoken as she repeated her question with a calmness that seemed out of place given the way she'd been when he'd entered the room. Her vacant stare set him on edge—like she was looking right into him, not the body he inhabited, but to *him* inside of it. For the first time since being dead, Michael felt cold. The skin he was in prickled all over with goose flesh, feeling like thousands of ants were crawling all over him and he found that he couldn't speak.

The lady placed both her hands on his arms and smiled up at him with such poignancy. Her deep blue eyes glistened with unshed tears as she spoke, "Please, take good care of him. Look after him until I get there."

Michael swallowed hard. What the hell was she talking about?

Then she kissed her own hand, reached up and placed it on his left cheek and nodded her head to him before walking out of the room.

After pausing for a moment, feeling quite bewildered, he followed her into the corridor and watched her walk into one of the hospital rooms. He walked over to the window and watched as the woman sat down on the chair next to a young dark-haired male lying unconscious on the bed. Her son, he assumed. That's why she'd been so upset. From the weak signals on the EKG machine just above his bed, and the respiratory machine that was breathing for him, he looked like he was barely hanging on. The woman placed her hand on his on top of the bed covers and leaned in close to his ear to speak to him. Just as Michael was about to walk away, the woman looked at him through the window and smiled. Then she went back to watching over her son.

The whole interaction had left Michael feeling confused and a little uneasy.

Before he returned to Lacy, he went over to the nurses' station and spoke to the same nurse who'd been there when he'd first arrived. "The man in room 3.10? What happened to him?"

At first it looked like she wasn't willing to discuss it with him and Michael prepared himself for the usual you're-not-a-relative speech, but after a sigh she explained. "He was hit by a car, a hit-and-run; doesn't look like he's going to make it. They're turning his life support off later." Her face was sympathetic. Even though she was probably well used to that kind of thing happening, the look on her face said that it was still hard to deal with.

"Is that his mother in with him now?" he asked.

"Yes. She's hardly left his side, the poor lady."

"She was pretty upset just now. You might want to send someone to look in on her."

She looked up at him, her smile grateful. "Of course. Thanks for letting me know."

He decided it was probably the woman's emotional state that had made her act that way and shrugged it off. He had too much on his plate right now to concern himself with other people's anguish.

He got back to Nina's room and as he clicked the door shut Lacy stirred. He walked over to her slowly, realizing he'd left the coffees in the waiting room. He figured they'd be cold by now anyway.

"Michael?" Lacy blinked quickly, placing her hand on her neck and stretching her head back. "I'm so sorry. I can't believe I fell asleep." Her voice was huskier than usual. He liked it. She shifted in her seat and put her hand to her mouth to cover a yawn.

"You look exhausted." He went to the opposite side of Nina's bed, checked out the reading on the EKG machine—which was a lot more steady than the poor guy's down the hall—then looked down at the young woman's face. She was pale, with no help from makeup, and even though she was unconscious and fighting for her life Michael noticed that she looked much better without it.

"How's she doing?" he asked.

"No change. She's out of it on pain meds at the moment." Lacy laughed a little and shook her head.

"What is it?"

She looked down at her hands as she twisted her fingers together in her lap. "I've prayed for her you know. Sat here and actually prayed."

"It's understandable."

She looked up at him, her expression somber. "But it's not easy when you don't believe in God. I haven't *believed* since I was a child. Religion, ghosts, life after death, all of it seems so story-book to me. I've never even been to church. What I was taught about God, I was too young to really understand. I think I remember my mother talking about God once, but she never cared about religion so I don't know why she even bothered. I think she thought it was just something she should do."

Ironic, he thought, considering she was standing talking to a dead guy.

"But I've prayed for Nina and I don't know why. I suppose it had something to do with what you said this morning."

He walked over to the window, looking out into the bland hallway of the quiet hospital wing. "It's just circumstance that's all. And there's nothing wrong with that," he said with his back to her. He'd never really had an opinion on God either until now. But there had been times in his life when he'd prayed and hadn't really known why. Sometimes, even if you weren't totally on board with the whole religion thing, just believing in the idea of it was a kind of comfort.

Now, however, he had a whole other opinion about it.

"But it didn't work last time." Lacy said, followed by a sniffling noise which made him turn around to see her wiping away a tear that had just rolled down her cheek. He frowned, not really knowing what to say. He knew it had to be hard for her seeing Nina lying in a critical condition in the bed in front of her. At least he understood now.

"The first, and only other, time I've ever prayed was for Beth; it didn't work. She died anyway."

He couldn't imagine how hard it was for her, being alone and having to deal with something horribly traumatic from her past. He wanted to reach out to her, but thought better of it. In the window's reflection, he saw Lacy get up from the chair and he turned to face her as she walked over to him.

"I don't feel right talking like this in front of her," she said quietly, looking back over her shoulder. She lowered her voice to almost a whisper. "All those years ago, I pleaded with a god that I hardly knew anything about to help my little sister live and yet she didn't. So why am I putting faith in that same god for Nina?"

Oh to hell with it. Pun intended. He reached down and took hold of her hand and placed it between both of his. He looked into her pale green eyes, which were now a little red. "Because you care, and deep inside you want to believe he exists just like the rest of us. You're a good person, Lacy. And the way you've cared for her"—he nodded towards the bed—"is proof of that."

They both stood and looked at each other for what could have been anything from five seconds to five hours, he wasn't sure. But he knew one thing: He was filled with a sudden urge to reciprocate what she'd done to him last night, but kissing her was really going to complicate things. He studied her face, noticing for the first time the faint freckles that dusted over her nose. Her long eyelashes curled up at each outside corner, reaching almost halfway to her neatly plucked eyebrows. His attention was drawn to a small, faded scar just above the left brow. He'd tried to ignore what he'd begun to feel for her. He couldn't possibly get involved with someone given his circumstances and the timing wasn't at all right. But right now—in this moment—she was drawing him in and he couldn't seem to stop himself.

Still holding her warm hand in his, he felt her edge closer. He didn't pull back, ignoring the shouting and screaming of his subconscious, which was now practically doing back flips trying to get his attention. He knew she was going to kiss him and he wasn't sure what to do about it. "Lacy. . . I. . ."

He was about to put his will power to the test and say something to stop her when she paused, breaking her gaze away from his to look over his shoulder. It was then that her whole body stiffened and her eyes widened as she inhaled a sudden gasp. "Jake," she whispered.

Michael spun around to see Jake moving away from the window quickly. He turned back to Lacy grabbing her by her arms. "Stay here for five minutes. Then I want you to go downstairs, jump in a cab and go straight home, okay?"

She nodded.

He was out of the door and running down the corridor after the SOB without even thinking about it. He reached into his inside pocket for his cell, flipped it open and dialled his buddy. "Evo! We have a visitor." Michael pushed through the door that Jake had just run through that led to a stairwell at the other end of the hospital wing. "We're on the far left side of the main building. He's no doubt heading for the fire escape at the bottom of the stairs."

"On my way." Evo replied, hanging up straight away.

On his descent, Michael leaned over the rail and saw that Jake had nearly reached the bottom of the stairwell and was headed for the door. Meanwhile, Michael was only halfway down, still having two more floors to go. *Screw this.* He placed both hands on the rail and leapt over the thing. He had no idea why, but he held his breath while he dropped down through the middle of the stairwell, seeing the tiled floor approach pretty quickly. He landed without even so much as a wobble, just in time to grip Jake around his neck before he left through the now open door.

"Where d'ya think you're going?" Michael growled as he tightened his grip on Jake's throat. The son of a bitch was trying his damnedest to wriggle free; nearly succeeding at one point until, from nowhere, a large fist came flying through the air. Before Michael could blink Jake flopped unconsciously onto the tiles.

"Huh! I expected more resistance," the large guy said as he squeezed his own fist with a look of pure satisfaction.

"Jesus! Evo. I had it under control"

"Even more so now." His face was smug.

"You ruthless bastard." Michael shook his head in amusement. Evo was right though, this guy was possessed so there's no way he should've gone down from just a punch to the face.

Evo crouched on one knee and rolled Jake's sleeve up.

"You need to be quick with this." Michael said as he watched Evo pull a small knife from a strap on his ankle. His buddy drew the blade over the palm of his own hand and, using the forefinger of his other hand, he traced along the wound. Next he reached over Jake and drew a symbol on his forehead in blood: a circle within a circle, then he finished in the middle with a hexagram. Michael had seen, and drawn, that very same symbol on more occasions than he dared to remember. It worked every time, though, trapping the demon or spirit inside its human host.

"Done!" Evo said as he placed his blade back under his trouser leg. Then he grabbed hold of Jake and threw him over his shoulder like he was nothing but a sack of laundry. "Let's get him in the car quickly."

CHAPTER TWELVE

As she paced back and forth in her living room—squeezing her fingers together like she was kneading Play-Doh—Lacy waited for word that Michael and Evo were okay, and that they'd managed to catch Jake. She was worried sick, almost to the point of actually throwing up. She took a few deep breaths and decided that if she was going to wear a hole in her blue area rug, she might as well do it with a mug of hot coffee in her hand.

In the kitchen, she placed the contents in her mug and opened the fridge door only to see she was out of milk. Dammit! Never one to drink her coffee black, and not wanting to nip out to the store just in case Michael called, she thought about pouring a glass of wine instead, cringed for a second, then thought better of it. New rule: She was no longer allowed to consume alcohol when under any kind of stress.

Mr Hinckley. Her sweet neighbor, and the only person in the street that she'd ever interacted with, would perhaps give her a drop of milk, though she didn't feel comfortable calling on him at this late hour. He was a nice old man. Lonely now after his wife had died four years ago. He'd popped by a few times with some fresh vegetables that he'd grown in his back yard.

Lacy grabbed her coat from the hook in the hallway and headed next door. A biting wind made her shiver as she walked down her path towards the street so she tucked her coat in tight to her chest to keep out any draughts. Although it would be early, it wouldn't surprise her if they had some snowfall before the night was through.

She reached Mr Hinckley's front gate, but before she opened it, she paused, feeling a familiar sense of unease like the other night when she was being watched. She looked down the street one way, then the other. No one there. Her neighborhood was always quiet at this time and tonight was no exception. There were lights on in most of the houses that she could see, their occupants savoring the warmth inside. She checked around again but there wasn't another soul in sight. Putting it down to still being a little spooked after the incident with Jake, she ignored it.

She knocked on the old man's door, noticing a small, hand carved, wooden angel that was severely weather beaten hanging next to the door. Just the kind of symbolism she needed to see right now. She heard the click of a bolt and the slide of a chain before the door opened and out popped Mr Hinckley's head from behind the door.

"Who is it?" he said, squinting as he pushed his glasses further up the bridge of his nose. "Oh. Lacy. Hello."

"Hi Mr Hinckley, sorry to bother you this late, but you couldn't spare a drop of milk could you? I can drop some in for you in the morning after I've been to the store." She blew on her hands and rubbed them together for warmth.

The old man had the kind of smile that made his eyes disappear. His thin gray hair was always combed neatly to one side with a little wave in the front. "Of course, would you like to come in for a minute? You look frozen stiff my dear." He opened his door wider and Lacy felt the warm air from inside hit her in the face. His house must have been stifling though the old man was wearing a thick, woolen pullover. Wine colored, to match his tie.

"No, that's okay. I don't want to keep you. Besides, I'm waiting for a phone call from someone so I can't stop."

"That's fine. Just give me a minute then, dear," he said, shutting his door to keep the heat in. After a minute or two, he returned with a carton that was a third full. "Is this much okay? I have another carton so you can take that with you."

"Oh, that's great. Are you sure you don't mind, Mr Hinckley?" She tried, but failed, to hold back a shiver.

He belted out a wheezy cough, his face turning plumb purple, and then finished off by patting his chest. She'd noticed his health had deteriorated over the last couple of months. "Don't be silly child. Now, is that all you need?"

She smiled. "Yes. Thanks. I just needed a coffee fix that's all. Busy day, you know. . ."

After saying good night, and after Mr Hinckley waited for her to get back to the house before going back inside, Lacy heard the muted sound of her phone ringing inside as she approached her front door. She cursed, grabbed her front door key from her coat pocket, nearly dropped it in a panic, and hurried to unlock the door. As soon as she stepped inside, the ringing stopped. "Shit!"

She rushed into the living room and saw that the red light on her answering machine was flashing. She pressed play and was relieved to hear Michael's voice coming through the loudspeaker.

"Lacy it's Michael. We got Jake. Figured the cops needed to speak to him, so we're gonna escort him to the station to let them know what happened. Just wanted to tell you everything's okay. Oh, and I'm gonna pop to my place before I head back to yours. Uh. . . Yeah, that's it. Bye."

Lacy sighed with relief, the tension draining right out of her shoulders. Thank God everything was okay. Mind you, she should never have doubted that it would be. She had a feeling both Evo and Michael were very capable of handling themselves physically, especially Evo who was the size of a WWE wrestler. There was no way Jake would have gotten away, not with how angry Michael had looked before he'd run after him.

And had they really nearly kissed? Just thinking about the way he'd looked at her back at the hospital filled her stomach with butterflies. Yep, she was definitely attracted to him. And going by what had almost happened, Michael must like her too. She couldn't help the smile that stretched across her face.

She realized that the cops were also going to want to speak to her about what had happened. If she left now she could meet them both over there. She grabbed her scarf, her car keys from the little wooden bowl on the sofa table in the hallway, and headed out.

It only took her ten minutes to drive to the County Sheriff's office in the middle of town. She came to a stop right outside the gray, unadorned, concrete building, but there was no sign of Evo's SUV anywhere. Perhaps he'd parked around the back. Inside the station, Deputy Teresa James, who Lacy had known since moving here, was sifting through files in one of the cabinets behind the front desk. She looked up and greeted Lacy with a smile. "Hey Lacy. . . Strange seeing you in here."

"Hi. How's things? It's been a while huh?"

"Yes, it has. I'm good. And you seem to lose more of that cute British accent every time I see you. You'll be one of us soon."

Lacy laughed and rested her arms on top of the counter. It was nice to see her friend after so long. It must have been over a year since they'd talked last—apart from the odd hi or hello in passing—just after Teresa had started work as a full time deputy after completing all of her training. She looked different now: older, without the makeup she used to always wear, and her deep brown hair tied back off her face in a tight bun. But she still had that same way of making Lacy feel welcome.

"Anyway, I'm guessing you haven't just popped in for coffee, as this stuff tastes like piss." She mumbled that last part so no one else could hear. "What can I do for you?"

"I've come to give a statement about what happened last night at work."

"Something happened at the college?" Teresa asked, raising a quizzical eyebrow.

She didn't know? Strange. "Yeah. Two friends of mine just brought a guy in that tried to attack me after I'd left my office last night," she explained, wondering why Teresa didn't already know. "He tried to get into my car before I drove off. We think he might know something about what happened to Nina Murphy."

Teresa still looked confused. "The girl who tried to commit suicide?"

Lacy nodded. She began to worry. It had to have been at least thirty minutes since Michael had called.

"Hold on. My shift only started fifteen minutes ago. I'll go through and speak to Don; he's probably got them in the back there in one of the interview rooms."

That'll be why. Lacy let out a relieved sigh. The sooner she got the statement over with, the sooner she could get home and flop into bed. What a rough night.

She took a seat in the waiting area and began to pick the chipped polish from her thumbnail. She jumped as the front door flew open and two officers hauled a man who was in cuffs inside. He was protesting loudly and two more officers appeared behind the desk. As the scruffy man with the dishevelled black hair got dragged passed her, he noticed Lacy sitting there and his leering smile made her physically sick.

"That's enough Milton." One of the officers ordered as they pushed him to the front desk.

Lacy wondered how Teresa could stand having to deal with this kind of thing every day. She'd only been sat waiting for five minutes and she wanted to bolt out the door and forget giving the statement altogether. But she knew she had no choice and managed to stay in her seat for another five minutes until Teresa finally returned. Avoiding the commotion at the desk, she sat next to her.

"Lacy, when did you say your friends brought him in?" Teresa asked with the same puzzled look that she'd had a moment ago.

"Would have been a little over thirty minutes ago. I guess."

"Don said no one's reported anything like that tonight, and your friends haven't been here."

What? Where the hell were they?

"Oh. . . Um, perhaps they've been delayed for some reason." Lacy said as she stood up from her seat, her mind began to think all sorts of things: What if Jake had gotten violent and hurt them? What if they'd been involved in an accident? She couldn't understand why Michael would lie about bringing Jake in. She had to call him.

"Are you okay? Would you like to make the report yourself? What happened at the college?"

She hadn't even realized Teresa was talking until she felt her place a hand on her arm. "Lacy?"

"I. . . I need to go home actually. I'm not feeling too good. Can I call in sometime tomorrow?"

"Sure. Or I can call round after my shift's finished in the morning."

She heard her friend's rushed reply fading away behind her as she hastily walked out of the station.

Lacy raced back to her house and immediately checked her answering machine. No new messages. She knew if Michael had turned up at the sheriff's office after she'd left, Teresa would have called her straight away. Not knowing what to do, the pacing started up again, but this time she was right by the phone, waiting for the damn thing to ring again.

CHAPTER THIRTEEN

At a motel just off I.52, Michael stood by the window of Evo's room watching his buddy, who was currently taking out his mood from lack of sleep on their captive's ass. Jake was all skin-stealing demon strapped in that chair, no question about it. It was staying silent, though. No matter how much Evo pressed, the bastard wasn't talking.

Evo turned away—his frustration clear by the way his lips were tightly pressed together—as he reached inside his jacket and pulled out a different knife than the one he'd used in the hospital stairwell. This one was much bigger, like a Bowie Knife on steroids. It had an unusual gold colored blade protruding from a black, leather bound handle. "Looks like I'm going to have to try another way to get this asshole to talk." His mouth curled up at the sides as he winked at Michael.

"What's that going to do?" was the first thing to come from the demon's mouth since they'd captured it. Michael sensed its enjoyment.

Evo smirked. "Well, lucky for you, you're just about to find out." He pulled the guy's sleeve up, placed the blade down on his forearm and cut a small slit down to his wrist. At first the demon looked totally unimpressed with what Evo had done. His eyes looked down at the sliced flesh, which Jake's blood was now trickling from, as though he'd just drawn a line down it with nothing but a sharpie. Jake smiled.

Evo stood perfectly still, watching the demon like he was waiting for some kind of reaction. After a couple more seconds, and just after Jake had started to grin up at Evo, the cocky expression changed dramatically. He looked down at his arm as if the thing had sprouted legs and was about to run away from him. His eyes widened, his mouth opened and his breath caught. Evo continued to watch with both arms folded over his chest without saying a word.

Michael wondered what the hell was happening and left his position by the window and approached slowly. As he looked down at the guy's arm it began to twitch uncontrollably. His skin looked like it was moving, then he noticed creeping black veins growing out from the fresh cut, spreading outward in all directions. He watched as the demon began to pant frantically, struggling against the tight restraints on his wrists and ankles. Jakes eyes widened with fear as they locked onto the arm that was now almost black all over. . . then came the hellish scream.

"What the..?" Michael had no idea what was happening. He'd never seen anything like it before and he'd dealt with many demons in the past. He looked at Evo waiting for some sort of explanation, but the guy just continued to watch with an eerily satisfied grin on his face. As the demon continued to react to whatever the hell it was that was happening, Evo began to repeat the line of questioning that he'd gotten no response to before.

All he got was a, "Fuck you!" then an "Arghhhhh. . . " before Jake's head flipped back with the pain that was now obviously shooting up his arm.

"Burns doesn't it?" Evo sneered. "I can make it stop, as soon as you cooperate." It was said with complete military composure—one of the things Michael admired most about his friend: his ability to interrogate his subjects with such prowess, whether human or not, was impressive. He had to hand it to the guy, he was no longer the nervous, scruffy, male that he'd met in that alley all those months ago. Now he was a warrior, a beefed up assassin that could hold his own with anyone or anything.

Yes. . . he was actually jealous of the guy.

But all that tough-ass came with a price. Evo was well known in the underworld and when you'd managed to carve out a reputation as lethal as he had in such a short time it got you noticed, and often by the wrong people, or. . . *things*.

"Arghh. . . " The demon possessing the man in front of them was having a hard time in there. Whatever it was that Evo had done to the SOB, it was having a profound effect. His face had begun to distort in such a way that his features were no longer Jake's own, and the screeching that was now leaving his mouth and filling the room could only be likened to that of a tortured animal.

His eyes flicked up to Evo as he continued to pant and growl like a rabid dog. "What have you done to me?"

"I'd be more worried about what will happen next." Evo smirked. "Start talkin' or things are gonna get much worse for you. You feel me?"

A deep rumble came from Jake's throat, which then erupted into a sinister laugh. The demon glared at him through evil eyes that had now turned crimson. He'd stopped panting by now and was looking Evo straight in the eyes. "You're playing with fire, boy." His voice had become deeper, and it sounded like two people talking, a mix between poor possessed Jake and the evil itself. Still, Evo wasn't fazed. "You have no idea who you're messing with. Your actions will lead to your deaths I assure you—you and your friend. . . "—he turned his head away from Evo and straight towards Michael—"Michael? Isn't it?"

Michael was momentarily aghast and noticed Evo glancing up at him with an equally shocked expression. "How the fuck. . . ?"

"How do you know who I am?" Michael asked through gritted teeth as he took a couple of steps towards the demon.

"Oh. . . we all know."

"What the hell's that supposed to mean?" The demon just smiled at him in a way which almost made Michael's borrowed skin crawl. "Tell me you son of a bitch!"

"You'll know soon enough. He's coming for you; sooner rather than later when I tell him where you are. And what a good demon I'll be, delivering that good news to him myself."

Michael's voice grew louder. "Who? What the hell are you talking about?" The demon said nothing. Only the sound of deep breathing was coming from the man whose eyes were still burning Michael.

"Enough of this. This bastard's full of shit." Evo said as he waved his knife right by Jake's face. "Are you going to tell us why you've been offing those students?"

Silence.

Before Michael could blink Evo had stabbed his knife through Jake's leg so hard, he heard the blade hit the wood from the chair below it.

The demon let out a vicious roar and black smoke began to rise up from where the knife had penetrated the poor, innocent young man's skin right up to the hilt. Michael knew Jake had no chance of living through this. They rarely survived possession anyway. If the demon had its way, it would make sure of it. Michael knew that from experience. Those wounds were sure to kill the guy. Besides, the first slice that Evo had given him had bled out all over the floor. He had no chance.

Poor guy.

"Talk!" Evo shouted over the deathly scream that was filling the motel room. He clamped his hand over Jake's mouth, halting the demon who was now scowling at him from under heavy eyelids. There was a long pause and then Evo pulled his hand away. He bent down so that his mouth was by Jake's ear "I said, talk!" Just as Evo looked set to pull the knife back out—no doubt ready to drive it into the other leg—the demon's face changed. He knew he was defeated. Damn his buddy was good.

"I have a debt to pay." The demon growled the words with fierce intensity and howled with pain again. "Remove it and I will tell you what you want to know."

Evo reached down and yanked the knife out, satisfaction evident as he looked briefly towards Michael for approval. All Michael did was roll his eyes. *Smug son of a bitch.*

"Continue. . . or this goes straight back in there." Evo ordered, assessing the guys weeping thigh.

"I am bound to Varesh. Indebted to him for a crime I committed more than a century ago. He feeds off human souls, they empower him, make him stronger. But the only way he can get those souls is if a human ends their own life: suicide, I think you call it. The Creator doesn't accept those who take their own life, so there's no going through the pearly gates for them. Instead, they go down, where Varesh intercepts them and can claim them for his own. And where better to find those souls than a place where there are lots of vulnerable humans. There are plenty of parasites in a college campus—depressed little whiners, hormonal, with nothing better to do than feel sorry for themselves. Places like that are full of them. I just gave them a bit of guidance, a *push* in the right direction."

His words enraged Michael. "You're not exactly giving them guidance by taking over their bodies and doing it for them." he bit out at the demon that had now calmed. "*They* are not choosing to end their own lives, *you* are!"

"But it's inevitable. I see what's in their minds, the way they imagine doing it. So I help them. It just saves time. The more souls I collect for my master, the easier my existence becomes. You see, I've always believed in self-preservation."

It took all of Michael's strength not to knock the guy's haughty expression right off his face, but what would be the point of striking him? He'd only further injure the innocent male who was being possessed, and besides, he knew it would take a lot more than that to affect the evil bastard. Why waste the energy.

"I've given you what you asked for?"

Evo stepped up in the guy's face. "Oh no. . . We've not finished yet." He flipped the knife in his hand and smiled at the demon as he held it over Jake's other leg. "What do you know of my buddy here?"

Michael had seen many demons before this one—had fought against them numerous times, knew their ways, their weaknesses—but there was something very different about this one. This one was a whole other level of evil; he could see it in those crimson eyes.

"I know this. . ." he warned, looking only at Michael. "Varesh has been looking for you for a very long time, but for some reason, you weren't to be found—hidden somehow. Then all of a sudden there were whispers amongst my kind that you'd been seen. We found out you were hunting us. My master has had his ear to the ground, so to speak. So after all of this time trying to find you, imagine my joy when you came wandering right into my hands."

Evo laughed. "You have a strange way of looking at things. From where I'm standing, you seem to be in our hands."

The demon smirked at Michael, ignoring Evo's words. "This news will be received along with great repute. Varesh will be most pleased when I tell him you are this close and when he finds you—"

"Who is this Varesh and what does he want with me?" Michael was done with the pleasantries.

A subtle laugh came from the demon and Michael thought he looked surprised for a moment. "You really don't know do you? I must say. . . Great look you've got going on there; although I did prefer you as a brunette," the demon mocked.

Michael walked around the guy that was tightly bound to the chair. He had no doubt that this demon knew exactly who he was. This was the first lead he'd come across. The demon might actually have relevant information which could help him find out the truth.

"Dammit! Just give me a straight fucking answer," he demanded. If he could just get him to say something, anything. . .

Evo snarled and began to lift the knife again but before he had a chance to do anything with it, the demon began to shake violently before snapping at Michael. "You'll find out soon enough."

Evo gave Michael a look that indicated he had nothing to do with what was happening. Both men slowly backed away as the shaking began to get more violent. Jake's skin began to glow from within as if someone had just hit a switch on his internal organs, lighting him up like a goddamn neon sign.

"Shit!"

Both Evo and Michael stood watching as the glow underneath the guy's skin grew brighter, his veins and arteries becoming visible under the surface. The demon continued to writhe, an evil laugh rising from deep inside his gut as an eerie chill filled the dark, damp motel room.

"You won't stop him!" the demon growled. "No one can. He knows who you are and he doesn't fear you."

What the hell was he talking about?

Michael threw a bemused glance at Evo, who now looked about ready to pounce on the guy. He wasn't sure if he should stop him, but soon had the decision taken out of his hands as the glow coming from the captive's body grew so bright that they both had to look away. Then, just like that, it was gone.

And so was the demon.

Jake's body was slumped forward. He wasn't breathing. Michael walked towards him, carefully assessing him before placing his hand on his shoulder and pushing him back.

"*Jesus,*" he said. Jake's face was contorted, eyes wide with no trace of color in them as they stared, lifelessly.

Evo let out a sigh as his fingers pressed against Jake's neck confirming that he was dead. "Poor bastard."

"Have you ever seen anything like that before, Evo?" Michael asked, knowing how much he knew about this stuff. Hell, Michael had sent enough of them back down where they belonged, but nothing like that had ever happened.

"Shit! No." he replied, brushing his hand over his short hair, looking as perplexed as Michael felt. "I have no idea what just happened." He wiped the blade of his knife on Jake's trousers before bending down to slide it back in its holster around his ankle.

"What is that thing anyway?" Michael asked as Evo pulled his trouser leg down over his boot concealing the knife once again.

"That's my fail-safe against those bastards. Or at least it was until tonight." Evo's eyebrows drew together as he looked over at Michael. "'He knows who you are.' What the fuck does that mean?"

"I don't know, but I'm going to do everything I can to find out." Michael drew out a long breath as he sat down on the bed, raising an eyebrow at Evo as he felt around the lumpy slab of concrete that was posing as a mattress underneath him.

"Seriously? This is the best you could do?" His eyes roamed around the room, taking in the dingy, old fashioned decor. The place looked like it hadn't been touched since the seventies: Leafy patterned wallpaper hung off the walls at regular intervals and the once red carpet was threadbare with dark, patchy stains.

"Well, I spent enough on the ride out there. Anyway, it has a bed and hot running water what more do I need?" he shrugged.

"A sense of smell." Michael scoffed as he sniffed the air. "It's like someone died in here way before we got here, for Christ's sake."

Evo's nose twitched. "That's actually quite possible judging by those stains."

"*Probable,* more like. C'mon! Grab your things. After we dump this poor guy, you're coming back to stay with me."

CHAPTER FOURTEEN

"Lacy. Let me in!"

Michael knocked on Lacy's front door for a third time. He'd been standing on her porch for God knows how long, but there was still no answer. Now he was worried, especially as the demon had managed to somehow evade them back at the motel. That bastard could be anywhere. He'd planned to drop Evo's stuff at his place, then for Evo to drop him straight back at Lacy's on his way to the hospital but they'd got sidetracked after Evo decided to make some calls to name-drop Varesh to some of his associates. No one he'd spoken to had heard of the demon, but they promised to ask around. He'd been much longer getting back to Lacy than he'd planned.

He decided to give one more knock and if there was still no answer, he was kicking his way in. No need. Just as he fisted the door it opened swiftly, leaving him knocking on nothing but air.

Lacy stood before him, rubbing her eyes. She looked at him for a moment, eyes narrowed, lips drawn tight, before turning and walking away from him. She looked. . . angry? She left the door wide open so Michael went straight in, pushed the door shut and followed her into the living room.

"What took you so long? You had me worried for a minute there." Michael said, his voice sounding calmer than he actually felt. "I thought that—"

"Where were you?" Lacy interrupted. She'd plonked herself on the sofa, squeezing her hands in her lap.

What was she so pissed about? "I told you we were taking Jake to the sheriff's office."

"But you didn't though, right?" She wouldn't look at him for some reason.

He hesitated, not really knowing what to say, but he had to think of something and quick. He couldn't tell her that Jake was dead, not without being able to tell her why. He hated having to lie to her, but he would if it was the best thing for her, which it was, without any doubt. She'd already been exposed to too much and there was no way of knowing where that demon was right now. At least when it was using Jake's body they stood half a chance, but now...

He took in a deep breath. "How did you know?"

Now she looked at him. "I went to the sheriff's office just after you called. I thought I'd meet you there—help you explain what had happened and give them my statement, but you never showed."

Shit! Now there was a real big problem. If Lacy had told them about Jake then things were about to get even more complicated as soon as they realized he was missing. "Did you tell them anything, Lacy?"

Her brow furrowed. "Yes. I told them what happened and they're going to want my statement. Where did you go? And where's Jake?"

"He got away." The lie just came out. What else could he do?

Lacy shot up from the sofa. Her hand went to her throat. "What? How?"

His skin prickled with guilt, but he lied for good reason. He also knew that if she thought Jake was still out there somewhere, she would have less of a problem with him staying at her house; he had to, to protect her from the demon that was now even more pissed off than it was before.

"We lost him at the hospital that's why I've been gone until now. We've been out looking for him. I told you everything was okay because I didn't want you to worry." He looked away from her. What the hell was he going to do about the cops? As soon as Lacy gives her statement they'll be all over it and it won't be long until they realize he's missing.

Unless he got Evo to recover the body and dump it somewhere the cops would find it; make it look like an accident. Yeah, that was the best idea. He didn't need the cops sniffing around the university any more than they already were.

He noticed that Lacy looked pale. "Are you okay?" He walked over to where she was leaning an elbow on the wooden fireplace, taking her by the other arm. "Here, sit down and I'll make us some coffee."

She sighed. "I'm worried, Michael," she said in almost a whisper.

"Everything will be fine. I'm here. I won't let anything happen to you." A promise he intended to keep. He was determined to keep her safe, now more than ever. He really didn't like it, but she was becoming more and more important to him. He couldn't believe that he'd nearly kissed her at the hospital. After battling so hard to keep his damn feelings in check, he'd nearly caved. He had to get himself under control not just for his sake, but for hers as well. No good could come of it; he knew that. So, he would execute better control around her, simple as that. *Yeah, right!*

Lacy's voice cut into his thoughts. "I'm not so worried about me. I'm scared that something will happen to Nina. What if Jake did have something to do with it and decides to silence her properly? She's so vulnerable in the hospital."

"Evo is there. He'll be watching the place overnight again." But perhaps it should be him. The sensible thing would be to tell Evo to stay with Lacy while Michael watched the hospital. That way he'd be away from her, and it would give him time to sort his damn useless brain out.

Coffee... He was going to make coffee.

"Michael?"

He stopped without turning around.

"I'm glad you're here."

He closed his eyes for a second, then went into the kitchen without saying a word.

* * *

Soft lips met his and began to kiss him slowly. Michael had been fast asleep on Lacy's sofa and was now being woken up in the most unexpected way. He was surprised, but didn't resist. His eyes opened slowly to see Lacy looking back at him, her eyes hooded and dark. She closed them and thrust her tongue inside his mouth meeting his and twirling it in the most intoxicating way, sending a fierce heat rushing through his whole body, lighting him up with a desire he knew he should be fighting but couldn't. He felt her climb on top of him, legs straddling his hips. He reached down and placed his hands on her soft thighs, stroking her velvet skin with his thumbs. She moaned softly and began to trail kisses down his jaw, his neck, and continuing to his chest.

"Lacy." he whispered, his heart pounding in his chest as he gave in to the feel of her lips pressing against his skin. Her hair fell over his chest, tickling him, caressing him as she kissed one of his nipples. He hissed, pleasure seeping through him.

Lacy sat up and pulled her nightshirt off to reveal a pretty white lace bra that matched her panties. Her hands stroked up his stomach and over his chest and she began to move her hips against him. She caught his moan with her mouth and he kissed her with more fervor this time, stroking his hands up her back and into her hair. She broke off their kiss again to run her lips over his neck. "You feel so good," she whispered into his ear, her warm breath prickling his skin.

He reached down and unhooked her bra, leaving it to fall freely by her sides, then he ran his hands all over her, feeling every inch of her as she continued to whisper things to him.

"I've wanted you for so long," she said, kissing under his jaw and across to his other ear. "Do you want me, Michael?"

He shivered this time and his breath caught before he answered. "Yes. I do."

She licked her tongue up his neck, but instead of relishing the sensation he paused. All of a sudden his instincts were on red alert. He wouldn't expect Lacy to act this way.

She softly nibbled at his ear. "Do you like that?" More kisses. "Do you like the feel of me?"

He didn't answer. His whole body stiffened, overcome with uncertainty. Something wasn't right.

"Do you want me? Do you Jack?"

What the hell? How did she know he was Jack?

Lacy sat up and when she opened her eyes, they were bright crimson.

Shit! The demon!

"NO!"

Michael sat bolt upright, unable to catch his breath for a second. But Lacy had gone. He scrubbed his hands over his face, then looked around, eyes wide. The small lamp on the side table by his head had been left on, the rest of the room in darkness but he could see he was alone. His racing heart began to slow, consciousness returning, making him realize that he'd just had the most vivid of dreams ever. Finally, he relaxed his shoulders.

Not real. Thank God!

There was a soft knock on the door. "Michael."

Lacy. "Yeah. Come on in," he croaked.

She was dressed in sweats and a T-shirt. No nightshirt, to his relief.

"I heard you call out. Are you okay? Bad dream?"

Well. . . Most of it was quite good actually. He looked down to make sure his lower half was covered just in case anything was going on down there. He cleared his throat. "Yeah. Kind of."

Her concern felt nice.

She sat down in the chair opposite and tucked her legs up under her. "I was just coming back from the bathroom when I heard you; thought I'd better check in. I'm having a little trouble sleeping."

He understood that. "Thanks." He scratched his head and tried not to look at her. He had to get those damn thoughts out of his head. He felt weird: One minute he was enjoying her on top of him on this very sofa, the next she was sitting across the room from him all innocent in her sweats. And what the hell was with those crimson eyes?

"It must have been a bad one, you're soaked with sweat."

Unusual. He didn't think he *could* sweat.

As he looked over, her gaze quickly dropped to the floor. Not wanting him to see her looking at his body he guessed. The thought of her doing so made his body heat a little. *Get a grip you idiot.*

The silence that followed was uncomfortable, but he couldn't think of anything to say. Why couldn't he think of something to say?

"I drink cocoa when I can't sleep." She was still looking down, her eyes glazed over as though her thoughts were somewhere else. Then she looked at him and her mouth curled up in a slight smile. "Beth, my sister, would sometimes wake in the middle of the night from a bad dream and I would always get out of bed, go downstairs and make us both a cup of hot chocolate. My mum would either be out working or in an alcohol induced sleep, so it was always me that looked after Beth when she was scared. We'd sit on our beds and tell each other stories, and I would stay awake until she went back to sleep."

Michael lay back down on his pillows. "You were very close?" More an observation than a question.

"Yes." She blinked as though snapping herself back to the present, then stood up. "Would you like a cup? Of Cocoa?"

He smiled. "Would love one."

Lacy went into the kitchen through the door that connected both rooms and Michael placed his arm over his forehead. The last part of his dream had disturbed him, leaving him with a gnawing in the pit of his stomach that he couldn't seem to shake. Obviously dealing with the demon last night was on his mind before he'd gone to sleep, but why the hell did it have to ruin a perfectly enjoyable dream? *Stop it. You've finally got yourself under control, don't start it off again,* his inner voice warned.

He placed his hand under the sheet, curious to know if anything *had* happened to his body. It was the first time he'd had feelings like that since being dead. He hadn't desired any woman or had any dreams which involved the opposite sex at all. In fact, he'd only had nightmares he could never really remember, and hadn't thought about whether his manhood would work or not.

Well, if it had, it wasn't now and he wasn't willing to try it out again, or see if it was capable of doing anything else.

Shit. He was in trouble. It seemed the more he tried to ignore what he was feeling for Lacy the more he felt. Now he was dreaming about her for God's sake. He was definitely going to have to swap roles with Evo after today, even though the thought of his womanizing buddy sleeping in the same house as her, the two of them alone, made him anxious in a way he couldn't describe. He knew how good his friend was at charming the females, and he didn't doubt that Evo would try working his magic on her, but it was something Michael would have to overlook if he was to try and spend less time in her company.

The door opened and Lacy came in with a tray that had two steaming hot cups on it. Michael pulled himself up to a sitting position, still careful to keep his bottom half completely covered, and after Lacy put the tray on the floor next to him she patted his leg with the back of her hand. "Scoot," she ordered.

She wanted to join him on the sofa? Michael reluctantly moved his legs back, making room on the edge and she sat down by his waist.

"I brought cookies too." She smiled at him; passing him a cup before taking hers followed by a chocolate chip cookie from the small plate. Michael wasn't in the mood for food. He was tense. With Lacy sat so close to him after what had just happened, he was having a hard time trusting himself right now.

"So what did you dream about?" she asked innocently.

He gulped a mouthful of cocoa and it went down the wrong way, causing him to momentarily cough his borrowed lungs up. He held his cup out trying not to spill the contents.

After he'd composed himself he thought of something quickly. "I don't really remember." It was all he could think of and oh, how he wished it were true.

"Happens to me all the time." Lacy smiled. She looked down into her hot chocolate and he watched her face straighten. "I was worried sick about you earlier. I thought something bad had happened."

He felt that pang of guilt, again, which unsettled him. He never thought that she'd go to the station, figured she'd wait here for him to return, and he would've called earlier if he'd known she'd be worried. He was so used to just getting on with things, and not having to think about anyone else, that he hadn't realized. He was uncomfortable with having to think of someone else's feelings all of a sudden.

"I'm sorry. I should have called sooner—"

"I know," she interrupted, "just hear me out for a second. When I was pacing the floor waiting for you to get in touch, my mind was thinking all sorts of things. I panicked when I'd convinced myself that something bad had happened and there was a possibility I would never see you again." She dropped her gaze and picked at her thumbnail. "I've been lying awake for the past hour trying to make sense of it all. I mean, we haven't known each other all that long, but it seems I. . . What I'm trying to say is"—she let out a sharp sigh and her shoulders slumped—"I care for you, Michael."

Oh, hell.

All the air left his lungs and he couldn't seem to think of a single word to say—stunned, for the first time ever. This woman in front of him had been in his life for only a little over a week and yet she'd somehow captivated him. He knew he was developing feelings for her and had tried so hard to deny them, but it seemed to have only made them stronger. What was he going to do? *Nothing! You can't let anything happen and you know it.* His inner voice seemed to have the right idea. *It wouldn't be fair on her.*

When he realized he'd been staring at her for far too long without saying a word, he tried to muster something. "Lacy, I. . ." What could he say to her that wouldn't hurt her feelings?

She reached out and took his cup from him, placing both onto the tray on the floor. She slowly leaned towards him and his heart rate increased, his own feelings playing tug of war as he stared into her hypnotic pale green eyes. She was so close he could feel her warm breath on his face and he almost weakened until something snapped him back to reality, reminding him of the hurt he would cause her when he eventually had to leave, which he would, without question. He wasn't human, would never be, so being with her wasn't an option.

He pulled back, his breath hissing between his teeth as he forced himself to ignore a potent instinct which would allow no room for rational thought.

"Lacy, we can't do this," he said, even though every part of him wanted to.

She dropped her gaze. "I'm sorry. I thought you felt the same way."

That feeling of guilt was hitting him a lot harder now. In fact, it had swapped its softball racket for a wrecking ball. "I can't deny that I have feelings for you, Lacy. And you can't begin to understand how hard it is for me to not kiss you right now."

"Then why?"

His reply was hesitant. "There are things you don't know about me." Things she could never know.

Damn. The way she was looking at him now made him nauseous. Hurt, fear, confusion, it was all clear to see on her face.

"What things?" she pressed.

Shit. He was sinking deeper into the hole that had appeared below him and it worried him that, without being honest with her, he wouldn't get out of it. "Things I can't tell you, but I assure you, you don't have to worry. I haven't done anything bad. Believe me, if there was any way I could tell you I would. You do know that, don't you?

He could no longer read her expression. She stared at the floor, her eyes blank behind those heavy eyelashes. He longed to know what she was thinking. Had he hurt her? It wasn't his intention but perhaps it would be for the best; better for her to be wary of him—to not trust him.

The silence seemed to last forever. Then Lacy damn near floored him.

"I do believe you."

It was her kind and trusting nature that had attracted him to her in the first place. Her willingness to care for a complete stranger such as Nina and the fact that she was accepting what was happening around her without question, trusting Michael to see her through it and make sure that everything was okay. Believing him now, after he'd meant to put doubt in her mind, was just a testament to her true nature. How was he going to stay away from her when every second he was with her, she pulled him in deeper?

"I'm glad because I would never intentionally keep anything from you unless it was to protect you." He placed his hand on her cheek and turned her face to him. "I would never hurt you, Lacy."

"I know you wouldn't, not only because of what you've told me, but because I can just feel it," she replied, and he could see that there was nothing but sincerity in her words. She'd never looked as attractive to him as she did at that moment. He was doomed.

"Michael, can I ask a favor?" She picked at her fingernails again. A habit, he'd noticed.

"Sure, anything."

She hesitated, biting her bottom lip. "Can I lie next to you? I don't want to be alone right now."

Anything but that! Jesus!

He stared into her eyes and saw a sadness behind them that he could relate to. He knew he shouldn't, that it was dangerous territory, but he felt the same way. After all this time of being alone, he suddenly didn't want to be either.

He held the blanket back for her and she climbed in next to him, lying down with her back to him, which was good. He only had a certain amount of control left and knew how thin the line was that he was walking right now. He kept his arms awkwardly by his sides, even though the temptation to put one around her and pull her into him was so strong. He tried not to breathe the sweet apple scent of her freshly washed hair in too deeply and ignored the heat of her body—which was way too close to his—as best he could.

If he could get through the rest of the night without touching her, he would take his ass out for a celebratory drink the minute there was a bar open. Who knew he would have this much control over himself?

"Good night, Michael."

He knew he should reply but honestly didn't know if he could speak. "Good night." he managed to say as he squeezed his eyes shut. This was one time he *needed* to sleep.

* * *

Lacy let out a contented sigh as she woke to a warm sensation at the back of her neck. As her eyes flickered open she realized soft lips were caressing her skin. As consciousness gripped her, she froze, making sure what was happening was real and that she wasn't in some crazy realistic dream.

She wasn't. *Michael.*

She felt his arm tighten around her waist, pulling her closer into his warm body as his lips travelled around her neck, softly caressing her as they slowly moved up to the flesh behind her ear. Her heart began to pound and when Michael gently sucked her earlobe, her eyes closed and she couldn't help the gentle moan that escaped her. Her breath caught and somehow she managed to whisper, "Michael?" as he continued to kiss her.

He didn't answer her.

My God. Is this really happening?

Her mind went foggy as the feel of his warm breath upon her skin sent a glorious shiver down the length of her body. She lay silent, afraid that if she moved she might wake up and realize that this was nothing but a dream.

His arm moved upwards and he placed his hand on her cheek, gently pulling her face towards him and kissing her softly along her jaw until his lips found hers. She closed her eyes, shifted her body around to face him as he continued to kiss her. His kiss grew more intense and just as she reached up and tangled her fingers in his hair, he whispered her name against her lips. Then. . .

Michael paused. His whole body had gone rigid.

He pulled his head back suddenly and she caught his horrified expression in the glow from the lamp. "Shit! Lacy, I'm so sorry." he said as he quickly sat up, nearly knocking her to the floor.

She followed him, swinging her legs off the sofa and sitting up beside him. She lowered her head, letting her hair fall around her face to hide her embarrassment. How could she be so stupid? Of course he was still sleeping. She should have realized when he hadn't answered her, but it had been a little hard to think straight.

The few moments that neither one of them spoke was almost unbearable.

Michael let out a sigh as he dragged his hand through his hair. "I didn't know what I was doing." His voice was almost a whisper and, swallowing her shame, Lacy found the courage to turn and face him. "I was dreaming. I'm. . . I'm so sorry."

She had to do something to make it right. As ashamed and embarrassed as she was, she had a feeling he felt worse. "Hey, listen. . . It's okay." When she was sure her cheeks had cooled down, she tilted her neck so he had no choice but to look at her. When their eyes met, she smiled and saw the tension ease a little from his shoulders. She nodded. "Really. . ."

He shook his head, leaning into his hand. "I feel like such an ass."

"Well, please don't. No harm done, I promise." She reached for the TV control not wanting to risk any more of that awkward silence. "Why don't we just watch some cheesy late night movie and forget about it?" She turned the power on and began to flick through the channels. "Besides. . . " She gave him a sideways glance, "I quite enjoyed it." Her face heated up and she couldn't believe what she'd just said. Then she looked up and caught the surprise on his face. They both laughed.

"Perhaps I should. . . "—he pointed with his thumb—". . . the chair?" He left the sofa and after settling on some eighties sci-fi b-movie, Lacy lay back down.

They were both silent.

* * *

Michael didn't really dream anymore. For the past year his slumber had only been filled with vivid images of his time in the pit. Jumbled nightmares filling the spaces between consciousness and anxiety were what usually woke him up with a start.

But again, not this time.

Only two times he'd dreamed properly since he'd died. Gone were the crimson skies and the blood and the slicing. Instead, for the second time in what must have only been a few hours, all he'd seen was Lacy. But the second time had seemed even more real than the first.

It was as though his mind had hit record on their whole conversation prior to him falling asleep, then replayed it to him in his sleep using an alternate ending, the one he'd really wanted to play out when Lacy had nearly kissed him.

Shit, it had felt good.

He watched as she slept on the sofa across from him. The movie had finished so he'd turned the TV off and could now hear the gentle sounds of the birds singing outside as they awoke to the coming dawn. He hadn't bothered trying to get back to sleep, not wanting to risk any more dreams, however pleasant they had felt. Hell, he'd stop sleeping altogether if that's what was needed.

This wasn't meant to be happening.

He promised himself that this was the last time he'd stay with her.

CHAPTER FIFTEEN

The smell of fried bacon filled Lacy's nose as she awoke from a deep sleep, but the minute she opened her eyes she panicked.

Where the hell am I?

The living room. *Her* living room. Panic over.

As her brain came back on line she remembered why she was lying on the sofa. She'd slept with Michael. . . Well, not *with* him, but next to him. Her sleepy eyes scanned the room, but there was no sign of him.

She closed her eyes and fought to rid her mind of Michael's horrified expression as he'd pulled away from her during the night.

And. . . *Oh, God.* What if she'd kept him awake after that because she'd been snoring or something? Never mind the shameful kissing and fondling moment, this could be far worse. She hadn't slept in a man's company for a long time. He probably couldn't take anymore and escaped before she'd woken up. Or what if she'd frightened him with her sleep talking? She knew she still did it now and again. She'd woken herself up with it. She couldn't take anymore humiliation.

The door from the kitchen opened slowly and in walked Michael, freshly showered by the looks of it and fully dressed. He was holding a tray. He smiled at her. *He looks so handsome when he smiles like that.* Her stomach groaned.

"You're awake?" he said with a gleam in his eye that made her melt inside a little. "I thought I'd fix some breakfast before I left."

She sat up and he passed her the tray which had a plate of bacon and eggs and a steaming hot cup of coffee on it.

She decided then and there that she could quite easily marry him. "Thanks," she managed to say past the warm glow in her chest. For God's sake, she was acting like a school girl with a silly crush.

Michael grabbed his coat from the chair and put it on. Soon after, a car horn sounded outside. "That'll be Evo. He wants me to take him to the Lake." He rolled his eyes. "He's such a tourist." The edges of his smile pulled down, turning his expression more serious. "Will you stay at home today?"

"What about Nina?" She'd planned to take some things up to the hospital for her, realizing when she was last there that the poor girl didn't even have any toiletries, or extra nightwear. It wasn't like anyone else visited her apart from Lacy and the hospital staff. She'd been in that standard issue gown since her operation and Lacy thought it was about time she changed into something more comfortable. Besides, she felt guilty as hell when she didn't visit, even if Nina didn't know her. Lacy believed that when she spoke, Nina could hear her and it would be better for her to hear a familiar voice when she did come around.

"Just until I come back, then we'll go to see Nina together. I'd feel happier knowing that you're here."

She understood. If Jake was still about then it *was* safer to wait. "Okay, I'll stay." She placed the tray on the sofa and followed him to the door. He stopped before opening it and turned to face her.

He surprised her when he leaned in and kissed her softly on her cheek. Her breath caught.

"Call me if anything happens, okay?"

All she could do was nod her head, then he opened the door and left.

Lacy finally released her breath. She placed her hand on her cheek and re-played in her mind what had just happened. That kiss, even though it had only been on her cheek, not her mouth like the others, it had almost stopped her heart. It hadn't been a polite see-you-later kind of peck on the cheek; his warm lips had lingered for a second, like it was more an acknowledgement of their feelings for each other.

She was so confused. Why had her feelings for him developed so quickly? She was never the type to fall for someone so easily, always cautious whenever she was dating someone, so why was this happening? It was strange to feel this way about someone so soon.

Last night when she'd laid in bed thinking about how concerned she'd been over Michael, she'd realized it wasn't just a crush like when she'd fancied Karl James back in high school. And it was certainly nothing like what she'd felt for Simon when she'd stupidly accepted his proposal before finding out about the cheating. She knew she never really loved him, just felt flattered that a man like him would want to spend the rest of his life with her. She'd learnt a very big lesson there.

No. this felt very different, like there was a strange connection between them. Michael felt too familiar to her; given the short time they'd known each other. She'd spent over an hour in her room trying to convince herself to go and talk to him, but had chickened out, deciding it could wait till morning. That was until she'd gone to the bathroom and heard his voice. Knowing he was awake, she couldn't go back to bed without talking to him first. It was a vice of hers: When something was on her mind it had to come out, no matter what.

She'd sensed that he felt something for her though—especially after what had happened, or nearly happened, in Nina's hospital room—but when he'd admitted earlier that he had feelings for her too, her heart had sung with delight only to clamp its mouth shut a few seconds later when he'd told her that they couldn't do anything about it.

So he had secrets, didn't we all?

He'd nearly let her kiss him. He'd hesitated before pulling away. And the way he'd kissed her in his sleep, even though he was just dreaming, it was obvious he desired her too. So what could be so bad he had to deny her? Perhaps it was also because he was only working in Oakland temporarily. Did he have someone to go back to? Her stomach sank at the thought of him belonging to someone else.

She could still feel his lips on her skin as if he'd left them with her. Then she allowed herself to think about their brief encounter again. She'd wanted him to kiss her so badly and couldn't believe that she'd awoken to him doing just that. She played the moment over and over in her mind and her body began to heat. *No! That's enough*, she told herself. She wouldn't allow herself to fall any harder until she knew what he was keeping from her.

After receiving a very pleasing phone call from the hospital informing her that Nina had woken up during the night and was doing well, Lacy had showered, dressed and was feeling a lot more positive about her day. The nurse had told her that Nina had even spoken and was aware of where she was; all positive signs that led towards the hope that she had no brain damage. She'd told Lacy that Nina was resting and would be having some tests this afternoon, so it would be best for Lacy to visit in the evening. Great! She'd go with Michael after dinner.

She was just stuffing some dirty laundry in the machine when her doorbell rang. Michael had only been gone a little over an hour, so she didn't expect it to be him. Besides, he never rang the bell.

It was still early. She glanced at the clock on the sideboard as she passed it on the way to the front door—eight-thirty, unusual for someone to call round so early, especially on a Sunday. Then she remembered: Teresa. She'd said she'd call in on her way home from her shift.

Lacy peered through the small, round window in the door and sure enough, Teresa stood on the other side of it blowing a cloud of warm breath onto her hands and rubbing them together. She quickly opened the door and greeted her with a smile. The cold air hit her straight away.

"Hi, come on in." After closing the door behind her Teresa followed her into the living room and Lacy gestured for her to sit down. "Coffee? Some pillows? You look about ready to drop." She had dark circles under her eyes and her shoulders were slumped.

Teresa pinched the skin at the top of her nose. "Busy night. I'll be glad when I'm in my bed. And yes, just some coffee would be great, thanks. I think I can hold off the pillows for a little while longer."

Two cups of coffee later and Lacy had finished giving Teresa her statement about what happened with Jake. Teresa had said that she found it hard to believe Jake would act so aggressively. Lacy had been surprised herself, even though she didn't really know him, she'd seen him on campus and he was usually pretty quiet; walked around with his hood up mostly not seeming to interact with many of the other students. Her deputy friend explained that he'd been in trouble in the past for petty things like pinching a donation box from the pet store in town. And once she'd caught him spraying the words SMOKING KILLS. WEED HEALS on the back of a bus stop but she'd never heard of any violence, couldn't even recall any fights he may have been involved in. She insisted that what happened with Nina, and then Lacy, was out of character.

Teresa closed her file and put her pen back in the inside pocket of her navy blue, duty jacket. "So you've no idea where Jake is?"

Lacy shook her head. "My colleague and his friend searched for him for a while after but no joy."

As Teresa got up to leave, she passed Lacy a business card. "Could you ask your friend to call me if he hears anything?"

"Of course," she said, taking the card and putting it on the table beside her. She walked Teresa to the door and after saying their goodbyes and promising to call each other to arrange meeting up for coffee, Lacy returned to her laundry in the kitchen. As she poured the detergent in the tray, she thought about what she'd do for the rest of the day. She had some assignments to mark, but wasn't in the mood, so they could wait until she got back from the hospital. She could clean the house, but that didn't sound very appealing either.

Maybe she would do nothing but watch movies until Michael returned, or even read a book, but something tense, a thriller, maybe, or a horror; definitely not a romance. Best not to feed that stupid fire she was determined to keep under control. Imagining Michael as the hero and herself as the love interest just wasn't going to help the situation at all.

She was looking through a pile of books she'd recently bought, over by the wooden bookshelf, when the doorbell rang again. Teresa had probably forgotten to ask her about something. She was normally sharp as a pin, but going by how tired she looked just now, it wouldn't be a surprise.

"Did you forget something. . . Oh!" The person standing on the other side of the door surprised her. Not Teresa but her neighbor.

"Mr Hinckley." Damn. She'd promised to get him milk this morning. "I haven't been to the store yet Mr Hinckley but if you still need some milk. . . " Her words trailed off as he walked straight into her hall without saying a word. His gaze was hollow, like he was looking at her but wasn't aware.

"Is everything okay? Mr Hinckley? You don't look so—" She never got to finish her sentence because the old man's arm flew up and he bashed her on the head with something heavy.

Darkness was all she knew after that.

* * *

"So, who is this woman again?" Michael asked Evo as they sped along Garrett Highway towards the airport.

He'd received a text from Evo earlier telling him he would pick him up at Lacy's because he had some good news. He still wasn't saying much; only that he'd been waiting on an important phone call and finally received it at four a.m while he was still outside the hospital. Now they were going to pick up some woman from the airport. Her flight was due in at ten forty-six. *She*, apparently, was a friend of a friend of Evo's who owed him a big favor after he'd captured a creature that was responsible for the death of the guy's son. That friend had agreed to talk to this woman and persuade her to meet with them. Something about her knowing who Varesh is.

But that was all Michael knew. He could pretty much guarantee that because this person was female, that Evo had already been there, but if he had, his buddy was keeping quiet about that too.

"I've told you once already. She's agreed to meet us to talk about this Varesh guy. I don't know what she knows about him, but anything's gotta help right now, huh?" Evo said completely unaware of the speed limit as he raced down the highway.

"How do you know she's trustworthy?" She could be on this Varesh's side. He hoped to God that wasn't the case or else she could be leading him straight to them.

"Oh, she's trustworthy. We have a mutual enemy: demons. So trust me, she's on our side." Evo had a smug look on his face. He was feeling proud of himself for some reason but while he was being vague, he was irritating Michael.

It wasn't really Evo's fault though. Michael had been antsy for two reasons since leaving Lacy's place: one, he wasn't happy about leaving her on her own, but Evo had insisted he go with him. And then there was the fact that he couldn't get her out of his mind and it was irritating the hell out of him. He couldn't stop thinking about last night. As he'd suspected, he hadn't been able to trust himself at all while Lacy lay next to him: As soon as he knew she was sleeping, he'd been stupid enough to stroke his fingers down her arm, enjoying the softness of her skin. Then she'd sighed and backed herself closer into him and he'd placed his arm around her before going to sleep.

His dream had felt so real. He felt really bad about the way he'd kissed her, not that he hadn't enjoyed it, *really* enjoyed it. He was so ashamed and annoyed at himself.

He'd spent the next few hours watching her sleep. The sound of her deep breaths had soothed him, and every now and again she would quietly moan words he didn't understand. It made him smile though. It was like she had her own sleep language. She made his goddamn heart swell. *Shit!* He hardly recognized himself at the moment.

When he looked out of the driver's side window, he was surprised to see the airstrip beside them. He'd been so lost in his thoughts, he hadn't noticed the distance they'd covered. Evo must have sensed his mood because he'd kept quiet for the last part of the journey which Michael was grateful for. He suddenly felt bad for feeling irritated by him, he hadn't deserved it.

Now Michael was back to being aware of his surroundings, he realized there was another reason he was glad he'd been pre-occupied by his inner-turmoil over Lacy: Evo's musical taste hadn't improved in their time apart. "What the hell is this you're listening to?"

Evo shot him a look of utter bemusement, like Michael was supposed to know who the female country singer coming out of the stereo was. "It's Faith Hill. . . What? She's talented."

"Jeez buddy. As soon as we get back, I'm buying you some new music." Thank God they were nearly there.

He needed a distraction and fast.

After checking the arrival time on the information screen—to make sure Evo's woman's plane would be landing on time—the two men walked through the small airport towards the arrivals lounge. They still had a little time until the plane was in so Michael ordered a coffee-to-go from the Wild Bean kiosk in the corner. They took a seat near the window.

"I have a feeling this Varesh is going to be a piece of work." Evo said, as he removed his sunglasses. It was the middle of October, and they were expecting snow any time, but Evo was always wearing those damned wraparounds no matter what. Usually only took them off at night when his vision was restricted.

"Yeah. How does your lady friend know so much anyway?" Michael was eager to know more about the woman he was about to meet. A little prior information would have been nice. Why was Evo being so vague about her?

"Alethia." Evo said.

"What?"

"Her name is Alethia. And she's not my lady friend. I've never met her before."

Michael's eyes narrowed. "Then why would she come all this way to meet us, and at such short notice?" It seemed strange that a complete stranger was willing to do that. He assumed Evo knew her. He guessed that corrected his earlier assumption that the guy had slept with her.

Evo sat forward, arms leaning on his knees. "I told you already, I'm owed a favor."

He was beginning to get on Michael's last nerve with his short, uninformative answers. "Not from *her*, though, right? Come on man, you're not giving me anything here. I'm about to meet this woman and I know nothing about her. I'm not comfortable with this."

Evo scrubbed his hand down his face and his eyes scanned around the lounge as if to make sure no one else was in earshot. "She's different."

Michael's eyebrow raised and he gave Evo a look that urged him to continue. "Different how?"

"She's... kind of powerful. And my *friend* said she may be able to help us. In fact, when I spoke to her on the phone, she was already on her way to the airport. She seems keen to meet us. This is a good thing Mike, buddy. You trust me, right?"

He never mentioned it was her he'd spoken to on the phone. And what did he mean by powerful? Someone working for the government powerful? He gave Evo a quick nod of his head. "Powerful like how?"

Evo's voice dropped to a whisper. "She's not human." Then he got up and joined the small group of people who had gathered waiting to greet the throng of passengers who'd begun to come through the exit doors, weighed down with luggage. Most of them had companions or were in small groups.

Michael went over and stood by him. The only person who had come through alone so far was a short, very round man with a thin mustache and a Yankees cap until...

Michael saw Evo's eyes light up as a tall, slim, brunette—who was dressed in a knee length, tan, double breasted coat with fur around the collar—came through the doors, pulling along a small suitcase. Her tight black pants were covered by brown, knee high boots. She was the picture of elegance as she stopped to fumble with her coat before her eyes scanned the room.

"That's gotta be her." Evo said before almost sprinting towards her.

God help her, Michael thought as he followed him.

"Alethia?" She looked straight at Evo and smiled tentatively.

Michael noticed she had a small dimple in each of her cheeks. She looked to be in her early thirties and very human, but then again, so did he.

"Yes. You must be Mr O'Reilly?" The woman outstretched her hand to Evo who took it immediately, gently shaking it while his gaze never left hers. "I've had quite an interesting chat about you with our mutual friend," she said wryly.

Evo seemed to like it. "Please. Call me Evo, and this is my good friend Michael."

She looked at Michael, her blue eyes narrowed with curiosity while it was his turn for the handshake. She lowered her voice. "Ah Yes. You're the one Varesh is looking for. He's not the kind you gain as an enemy easily. You must have really pissed him off."

Michael was surprised by her words. So she did know who Varesh was? Well, that was a start. The fact that she was here with no hesitation, worried him though. Three things he would need to find out about her before he trusted her: one, how well did she know this Varesh? He needed to be sure that she wasn't working with him and had come here because she planned to deceive them. The second thing, Is she as powerful as Evo said? And finally, if she's not human then what the hell is she?

"I haven't done anything to him." Michael replied coldly, informing her where he stood with the trust issue.

Her eyes narrowed with her irreverent smile. "I highly doubt that," she said before turning her attention back to Evo. "How long till we can eat? I'm starving." She began to walk towards the exit, suitcase in tow, not bothering to look back to see if they followed.

They did though.

Michael looked at Evo who was happily enjoying watching her walk on ahead. "I think I'm in love with her which is bad." Evo said, to which Michael rolled his eyes.

"No, I'm serious. I mean, how am I going to concentrate on anything she has to tell us when she looks like that?"

Michael shoved his elbow into Evo's arm. "I'm sure you'll manage, you sexed up asshole."

* * *

The journey back was an interesting one. Michael had learned nothing more in the time spent with Alethia and Evo, except that Evo's flirting was something to behold. . . Or not, in Michael's case. His buddy had tried every which way he could with Alethia but she wasn't succumbing to his pretty impressive—as much as it was hard for Michael to admit—attempts to woo her. He'd never seen Evo have to try so hard. Alethia seemed amused by him, not at all bewitched, which was the case for most females who got in the way of Evo's infamous charm. Poor bastard wasn't used to it.

Michael hadn't quite figured the woman out yet. She was a peculiar character; that much he'd already established. Sometimes when she spoke, she sounded mature, wisdom poured from her suggesting she was much older than she appeared. Other times she was playful. The way she teased Evo, playing him in a mischievous way, resembled the behavior of a teenager. Not unlike Evo himself.

They finally arrived back in Oakland. Michael had said he wanted to swing by Lacy's before anything else, to make sure she was okay. He'd promised he'd go with her to the hospital and he still would, but it would have to be later on tonight. The meeting with Alethia was number one priority; if he was going to let her help, then he wanted to know everything about her first.

As the SUV pulled up outside Lacy's, it took less than a second for Michael to realize that her car wasn't in the drive. She'd promised him she'd stay at home until he got back and she wasn't the type to go back on her word. Even though she could've just popped to the store, or something as simple as that, his instincts were telling him there was something wrong, and he usually trusted them.

"Evo. Buddy. Have you got that special knife on you?" he asked, his heart rate increasing slightly, preparing for the worst.

Evo turned to him. "What's wrong?"

"Just being cautious, that's all." As he walked up Lacy's driveway, he heard the sound of two doors closing shut behind him, then the footsteps of Evo and Alethia following him to the house.

He got to the front door which was open slightly. By this time he'd slipped his own knife out from inside his jacket and, holding his breath, he slowly pushed the door and walked inside. "Lacy?"

Silence.

He pointed down the hall, silently gesturing for Evo to check the other rooms which his buddy did with no hesitation. Michael went into the living room, still no sign of her. He noticed a cup on the coffee table which was half filled with coffee. He reached down and touched it with the back of his hand. Cold, so it had been there a while. He didn't like it one little bit.

"Lacy. Are you here?" Again there was no reply. He checked the kitchen. Then a woman's voice called out from the hall. Alethia's.

"Uh, I think you need to see this."

Michael raced out of the room catching sight of Evo doing the same thing at the other end of the hall. Evo shook his head as he left Lacy's room, confirming she wasn't there. When Michael looked down at what Alethia was pointing to on the floor, he sank to his knees. He stared at the droplets of blood trailing off towards the door where they stopped suddenly. Michael found it hard to breathe as he imagined

Lacy being hurt and then probably carried out to her own car and taken somewhere.

He barely registered Evo as he spoke. "Shit. Man. That doesn't look good."

"Does someone want to tell me what's going on?" Alethia asked.

Michael couldn't seem to find his voice for a moment, but through the deep mixture of anguish and rage now pulsing through his veins he managed to produce some sort of sound. "That bastard has her, Evo."

"Who?" Alethia demanded, her voice ringing in Michael's head.

Evo was quick to answer her this time. "That shit of a demon we captured. He must have taken Lacy and no doubt"—he hesitated—"Varesh will have ordered it."

All of a sudden Michael couldn't hear beyond his own thoughts. *How long has she been gone? What if they'd killed her already?* His head started to pound. He was so filled with fury that his vision began to distort. Then his whole body started to vibrate. The walls around him appeared to rumble and through the haze he heard Evo's voice.

"What the fuck. . . ?"

What was happening to him?

Evo's voice cut through again, this time with the kind of urgency that he'd never heard coming from his friend. "Do something Alethia!" He sounded. . . scared?

The vibration continued, like he had two thousand volts of electricity travelling through every inch of his skin. Through his now severely reduced vision, he saw the walls moving. He was hallucinating, had to be. No. Wait. . . This was real. He caught the fear in Evo's eyes, his shocked expression confirming that Michael wasn't the only one seeing what was happening.

Michael gripped his head on either side as a strange pressure began to build inside of it, as though someone had a foot pump on his brain and was seeing how far they could inflate it before it burst. He couldn't stop it. Whatever was happening was beyond his control.

Everything seemed to blur into one, spinning around faster and faster until he couldn't make anything out anymore. It was like he was in the eye of a hurricane with everything rushing, circling around him then. . .

Darkness.

Silence.

Nothing but the sound of his hitched breaths in his ears.

Then he was consumed by light; bright, white hot light that stung his eyes. He threw his arm over his face and heard his friend's voice groan beside him. When Michael removed his arm, and after blinking a couple of times until he could see properly, he looked down to see Evo crouched over, his guts doing a damn good impression of Niagara Falls.

"What. . . the. . . fuck. . . just happened?" Evo said in between retching.

When Michael looked around, he saw that they were alone in a long bright room with alabaster columns running along each side. The floor was covered in marble, also alabaster, and there were pale, delicate drapes across the far end.

Where was Alethia?

Michael turned to help Evo. "You okay buddy?"

"Yeah," he moaned as he got to his feet while still clutching his stomach. "Man that was a bitch of a ride. Where the hell are we anyway?"

"I've no idea. And what happened to Alethia?"

"Beats me. . . One minute she was standing there with her eyes closed, gripping hold of something that was on the end of her necklace, the next I felt like I'd been sniffing PCP." His buddy's eyes narrowed as he looked at Michael. "Let me see you man."

Michael sensed concern in Evo's tone as he walked right up to him and placed his hands on his shoulders. His gaze was intense. "Thank God. Your eyes are back to normal. Are you feeling okay?"

Michael frowned. Why was he asking him that? His eyes always changed when he was really angry. "Why the concern? Not like you haven't seen my eyes change before."

Evo nodded his head and dropped his hands from Michael's shoulders. "Oh, I know I have. . . but not the rest of your body glowing white I haven't."

"What the hell are you talking about?" It had to be the hallucinations. Evo must have had one too. He was getting confused. Had to be.

"And before you say it, it was before all of that spinning started." His friend said as if he'd read his mind.

He wasn't convinced. "How can you be sure?"

Evo paced around the big empty space. "I was well aware of my surroundings at that moment. And Alethia was still coherent. She seemed as surprised as I was. It was only after that happened that she actually listened to me and went into a trance. Then she started chanting or praying or some shit." Evo stopped and faced him again. "Oh yeah, there's something else I forgot to mention too."

Michael didn't know how much more of these revelations he could take right now. What else? He grew horns. . . A tail? "What?" he snapped. It came out more harsh than intended. Evo ignored it.

"Your rage made the walls shake."

Now Michael was certain Evo was mistaken. How could that possibly happen? He'd been like he was for almost a year now and neither of those things had ever happened before.

Evo must have sensed his denial. "I'm telling you man, that spinny, stormy crap that just happened? That was Alethia—and remind me to thank her for making me hurl my guts up next time I see her, by the way—but the wall shaking thing. . . all you buddy." he said all matter-of-factly.

Before Michael could respond, the veil of drapes at the other end of the room parted unhanded and two figures walked through, one being Alethia, the other a tall man with wavy brown hair that fell to his shoulders. His clothes were unusual: white linen trousers and a sleeveless drape of the same color, which fell over his hips, held together with a sheer gold cummerbund around his waist. He wore white sandals, their ribbons wrapped from his feet to his ankles.

The man had both hands behind his back as both he and Alethia gracefully ambled towards them. It was mature Alethia that faced them now as they stopped right in front of where he and his buddy stood; no sign of the playful female that had teased Evo earlier. Michael noticed Evo stiffen, but thought nothing of it.

Alethia spoke first. "This is Valtas. God of shadows."

The stranger held out his hand, a golden cuff covered his wrist. "Welcome, gentlemen," he said in a slightly accented voice that Michael couldn't place. He shook Michael's hand, then moved to Evo who now looked as pale as the guy's clothes.

"Is this Heaven?" Evo asked, seeming to be awed by the man currently shaking his hand.

Michael almost choked at Evo's strange question. But Valtas simply smiled and shook his head. "No. You are in Asirus. No longer are you on Earth, though you are not yet in heaven."

That's what all of the spinning was about. Alethia had somehow materialized them here. But where exactly was here? Were they amongst the clouds or further beyond? He was stunned for a moment. Not only had he been to Hell, but now he'd visited the heavens. As a dead guy he'd seen a lot of strange shit and knew from experience that there was an afterlife and spirits and monsters. But this seemed too surreal;

too impossible, even for him to get his head around. He couldn't quite believe that he was standing in front of a god, a living breathing god. Now he understood why Evo was acting all polite and self-effacing around the guy. Bastard knew everything.

Valtus began to pace a little, hands behind his back and accentuating the thick muscle that covered his bare arms. He was powerful and stood easily at six and a half feet. His physique resembled Evo's only he was much larger, as you would expect of a man of his stature.

"You are honored gentlemen. Only the gods enter Asirus. We do not allow for visitors of any kind in our realm,"—he turned to face Michael, caramel eyes locking onto his with a fierce stare—"Especially those who have returned from Hell. You are only permitted here now because my daughter tells me we have a mutual enemy and that you seek her help."

His daughter? Whoa! Evo hadn't lied when he'd said she was powerful, only powerful didn't quite sum it up. She was a fucking goddess. Only Evo could enlist the help of an all powerful deity. He almost wanted to kiss the shit out of him.

Valtus continued with his gaze fixed solely on Michael. "Tell me. How is it that you managed to leave the underworld that you were banished to? It's not easy to leave such a place unaided."

The question was unexpected and plagued by suspicion. "I can't give you an answer because I don't know." It was the truth. He had no memory of how he'd returned. Only the intermittent memories of his torture, but even they weren't clear. The pain was, though. He didn't think he'd ever forget that.

"Father," Alethia said. "It's Varesh. He has returned. I believe he has taken a human woman hostage and he's done it to get at this man." She held her hand towards Michael.

Valtus's eyes narrowed. "Why would he be after you?"

Michael remained stoic. "Again, I have no answer. I'd never heard of him until we captured one of his demons who then spoke about him to me. He told me Varesh had been looking for me for a long time. I don't know this demon." But he would do soon, of that he was certain. Whoever, or whatever, he was, he would pay for taking Lacy. "Look, as much as I'm enjoying our little meeting here, I have something more important to do. Every moment wasted talking to you could be spent searching for my. . . for Lacy."

"And how can you be sure you'll find her? Alethia says you've requested her help, which I'm reluctant to allow." Michael noticed Alethia fight back a frown. "My daughter is too important to me to get mixed up in some human's unfortunate affairs, but you, I am intrigued by. Varesh has been our enemy for thousands of years. He is powerful and unfortunately wants to be more so, which is why I question what he wants with you."

Michael remained still as Valtas stepped closer. The god's stare penetrated him intently as though he was trying to see right into his soul, if he still had one. No one said a word. Through his peripheral vision Michael saw Evo tense. He'd remained uncharacteristically quiet through their whole meeting. His buddy had his hand perched over one of his guns, as if a gun would do any good against a god. He looked like he expected things to turn sour at any minute.

Valtas was so close to Michael now that he felt his breath on his face as he spoke. "Because of my daughter's persistence, Alethia will assist you in finding the human woman, but once you do, you will not call on her again. Am I understood?"

Michael's gaze flicked to Alethia and back to Valtas. "You have my word," he replied and as Valtas stepped away, he relaxed his shoulders and allowed himself to breathe again. Jesus, he'd felt the male's power pouring off him, a power he wouldn't want to be on the receiving end of that's for sure.

He noticed Evo relax too. His buddy raised his eyebrows at Michael and also let out a relieved sigh. He'd obviously felt that power too, his pasty color was evidence of that.

Next, Valtas walked up to Alethia. Without speaking, he held out his hand. A small glow of bright light formed right above it and after it faded, a jewelled, silver ring appeared in his palm. He brought it down in front of Alethia whose mouth curled up in what looked like a wicked smile before she took it from him and placed it on the middle finger of her left hand. The damn thing resized on its own until it fit.

"I trust I don't have to tell you to take very good care of this?" Valtas said. "Only you are to use it. Its captives will be dealt with accordingly."

Its captives? What the hell did he mean?

Valtas turned on his heels. "I expect you to keep me informed, Alethia," he called out over his shoulder as he walked away. The woman remained silent until her father had left the room.

"Pompous ass!" she whispered. Evo fought a laugh. "Let's get out of here," she said as she grabbed the pendant around her neck and the room began to spin.

CHAPTER SIXTEEN

". . . I'm sure. I've seen the way he looks at her."

Silence.

The ache in Lacy's head was pretty intense as she awoke from what seemed like a very real nightmare. Was it a nightmare? And who was that she could hear talking? Through the haze and confusion, she thought she'd heard a male voice, but that too was probably part of her nightmare. She felt groggy, nauseous, in fact her whole body felt heavy, weighed down by something strong.

"You have my word, my lord."

There was that voice again. She heard no reply so assumed whoever it was was talking on a phone. It hurt to move her eyelids. She slowly opened them, but everything was blurred. Blinking once, twice, her vision began to clear but she still strained to see her surroundings. She blinked again until the room slowly came into focus.

At first she was confused, her brain refusing to work through the throbbing pain in her head. She inhaled a deep breath and almost choked on the heavy stench of urine and God only knew what else.

Then a vision flashed in her mind, a memory so vivid yet so hard to fathom: Mr Hinckley. Oh, God. . . Mr Hinckley had hit her? Hadn't he?

She realized she'd been abducted.

No! She fought to stay silent even though every part of her wanted to scream, but she managed to compose herself.

Where the hell was she?

She was lying on a bed but she couldn't move. Her arms were stretched above her head tied together by her wrists, probably to the headboard. Her feet, the same: bound at the ankles. She summoned the strength to lift her head slightly, wincing, and saw that she was in a large room, some sort of disused warehouse it looked like.

There was a lamp with no shade to her left on what looked like a metal hospital trolley. It was hard to make out anything beyond the shallow pool of light that fell over her, but she thought she could see dirt and debris covering most of the surrounding floor. She noticed a room just off to her right side—door ajar, light on. That was where the voice had come from. She heard metal crashing from inside which startled her. Soon after, the door swung open.

Shit!

She closed her eyes and pretended she was still unconscious.

"I know you're awake. I can smell your fear," a raspy voice said. Lacy couldn't will her heart rate to slow down. She ignored him and kept her eyes closed.

"Hey. Bitch!" He was closer this time.

SLAP!

Lacy cried out at the sudden pain on her cheek as her head whipped to the side. She tried desperately to keep the tears inside her eyes but failed as they rolled down either side of her temples, wetting her ears. Her head already felt like it had been kicked around a school yard and now one side of her face burned like hell too. She looked at the man without saying a word, taking in as much of his appearance as she could through her watery eyes.

He looked to be about forty. His eyes were deep set, though she couldn't tell what color, framed by thick dark eyebrows. His hair was short, recently cut and black, but dusty—much like his face. She found his clothing strange: navy suit under a tatty gray coat with a dirty white shirt and a matching blue tie. It wasn't the kind of clothing she'd expect a kidnapper to wear, not that she'd had any experience with one before. He looked ready for the office.

He stood sniggering at her.

Somehow she managed to speak. "Where is Mr Hinckley?" Her voice was hoarse. She swallowed to try and help it, but her mouth was bone dry. "What have you done with him?"

The man frowned as though he didn't know who she was talking about, but then seemed to remember, "The old man? I got rid of him."

Lacy choked back a sob, determined not to let him see a weakness.

"He served his purpose." He put his hand near her face like he was contemplating stroking the very same cheek which he'd just slapped—*Oh, God No. . . Please*—but he pulled away. He swung around, grabbed an old, wooden chair and sat on it the wrong way round, leaning his elbows on the back and leering at her. She hadn't noticed he had a knife, but he was now twiddling it through his fingers. The way he stared at her sent a chill through her blood.

"What do you want with me?" she asked, trying to hide the fact that she was trembling.

He grinned. "What I want, and what I'm allowed, are two very different things." He licked his bottom lip, eyes narrowing as they looked over the length of her body in a way which made her skin crawl. "Unfortunately, for now, I have to use you as bait, but while my master is away that don't mean I can't have a bit of fun while we wait." He reached over and ran the blunt side of the knife down her cheek. She inhaled sharply, and clamped her jaw tight to stop herself from crying, as the back of the cold metal blade scraped down her flesh.

The man's eyes widened as he sensed her fear; he enjoyed how frightened she was. She had to put a stop to that right now so she forced herself to exhale slowly and tried her damndest to push her fear to the back of her mind.

Bait? What for?

She couldn't bring herself to ask the question, but she didn't have to.

"So how is your teacher friend? Do you think he cares for you enough to come save you?"

Lacy's stomach sank, a deep dread washed over her as she realized. . . Michael. No. What did he want with. . . ?

Suddenly, Michael's words from last night rushed through her mind, *"There are things you don't know about me. Things I can't tell you."*

Oh, God. He must be involved in something really big for someone to have kidnapped her over it. That's why he couldn't tell her. Was it drugs? Gang related? Michael *and* Evo? They were in some deep shit she was sure. She closed her eyes, unable to cope as all of the thoughts of what he could be involved in spun through her mind. *"You don't have to worry. I haven't done anything bad."* he'd said.

She turned her head to face her kidnapper. "Who are you and why are you after Michael?"

The knife touched her again, starting from the top of her temple, only this time it felt sharper. "It's not me that's after him, although, he'd be much better off if it were. I would just end him. When my master gets a hold of him, he'll wish that I had." As he spoke his eyes glazed over like he was imagining something. She gasped, holding her breath again as she felt a sharp sting as he pressed the knife down harder, slicing her skin just by her eyebrow.

Her captor paused as a cell phone began to ring from the other room. He grunted, then shot up from the chair and disappeared from view.

Air burst from her lungs and she began to feel light headed. *Don't you dare pass out!* She warned herself. *You don't know what he'll do to you.* She felt a warm trickle of blood roll from her temple and a familiar feeling of panic began to rise up from her toes. She closed her eyes tightly and tried to think of something that would take her mind off where she was. Last thing she needed was to lose it here.

A vision of Michael's face sitting across a table from her filled her mind. He was laughing, his blue eyes sparkling like sapphires over the flame of a candle. She wished she was back at Carlito's, back at that night when they'd both first spent some time together. She'd liked him from the start. He'd seemed kind and gentle and hadn't taken advantage of her when she'd so stupidly thrown herself at him. Where was he now? She wondered. Had he returned to find her gone yet? She hoped so. Maybe he'd informed the cops and they were now looking for her. But what if they couldn't find her.

She heard the door open and her kidnapper came rushing through holding a piece of paper. He returned to the chair that he'd occupied before, but moved it closer so that the back of it was touching the mattress. His twisted grin chilled her to her very core.

He flipped his cell phone open and began to dial a number from the piece of paper he was holding. He waited.

She could just about hear the voice answer on the other end of the line.

The kidnapper spoke. "I have something you want."

Lacy's heart sank. She suddenly found it hard to breathe. Michael's voice bellowed through the phone's speaker. Her heart pounded so hard in her ears, she had to struggle to make out what he was saying.

"Where is she you bastard. She better be okay or I swear I will make sure you suffer you son of a bitch!"

Her tears were back. She thought of him returning to her house to find her gone and couldn't bear it. How would he find her? How long had she even been there?

Her thoughts were cut off when her kidnapper laughed at Michael's words. "Met my mother have you? She was more of a bitch than you could ever imagine," he mocked. "You think your words scare me? Don't bother. You want to see your woman again, you better listen carefully. My master wishes to do a trade. Her for you. That's the only way she gets to live."

"You fucking asshole!" Michael's words came thick and fast.

"I am indeed. And you're being offered a chance to save someone you care about. We both know you will come."

"Oh I'll come, and I'll end you and your master. I promise you that."

Lacy's eyes widened as she listened, wishing there was something she could do to prevent Michael from putting himself in danger. She almost screamed with frustration. She was the one who'd put Michael in this position. If only she'd been more careful, but how was she to know that Mr Hinckley was there to hurt her? What had happened to him to make him hit her? When she'd looked into his eyes as he'd stood in front of her they'd looked blank, dead even, like he'd been in some sort of trance. Someone must have forced him to do it, but how?

All those questions weren't helping right now. She was here, and Michael would come as her captor demanded.

Another laugh escaped the man who was now standing at the bedside.

Michael's voice was stern. *"I want to speak to her. I want to know she's still alive."*

The man didn't answer him; instead, he put the cell to her ear. "Speak!"

She struggled for air. At that moment she wanted to bawl into the phone, to tell him not to come for her because she feared if he did they would both be killed. She had to sound strong. She would. "Michael?"

"Lacy, are you hurt?"

"No, I'm okay," her voice trembled beyond her control.

"I'm coming to get you. I promise. Stay strong—"

"No!" she cried as his voice was pulled away from her ear. More tears streamed from her eyes as she tried to hold on to it, to keep the sound of Michael's voice in her head, trying to filter out her captor's voice as he continued to speak on the cell. Would she ever see Michael again? That she didn't know but whatever happened to her now, she would keep his voice in her memory right up to the point of her inevitable death, holding on to him with everything she had.

The man's voice grew louder, more savage, pulling her from her thoughts. Now she had no choice but to hear him as he spat his venomous threat into the phone.

"If I even sense that you haven't come alone, believe me when I say that your bitch will die in the most horrific way possible, which I'll enjoy immensely, after what you attempted to do to me last night." that sickening laugh again "What a shame you failed."

Last night? What did he mean? Michael and Evo had encountered this monster before? So many questions swirled around her head, sending her into a tailspin. This must have been the kind of trouble Michael was in, the reason why he'd said he couldn't be with her. Now she was starting to wonder if they'd looked for Jake at all last night. Perhaps they were too busy dealing with this other problem instead.

Her abductor ended the call and peered down at her. He no longer had his creepy smile, just a deep scowl twisting his features, turning him into something much more sinister than before. "Let's see how much he cares for you, shall we?" he hissed, before reaching down and taking hold of a chunk of her hair, fanning it through his fingers.

What was wrong with his eyes?

She swore she'd just seen the slightest hint of red glowing around the edges of his irises, bleeding out into the white before disappearing again. It was probably a reflection from the lamp or something.

He walked away from her and went back into the other room, pushing the door closed behind him.

Lacy closed her eyes and immediately saw Michael's face again. He would be coming here for her now and she really couldn't let that happen. She had to at least try and free herself. She began pulling her wrists as hard as she could, but all that did was cause the rope to burn as it rubbed against her skin. She tried twisting and pulling this time, holding her breath and squeezing her lips tightly together to stop from screaming out at the pain. . . Still no use.

She tilted her head back to look at the headboard that she was bound to. The rope was twisted and tied over and over again through the metal slats that were welded to the frame.

No way was she getting out of this.

She strained her head to look at her feet and almost screamed in frustration when she assessed the thick metal chain that bound her ankles in much the same way. She began to wiggle her feet anyway. Pulling and twisting, but again, it was no use. The chains were even tighter than the rope. She bit back a curse and blinked her eyes a couple of times to stop the tears—tears of anger this time—that had begun to fill her eyes. She huffed, lifted her head and narrowed her eyes as she tried again to see beyond the glow of light around the bed.

It was still too dark to make anything out. Distant shadows were all she could see, of furniture or equipment of some sort. She knew wherever she was, it was big, going by how her and her abductor's voices had echoed, his more so than hers.

A noise, like metal clanging on concrete, flicked her head to the side. Her eyes widened as she waited with baited breath for something to come into view. Her heart pounded loudly, the only sound in the silence that followed.

Nothing.

She began to slowly breathe again as she told herself it was probably a rat or something, hoped it was anyway. No. Not hoped. . . she hated rats.

Something caught in her peripheral vision, the opposite side from where the noise had come from. She reluctantly turned her head, but there was nothing there.

There it was again. A little over to the right this time. She jerked her head to look for whatever was catching her eye but still. . . nothing.

She was losing her mind. That had to be it. The surrounding darkness was playing tricks on her and she didn't appreciate it. She was scared enough as it was without scaring herself to death as well.

This time she saw it. A shadow moved past the bed so quickly she nearly missed the damn thing. Her breath caught. What the hell *was* that?

Then a figure appeared from the darkness at the foot of the bed. A woman, dressed in a long white nightgown, her long brown hair ran down past her shoulders, curling at the ends. She looked to be in her early twenties maybe, it was hard to tell, she wasn't exactly solid.

Lacy groaned. Not another damned hallucination. Now really wasn't the time.

The woman began to walk towards her, her form flickering ever so slightly, like Lacy was watching an old video tape that was damaged. Suddenly, Lacy felt her whole body go cold. She shivered, goose flesh tingling all over her skin, and watched with gritted teeth as the woman reached out a hand toward her.

This is all in your head. She's not real. She's not real.

Lacy blinked hard over and over again, hoping that one of the times when she opened her eyes the vision would be gone but no such luck. Her mind was determined to destroy what little amount of sanity she had left.

Please, just go away.

The figure came closer to the bed, her arm outstretched in front of her like she was reaching out for something. Her face was gaunt, eyes glazed over as she stared at Lacy.

Something wasn't right. If this was a hallucination, it was very realistic.

All of a sudden the woman's hand came down and grabbed Lacy's ankle. Shit! She was real all right. Lacy bit down on her lip to stop herself from screaming as the woman's grip got tighter, causing her ankle to sting from the pressure.

What the hell? She didn't dare speak the words through fear of her abductor returning so she remained as quiet as possible, forcing her mouth to stay closed. She felt something snap—praying it wasn't her ankle—and almost cried out with the last sudden jolt of pain.

Then...

The pressure and pain eased and she felt the chains fall away from her.

Before Lacy could register what had happened, the woman had moved to the head of the bed so quickly Lacy hardly even saw it. She noticed how pretty the woman was now that she was closer. "Who are you?" Lacy asked in the faintest whisper. The woman's head angled to the side as she looked down at her. She didn't speak, only proceeded to do the same at her wrists as she'd done at Lacy's feet.

Lacy held her breath in anticipation of the same pain she'd just felt.

Snap!

Her hands were now free. She rubbed at her wrists.

In spite of her complete shock at what had just happened, and at the realization that maybe, after all this time, the visions she'd always seen were never actually hallucinations, she still somehow managed to climb off the bed and stand up. When she looked around to thank the woman she'd disappeared. Before her mind began trying to convince itself that the woman hadn't been real after all, and that she *was* actually losing her mind, Lacy reminded herself that imaginary women in their nightgowns could not snap thick rope and chain with their hands.

She shook herself. No time to think about it.

Now she had to move, and fast.

She looked over at the door to the other room and to her relief it was still closed. Forcing her eyes to focus she hurried through the large space, careful not to kick anything or trip over as she struggled to navigate through the dark, thick shadows without making a sound. Up ahead, she noticed there were a few small windows that had been blackened out, one of which had a beam of pale light bursting through a small gap in the paint. Was it still daylight? As it was the only source of light, she headed in that direction and as she got closer, two large metal doors became visible.

Please don't be locked. Please don't be locked. Her pleas went unanswered. Her stomach sank when she saw a thick chain, much like the one that had bound her ankles, threaded through the slide lock and held in place by a large padlock.

Shit! Her eyes frantically scanned the darkness. She didn't have much time until that bastard returned to find her gone and when he did he would surely be pissed. God knows what he'd do to her. Besides that, another reason was spurring her on: If she managed to get away, it'd save Michael from risking his life to rescue her. She inhaled a deep breath and willed herself to a relative calm so she could focus for a minute. When she did, she noticed that one of the large doors looked slightly different to the other and then she saw why: a smaller door, normal height, was inside of it.

Oh, my God. Through all of my damn stressing I almost missed it. She thought to herself as she quietly undid the bolt at the top. She noticed another towards the bottom, unlocked that one too and then pushed. It didn't budge. Her eyes narrowed, focusing on a keyhole. Shit! It must be locked. She pushed again, but it was no use.

Tears began to sting her eyes. How cruel was it that she'd been set free from her binds, but was now locked in the damn building? There had to be another way. She was about to turn around, but froze as she was hit by a familiar sensation. Her body had gone cold as it had on the bed, and no sooner had she realized why, an arm reached past her, its hand flattening against the lock. She turned to see the brown haired woman standing next to her. Immediately, a faint click sounded and the door pushed open to reveal the blackened night outside; a rush of sweet, chilled air hit her instantly. Maybe she was going to make it after all.

She turned to the spirit and whispered, "Thank you," then watched as she faded away.

Lacy shot out of the warehouse and into the grounds of a junk yard. The light she'd seen through the window was caused by floodlights that lit up the whole yard. Twisted metal heaps that were once cars were piled up high in organized rows stretching out as far as she could see. She never thought it possible to feel claustrophobic in such a vast open space but she did.

Suddenly a loud roar came from inside the building, the echo of which filled the expanse of the disused warehouse until it reached Lacy, hitting her full in the face. Fear spiked through her veins and she ran. As fast as her legs were able to carry her, she ran for her life.

Her breath rushed in and out as she ran through the tall maze of metal. The moon reflected on the damp floor of the junk yard, helping to illuminate the way. She reached the end of the aisle only to be faced with more of the same. She looked both ways and couldn't see an end to the rows upon rows of stacked up cars.

There has *to be a way out of here.*

Lacy gasped as she heard her captor's malevolent laughter filling the air as though it was flying around, travelling on the cold night breeze. She picked a direction and ran, hoping that she'd find a way out of there. It had to end somewhere, right?

Her head whipped around to the sound of the man's sinister laugh in her ear, much quieter and a lot closer, as though he was running beside her, in fact, she could have sworn she'd felt his breath stroke her neck but he wasn't there. Her heart began to race and freezing cold tears flicked off her cheeks as she fought to stay upright on her weakening legs. She kept checking behind to see if he was following but there was still no sign of him. She could only hear his voice. Somehow he was projecting it, tormenting her. Her lungs burned, her chest ached but she didn't stop running.

After checking over her shoulder once more she went ploughing into a dark figure: her captor. His laugh was the same as she'd just heard only his face was still. The sound wasn't coming from his mouth, but yet she still heard it echoing all around the junkyard. She screamed and he spun her so she faced away from him, locking his arms around her.

"Get off me," she cried, frantically trying to break free from his hold. Her energy was fading and she struggled for breath. "Please."

His hand covered her mouth and he whispered next to her ear. "Now I get to hurt you." His raucous laughter grated in her ears.

She attempted to scream, for all the good it would do, but it just came out as a muted grunt. She knew she'd signed her death warrant when she'd decided to run. If her kidnapper had planned to let her go in exchange for Michael she highly doubted that would be the case now. He was pissed off.

She still struggled in his grip; no way was she dying without a fight. Not after how close she'd come to escaping.

"Stop it bitch or I'll just snap your neck right here." His voice sounded a lot deeper than usual and almost like there were two of him speaking.

She doubted he would. If he killed her now he'd lose his leverage.

It wasn't her kidnapper's ominous threat that made her body freeze. It was the voice that came from the shadows, a voice that both filled her with hope and fear.

"Don't you fucking dare harm her you son of a bitch!"

Michael. She feared for them both now.

"Well, well." her captor said, keeping his grip tight over her mouth. "Didn't you show up just in time? Shame though, I was about to have some fun. Perhaps I still will, now you're here to watch."

He brought his arm up and Lacy felt something sharp dig into her neck. She inhaled sharply through her nose and her eyes widened and locked onto Michael's.

Michael's hands went up as if to show he had no weapons. "Easy. I'm here just like you wanted." His voice had lost all the anger. He took a step closer then paused. "You hurt her, the deal's off."

"And you're alone?"

"You know that already. Now summon him."

Michael's hands remained where they were. Lacy could see in his face that he knew with the knife being so close to her throat, one wrong move and she was dead. She tried but couldn't stop trembling and could hardly breathe due to the fact that every inhale pushed the blade deeper into her skin.

"I said summon him." Michael demanded.

"I don't have to. He's already here."

Lacy saw a large figure appear behind Michael. From out of nowhere! She tried to shout, to warn him. Then felt a piercing sting as the knife cut her. It worked. Michael whipped around, but was immediately thrown backwards by some sort of invisible force.

What the hell?

Lacy was suddenly thrown free. She hit the ground with a thud, but managed to shuffle herself into a corner out of the way where all she could do was watch with absolute horror as the two men descended on Michael.

CHAPTER SEVENTEEN

"Now is as good a time as any, Alethia."

Michael called out right before he got a heavy boot in his abdomen. He flew through the air, landing against a hunk of metal which caved under the weight of him. He jumped to his feet as quickly as his legs would let him and ran at Varesh. He knew he was only fighting to hold him off until Alethia intervened in whatever way she was planning, and wished to hell she'd hurry up about it.

Just as Michael was about to charge into Varesh's six feet seven—at least—frame he disappeared into thin air leaving Michael to crash into his minion instead. Whatever. . . Either one would do as long as he kept them both away from Lacy.

They hit the ground and skidded along the asphalt. Michael swung at the bastard who—and he had no idea why he noticed at this moment—was wearing a suit. Some poor office bloke on his way to work that he'd found no doubt. He connected with his jaw. Of course all that did was jerk the demon's head back a little and make it even more riled than it already was.

The demon maneuvered his leg under Michael and kicked out, once again sending him backwards through the air. When he landed, he cracked the back of his skull. He lifted up onto his elbows and shook away the stars that had filled his vision temporarily. He reached around his head and felt a wet patch in his hair. When he looked at his hand it was soaked with blood. "Son of a—" The demon charged towards him.

Michael jumped up, but the bastard crashed right into him, the force pushed him back until his back got slammed up against a wall of scrap metal. He felt something sharp puncture his skin above his right kidney just as he heard Lacy crying out his name. He looked down to see that he'd been impaled on a piece of metal tubing, a goddamn tailpipe?

He glanced over to where Lacy was huddled between two cars. When his gaze met hers, she gasped. Her eyes widened, her face filled with bewilderment as her hand slowly covered her mouth. When Michael flicked his eyes back to the demon minion who was now snarling in his face, he knew why Lacy had reacted that way. The demon's face was illuminated by the white glow Michael was now emitting from his eyes, which was always the case when he was angry.

She'd seen them.

He didn't have time to worry about that now. Besides, she'd also seen his back eat the end of a tailpipe and was about to watch him walk away from it unaffected so, yeah, he knew he'd be having a certain conversation with her once this was over.

He pushed the demon backwards with all of his strength and managed to free himself from the metal. Without hesitation, he punched the guy under his chin and before his head had chance to correct itself he punched again, then twice more. The demon only stumbled backwards a couple of steps, but it was enough for Michael to gain back his momentum. As the demon looked back at Michael he wiggled his jaw, his eyes now glowing crimson, just like he'd seen in Jake's and another demon's eyes in the alleyway all those months ago when he'd saved Evo. This bastard was as strong as that one had been too.

Michael braced himself for what would come at him and sure enough the bastard pulled out a knife.

"When you are mine, I'm going to enjoy slicing your flesh from your bones," he hissed as he began to pace around Michael like a lion circling his prey.

Michael looked at the knife, then smiled. "You think that will hurt me?"

The minion laughed. "Maybe this won't. But *that* will."

"MICHAEL!" Lacy cried out.

He was just about to turn around when a white hot pain shot through his entire body, burning every inch of him like he'd imagine hot molten lava to feel if it were poured over his skin. He would have fallen to his knees in agony, except there was something stopping his body from collapsing. He looked down and...

What. The. Fuck?

A glowing hand protruded from his stomach. Despite the intense pain Michael turned his head in stunned silence to see Varesh was standing behind him. He'd pushed his hand right through his stomach. *Fuck!*

Michael let out a pained roar.

Varesh laughed with deep satisfaction. "I have waited for this day for a long time. I must thank you for making it easy for me. I expected a much harder battle with you given the power you are rumored to possess. Now, you have a choice to make. Die, or join us."

Michael couldn't think past the acid heat that was now surging through his entire body. He heard Varesh's words, but nothing he said made any sense. He tried to speak, but it was no use.

The distant cries of a female voice confused him. It was familiar, but he couldn't quite place it.

"*STOP!* You're killing him," she pleaded.

Then he remembered. *Lacy!* He had to keep her safe, but his body was paralyzed.

Varesh's voice shouted out to his minion. "Kill her!"

"NO!" Michael roared. He managed to open his eyes and saw the other demon stalking towards Lacy. The fear in her eyes pained him more than what Varesh was doing and when he tried with all of his strength to move he couldn't. He was helpless.

In the next instance, his vision began to change. Everything around him grew brighter and began to spin.

NO! This can't be happening. Not now.

But this was it. He was finally dying and there was nothing he could do about it. Nothing he could do to save Lacy either. As his vision began to fade he heard muffled voices shouting out.

"What's going on?" A male voice penetrated the fog now filling Michael's mind.

"Alethia!" another voice shouted. *"What business do you have here, Alethia?"*

Then a feral growl filled the air. The sound was close to him so it must have been from Varesh. *"You will die for this,"* the demon shouted.

He forced his eyes open and everything was brighter now. This was what he'd longed for through his torture all that time ago, the light that he'd heard appeared before you died. He felt the burning beginning to ease, a peace rushing through him like a waterfall dousing the flames that had been so rampant over his skin and through his veins. Then everything went quiet and he felt like he was floating. Flying through an expanse of nothingness, unable to see or hear, just feel. This weird sensation must have been his passing. He was finally going to where he was meant to be. *If this is what true peace feels like, I'll take it,* he thought. And in that moment he didn't want anything else.

His weightless body touched down onto something solid, then he felt something touching his arm. As he slowly opened his eyes a blurry shadow appeared over him and a voice grew louder in his mind. ". . . wake up. Michael." He knew that gentle voice, but it took him a moment to place it. Lacy. He blinked and his vision began to clear. Lacy was leaning over him, her face was like an angel's. Was she an angel? Had she died too?

"Michael. Talk to me. We're safe." The moment his brain kicked into gear, like someone had jump started the thing and begun to rev the engine to give it more power, everything came back to him. He sat up quickly and looked down at his stomach, feeling panicked and a little dizzy.

"Where are we?" his voice croaked.

Lacy placed her hand on his shoulder. "It's okay. We're at my place. We're safe." She reassured him again.

"Where's Alethia?"

"You mean the woman who helped us?" Michael nodded. "I don't know. I saw her appear from nowhere and then she did something impossible and those men disappeared right in front of my eyes. I don't really know what happened after that. Then suddenly we were here, just the two of us." She shook her head in disbelief. "How. . . How is any of that possible?"

He placed both his hands on Lacy's face. "Are you okay?" Remembering the last thing he saw was the demon prowling towards her.

She nodded her head slowly. "Yes," she whispered. But there was something in her expression that he couldn't place. *Shit*. She'd seen his eyes. Before he could say anything to her, she placed her hands in his and pulled them away from her face.

"You're wounded." She reached down and pulled at his coat to get a better look. He twisted his head around to see a bloody hole in the fabric where the tailpipe had penetrated him. *Shit!* He pulled himself up from the floor. Lacy followed him, grabbing hold of his arm to steady him when he wobbled a little.

"Thank you." he said to her, noticing a kind of sadness in her eyes.

She reached down to grab the hem of his shirt, which was soaked with blood, but he put his hand on hers to stop her. "It's nothing. I'm fine."

Lacy's eyebrows pulled down into a frown. "I saw what happened. You need to go to the hospital and have it looked at. You're bleeding a lot."

"Really, I'm fine."

She pulled the shirt up anyway and gasped. "Oh, my God." Her hand covered her mouth and her eyes widened. "We need to call an ambulance, now." She went to turn around and Michael grabbed her shoulders, holding her still in front of him. "Jesus, Michael. You have a big hole in your back and—"

"Lacy. Listen to me," he interrupted. "I'm fine. I promise you." She looked confused, bewildered, which was understandable. She inhaled as though she was about to say something, but stopped herself. Instead, she stared into his eyes for a moment and then the expression on her face suddenly changed to something more like disbelief which told him she'd just remembered what she'd seen.

"Your eyes. . . What happened to your eyes back there?" She stepped away from him.

There was no hiding it any longer.

He knew he had no other choice but to be honest with her. He owed her the truth and now he was going to tell her. Everything. Maybe she would understand why he'd run from her at every opportunity. Maybe she would run from him once she knew. The latter was probably for the best.

He began to move them over to the sofa. "What the hell is going on, Michael?" She walked with him and they sat down next to each other. "None of that could have been real right? It's not possible that any of that really happened. Tell me I'm completely crazy and I'll believe it right now."

He shook his head. "You're not crazy, Lacy."

Where to begin?

He inhaled deeply and let his breath out slowly struggling to find the right words. In the next few minutes she was either going to think he was a nut job or that he was some sort of monster. Neither one he was prepared for but it couldn't be avoided anymore. She'd seen too much to accept some lame attempt at a logical explanation, and he knew she wasn't stupid enough to believe it anyway. He had no other choice but to come out and say it.

"I'm not human."

He watched her face for any kind of reaction, but her expression remained blank. He continued. "The men who abducted you aren't human and neither is Alethia." He took one of her hands in his and covered it with his other. "Before I explain things I want you to know that everything I tell you now is the god's honest truth. And that I have only kept this from you to keep you safe. Okay?"

She looked up at him through her long eyelashes and nodded her head.

"A little under a year ago something happened to me. I was murdered."

He heard her sudden intake of breath.

"I don't know who did it or why, all I know is that I didn't pass over to where I should have, instead I ended up in Hell. I don't really remember my time there, and I am pretty sure that's for the best. I don't even know how I got free, but ever since I did, I've been trapped here on earth as a spirit of some kind. Or even a demon. Hell, I don't know what I actually am but I don't think I'm the same as those demons who took you.

"Anyway, I figured I must be like this for a reason, but what that is I've yet to figure out. The next thing I'm going to tell you is going to be even harder to believe. You know the monsters and ghosts you read about when you were younger and some of the things you've seen in movies, they're real Lacy, they exist in a different plain which is not really part of our world but sometimes those monsters cross over and end up right here on earth. I don't know how but it's true. I've spent the last year hunting and tracking them down and sending them back to wherever they came from.

"I came to Oakland because I suspected something supernatural was killing the students here and I was right.

They didn't just decide to kill themselves, they were pushed to do it by a demon. It possessed each of them and made them jump to their deaths. Just after Nina had jumped and we found her lying on the ground I saw the demon leave her body. It had possessed Jake which is the reason he was acting so strange. It's also the reason he came after you. I believe he would have killed you if you hadn't gotten away."

Lacy's other hand had moved to her mouth. She choked back a sob. "Oh, God."

"The man that took you is that same demon, and the other one is his master, who, from what we know, is very powerful. I don't know why they are after me, but I do know that I'm the reason they took you and I'm so, so sorry about that."

"We? You mean Evo knows about all of this too?"

"Yes." As he looked into her eyes, which were now glistening with unshed tears, his chest tightened with the tremendous guilt he felt over what had happened to her and what she now knew. He needed to help her process the things he was telling her; help her understand that, even though these things existed, and knowing this meant her life would never be the same, he would do anything to keep her safe.

She just stared at him with a complete look of despair on her face. Her lips parted and for a moment it seemed like she didn't know what to say. She only managed a whisper. "Is Evo also. . . "

"No. Evo's human just like you."

"How. . . " she cleared her throat and shook her head, "How can I believe any of this? I've seen things today that I truly can't explain, but how can I accept that what you're telling me is true?"

Michael swallowed hard. "I understand how hard it must be for you. It took me enough time to accept what had happened to me, but it's true, all of it."

A tear fell from her eye and he reached up and wiped it with his thumb.

"How can you seem so. . . real? I can touch you, feel you. I kissed you. . . "

"Because this body is real, but. . . " For some reason the words stuck in his throat. He was hesitant because he feared that as soon as he told Lacy the next part, she would run from him. And even though it would be the safest thing for her to do, he didn't know how he'd feel once she was gone. Truth is, since he'd met her he'd been able to pretend he had some kind of a life, a purpose, and that he truly was Michael Warden, just a normal guy who worked at the university. A guy that Lacy wanted to be with and who wanted to be with her. He'd considered it. Imagined them being together; imagined kissing her properly, making love to her. But none of it was real. It could never be.

"But what?" she pressed.

He lowered his gaze, unable to look her in the eye. "But it's not really mine."

The instant he heard her gasp his heart sank.

Now she knew.

Everything.

He couldn't be a coward, so he looked at her again. "I kinda took it from someone who was dying. I'd used other host bodies, but there was one consequence of that that I couldn't deal with: it was dangerous, could kill the person, or if it didn't kill them it damaged them in some way. I couldn't do that anymore, so I waited. And in the end it paid off." He watched Lacy as she listened intently, a small crease settled between her brows. "One night, I happened to stumble across a man who was in a bad way, close to death, slumped under a bridge. It looked like the poor guy was a heavy drug user and he'd overdosed. There was nothing that could've been done to save him. His death had been inevitable, which meant his body was no longer any use to him. So, I figured I'd wait, and at the very last second, I took it."

Lacy's eyes shimmered with her unshed tears. She was silent, her lips pressed together as though she was struggling to process what he'd just told her.

"So, you see. . . I'm not even real, Lacy. Michael Warden is a walking dead man and I'm just hitching a ride. And now you know why I couldn't kiss you last night."

She stared into his eyes, her gaze never wavering. Then her brow creased and when she pulled her hand from his, he thought she was going to bolt, but then a rush of breath left her and she put her head into her hands. After a moment, when she looked at him again, her frown had gone. She looked strangely calm.

She must have seen the despair on his face as he waited for a response because she reached up and placed her hand on his cheek. Another tear fell from her eye as she stroked his face with her thumb and whispered, "You are real to me."

He almost stopped breathing. After everything he'd just told her she should have been running out the door as far away from him, from this whole nightmare, as she could. But instead she was looking at him with adoring eyes like she had done last night before she'd gone to kiss him.

"Michael, I don't know how to deal with all of the things you've just told me. Part of me, the little girl in me, wants to run away and forget any of this ever happened, but what good is that going to do? It'll probably only drive me mad in the end anyway. What I do know is this: no matter how hard this is for me to deal with right now, it can't be anywhere near as bad as it is for you."

Shit. Before, she'd just been knocking on the door to his heart, but now, after that speech, she'd gone and moved herself in, kicked off her shoes and propped her feet up on the sofa. Now she wasn't going anywhere.

He couldn't speak.

"You're not one of those demons, you're not evil. I can feel your compassion and your kindness, that's the reason I care for you. You came to rescue me at the risk of your own l. . . " She stopped herself from saying the word *life* and then looked away from him to hide her embarrassment. "I'm sorry."

He pulled her chin around so she was looking at him again. "Hey. Don't apologize. I've had a year to deal with this, and even though I still don't have any answers for why I'm like this, I'm kind of used to it."

Her lips curled up in a faint smile. "You are real to me," she repeated, then surprised him when she leaned across and hugged him, resting her head on his chest. He hesitantly placed his arms around her and rested his chin on her head. He closed his eyes.

He rubbed her back while he thought of how well she'd taken everything. Perhaps he could have been honest with her sooner. He doubted it. If she hadn't just witnessed what she had there's no way she would have believed him. And who would blame her for that? He found it hard to believe himself and yet he was smack bang in the middle of it.

"I don't think this whole ghosts and spirits thing is so crazy, not now anyway." Lacy said, her head still on his chest.

"Oh, yeah? Why's that?"

She sat up, but he kept his arm around her. "As crazy as it sounds coming out of my own mouth. . . a ghost helped me escape tonight."

What was she talking about? He gave her a questioning glance. "I don't understand."

"I was bound to a bed by my ankles and wrists and had no way of freeing myself. A woman appeared in front of me, a spirit, and she helped me get free," she explained.

What? He thought the only reason he could see spirits was because he was also dead. How was it possible? And more importantly, why would a spirit help her? He hardly ever interacted with ghosts because they were never easy to communicate with.

"How?"

"Somehow, she was able to break the chain and the rope. Then I ran. But when I got to the door of the warehouse it was locked. The spirit helped me again by placing her hand on the door which unlocked it. There's no way I could have broken that chain myself so I couldn't have imagined it, I swear I—"

He placed his hands on her arms. "Lacy, I believe you." It sounded like she was trying to convince herself more than him. "I just don't understand it."

She smiled and looked down. "I don't either. But I think, after all these years, I've finally realized I'm not crazy."

She seemed to be talking to herself rather than him. She wasn't making sense. "Lacy, what's going on?"

She chewed on her bottom lip for a moment. "I've been seeing things I can't explain since shortly after my sister's death; people who have tried to talk to me, to show me things. My grandma, and the doctors I spoke to about it, put it down to post traumatic stress. And that's what I've thought ever since. I thought I was having crazy hallucinations, worried that perhaps I was losing my mind. Hell, I've paid enough out on therapy bills because of it, even spent years trying to psychoanalyze myself to no avail. I hadn't had one for nearly five years, until a couple of weeks ago when I was on my way to work. I saw something in the road and swerved to miss it. When I checked, there was nothing there. I think that, after all these years of thinking I was a little crazy, I've actually been able to see the dead."

She let out a heavy sigh, but surprised Michael when she laughed. "This has been one hell of a crazy day, huh?"

He couldn't help but admire her even more over her attitude to everything especially this new revelation. Well, well. . . So she was gifted as well as beautiful.

He couldn't help but pull her into his arms again. "You're amazing, you know that?"

"Why? Because you're not hauling me out of here in a straight jacket?" she said as she rested her chin on his shoulder.

Michael felt a slight breeze and a shift in his senses. He looked up to see Alethia standing in the doorway of the sitting room.

"What the hell took you so long back there?" Michael suddenly snapped. He and Lacy had been seconds away from death.

Lacy pulled away from him. And he realized how angry he'd just sounded.

Alethia's face was pale and she didn't seem herself. "Yes, I'm sorry for that. I had to wait until Varesh was weak. What he was doing to you was draining his power and I had to wait until the right moment before I could use my powers on him. He's strong and I needed to make sure he was vulnerable."

He calmed himself, remembering that she was the reason they were both still here. "What *was* he doing to me? That hurt like hell."

"That's because it *was* Hell. He was using Hell's fire to dampen your powers so that he could rip your soul out."

"What fucking powers? Demons keep telling me that I'm someone I'm not, and now he's convinced I have powers? There is some sure fucked up case of mistaken identity here and I need to clear this shit up before he hurts anyone else I care about." His eyes flicked to Lacy for a moment and he saw her eyes widen slightly. Yes, well, he was all about the truth right now.

Alethia remained quiet.

"Are you okay?" Lacy asked as she walked over to her and placed her hand on her arm. "You look awfully pale." She led her to the sofa.

"Uh, yeah, sorry. Alethia, this is Lacy. Lacy. . . Alethia." Michael motioned his hand back and forth between the two. "Alethia is a goddess." He waited again for a reaction from Lacy but she was more concerned with helping the woman, who actually did look a little sick.

Alethia sat down, shoulders slumped. "Nice to meet you. I'm fine, really, thanks."

"Are you sure?" Lacy threw Michael a quick look and he shrugged his shoulders.

"Truly, I am. Dematerializing someone usually drains me a little, but, like I said, Varesh is powerful. It took a lot out of me that's all. I'll be fine once I've rested."

"Where is he now?" Michael asked as he pulled out his cell ready to text Evo to inform him that they'd made it back okay.

"I sent them both to see an old pal of theirs. Lucifer will enjoy his company for a while, but I wouldn't count on it being for long. At most, it might buy us a day or two." Alethia began to cough, her pallor now a pasty gray. She leaned back and closed her eyes.

Michael hadn't even thanked Alethia for what she'd done. If it wasn't for her, Lacy would certainly be dead and who knows what would have happened to him. He had a very bad feeling about all of this. Why was this powerful demon after him? What kind of threat did he think Michael could impose? The whole situation was just getting weird.

Was it a case of mistaken identity? Perhaps that's why he was killed in the first place, because whoever it was thought he was somebody else. He could think of no other reason so it had to be that.

"Would you like to have a lie down on my bed, Alethia?" Lacy's voice pulled him back from his thoughts and her soft, caring tone warmed him. Thank God she was okay. "You look like you could use a soft pillow right now and I have lots of them on there."

The deity gave Lacy an appreciative smile as she managed to nod her head. "I'll show you to my room."

Michael watched as Lacy put her arm around the deity and helped her towards the door. "Alethia," he called. She looked back at him over her shoulder. "Thanks."

"That's okay. I like diamonds by the way." She winked at him and smiled a little before they disappeared down the hall.

He was amazed at how Lacy was handling everything. She seemed completely unfazed by what had happened and what she'd learned about the world she thought she knew. And now she was taking care of a powerful goddess without even giving it a second thought. Like it was just something she did every day.

But he couldn't shake the feeling he had. It seemed he was to blame for everything she'd been through lately. If he'd just stayed away from her none of this would have happened. Yeah, instead of sticking to his normal routine of keeping his distance and getting on with the job he was there to do he'd weakened. It was an innocent slip that had materialized into something that was now way beyond his control. He cared for her, and knew she felt the same and wasn't that just a ball ache?

He had to stop it. There was no choice.

He had to stick to his plan of Evo staying with her from now on. As soon as his buddy got back, he'd inform him of the new plan, then Michael would go to his place, pick up a few things and head over to the hospital. He didn't think Nina was still in danger but wanted to be sure.

His phone vibrated in his hand. It was a reply from Evo: *On my way. Will get takeout.*

Michael exhaled hard. Now he had to prepare to give his friend the next bit of bad news: they'd left the MERC behind.

* * *

After fetching a fresh towel from the closet in the spare room, Lacy returned to her room to find Alethia sitting on the edge of the bed, eyes closed, head tilted back, and a rush of whispers coming from her lips. Lacy approached slowly, wondering what language it was that she was speaking. Not wanting to disturb the strange ritual, she quietly walked to the armchair in the corner next to the window and placed the towel on it.

"I was just talking with my father." Alethia said unexpectedly.

Lacy turned around to face her. "Wow. Impressive. Your cell phone bills must be nonexistent. Do you even need one at all?"

Alethia smiled. "Not for our conversations. It's one way my kind communicates with each other when we're not together."

"I see. Like a form of telepathy?" Lacy asked, still trying to understand all the bizarre stuff that had happened in the last twenty-four hours.

Alethia nodded. "Yes."

It was hard to see the deity as anything more than normal—human. If Lacy hadn't witnessed her power first hand, she would never have believed it. She was very pretty, in a sophisticated way; dark eyebrows framed unusual caramel colored eyes. Her black hair hung straight with the slightest curl at the ends.

"I brought you some clean towels in case you want a shower. Feel free to. The bathroom's just across the hall." Lacy paused as she noticed how off color Alethia looked. "Are you sure you're okay?"

"Yes. Really, I am. It's just. . . it's been a while since I've used that much power." Alethia shifted herself until she was lying down.

As Lacy thought back to when she'd appeared from nowhere in the junk yard and used her powers the way she had, she remembered seeing how much the woman had struggled. Whoever, or whatever, that being was that had nearly killed Michael it was certainly very powerful, and to think that she'd been captured by such a thing brought the dread sweeping back over her. She worried for Michael—worried for all of them. If using her powers on such a creature when he was weak had drained Alethia as much as it had, she dreaded to think what would happen if Varesh was at full strength.

She didn't want to keep her any longer so she headed for the door. "Well, let me know if you need anything okay." She was about to leave when. . .

"He cares for you, you know."

Lacy paused with her fingers around the door handle as Alethia's words surprised her. She turned around, a little taken aback. "I'm sorry?"

"Michael. He has feelings for you. I sensed his sadness when we first met at the airport and I saw a vision of you in his mind. Then just now, his guilt over what happened to you."

Lacy walked back over to the bed not really sure what to say so she just sat on the edge. "You can read minds?"

"Yes. Look, I try not to invade people's thoughts, but sometimes it just happens. He's scared to let himself feel for you because of what he is and. . . " She paused. "Shit. I just thought you should know. I'm sorry. Perhaps I shouldn't have said anything. See, this is exactly why I'm normally strict with myself when it comes to hearing people. I can't ever keep my damn mouth shut."

Lacy placed her hand on Alethia's arm and gave her a smile. "Hey. It's fine. I kind of knew anyway. I kissed him last night and he told me then." She didn't know why she wanted to talk about this with someone she'd known for all of five minutes but the truth was she really did. She felt quite calm, strangely comfortable in her presence even though she was practically a stranger. Must be the goddess thing. "I just don't know what to do about it. When I saw that. . . *thing* nearly killing him I wanted to run to him, to help him. I couldn't bare it." Oh, God. She'd fallen for him. Hard. Well, wasn't this a revelation?

Alethia pulled herself up to a sitting position and Lacy saw genuine compassion in her face. "Can I give you some advice?"

Lacy nodded.

"Just be patient with him. I understand his concern about the two of you and if I were in his position I would feel the same. He isn't human anymore." She let out a sigh.

"I know we don't know each other, but you need to know that I'm quite good at detecting when someone is pure of heart. I sensed it about you, even Evo." She must have seen Lacy's eyebrows rise because she laughed a little. "I know he's a horny, womanizing snake—Yes, I've been in his head too. Don't judge me—but his heart is in the right place when it needs to be. With Michael though, I sensed it the most. I don't know how to explain it, but I just feel that he's here for a purpose. There's a reason he came back from Hell. I don't know why he's been targeted by Varesh, and I don't know why he was killed, but everything happens for a reason right?"

It was a philosophy that Lacy wasn't entirely on board with, at least she hadn't been until now, but maybe Alethia was right. She didn't really understand any of this, in fact, her head was beginning to spin with the events of the past few weeks, but she knew Michael was a good man. She'd sensed it too, in her own way, and that's why she felt the way she did about him.

Why couldn't she have met him when he'd been alive?

The two of them sat in silence for a little while. Both of them clearly affected by this evening's event, but in very different ways. She was sitting next to a powerful goddess who had exhausted her powers on some evil demon, and in the other room, was a man (she refused to call him anything else) who had experienced severe tragic circumstances—resulting in that same demon hunting him down—who she now had feelings for.

What a mess.

Lacy looked up at Alethia who now had her eyes closed. "I'll leave you to rest," she said as she stood up. She headed for the door, but before she opened it, she turned back around. "Thank you, for the chat."

"Mmhmm." Was all Alethia managed along with a slight nod of her head.

Lacy closed the door behind her and when she returned to the living room, Michael wasn't there. Before she thought anything of it, she heard movement coming from the kitchen. When she walked through the door, he glanced at her over his shoulder and gave her a faint smile. "Thought I'd make coffee," he said as he placed the jug that he'd just filled with water in front of the machine.

She walked over and leaned against the counter watching him gather the cups and the sugar bowl from the cupboard above his head. He put one sugar in each of the two cups leaving the spoon inside the last one. He stood motionless with both hands on the counter, his head hanging low. He didn't look at her as he spoke. "I'm sorry."

She straightened. "Sorry? What for?"

He stayed with his back to her while the noise from the coffee machine increased in volume. "For everything. All of this is my fault. I should never have brought this to your door."

She thought about what he'd said to her in the living room when he'd confessed to what he was. "You told me you came here to help the students. To find whatever was killing them didn't you?"

"Yes," he answered quietly.

"And you had no idea that this demon was after you, and that he had something to do with what was happening on campus?"

"That's right."

"Then how is any of this your fault?"

His voice rose slightly. "If I'd stayed away from you then you wouldn't have been dragged into it. You wouldn't have been abducted and almost killed." He slammed his hand down on the counter.

She didn't say anything. Couldn't. Instead, her thoughts went back to being tied to that bed, terrified she would never see anyone again: her friends, her colleagues, but most of all Michael. The whole time she'd laid in the darkened warehouse she'd thought of him—the only reason she'd gotten through it.

He turned around and took up the same position as she had, arms crossed over his chest. "I'm not used to this, Lacy. For the past year I've had nobody but myself to worry about. But now, I've somehow managed to drag Evo deeper into this shit than he was in the first place; Alethia, who Varesh now knows is involved as well; and worst of all you... I've put you in danger and it was purely because of my selfish actions."

"What do you mean, selfish actions?"

He seemed to hesitate as though he was finding it hard to say his next words.

"Because I allowed myself to feel. I just wanted some normalcy, just to feel for a moment like I wasn't the guy who'd been murdered, that I was just me. Because you, Lacy, you made me feel human again." A tendon twitched as he tightened his jaw. "*I* put you in danger."

Lacy bit back the tears that were threatening to form and walked over to him. He looked her in the eye as she reached up and stroked her hand down his cheek. The coffee machine had run through its cycle, leaving nothing but silence as the two of them stood and looked at each other.

Michael tucked a stray hair behind her ear and surprised her when he reached up and placed both hands on her cheeks. "I'm sorry." He whispered it this time, but before she had chance to tell him to stop apologizing, he bent his head and placed his soft lips on hers.

Stunned at his unexpected kiss, she closed her eyes, allowing herself to get lost in the feel of him. A warm flush filled her cheeks.

He broke contact and pulled back slightly, just enough to look at her. His piercing blue eyes scanned her face and she couldn't quite place his expression. Her heart began to race; her whole body had warmed with a sudden glow that soared through her veins as she stared back at him unable to speak. But she didn't have to. He kissed her again, this time licking his tongue over her lips and pushing inside. She opened up to him and he moaned as their tongues met and began to twist around each other. His hand stroked through her hair to the back of her neck and he walked her backwards until her back hit the other countertop.

She stroked her hands up his back. *Oh, God.* This was what she'd wanted, needed from him. Her body was filled with a rush of sensation as Michael's tongue continued to massage hers, the taste of him making her head spin with desire. At that moment she wanted everything from him, she wanted to feel his flesh on hers, their bodies lying together with no barrier between them. The thought of it heated her core.

Her thoughts were cut off when the doorbell rang and Michael immediately broke contact and pulled away from her. He was panting in much the same way she was, and he swallowed hard before he eventually spoke.

"That'll be. . . "—he cleared his throat—"That'll be Evo." His brows dipped slightly and then he was out of the door before she could blink.

Lacy stood in the same spot while she heard Michael letting Evo in. Feeling bereft, she put her hand on her chest and felt the rapid beat of her heart. Even though she'd craved Michael's kiss again, the glow quickly began to dissipate and she felt her chest tighten as a sudden sadness washed over her. For some reason she feared that might be their last.

* * *

In Lacy's bathroom, Michael had just finished splashing water over his face and was now towelling it off. He'd let Evo in with his big bag of takeout and made like he was desperate for the toilet, but not before catching the concerned expression on Evo's face. Never missed a thing that man.

Hands propped either side of the basin, he stared at his bruised reflection. He tried to replace what face he saw with his own, but the truth was, the memory he had of his real self was fading. He'd been in this body for around ten months, but with everything that had happened since then, all the battles he'd fought, it felt more like ten years.

He thought back to how simple his life had been. Even though he'd been CEO of his own company, and it had been hard and very stressful at times dealing with the many staff who worked in his building and the general day to day responsibility of running things, his biggest worry right before he'd died had been whether he was going to be able to make it to his damn conference in Connecticut.

Things couldn't be more different for him now.

Now, at this very moment, he was faced with the harsh reality that he was falling too hard for a woman he could never have, and didn't deserve; a woman whose life he'd selfishly endangered and who, he suspected, felt the same for him despite now knowing what he really was. Part of him had hoped that when he'd confessed everything to her, she'd have been so freaked out she'd have had no choice but to distance herself from him, but in fact it had done quite the opposite.

And now, not only had he succeeded in making her feel sorry for him, with a moment of complete madness he'd just made things even worse.

God, that kiss had damn near torn him apart. He closed his eyes for a second and allowed himself to remember it. Her lips had been so soft; her sweet floral scent had made his head spin with desire for her. He was surprised that he could feel all of those sensations given his situation, but feel them he had. The buzz of desire had run through his very core lighting him up, making him feel as real as he had before he'd died. In fact more real than he'd ever felt.

He inhaled deeply and let his breath out in a long drawn out sigh. He had to get his head together. It had been lovely, had exhilarated him, but it was a moment of weakness that he couldn't, and wouldn't, allow to happen again.

He flushed the chain for effect and went through to the kitchen where Evo and Lacy were playfully arguing over what looked like egg rolls?

"You've got the extra bit of shrimp toast so it's only fair that I get that extra roll." Lacy snagged it from Evo's plate before he could argue back.

"You, woman, are a pain in my ass," he grumbled. "You're—HEY, buddy."

Michael managed a smile. "Hey." He went over to the counter where all the plating up was happening.

"We've shared it out equally." That last word was said with gritted teeth and a look towards Lacy, who shrugged her shoulder at him as she sat down at the dining table with her plate piled high. "Yours is over there," he gestured. "I just shoved a bit of everything on your plate."

Michael wasn't really in the mood, but he grabbed the food anyway. "Cheers, man." He went over and sat opposite Lacy, who glanced at him briefly and gave him an awkward smile. She'd obviously sensed something was off with him. Not surprising since he'd practically run away from her just now. Better that she did. It was time for him to stop this nonsense. He would apologize to her for what happened and then move on. He had much more important things to do right now than battle with himself over a woman. Yes, he'd made up his mind and was determined to stick to it.

Evo sat down next to him and before he spoke, his friend glanced at Lacy then back to him. He knew something was up, but to Michael's surprise, he didn't mention it. "So. . . You going to tell me what the hell happened over there?"

* * *

After they'd eaten and Michael had filled Evo in with all the details from Lacy's rescue, Michael decided he needed to go back to his place. It wasn't going to help his situation hanging around Lacy when he didn't have to, so he and Evo had left pretty much straight away. Besides, he had something else he needed to do.

Alethia had agreed to stay behind. Going by what he'd seen so far Lacy would be very well protected by the deity should anything happen. There was no need to continue staking out the hospital because Lacy's friend had informed her that an officer was now watching her room in case Jake returned, and the chances of Varesh or his sidekick bothering her now were very slim.

Michael knew Evo wasn't going to be happy when he found out what he was about to do, but he had no choice, and had no idea how to do it on his own, which was the only reason he had to involve his friend, as much as he hated to.

After retrieving Evo's MERC—after the guy had insisted—and Lacy's Focus from the breaker's yard, they were now at Michael's apartment. He grabbed a clean shirt from his closet and did a quick change, throwing the ripped and bloodied one in the trash. He returned to the sitting room where Evo was sat on the sofa fiddling with one of his guns. "So, what now?" his friend asked as he flicked the safety on one of his SIG SAUER pistols.

"You help me," Michael said as he watched Evo's eyes narrow towards him.

Evo placed his pistol on the table in front of him without looking away. "Help you with what?" His voice was thick with suspicion.

Michael held his gaze. "First, I want you to promise you'll hear me out before you say anything, okay?"

Now he frowned. "What is it?"

"Evo," he pressed.

"I promise," he said through gritted teeth. "What do you need me for, man?"

Michael paused. "I need your help. . . to get into Hell."

CHAPTER EIGHTEEN

"Oh no. No! No way... Not happenin' my man." Evo said as he began to pace the length of the small living room.

Michael wasn't at all surprised by his reaction and the least he could do after dropping such a bombshell on him was keep quiet until he'd finished his rant. Not that Michael was paying much attention.

"... only thing you'll succeed in doing is being skinned alive," he went on. "And I, for one, am not going to play any part in helping you get there. You got me?"

Silence.

"Have you finished?" Michael asked as he leaned his back against the apartment door.

"Well, that depends... Have you changed your mind?"

"No. And I'm not going to either."

"Then no. Have I *fuck* finished!" Evo scrubbed at the stubble on his chin. He stopped to face Michael placing both his fisted hands on his hips. "Okay. So... let's say I did help you, what is it that you plan on doing when you get there?"

"Talking with Lucifer."

Evo's eyes widened before he began to laugh until he saw Michael's stoic expression and realized he was deadly serious. The laughing ceased and his face paled. "You're out of your goddamn fucking mind."

Michael brushed past him. Maybe it was a dumb idea. Maybe he would be facing a fate worse than death. But the way he saw it, he had to do something about Varesh and maybe speaking to Lucifer was the only way.

"Think about it. He's after that demon piece of shit just as much as we are, remember. What if we can help each other?"

Evo was looking at him like he'd lost his mind, the horror at the fact that Michael had even suggested looking for Lucifer clear on his face. "Can you hear what you're saying right now? You're suggesting teaming up with the king of Hell, and you expect me not to have a fucking issue with that?"

"No. I'm not expecting that. I understand why you do, but you need to understand that this might be the only way. I've already seen some of Varesh's power, hell. . . even his demon minion was more powerful than any other we've encountered. For whatever reason he wants me to team up with him or he wants me dead, I mean *really* dead. I'm not joining him, so do you think he's going to stop until he gets his wish? We don't stand a chance against him on our own Evo."

Evo dropped his head and let out a sigh. His voice had calmed and the weight of his friend's grave expression was evidence of how dangerous Michael's plan actually was. "There has to be another way, Mike. This has to be the stupidest. . . Jeez, I don't think even I would have come up with something as crazy as this."

"I told you what Alethia said. It's not going to be long until he returns and he's going to be more pissed than before. We have to try this."

"What about Alethia's ring? The one her father gave to her. I thought it was supposed to capture demons."

Michael sat on the sofa and rested his foot on his knee. "She tried. He was too powerful. All she could do was send him away and that nearly killed her."

"But it *will* work on other demons right?"

"Apparently so."

Evo didn't speak. Instead, he sat staring at the coffee table for a moment until he eventually looked back up at Michael with a smirk. "Then we're not going down there without that ring. There will be plenty of other things in that place to worry about besides Lucifer."

* * *

After about an hour of trying to convince his stubborn jackass of a friend that he wouldn't be going with him, Michael had finally given up. Evo was a determined SOB and when he decided he was going to do something, there was nothing Michael could ever do to stop him. This time was no exception. Evo was going with him to find Lucifer and that was that.

Meanwhile, after his friend had gone out for some supplies, Michael played back the answering machine message that he'd just listened to. It was from Lacy. She'd called twice since he'd returned to his apartment and both times he hadn't answered.

Fucking coward!

The second time she'd left a message: *"Hi, it's Lacy. I. . . I was hoping you'd be back home by now. I just wanted to speak to you about earlier. I figured that's the reason you left so quickly but. . . Michael I. . . "* Pause. *"I just wanted to say I'm sorry. Call me if you want to."*

Michael stood with his finger on the delete button. *Shit!* She had no reason to be sorry. He should have called her back. Damn! He really wanted to, at least to tell her that everything was okay. But he didn't. When he heard the key turn in the lock he knew Evo was back. He pressed the button and erased the message. They would talk and he would tell her that nothing could happen between them, but it would have to wait.

Evo walked through the door looking like he'd had a fight with a mud wrestler and the mud wrestler had clearly won. His coat was covered in dirt, but that wasn't all, he had smears of the stuff all over his face too.

Michael shot him a quizzical look. "If this is your attempt at camouflage. . . Well, I can still see you."

Evo's responding smile was full of sarcasm. He dropped a small backpack, which was just as dirty as he was, onto the floor in front of the coffee table. "I hope you've got plenty of Jack," he said as he removed his coat and slung it onto the chair in the corner of the room.

Michael didn't even bother to ask where he'd been and instead, retrieved two glasses from the cupboard and a large bottle of whiskey from on the unit. He walked over to where Evo had now placed a pile of items on the floor and watched as he grabbed his Bowie knife from his ankle and began to cut away at what looked like a tree branch. Again, Michael didn't ask. He'd seen his friend do this kind of thing many times before and never really understood any of it.

He poured them both a glass of Jack Daniels and sat quietly on the sofa watching Evo go to work on the branch. Finally, after about twenty minutes or so, it resembled some kind of. . . wand? Evo held it up and studied it for a moment. "It's a branch from one of the trees in the cemetery. Has to be from sacred ground."

Michael nodded and took another swig of whiskey. "You gonna drink that?"

His friend didn't answer and got back to work. Now he was carving something into the thicker end. Some symbols, four of them. When he was done, he took a swig of his drink and looked at Michael, eyes narrowed. "I've no chance of talking you out of this have I?"

"No," was all Michael said as he put his glass to his mouth and took another large sip of Jack.

Evo chewed on the inside of his cheek and nodded his head. He picked up a dirty piece of cloth and ripped it into two pieces.

"What's that?" Looked like something he'd grabbed from a dumpster.

"Part of a shroud." Evo answered.

Michael frowned. "Please don't tell me that was wrapped around someone at some point."

His buddy's eyebrows rose. "Then I won't. But it won't change the fact that it was"

Nice. Just what the hell else was he going to produce from that bag? His answer came next when Evo pulled out a dirty bone. Michael guessed it hadn't belonged to an animal. That would just be too acceptable. "Human?" he asked, not surprised when his buddy replied, "Yup." before cutting through it. "I need two small bowls."

After Michael retrieved what he'd asked for from the kitchen, he poured himself another whiskey and resumed his place on the sofa.

"Make sure you save some of that." Evo said, nodding towards the now half empty bottle. He then placed the small portion of bone he'd cut into one of the bowls.

"I've poured you one, remember? Ain't my fault if you don't keep up."

Next Evo pulled a lighter from his shirt pocket and lit the bone on fire, watching the flame crackle and burn before placing a piece of the shroud inside. "Not to drink. We're gonna need it for something else shortly." He then pulled out a clear bag, which looked to have dirt in it, and placed it on the table next to him. When he blew the flame out of the bowl, he crushed the charred remains with the back end of his knife, and then added the contents from the bag. He reached into the backpack again and this time pulled out a hip flask, unscrewed the top and emptied what was inside into the same bowl. "Holy water."

Of course it was. The main ingredient for most of the rituals he'd seen Evo perform.

"I need your arm." Evo said as he rolled up his own sleeve. "And bring the whiskey."

As soon as Michael handed him the bottle, Evo poured some of the stuff onto his own forearm, then without hesitation, he sliced through his skin and held it over the other empty bowl. Shit, it was deep. He clenched his fist and watched as a steady stream of dark crimson dripped from his arm, a stark contrast against the bright white porcelain of the bowl. When he was satisfied, he wiped at the wound and then the blade with a piece of torn cloth and handed the knife to Michael, hilt first. "Make sure it's deep," he ordered.

As he took a hold of his friend's blade Michael felt a pang of uncertainty rush through him when he thought about all Evo was willing to do to help him. He knew he was loyal through and through, but this was worse than anything they'd ever encountered. Michael's decision to confront the most powerful being known to man, and... everything else, to ask for his help was most likely a suicide mission, but one that he was willing to partake in to see that that bastard demon got what he deserved. His own life had already been taken from him, but he wasn't happy about being the cause of Evo losing his.

Nothing could be done, though. Once Evo set his mind to something, there was no talking him out of it, even something as stupid and dangerous as this.

As he held his arm over the bowl, Michael glanced over at Evo, placed the blade on his forearm and began to draw it deep through his skin. No pain. Just a strange pulling sensation as his flesh parted and blood that wasn't his own began to drip from the wound and into the bowl, merging with Evo's.

He had no clue what his friend was doing and quite frankly he didn't care. He was focused and willing to do what he must. A vision of Lacy popped into his head, her smile lighting up her face as she sat across from him in the restaurant. Then that nice vision quickly changed into the grim sight of her cowering away in the junkyard, her face bloodied. Her fear had almost broken him apart. She was the reason he was determined to see this through. No matter what became of him he had to make sure she was safe and getting rid of that son of a bitch and his minion was priority one. The rest would follow.

After enough blood had left Michael's vein, Evo passed him a torn piece of cloth to hold over his wound to stop the bleeding and continued with his ritual. Next he combined the ground bone, earth and holy water to the blood and mixed it together until it became a paste. Michael screwed his nose up. It was pretty gross.

Evo retrieved the make shift wand from the table, looked at it for a second and sighed. "This is the final part of the ritual," he said still looking down at the thing. "There's no going back from this. I can give you more time to think about it before we do it. Just so you're sure." Evo's eyes flicked up to meet his. The intense stare from his friend cut deeply, knowing they may not return from this yet, selflessly, Evo was ready to go in guns blazing. The concern on his face wasn't for himself though.

Michael closed his eyes for a second and again, his mind was filled with more visions of Lacy. Her pale green eyes staring back at him full of concern. Then his vision shifted to her flushed cheeks and hooded lids just after they'd kissed. He tried desperately to fight away her image, to pretend that she meant nothing to him and get his mind fully focused on what lay ahead but it was impossible. His feelings for her were more than he'd anticipated and the thought of leaving her without saying a word and throwing himself into certain danger was proving too difficult.

He heard her voice echoing over and over through his head. *"You are real to me." "I'm sorry." "You're not evil. I can feel your compassion. . . "*

Evo's voice brought Michael back from his thoughts. "Look buddy, if you've changed your mind, I'll gladly burn all this sh—"

"No." Michael said harshly. "I haven't. I just. . . I just need to go out. There's something I have to do first."

He got to his feet and headed for the door. He had to tell Lacy what he was about to do even though he didn't want her to worry about him. He had to let her know how he truly felt.

"Oh. . . I'll just hang here then." Michael heard Evo shout in a derisive tone as he pulled the door closed behind him.

* * *

"I'll take a seat out here in the hall." Alethia said softly.

Lacy nodded her head as she reached down for the door handle and walked quietly into the hospital room. Nina's head shifted around from her gaze out of the window. Her mouth turned up into a light smile as she looked at Lacy. "Miss Holloway?" Her voice was hoarse.

Lacy smiled at her. "Hi. Please. . . it's Lacy."

The head of her bed was raised so that she was nearly in a sitting position propped up on a bulk of pillows. She looked weak and her skin was pale which only accentuated the dark shadows under her eyes. But she was awake and the doctors had said that she was responding well, which was all Lacy needed to hear.

"I brought you some things." Lacy said as she held up a sports bag that she'd filled with toiletries and some clean night clothes. "How are you feeling?" She walked over to the large chair beside the bed, eyeing the uneaten food on a tray across the other side before sitting down.

"Thanks. Strange." Nina said. "I can't really remember much of what happened. It's all fuzzy."

"That's understandable."

Nina looked down at her hands as she picked at her nails. "I remember thinking I was dying, but I wasn't scared. All I could hear were echoes of distant voices all around me and then they began to fade and I could no longer feel my body. I just felt relief. It was like something was telling me that I was going to see my boyfriend, Danny, again and that's all I was waiting for.

"Then everything went dark and all I remember after that is waking up feeling really groggy in this room." She closed her eyes and frowned. It was hard to ignore the sorrow in her voice. The poor girl had been through hell and back. "The nurses say that you stayed with me."

Lacy nodded. "I couldn't let you go through this alone."

"Thank you," Nina said, trying her best to smile.

Lacy reached over and placed her hand over Nina's. "You don't have to thank me, Nina. You just get yourself better."

Noticing the sorrow on Nina's face, Lacy wondered if she should leave her to rest. After all, she hadn't been conscious that long and the whole situation must be quite overwhelming to say the least. She was just about to say her goodbyes when Nina spoke.

"What do I do now?" she asked in a low whisper. "I have no one left." Her eyes began to glisten before she turned her head away.

Lacy thought back to when she'd first arrived in America. Being from a little place in England, and never venturing much further than the end of her street, everything had been so different. She hardly really knew her grandparents and didn't really fit in well at high school, so *alone* was a very familiar feeling for her. After her grandparents died, she had no choice but to deal with the way things were, and she did. But even though she was around people every day at work, there was always a void in her life she could never seem to fill.

Lacy noticed a small box of Kleenex on the cupboard beside her. "Hey," she said, taking one from the box and handing it to Nina. "I promise that you won't be alone." And somehow, she would make sure of it.

Lacy felt the vibration of her cell phone in her pocket. When she looked at the screen her heart skipped. She read the text message from Michael:

At yours. Where are you? Need to talk.

She quickly typed back:

With Alethia at hospital. Nina doing well x

K. Pick u up in 20 mins outside main doors, he replied.

It wasn't totally unexpected to hear from him. They'd hardly said two words to each other before Michael had left earlier. But it was the ominous *"Need to talk"* part that unnerved her.

Everything okay? she asked.

Yes. See u then.

She put the cell back in her pocket. Everything wasn't okay. She knew they would have to talk about what happened earlier, but for some reason she had a feeling it was more than that.

She said her goodbyes to Nina, promising to visit again tomorrow evening. She explained to Alethia that Michael was coming to pick her up, and that she could take her car, and then made her way down to the lobby.

CHAPTER NINETEEN

The ride home from the hospital was a quiet one. Lacy felt a distinct tension in the air and was growing more and more anxious by the minute about what would become of her and Michael's impending *talk*. Many times she'd gone to say something, but couldn't seem to find her voice. After Michael had asked her about Nina, and she'd told him what the doctors had said, he'd shut down and neither of them said another word until they pulled up outside her house.

"I've told Alethia that I'll text her when I leave. She'll stay with you tonight," Michael said, his voice so void of emotion that Lacy found it hard to even answer him.

"It's good of her to help us."

Michael remained silent as they approached the house. She couldn't bear it much longer. Never before had she felt so nervous over a coming break up. Not that she could call it that. One proper passionate kiss was all they'd shared—hardly relationship of the century—but she knew she would pine after him once he'd finalized things, nonetheless. Damn, her emotions had been all over the place the last few weeks. She was a mess.

Lacy removed her coat and scarf and hung them on the hook in the hall. Michael left his jacket on and went straight to the sofa in the front room and sat down. He clearly wasn't planning on staying long and that was probably for the best. She just wished he'd speak and get it over with.

She couldn't take the silence any longer. "Can I get you coffee?" Jeez, her voice was trembling. What the hell was the matter with her?

Michael didn't look at her. "No. Thanks." He scrubbed the short stubble on his chin anxiously and then glanced up at her. "Would you sit? Please." He motioned to the chair, clearly not wanting to be too close to her. Lacy did as he asked, pushing her hands between her knees.

"About what happened earlier, I'm sorry for my behavior. That should never have happened." His eyes found hers, full of sorrow, guilt, confusion? It was hard to read him. Just as Lacy was about to speak, he continued. "Unfortunately, I let my emotions get the better of me and I shouldn't have. I'm finding things a little hard to deal with and had a moment of weakness. It won't be happening again." It was said so matter-of-factly, it actually made her feel a little annoyed. His face was serious, eyes narrowed as he looked at her, obviously waiting for some kind of reaction from her.

A moment of weakness? Well. . . he was going to get a reaction all right. She was sick and tired of the emotional roller coaster they were both on. She didn't appreciate the way he'd made her feel in the car on the way home and even though he'd said the reason they couldn't be together was to protect her, she couldn't help thinking it was bullshit. If he didn't want her, then he just had to man up and tell her.

"You're right," she thundered as she got up from the chair and began to pace up and down in front of him. His eyes widened at her sudden outburst. "It won't be happening again. I've had enough of you playing with my emotions. It's not fair. You tell me you want to be with me but nothing can happen between us. I try to deal with that. Then I wake up with you kissing me and you tell me it was a mistake because you were dreaming, which also tells me how much you want this if you're dreaming about it. Again, I try and deal with it. Then you kiss me the way you did this afternoon." She stopped to face him, her voice lowered to nearly a whisper. "Just. . . stop using me as an excuse."

She lowered her head and let out an exasperated sigh. It was hard to feel the way she did about him knowing that she wouldn't be able to have any more. Why did she let herself fall for this man? She couldn't bring herself to look at him and kept her gaze to the floor.

It was a few minutes before either of them spoke and then. . .

"It was me." was all Michael said.

She looked at him, confused. "What?"

He scrubbed his hand through his hair and met her gaze. "The boy who helped you in high school. The one who got beaten up and put in hospital? That was me."

Whoa! So that's what a ton of bricks landing on your chest felt like. She froze, breath caught, mouth wide open as she repeated his words over in her mind to make sure she'd heard them right.

"What?" she whispered so quietly that she barely even heard it. She walked over to the sofa in a daze and sat down next to him. They looked at each other without speaking. She couldn't seem to find her voice or her brain was refusing to function or something. Finally, she managed to force out some words. "You? How. . . "–she swallowed hard–"how can that be?"

Michael shifted his body so that their knees were nearly touching. "I was brought up by foster parents in Lawrence County."

"I can't believe it," she gasped. "Jack? That was really you?"

She watched as he reached into his inside pocket and pulled out a black leather wallet. He opened it and slid a crumpled picture out from one of the pockets inside, looked at it for a second and then passed it to her.

Oh, God. A handsome face stared back at her. Dark brown/black hair styled neatly to one side, blue eyes framed with thick dark brows, a strong jaw. . . It was Jack Pearson, just as she remembered him only older. "This was really you?"

He nodded and closed his eyes.

She felt deep sorrow as she looked back at the photo. It was hard to imagine his situation. Having not only your whole life, but your body being suddenly ripped away from you was inconceivable. After she'd processed the news, she thought back to the day he'd saved her. "I thought about you a lot after what you did for me. I hated the fact that I couldn't say thank you. Your parents—"

"They weren't my parents, not really. I'm sorry for what they said to you. I never knew you came. They never told me."

Lacy knew she shouldn't do what she was about to, but was past caring and did it anyway. She leaned across and softly kissed his cheek. "Thank you for what you did," she said, quickly resuming her position.

Michael's eyes widened and for a second he looked tense. After a moment his shoulders relaxed and he smiled at her. "You're welcome."

"How did I not know you? I don't remember seeing you except for that one time." Clear View High wasn't very big, so she wondered why she'd never noticed such a good looking guy.

Michael sat back, visibly more relaxed than he had been since he'd picked her up. "I didn't really mix with the kids in school; never really had the time. Each day I'd leave after last class and go straight to work so I never had any kind of social life. I'd seen you around. Never spoke to you though because what was the point?" He smiled. "Didn't think I'd be your kind of person."

She couldn't help but smile back at him. It was a rare thing lately to see Michael without a permanent crease between his brows. Not that she could blame him. The dangers that she now knew existed, dangers that were after both of them, were enough to undo the strongest of people. Add the fact that he'd been turned against his will into some sort of unknown, inhuman being and it was a surprise that he could smile at all. But he was and it invigorated her.

"And why not?" she asked playfully with an eyebrow raised.

He smirked. "Because I saw the kind of guys you hung out with; the hard working geeky types, the ones who would hang around the library on a Saturday afternoon to get their recreational kicks. I certainly didn't fit that description."

"Hey, are you saying you thought I was a nerd?"

He laughed. "Noooo, I'm. . . just saying you were a hard worker that's all."

"Oh! That's all, huh? Well, maybe you shouldn't have assumed that I wouldn't be interested in you." Lacy grew serious at the same time Michael's face straightened. His gorgeous blue eyes stared into hers and she was instantly mesmerized by them. Her chest tightened. Why did things have to be so difficult?

She sensed the door had just slammed shut on his emotions again and Lacy knew that their playful moment was over. She looked back at his photo before giving it back to him.

After putting it back in his wallet he stood up and walked over to the window. She watched his shoulders rise, then fall before he spoke. "Lacy. We can't be near each other anymore."

There they were, the words that she knew he would say. Her heart sank in her chest and she honestly didn't know what to do. Maybe it was for the best. Maybe Michael having to battle with his feelings was no good for any of them. She knew it was a huge distraction for him and the last thing she wanted was for him to be vulnerable when it came to fighting Varesh. Because that was what he intended. She knew that much.

But how could she just let him go? Knowing what they both felt for each other, how could she let him walk away from her?

"I don't want to stay away from you," she said before she could stop herself. He turned around to look at her, a deep frown on his face.

"We have no choice."

Lacy got up and walked over to him. "Why?"

"How can you want to be with me knowing what I am? I'm not even alive, Lacy. And who knows how long I'll even stay this way. What if I just stop existing?" He took her hands in his. "I don't want you to get hurt and that's the reason I came over tonight. I had to see you, to clear things up before I leave. There's something I have to do and I don't know if I'll even survive it."

"What. . . What is it?"

He took a deep breath and she braced herself for what she was about to hear. "I'm going back into the pit. . . into Hell."

Lacy broke contact from him and backed up a couple of steps. "What the. . . Why? Are you crazy?"

"No. It's the only plan I have. I know that Varesh has a very powerful enemy, Lucifer, and I want to make him an offer."

Holy Sh. . . No! Panic took over. Lacy felt light headed all of a sudden and began to lose the feeling in her legs. She practically floated over to the sofa and sat down before she fell down. It took her a moment to catch her breath. This was a different kind of panic than what she was normally used to. This was caused by sheer terror. Michael was throwing himself into the fire—literally. She didn't even know how that was possible; didn't feel the desire to ask.

"Evo knows a ritual that will get us there." Michael answered as if he'd heard her thoughts.

Her head snapped up to look at him. "Us?"

"Me and Evo. He's insisting he comes with me. I couldn't talk him out of it."

Her legs tingled as the feeling began to return. "Then he's as crazy as you are," she said before dropping her head into her hands.

"Lacy, listen to me. Lacy." she felt the sofa dip under the weight of his body as he sat down next to her. Then he was turning her to him and pulling her hands from her face. "Look at me." He ducked his head to look into her eyes. "Varesh is dangerous and for whatever reason he wants me dea. . . gone. He clearly doesn't care who he uses to get to me and I'm not about to sit around and do nothing. Not when yours and Evo's lives are at risk because of it."

She bit down to stop the tears that were threatening to form. "Then we'll run."

Michael looked momentarily stunned. "And where would we go? You can't just run from a power hungry demon. He'll always find you." He reached up and tucked a stray hair behind her ear. "You would really run away with me?" he asked, his voice broken.

She didn't hesitate to answer. "Yes. I would."

He stroked her cheek and she nestled into his hand, closing her eyes and savoring the soft touch of his fingers. She let out a long drawn breath and wished that she'd known him before, when they were younger, when he was Jack Pearson and she was just a girl in high school and the only demons she had to deal with were the seniors who never thought her face fit.

When she opened them again Michael was burning her with his sapphire stare, his brows drawn low. She could tell he was battling with himself. He wanted her, but was refusing to allow himself to have her.

"Michael, I don't know why, but I can just feel that there's a reason why we found each other again after all this time. You are the one who speaks about destiny and fate.

What if we're just meant to be together?" She reached up and swiped at her left eye before the tear fell. "There's something between us I just feel it, and I know you do too."

He sighed as he closed his eyes. "I can't—"

"Then stay with me, here, tonight." There she goes again, speaking before she has time to think. She couldn't believe the words had just left her mouth, but she held his gaze, wanting him to see how serious she was, and to understand her meaning. What the hell did she have to lose anyway?

She guessed she'd shocked the hell out of Michael too as he hadn't said a word. She could tell he was having some sort of internal battle with himself and expected the rational part of his brain to win. She was mentally preparing herself for the knock back when. . .

"Okay."

What? He said yes! Her heart began to sing as he smiled at her tenderly but her elation was short lived as she soon realized this could very well be the last time she saw him, the only time they would get to spend with each other before he committed suicide, or the already dead version of it.

"I just need to call Evo. He was expecting me back. You'd better tell Alethia too," he said as he got up from the sofa and headed out of the door.

She grabbed her cell from out of her coat pocket in the hall, noticed through the little window in the front door that Michael was on the porch, and headed for the bathroom. Shit. She had like. . . zero seconds to freshen up and make herself at least half decent if she was spending the night with Michael. It may be their one and only, but she was going to make damn sure that she was at least half presentable.

She paused. *Oh, God!* She was spending the night with Michael, actually *with* him. Her stomach began to do back flips with a mixture of nerves and excitement. No time. She sent a short text to Alethia explaining what was happening and asking her to drop the car on the drive whenever she liked, hoping she sensed the hidden do-not-disturb message that was in there, and quickly brushed her teeth. Then she threw off her top, splashed her armpits with cold water, dried them, and sprayed some sweet scented deodorant under each one before putting her top back on.

Her cell went off. Quick check, reply from Alethia. She was back at her hotel and she'd see her tomorrow. She ended it with, *enjoy yourselves :-)*.

Lacy smiled.

She practically ran from the bathroom across the hall to her room, pausing halfway to check that Michael was still outside. She heard his muted voice from the other side of the door and then continued into her room. She quickly undressed, pulled some plain gray sweatpants and a white string top out of her closet, some fresh, matching underwear—white panties and bra—from her drawer and threw everything on. Finally, she ran a brush through her hair and pinned the front, back out of her face.

Just as she was walking back down the hall, Michael came through the door. He stopped short and looked her up and down, noticing that she'd changed. "I like to wear my sweats in the evening," she said all nonchalant as though all she'd done was change her clothes. "Did you talk to Evo?"

"Yeah, he's cool being at my place. Says he has something to do anyway," Michael replied, he looked a little awkward then removed his jacket.

"Just stick it up on the hook," Lacy said awkwardly. Why the hell did she feel like a school girl on a first date all of sudden? And by the looks of things Michael felt the same. This was ridiculous. They were both adults. And anyway, it wasn't like they hadn't spent time together before. Only that was when things were just casual, when they were work colleagues who'd become friends. This was. . . different. "I'll just make that coffee now."

Thankfully, after a short time, things had become a lot less awkward between them. Lacy had made them both omelettes and they'd watched and laughed at some cheesy horror comedy on the horror channel. It was nice, relaxed; comfortable. They'd sat beside each other on the sofa and half way through the movie Lacy had nestled into Michael's side and he'd lifted his arm and placed it around her. She was still in the same spot when the credits began to scroll up the screen only now Michael was lightly stroking her arm. Her head was on his chest. She breathed him in; the scent of him was intoxicating, like dark spice mixed with an ocean breeze. She knew she would want to hold on to it, remember it for as long as she could.

Michael must have sensed her anguish. His voice vibrated in her ear through his chest. "Don't think about it," he said as he stroked his hand up her bare arm and over her shoulder.

Reluctantly, she sat up so she could see his face. "How can I not? There's a chance that I'll never see you again after tomorrow. I'm having a little trouble dealing with that."

He turned his body to face her. "Lacy, I know it's going to be dangerous, but I'm not planning on staying down there. It may seem to you like a suicide mission, but it isn't. I promise I have every intention of returning... to you."

She closed her eyes and whispered, "Please do."

Michael placed his finger under her chin and lifted her head. "I will."

He pulled her into his arms and she wrapped hers around his back. They simply hugged each other for a couple of minutes. Michael's chin rested upon her head. She was at home within his arms, never wanting to let him go. But she had to. It was going to kill her, but tomorrow she would say goodbye to him as though she would never see him again.

Michael pushed her back gently, his hands falling to her arms. "Hey, don't think about it tonight, okay? Let's just be together."

She bit her teeth together to force back tears. She nodded her head. Then Michael leaned in and softly placed his mouth on hers. As soon as their lips joined, Lacy's heart began to pound and she instantly melted into his kiss. His tongue pushed into her mouth finding hers and twining together in a sensual dance.

When he broke off, he leaned his forehead against hers. She saw him close his eyes and he whispered, "I don't want this to be the last time I kiss you, or hold you."

"Then come back to me."

He began to kiss her again, wrapping his arms around her and stroking one hand up her back and into the nape of her neck, his fingers weaving into her hair. She was lost in him, the feel of his warm, full lips, his tongue massaging hers. He was like a drug that caused all her nerve endings to tingle with desire.

Next minute she was being picked up, Michael's strong arms carrying her while he continued with his hypnotic kiss. She hadn't realized how far he'd walked until she felt herself being placed on a bed, her bed. Michael followed her, his lips still fused with hers. She felt the weight of his body press down on her and she wrapped her arms around his back, feeling his muscles move under the material that she so wanted her hands to be under. She moved them down, found the hem of his sweater and slid her hands underneath and. . . *Oh God!* His skin was so soft she just had to feel it touching hers.

Michael's mouth left hers and moved down to her chin. He kissed all the way around her neck. She closed her eyes uncontrollably at the sensation of his little soft kisses on her skin. He kissed up the other side to her ear where he gently sucked on her lobe. His name left her lips in a breathy whisper and his sharp exhale tickled her ear, sending goose bumps all over her body.

All they had done was kiss and she was totally lost in him, drowning in the pleasure of him. She needed to be closer, skin to skin. She pulled his sweater up the rest of the way and Michael took the hint and pulled it off over his head. He paused to look at her—his heavy eyes pinning her with an erotic stare that was almost her undoing. There were no words between them; there didn't need to be. They both knew that this was probably their only night together and they were going to make it last, at least if Lacy had her way.

She sat up slowly and began to remove her top, but was quickly stopped from doing so by Michael's hands. "No," he said, shaking his head as a tortured look of shame suddenly washed over his face.

Lacy froze. Where had this come from? A few seconds ago he was just as lost in her as she was in him so what just happened?

She placed her hands either side of his face and looked him straight in the eye. "What's wrong?" She tried to sound coherent, slowing her panting breath.

"I can't do this. It doesn't feel right," he said.

* * *

Lacy's hands slowly left Michael's face and as he sensed her sorrow his chest tightened. He felt confused. How could this be happening? A month ago, he was a loner, as he was meant to be, unsure of why he was here but accepting things as they were. Finding answers was all he had to exist for; all he'd cared about. Hell, he hadn't felt anything but anger for such a long time—not even sure if it was possible to feel anything else, until now.

Now there was something much stronger than anger growing inside of him, and he felt it right in the center of his chest. His heart felt twice the size and, he didn't know how, but Lacy had managed to somehow climb inside of it.

"I just don't want you hurting if I don't make it back. If we do this it's just going to be so much harder. . . for the both of us. I'm already close to losing my mind over you, Lacy." He was already worried about his sanity if he ended up trapped down in the pit like he feared. But spending the rest of his existence in that place craving her touch any more than he already did would be his downfall.

A stray tear escaped and ran down Lacy's cheek. As he wiped it with his thumb, she closed her eyes and held his hand to her face. She whispered, "I want you, Michael. So much it. . ."

What little control he had snapped in that instant. He cut her words off as he placed his mouth over hers, kissing her deeper this time, savoring every touch of her lips on his. He licked his tongue softly over her bottom lip and when she opened for him, he slid it inside meeting hers for a moment before retreating. She moaned into his mouth, causing desire to enrapture his whole body. He threaded one hand through her hair while the other one stroked slowly down her neck. He revelled in the sensation of her silky smooth skin under his fingertips, and of her warm, soft lips against his.

He knew it was wrong, but there was no going back now. What little strength he had to stay away from her was gone.

"*Shit*," he said suddenly, breaking their contact for a moment and sitting up on his knees at the side of her. "I don't even know if I can. . . if everything's working okay, physically I mean." He saw the confusion on Lacy's face. "I haven't *desired* anyone since I've been in this body. I haven't been interested in having sex at all. I don't even know if I can. . . "

"Then we'll have to try it and see won't we," she said behind hooded eyes as she joined him on her knees and placed a soft kiss on the corner of his mouth before pulling back to look at him again. Her enticing smile was enough for him to toss his concern aside.

His mouth was on hers again in an instant. *Shit!* If he was going to do it, then he was going to make damn sure that neither of them ever forgot this night.

* * *

Lacy's heart raced as she got lost in the sensation of their tongues twisting around each other. The feel of his strong arms wrapped around her as they both remained on their knees on top of the bed was glorious. Her arms went up around his neck and she ran her fingers through the soft hair at his nape. She felt his hand slide down to the arch of her back and he pulled her in closer. Her breath caught as she felt his erection press against her hip. He paused, then she felt him smile against her mouth before he continued to kiss her in such a heavenly way.

Thank God, she thought. His body was working just fine.

He lifted her top and she held up her arms for him to remove it, and he did it in such a way that his hands stroked over her flesh before he threw it to the floor.

She ran her hands over his shoulders and down his arms, feeling every inch of him, pausing to squeeze his thick biceps before she moved them to his stomach. His tight muscles were like ripples of hard iron under soft silk as she slid her hands up his torso. He watched her as her eyes drank every inch of him in. As her fingers stroked over his nipples, hardening them, he inhaled sharply, then placed his hands either side of her face and kissed her over and over again.

God, she loved the feel of his mouth on hers. She'd wanted this for so long, had been too afraid to admit to herself how deeply she was falling for him until now. He was everything she'd imagined him to be and more. He made things happen inside her body that she'd never dreamed she could feel; a desire she never thought possible. She ached for him.

His hand brushed up her side and she moaned into his mouth as he cupped her breast and began to knead her nipple between his thumb and finger through the lace of her bra. He unclipped the front clasp, freeing both of her breasts, then slid the straps down her arms. After dropping it onto the floor, he stroked both hands up her arms, his eyes raking over her goose flesh, watching as she felt her nipples hardening instantly.

He leaned into her. "You're so beautiful," he whispered into her ear before lightly kissing the flesh under it. She closed her eyes and melted under his warm breath as he trailed his kisses down her neck, across the front and up the other side. Suddenly, she forgot how to breathe. The feel of his lips on her skin sent flames of desire rushing around her body.

He pressed his groin into her, his moan sending her crazy. He began to trail kisses down her neck, then her collar bone, pausing again to look at her he said, "Jesus. Lacy. You're perfect." His voice was husky making him sound even sexier than he already did. He made her feel perfect, beautiful, and she loved how he looked at her.

She inhaled deeply, arching her back as his mouth latched onto her breast and his tongue began to swirl around her nipple, sending intense waves of heat, like nothing she'd ever felt before, rushing through her body.

"Michael," she whispered as she played her fingers through his hair. His hand reached for her other breast, massaging it as his tongue continued to lap at the other, then he sucked, and kissed and licked her until she was sure he would tip her over the edge. Dear God, she was close to it already and he'd only gotten as far as her breasts.

She needed more.

Bravely, she pushed herself into his groin, feeling his hard length press into her, rubbing her in exactly the right place. She reached down between their bodies and began to unbutton his jeans. He moaned as her hand brushed his erection and he reached down to place his hand over hers, rubbing himself through his jeans. Then he was back at her mouth, pushing his tongue inside of her again, repeating that sensual kiss from before only now with more intensity. She freed her hand from his and pushed his pants and boxers down his thighs. Michael reached down, pulled them over his knees one by one and kicked them on to the floor.

Oh my... He was beautifully naked.

She didn't have much time to admire him as he was easing her down onto her back then he was on top of her. He began to feather more of those sensual kisses down her throat, over one of her breasts and down her stomach and when he reached the top of her sweats he looked up at her through hooded lids as he slowly pulled the material down over her hips, her legs, dropping them to the floor followed by her white lace panties. Finally, there were no more barriers.

* * *

Michael's breath caught as he knelt in front of Lacy, who was now lying naked in front of him. His eyes roamed around her body taking in every inch of her rosy skin. She smiled up at him, her beautiful pale green eyes locking onto his. Her cheeks flushed from her arousal, which made him even harder as he anticipated what was about to happen.

Lacy slowly lifted one of her legs and slid it outwards, giving him one hell of a view. She stroked her hand over her breast and down her stomach towards her sex, her gaze never leaving him, once again causing his control to snap. He bent down between her legs beating her hand to its destination with his mouth. She cried out as he softly licked at her core, soaking up her wetness, tasting every inch of her. Jesus Christ, she tasted so good. She writhed with pleasure as his tongue flicked over her flesh. He knew exactly when her orgasm hit because she cried out as her whole body began to spasm and she grabbed the sheet in both of her hands. Lacy cried out his name as he felt the muscle of her sex contracting against his tongue.

In an instant he was on top of her, needing to be inside of her. He pressed the blunt head of his erection against her warm flesh, but before he went any further he paused to look at her. This woman who was lying beneath him had somehow captivated him. He was completely enthralled by her. He knew that after tonight there was no way he could stay away from her—be without her. He would make sure he survived his little trip into Hell and then he would protect her for however long he could.

"Michael. Are you okay?" Her voice snapped him away from his thoughts, bringing him right back to the beautiful face that was staring up at him.

He smiled at her as best as he could, stroking her damp hair from her face. "Right now, Lacy, in this moment with you, I couldn't be happier."

As he kissed her he eased himself inside of her, joining their bodies for what may be the only time. She cried out as he pushed himself to the hilt feeling her warmth around him as their pelvises met. Heat rushed over him, melting him, his heart. He withdrew slowly, almost all the way, then slid back inside feeling her walls rub him, squeezing him. Even though he was dead, he'd never felt so alive. His greatest fear now was that he'd never feel this with her again.

Lacy gasped as she looked into his eyes and he instantly knew why. The white glow from his irises softly illuminated her face, making her skin appear luminous. Her beauty overwhelmed him. He kissed her deeply, his tongue stroking hers, her breath caught every time he pushed into her. Her hands pressed into the cheeks of his ass pushing him deeper inside her with every thrust. Her moans grew louder as he increased the pace.

"Jesus, Lacy!"

He couldn't be gentle any longer and a need took over him, but he knew she wanted it that way too, just as much as he did as her nails dug into him. "Oh, my God, Michael." Her breath on his skin warmed his whole body with a heat he'd never felt before.

He drove into her, retreating and thrusting again, faster, harder until he could feel his own release rising through him with an electrifying intensity. "Fuck!" He let out a loud groan as he came, filling her with his orgasm as she found her own release, milking him, squeezing him with her thighs as he felt her whole body tense with pleasure beneath him.

"Oh, God."

He buried his head in her neck. Inhaling her scent for a moment as his body relaxed on top of her. He was still inside her as they lay panting in each other's arms. He wanted to stay joined to her for as long as he could, scared that he might never get this chance again.

He brushed her hair from her face, kissing her forehead, her cheek, and when he kissed her mouth he felt her smile against his lips. He pulled back to look at her as she gave him the loveliest smile he'd ever seen.

He rested his forehead on hers. "Everything seems to work okay," he said playfully, still catching his breath.

"Are you kidding me?" she replied, her voice slightly hoarse. "Okay? More than okay."

They both laughed and Michael shifted onto his side, pulling her with him and wrapping her in his arms. The realism of what he was soon to do kept threatening to consume him as he lay silently holding her, but he pushed it from his mind. He needed to be here with her in this moment for as long as he could, and he wasn't about to let anything ruin it.

They lay silently gazing at each other; faces inches away, their warm breaths merging in the small space that separated them. They didn't need to speak, the silence said it all. Michael stroked his fingers up and down Lacy's back and watched as her eyes blinked with dreamy languor and she eventually fell asleep. He kissed the end of her nose.

CHAPTER TWENTY

"Laaacy!" Her blond hair hung over her face as she bent over Lacy.

Ghostly features stared with such intensity. Her face was mere inches away. Lacy tried to look away, but the ghostly figure somehow held her within its glassy gaze, unable to move. "Laaacy!" she repeated. Lacy wanted to call out, to ask her what she wanted, but when she went to talk, no sound came out. Suddenly the woman backed up out of view. When Lacy lifted her head to see where she'd gone, she was at the foot of her bed. Her torn clothes hung from her and her arms were outstretched towards Lacy. Her head tilted to the side before she shot backwards and through the bedroom wall.

Lacy saw something written on the wall right where she'd disappeared. She squinted to read it, but when she did, her stomach sank. . .

The two words written in black simply read:

HE'S COMING

Lacy's eyes sprang open. She could have sworn she heard someone whisper her name. She blinked a couple of times and a vision of a blond woman flashed into her mind. She tried to remember the dream she must have just had that had made her heart pound in her chest, but couldn't. After a few seconds, when her brain had kicked into gear, she smiled and cuddled into Michael's arm that was wrapped around the front of her across her breasts. She must have turned around in her sleep because she now had her back to him and could feel his warm body tucked around her. She sighed, content in the moment until. . .

"No. . . Can't. . . . . . out!" Michael murmured. She felt his whole body tense around her. "Lacy. . . Need to. . . Help her!"

She slowly maneuvered herself around under his heavy arm so that she was facing him. "Hey," she whispered, shaking him softly, careful not to startle him. "Michael, wake up."

"He'll. . . Kill. . . " He tensed again. She felt his body tremble.

Oh God. "Michael. . . Hey." His eyes snapped open, startling her for a moment. "You were having a—"

Before she could finish he was pulling her into him, his head burrowed into her neck. "Hey. It's okay. It was just a dream."

She felt him tighten around her and she squeezed him back. Whatever it was that he'd just seen in his nightmare had clearly freaked him out. "Are you awake now?" she asked in a tentative voice.

"Yeah," he murmured into her neck before pulling back to look at her. He blinked a few times, clearing his sleepy vision. "*Shit!* That was weird. It felt so real."

She brushed his sweaty hair from his forehead. "Well, it wasn't. You're here with me." He kissed her amorously and then resumed his hug. She closed her eyes, feeling overwhelmed by his tenderness.

After a moment, Michael pulled away just enough to look at her while keeping her in his arms. "You were dying. Varesh had taken you again and he was torturing you to get at me. He was using his fire to burn you just like he did with me only you couldn't take it. I couldn't get to you because I was trapped in the pit, but Lucifer took great pleasure in showing me what Varesh was doing to you." His voice was shaky. He paused and swallowed hard. "I felt everything you were feeling and there was nothing I could do to get to you."

Lacy reached up and placed her hand on his cheek.

"It felt so real." Michael closed his eyes for a moment.

Her vision went blurry as her eyes filled up with tears. This time *she* pulled *him* close. She couldn't bear to see his anguish. It hurt her so much to think that he may not make it back. To feel so strongly for him in such a short time astonished her. How had this happened? How had she fallen so hard for someone she barely knew?

"I need you to come back to me," she whispered.

Michael lifted his head, looked into her eyes and then kissed her in such a tender way she nearly lost her mind. She tried to push away the thought of him leaving her in just a few hours and focus on this time with him, here in his arms, loving him. *Oh my...* did she love him? Was it possible to love somebody so quickly? All she knew was that she would ache for him when he was gone.

Michael made love to her again, twice.

* * *

Lacy woke up with a smile on her face. That was until she reached around expecting to find Michael beside her, but the bed was empty. She sat up quickly. "Oh, please. No." She panicked thinking that he'd left without saying goodbye, but then paused when she heard something drop to the floor in the kitchen. Soon after, she realized she could smell bacon. She let out a relieved sigh and lay back down. Last night had been the most perfect night of her life, and even though she knew her afterglow would be short lived, she couldn't help the big grin that filled her face as she thought about what had happened between the two of them through the night. Never in her life had she had sex even twice in a row let alone three times. When she moved on to her side, she ached. Oh, but it was a good ache. The muscles in her thighs felt tender but she loved it. The pain was lessened due to the cause: mind blowing sex. Sweet lord Michael knew how to please.

Her erotic thoughts were interrupted when the door opened and in he walked, gloriously naked from the waist up, with a tray in his hands. He had the most handsome smile as he walked over to the bed.

"Good morning. I made you breakfast," he said. Could he be any more perfect? She pulled herself up to a sitting position, bringing the comforter with her and tucking it under her arms. For some reason her modesty had returned and she felt a little shy. Why the hell did she feel shy?

"Morning." She beamed up at him.

Michael sat down on the edge of the bed and passed her the tray, leaning over to kiss her as he did. Her stomach did a little growl and she felt his lips curl up into a smile. "Someone's hungry," he said, and kissed her once more before he pulled away. She looked at the food on the plate: bacon, eggs and two slices of toast accompanied by a glass of coke?

"You didn't have any fresh juice so. . . " They both laughed. It was hard to act normal, though. Reality had returned and her conflicting emotions were hard to ignore. As much as she wanted to revel in her joy at having spent the whole night with Michael—him bringing her breakfast followed by a tender morning kiss—she couldn't. The whole wonderfully perfect situation was overshadowed by the dread that was looming over her.

If Michael noticed her glum face, he didn't say anything. "Enjoy your food," he said as he stood up. "I need to call Evo for him to come pick me up. I'd prefer to leave my car here if you don't mind."

Lacy managed a nod as she pushed a piece of bacon in her mouth, which suddenly tasted like cardboard. Michael's words had just instantly killed her appetite. She was no longer in the mood to eat but would do so. Michael had been kind enough to make her breakfast so she wouldn't disrespect him by leaving it, even if she had to throw up afterwards. His eyes lingered on hers a moment before he turned and left the room.

The clock was ticking. Soon they'd be saying goodbye to each other, but while he was still here in her house she could pretend he wasn't going anywhere.

After finishing the breakfast that she surprisingly ended up enjoying, Lacy was now dressed and at the sink in the kitchen filling the jug for the coffee machine. She hadn't showered; that would have taken up too much time. Instead, she'd picked out some fresh clothes, tight black jeans and a midnight blue T-shirt, and hurried to the kitchen in her slippers, picking up the car keys from the mat by the front door that Alethia must have posted during the night. Michael had flashed her a tentative smile as she'd passed him in the front room while he was speaking to Evo on his cell.

"He's on his way," Michael said quietly behind her, sounding as dejected as she felt as he joined her in the kitchen.

She placed the coffee jug down on the counter. It was too soon. She wasn't expecting him to leave straight away. Her shoulders dropped. "I was about to make coffee too."

Suddenly, strong arms wrapped around her and Michael placed a kiss on her neck before resting his chin on her shoulder. *Oh, God.* She couldn't do this. She closed her eyes.

"We can have coffee," he murmured next to her ear. "Evo'll just have to wait."

He turned her around to face him, lifted her chin with his finger and then kissed her mouth tenderly. Then she hugged him and rested her head on his chest, discreetly rubbing away the unshed tears from her eyes.

Their embrace was short lived when there was a hard knock on the front door.

"That'll be him now." Michael gave her a half smile and left to answer it.

Lacy carried on making the coffee, filling the jug a little more assuming Evo would want one too. She took a few deep breaths in an attempt to compose herself as she heard Michael and Evo's voices growing louder as they approached.

"Hey," Evo said over the noise of the coffee machine, "do I time things right or what? Black, two sugars please." He winked at her as he sat at the table.

Normally he irritated the hell out of her, but strangely enough, she welcomed his buoyancy with open arms today even though she didn't understand it. After all, he was accompanying Michael on his little trip, but didn't seem to be at all concerned. She would never figure the guy out.

"Do I smell bacon?" Evo asked, leaning back and kicking his ankle up onto his knee. His arm was flung over the back of the chair.

Michael grabbed something from the fridge. "You did. Here," he said, throwing something at Evo. His friend caught the packet of raw bacon with a look of disgust on his face. "You're welcome to cook some."

"Charming. I'm throwing my life on the line for you today and you can't even cook me some damn bacon."

Michael leaned against the counter and stroked Lacy's arm with the back of his hand, making her realize that her whole body had tensed at Evo's flippant words. "I'd rather go it alone than wait on you like some dumb shit," he replied.

Lacy couldn't hold back her chuckle as she stirred the three cups of coffee. She carried one over to Evo, who was reaching into the inside pocket of his black leather duster, and placed the mug down in front of him.

"Thanks," he said in a low voice and then winked at her. She wasn't sure how comfortable she was with that, but soon realized it was for a reason.

"Well, see. . . then you wouldn't have this." Evo held up a small silver ring which had multicolored jewels encrusted all around it. His proud smirk made Lacy raise an eyebrow.

"Shit! Evo, that's Alethia's ring. How did you get it?" Michael immediately went to Evo and took the ring from him. He was clearly surprised by the small, non-descript looking thing but why? What was so special about it? And yes, how *did* Evo get it?

His cocky face remained the same. "Let's just say I'm good with my hands," he winked again, at Michael this time.

"You didn't. . . Is that where you were going when I spoke to you last night?" Michael's face was a mix of shock and admiration. Evo didn't answer, just carried on looking smug.

"What's going on?" Lacy asked, confused by the whole exchange.

Michael answered. "This ring was given to Alethia by her father. It catches demons somehow. But we don't even know how to use it." That last part was directed at Evo who was now gesturing with his fingers for Michael to give it back. "*You* may not know. *I*, on the other hand, do." He flashed Michael a proud grin while taking back the ring and tucking it back safely inside his pocket.

"And how the hell did you manage that?"

Evo raised an eyebrow. "You have to ask?" was all he said, and she was pretty sure they both knew what he meant. Lacy was actually a little surprised that Alethia had succumbed to Evo's charms. Granted, she hadn't known her longer than five minutes, but even so, Lacy thought her wiser than that. Evo was obviously better than she thought.

"Uh, Michael, don't want to rush you buddy, but we really should get going."

As soon as the words had left Evo's mouth, Lacy felt her knees buckle a little. In an attempt to distract herself from her imminent anxiety attack, she busied herself by grabbing the cups from the table and she placed them in the sink. She turned the faucet on and heard Michael mutter something to Evo. "Take care Lacy. Oh, and when we get back, I want some of that bacon," Evo said as he left the room.

After filling up the sink, she turned the faucet off to a dead silence.

"Hey." Michael said after a few moments as he placed his hand on her shoulder and turned her to face him. As Lacy looked at his beautiful pale blue eyes, she choked back a sob. His expression was as pained as hers. The feeling that this was goodbye as evident on his face as it was in her heart. He pulled her into him and wrapped his arms around her tightly. She did the same to him and in that moment, his warmth, his scent, his closeness broke her resolve.

She lost it.

Tears began to stream, dampening Michael's sweater. He must have heard her hitched breaths because he tightened his hold on her, kissing the top of her head. She didn't know how long they stayed like that in each other's arms, but when Michael eased her back so he could look at her she knew it hadn't been long enough.

He wiped at her tears with the tips of his fingers, then tilted her chin, covering her mouth with his in a lingering kiss. "I have to go," he said in a husky voice, while resting his forehead against hers. He closed his eyes and let out a slow ragged breath.

When he moved to leave her, she managed to speak, "Michael—" but her words were cut short when he placed his hand over her lips and shook his head. "Don't. . . "

Another tear escaped and ran down her cheek and she swallowed hard. Aside from burying her sister, saying goodbye to him truly was the hardest thing she'd ever had to do in her life.

"I'll see you soon, okay?" His eyebrows raised a little and he looked at Lacy with reassurance.

"Promise?"

Michael placed his hand on her cheek. "I promise." He gently kissed her forehead, turned and left.

Lacy stayed in the exact same spot for what could have been a few minutes, a few hours, she didn't care. The man who she feared she was falling in love with had just said goodbye to her for what could be the very last time. She was numb, devoid of all feeling.

When she finally managed to move her legs, she grabbed the phone, called work and told them she had a severe stomach bug—no way she could face it today—and snuggled on the couch with a blanket with the intention of watching trash TV in the hope it would take her mind off things. It didn't. Instead she just sat and stared.

Lacy had no idea how long she'd been transfixed on the TV screen. The show that was on when she'd first sat down had finished and Extreme Makeover had taken its place. She hadn't even noticed that the sound was down until now. She wanted to get up from her zombie-like state and at least take a shower, but she had no chance of willing her body to move. This was worse than she'd anticipated. When she'd imagined Michael leaving and the state she'd be in, it hadn't been this bad.

She groaned and pulled the blanket right up to her chin suddenly feeling the air turn chilly. Oh well, at least she'd have no choice but to move soon when she'd have to turn the thermostat up on the heating. The temperature must have dropped outside.

She pushed the blanket off and was just about to get up from the sofa when a sudden humming sensation began to sound from over by the door to the hallway. She paused to listen. It grew louder and then, in the exact spot that her eyes were fixed, a swirling gray mist formed from nowhere. Before she could do anything other than freeze with fear, a familiar figure appeared and the gray mist dissipated as quickly as it had formed to reveal a tall, dark-haired woman, dressed in navy blue tight jeans and a black figure hugging turtle neck top under a tan knee length coat, with a very troubled look on her face.

"Alethia?" Lacy gasped as she rushed over to her, taking her arm and walking her to the sofa. "What's wrong?"

Alethia blinked and shook her head as if to re-load her batteries. "Where are they?" She grabbed hold of Lacy's arms, her desperation, causing Lacy's heart to race with concern. "Evo and Michael, where are they?"

"They left about an hour ago, I think. Alethia, Evo is performing a ritual that will let them enter Hell. I'm so s—"

"Where? Where are they performing the ritual?" Her unusual caramel colored eyes were wide, staring right into Lacy's.

"They were going to Michael's apartment at the university."

"We have to stop them."

Lacy instantly felt nauseous. The fact that Alethia's usual calm had abandoned her was a huge cause for concern. "Why. . . Alethia, what's wrong?"

"The ring. . . *Shit*. He can't use it. There will be terrible consequences if either one of them try."

"What? The ring that you gave to Evo? What consequences?"

"I didn't give it to him. He took it from me."

"What consequences, Alethia?" Now Lacy was the one who was frantic.

The deity's shoulders slumped as she began to explain, talking so fast Lacy could only just understand her. "It was created by my father and only he can decide who can use it. It was designed in such a way that if it happened to fall into the wrong hands it would—" She paused mid sentence.

"What? Alethia, tell me please."

"If Michael or Evo use that ring. . . instead of trapping the demon they are wielding it on, it will reverse the process."

"Annnd?" That didn't sound good.

"By trapping the person who uses it instead."

Lacy's breath left her lungs in a rush and she suddenly felt quite dizzy. "Oh. My. God! We have to stop them." She rushed to get into her coat and scarf, shoved her warm camel skin boots on her feet and grabbed her car keys.

As she headed for the front door, she was stopped in mid-stride as Alethia grabbed her arm. "There's no time for that. We'll have to go my way." She took hold of Lacy's upper arms, wrapping her hands around her tightly. "Hold onto my arms. And your stomach."

"My stomach, why?" Lacy asked as she placed her hands tentatively on Alethia's arms in the same way.

"Because you're probably about to lose it. Humans don't usually cope well with this. Now hold tight."

Before she could respond, Lacy was being swept into a swirling black mist, suddenly losing all sense of where she was. The disorientating rush of dizziness that consumed her in the next moment was sickening. No wonder Alethia said to hold on to her stomach. She honestly felt like she was about to throw up her whole insides not just her stomach. The feeling was much worse than last time. Probably because last time she'd been so preoccupied with everything that had gone on she hadn't noticed. Just as she felt she was about to pass out, the swirling began to slow and the darkness that surrounded her a moment ago began to fade. Alethia came into view and Lacy realized she was still gripping onto her arms for dear life. White and blue painted walls began to appear either side of them and when the last bit of gray haze had disappeared, she recognized where they were: standing in the corridor outside Michael's front door.

Alethia helped her regain her balance. "Feeling okay?" she asked, still holding on as if to make sure Lacy was okay.

Lacy waited a moment before answering. "Yeah. Actually, I feel fine."

Alethia shrugged her shoulders. "You're stronger than you look." She smiled slightly, but then it quickly disappeared and she turned to face the apartment door. "I couldn't get us inside. He must have spelled it with something."

Lacy didn't care and rapped her knuckles on the door. "Michael! Michael, are you in there?" No answer. She knocked again, harder this time; still no answer. "Oh, no! They must have done the ritual already."

Alethia grabbed Lacy's shoulder and pulled her back from the door. "Allow me." She crossed her arms over each other in front of her chest and bowed her head, eyes closed. After a couple of seconds Michael's door flew open.

Shit! She was good to have around in situations like this.

They both walked into the living room where a pile of unusual looking items was scattered around the coffee table, including what looked like a bowl with blood in it and another with what appeared to be burnt ashes. Lacy went cold. She wasn't usually one for cursing, but with a trembling voice she said, "Alethia, what the fuck are we going to do?"

CHAPTER TWENTY-ONE

It wasn't the blood soaked walls of the many caves, nor was it the horrific, blood curdling screams in the distance that made Michael's skin crawl as he remembered his torturous time in the pit. No, it was the stomach churning stench of burning flesh that was at the forefront of his memories. The familiarity of that alone was why he felt as uncomfortable as he did at that moment. Both men made their way down a long tunnel cut through a large rock formation that they'd suddenly appeared in front of after completing the ritual—which was downright weird by the way.

It hadn't been as bad for Michael, but how Evo had managed to endure the pain—which he could only imagine—of slicing his own flesh and then stuffing his wound full of the pasty blood and ash mixture, all the while chanting strange sounding words, was unimaginable. It was only when he cauterized the sliced flesh back together with that strange looking wand that his buddy screamed like a bitch.

Couldn't blame the guy though.

"Man, this is some freaky shit," Evo said as he walked a few steps ahead with a burning torch that he'd grabbed at the entrance of the tunnel. He was passing it over the seeping walls inspecting every inch of them with the light from the flame. "I don't even want to know what that shit is." His nose curled up at the sight of some black ooze that was about to drip down from above him. He moved his body out of the way just in time.

Michael hadn't known what to expect before they'd arrived. His memories of his time in Hell were very limited, but he was pretty sure he hadn't been given a grand tour of the place. No, instead he'd been locked away somewhere and forced to endure things that even the devil himself would have squirmed at.

He stayed behind his friend, eyes scanning the shadows, as they continued deeper into the tunnel. Evo had his not-so-demon friendly knife in his right hand, ready to stick it into anything that came near, while Michael had stuck to the regular type, but he'd opted for one in each hand.

It was too damn quiet.

The distant screams had quietened down the further into the cave they'd gotten, and apart from dripping sounds and the occasional curse from Evo, there was deadly silence. Michael didn't like it at all. Neither one of them had a clue how to find Lucifer, or what dangers they were heading for, but Michael was prepared for anything and had a feeling that the evil bastard, if he didn't already, would know he was here soon enough.

The silence was unnerving.

After Michael and Evo argued the toss about which way they should go when they reached an intersection of tunnels—straight on, right or left—they ended up taking a right and it wasn't long until they found a small archway in the rock. As they cautiously entered what looked like a dark cavern, bizarrely, and in the blink of an eye, they found themselves in a room that was almost. . . normal. Aside from the fact that the walls were nearly black with dirt, as well as the worn floorboards and the remains of old furniture, the room looked familiar.

"The Fuck?" Michael heard Evo say as they both stood in the middle of the room. It was like they'd just stepped through a portal that had led them straight out of the pit and. . .

Wait. Michael had been here before. As he looked closer he realized why the interior looked so dirty: it was the remnants of a fire and now he could even smell it, the harsh scent of the charred surroundings began to sting the back of his nose and throat. But where was this place?

As he walked out of the door that had now replaced the archway they'd both just come through he gasped, awash with confusion at the fact that he hadn't returned back to the cave. Instead, he was in a hallway that was much more of the same: blackened walls with burnt out pictures hanging up on them. A strange pull was leading him down towards three doors at the end: two on the left and one on the right. It was the one on the right that he went to.

"Hey, Mike. Wait up," he heard his buddy call out as he placed his hand on the door handle. Dread hummed through every inch of Michael's body, yet he didn't know why. All he knew was that something terrible waited for him on the other side of that door.

"Uh. I'm not so sure that's a good—"

He didn't wait for Evo to finish. He turned the handle and opened the door, but as he did, the realization of where he was, nearly had him face planting on the ground. He grabbed hold of the door jamb for a second before catching his breath. Then he noticed something on top of the burnt bed over the other end of the room. In the next second he heard a pained roar rip through the room and soon realized it was coming from his own lungs.

"NO!" he screamed as he ran towards the bed where the charred remains of a female form lay upon the blackened mattress. He grabbed the body and cradled it knowing exactly who it was.

"Michael. No! Don't touch it."

It was Lacy's house they were in. That's why it was so familiar. Only it wasn't the same neatly decorated place he was comfortable in—the place he'd had a hard job leaving before he'd done the ritual—no, there wasn't a thing that hadn't been destroyed by fire, including. . . NO! Not while she'd slept.

"Lacy. Please, God. No. . . NO!" he heard himself say as he rocked back and forth with her burnt body in his arms.

She was dead. Lacy was dead.

Her precious, soft, alabaster skin was now black and blistered.

He felt something trying to pull him away from her, strong arms, trying to pry his own from her body.

"Michael, you have to let go of her. It's not real. . . None of this is real."

He heard his friend's words, but couldn't process them; didn't matter. He didn't care. All he knew in that moment was heartache. His Lacy had died in such a horrific way and he hadn't been there to save her. *Oh, no. NO! Why didn't I just stay with her? I could have saved her.* A distant voice pulled him from his inner torment and he realized he was crying. Shit. Why her?

"Michael. . . *Michael.* Listen to me. Hey." He managed to lift his eyes to his friend who was now leaning over Lacy's body and had gotten right up in his face. "This is *not* real," Evo said again. Michael just stared into his hazel eyes, which were now frantically piercing his own. "You have to let go of her. Now!"

When Michael looked back down at Lacy he tried to will what little strength he had to believe what his friend was saying. But she *was* real. He held her tightly to him. She felt as real as. . .

He couldn't fathom what happened next.

Lacy's head slowly turned towards him. Her eyes suddenly opened wide, shocking the hell out of him as she looked directly at him. "Fuck!" he yelled as he threw her body away from him and jumped up from the bed.

He heard Evo's gasp.

Completely dumbfounded at what he was witnessing, Michael began to back away at the same time that the charred body rose up onto its knees and began to crawl towards the end of the bed. She reached out one arm to him. "Michael. Help me!" she rasped.

Evo was right. This wasn't Lacy. He continued to walk backwards; joining his friend—whose mouth was now hanging wide open—over the other side of the room.

She slowly climbed down from the bed and straightened, bright white eyes—a stark contrast to her blackened skin—bore into his as she walked towards them.

"Jesus. Fucking. Christ." Evo said in a shaky voice beside him. "We have to get out of here."

They both turned towards the door, but as Michael grabbed for the handle he was grabbed by his arm. He turned his head to see the corpse had latched onto him and was trying to drag him backwards. It was working too. He tried to prize her away, but she was strong and continued to pull. Her grip got harder and she managed to tug his body back a few feet. Just as he thought his flesh would be pulled from his arm, Evo swung something at her head, connecting with it and nearly knocking it clean off her shoulders. The body lost its grip on Michael and slumped to the floor.

"Weird, crispy bitch!" Evo growled as he threw the now broken lamp base to the floor. "Let's go."

This time they both made it out of the door and as Michael began to pull it closed, he paused and looked back catching sight of the body trying to drag itself across the floor towards the exit. He slammed it shut and they both leaned against the wall across from each other gasping for breath. Michael looked at Evo whose look of disbelief must have mirrored his own. "What the. . . " he swallowed hard, "what the fuck just happened?"

It took a minute for Evo to reply as he crouched over, both hands on the tops of his thighs, fighting for breath. "It's this place fucking with us."

"Yeah? No shit."

"I've got a feeling that won't be the only time something like that happens."

As Michael tried to shift the disturbing vision of what he'd first thought was Lacy from his mind, something began to happen. Their surroundings switched from the dingy burnt out hallway to the seeping walls of the cave that they'd been in prior to their altercation. Evo leapt up from his lean against the wall. A quick shiver ran through him as he looked back over his shoulder with disgust at what had returned. "Let's go," was all he said, brushing both of his shoulders as he walked off towards the darkness.

* * *

One thing Michael realized was that in Hell there was no sense of time. He had no idea how long it had taken him and Evo to get from the tedious caverns of the mountain to where they were now, but what he did know was the fire he could see lighting up the crimson sky ahead couldn't mean anything good. The mountain was now long behind them and thankfully so was that awful nightmare they'd found themselves in. They were out in the open now, walking through a clearing that was surrounded by tall blackened trees, the dark woodland seemingly out of place amongst the crimson landscape. Every so often Michael would notice, through his peripheral, things moving through the underbrush.

He knew they were getting closer to danger as the demonic cries that filled the air began to sting his ears once again as they increased in volume. He felt a profound disquiet wash over him as he began to imagine the cause of those screams, knowing that at one time his voice would have carried through the air in extreme agony just as those were now. He pushed it aside, refusing to let the memories from that time overcome him, locking them away deep into his subconscious just like he always did.

He couldn't afford any distractions at a time like this. No matter how tough his recollections were, nor how vivid those memories became, he had to stay focused for both of their sakes.

A deep, ear-splitting howl pulled him back from his thoughts and he immediately saw Evo's body stiffen; the big guy's sudden change in stance said he was on high alert as he too must have sensed that something was about to happen.

Michael could feel the ground begin to vibrate and his eyes darted around trying to get a visual on whatever it was that was about to attack them. *Shit!* The noise was coming from all around them: one minute to their left, the next in front, then from behind. Whatever it was was moving fast, toying with them, and all the while keeping out of view.

Suddenly a dark, formless shape rushed by Michael causing him to duck down low. He saw Evo do the same as another flew by him, but he wasn't quick enough. "Shit!" Evo exclaimed as his hand went to a fresh wound on his cheek. It didn't look like it had sliced him but. . . was that a burn? "What the f—"

Michael noticed more heading straight towards them. As soon as one of the black demons got close, on instinct Evo sliced at it with his knife. The demon squealed and sparks flew off it as soon as the blade connected. Evo raised his eyebrows at Michael, clearly surprised by the fact that he'd wounded it, all be it temporary. But temporary was better than nothing right now. Then Michael remembered the ring. Alethia's ring was supposed to capture demons somehow. He felt a small whisper of hope at the thought of maybe getting out of this situation.

"Evo, the ring."

His friend threw a smirk his way after Michael had reminded him that he probably held the key to ending the onslaught, but when Evo looked back at Michael, his face had paled and he had an odd expression. "Evo. What's the delay? Use the ring."

"That might be a little difficult," he shot back just before ducking out of the way of a demon.

"What are you talking about?"

He raised his hand to Michael and wiggled his pinky finger. "I don't have it." As it didn't resize like it had for Alethia, the only finger that had been small enough to wear it was empty.

The ring was gone.

Shit! Not only were they screwed right now, but even if they did somehow manage to survive the attack, he wasn't sure Evo would survive Alethia when she found out he'd lost the damn thing.

It was Michael's turn to duck out of the way this time and when he looked back at his friend, who was now in a panic, eyes scanning the dusty floor, he. . .

"EVO!" Michael cried, warning him just in time. A demon was heading straight for him and two more were on its tail. Evo managed to slice that one too, but Michael had no such knife and watched as the other two demons changed course and were now headed straight for him instead. *Oh, fuck!*

Evo darted in front of him, slicing one of the demons before rolling on the ground, but the other went straight after Michael. Knowing that the knives he had would do nothing, he put his arm up to protect himself and cursed out loud as the demon connected and flew off as quickly.

"Fuck! That burns," he gasped, surprised by the pain as he quickly inspected his arm. He could see his pink flesh under his coat where the demon had burned right through. He made a quick mental note not to let one of those things touch him again as he was now aware that he could feel physical pain down here.

The demons were playing with them. He knew that they could attack properly whenever they wanted to and then neither of them stood a chance.

Evo must have read his mind. "We haven't a hope of defeating these things, Mike," he shouted between slices. Michael continued to duck out of the way by his side. "My knife seems to be stunning them momentarily, but that's about it. We're screwed here, buddy."

He knew Evo was right. Michael couldn't see a way out of this. Evo was managing to keep the demons away from both of them at the moment but for how long?

"Uh. . . Mike?"

Shit. Three more had just joined the party.

Instead of swooping down on them like the others were, the new additions begun to fly around them and to their surprise the rest joined them. The five demons circled them in the air. Now Michael was able to see them properly, noticing their skull-like features and the black mist that represented their bodies just like the demon he'd seen at the university, the one which had possessed Nina and then moved on to Jake.

They began to move faster until they appeared to merge into one, forming a black ring around them as they stood as prey in the center.

"I don't like this." Evo shouted over the wind that was now hurtling around them. "What do we do now? Can't you do that shit you did at Lacy's house—whatever the hell that was—and get us out of this?"

"I don't even know *what* happened, let alone how to make it happen again."

"Well. . . great. We're going to die. I mean, I am anyway. You're already dead."

"I don't need a reminder."

Just then, a deafening screech tore through the air and immediately the demons began to scatter, leaving Evo and

Michael perplexed in the silence that followed. Only the eerie quiet didn't last long.

Another screech. Closer this time.

Michael and Evo now stood back to back in the middle of the clearing, both with weapons held out in front of them, ready for anything. At least he thought they were until what he saw emerge from the black trees right in front of him made him think again. He took an unnecessary deep breath in anticipation of what was about to happen.

"Uh. . . okay, more trouble," his friend said. Michael threw a quick glance over his shoulder to see that Evo was facing the same thing. Then he heard a movement off to the side and saw another of the large beings, dressed in black robes and on horseback, stalking towards them.

The horses let out a loud screech.

"We mean no trouble," Michael shouted to the robed figure in front of him. "We're here to speak with Lucifer."

A deep laugh resonated right through to Michael's very core. "*You*"—he looked at Evo—"secured trouble when you trespassed into this realm." The horseman then turned his gaze to Michael. "*You,* however, should never have left."

Michael swallowed hard at the horseman's recognition, but all he could do was hold out his knives and, keeping his gaze fixed onto the one who seemed to be in charge, he slowly crouched to the floor letting the horsemen know that he didn't want any trouble. He nodded to Evo to do the same, but his stubborn friend didn't look too impressed about it. He knew Evo wouldn't be happy letting go of his knife—hell, he was so fond of the thing he'd all but given it a name—but they needed to show that they weren't the aggressor. He lay both weapons down on the dusty floor and returned to his position just as slowly.

He saw Evo eyeballing his blade on the floor, ready to grab it at any chance he got should shit start to go down. Good job the horseman didn't know what that knife could do, their lack of concern over it showed that they had no idea, or else the chances of Evo retrieving it would have been slim to none.

The demon in front of him began to look impatient.

"We're just here to speak with Lucifer," Michael repeated.

All they got back in reply was a deep wheezy laugh.

"We have information for him about a mutual enemy. I think he would be interested in what we have to propose." The fact that a proposition didn't actually exist, and that Michael and Evo had no idea what they were going to say to the powerful fallen angel, remained unsaid.

Michael saw Evo change his stance so that his legs were wider apart; so wide, in fact, that he looked quite uncomfortable. His face was stoic but Michael sensed something was off with him.

The demon was silent as it assessed them both. It glanced at the weapons on the floor. "You may retrieve your metal; they are of little use to you down here."

Michael didn't agree.

As both men crouched to grab their knives, the reason for Evo's strange behavior was revealed: After he'd picked up his knife, pulled up his trouser leg and replaced it into his ankle strap, Michael saw him retrieve something from under his boot. Evo clamped his fist tightly, then his mouth curled up slightly at one side in a grin meant only for Michael's eyes.

He'd found the ring.

No sooner had they stood up than they both found themselves restrained by two horsemen who had dismounted their horses and now had each of them in a tight headlock facing their leader awaiting instructions.

The demon remained silent, black eyes bearing into them in turn as it seemed like it was deciding on a course of action. Michael stared at the demon whose face was almost skeleton-like. Its pasty diaphanous skin was almost nonexistent over the bones that it covered. Michael's composure began to dissipate the longer they faced the creature as he sensed something bad was about to happen. Was it now that he would finally meet his fate? Was this the end of the road for him and Evo?

When the horseman began to move towards them, Michael slowly closed his eyes. A vision flashed in his mind, Lacy, almost as clear as if she were standing in front of him. He held on to it for a moment before inhaling a deep breath and opening his eyes again. When he did, a large, black robed, skeletal hand came crashing down towards him. Just before it made contact, Michael flashed a look to his friend who was calling out his name with a look of sheer terror on his face. When the horseman struck, it was the last thing Michael remembered before everything went black.

* * *

A deep laugh penetrated Michael's ears as he roused from unconsciousness. Feeling like he'd been the unfortunate one at the bottom of a huddle during a football game, he managed to open his eyes to see his friend lying unconscious—at least, that's what he hoped he was—on the rocky ground next to him. As well as Evo, Michael was also on his stomach. He began to pull his body up and when he was on his knees, he got a good look at his surroundings.

Black.

All around him was black: black clouds in a black sky, black rock underneath them leading to a cliff face to his right and what he guessed was a sheer drop to his left. They were on the edge of a mountain, wind howling through the air, sending piercing chills right through Michael's skin. He was about to assist his friend when he froze, sensing something powerful. They weren't alone, there was something behind him and he almost didn't want to turn around. But he did.

Slowly.

Then, what Michael saw was inconceivable.

Impossible!

It had to be his mind playing tricks on him again; pushing him into a memory from his life in order to confuse him. But, like the vision of Lacy's charred body, the female standing in front of him looked very real.

She couldn't be real.

Could she?

"Jessica?"

The brown haired woman whom he once knew was being flanked by two of the horsemen. Not being able to judge their size while they'd surrounded him and Evo earlier, he was surprised to see the sheer magnitude of the demons as they faced him now minus their horses.

"Ah yes, about that. . . not my real name."

"Where's Lucifer? It was him I requested to speak with."

The woman's mouth turned up at the side as she leered at him with dark brown eyes. "He's unavailable right now. And will be for the foreseeable future."

What?

Michael got to his feet and faced them. The more this was playing out in front of him, the harder he found it to trust his own mind. Lucifer was gone? Where? Jess was here? No. It just couldn't be happening. "This isn't real. *You're* not real. It's this place. . . it's messing with my head again." He threw a quick glance at Evo who was still unconscious, but was relieved to notice a slight movement in his back. He was still alive. Thank God. But why was he still face-planted on the floor?

"Afraid not. I'm very real. As real as the last time you saw me. The night we spent together."

"What the hell are you talking about?"

Jess looked strange. She hadn't really changed from what he could remember, but there was something about the way she was regarding him. She looked arrogant, cocky, a trait that was never a part of her demeanor when she'd worked for him. That was one of the reasons he was refusing to believe it was really her.

She began to walk towards him as she answered. "Oh, silly me. I almost forgot. The suppression."

"What. . ."

Suddenly, Michael gripped his head as memories began to fill his mind; a whirlwind of images flying through his head like a video on fast forward: both he and Jessica laughing together at the office, sitting opposite each other in a restaurant, walking through the park, her arm linked through his. They were affectionate towards each other. Still gripping both sides of his head, he paused when he realized the memory of his old self that followed wasn't a familiar one.

Jack stood with Jess in front of the fireplace in his apartment. He thought she looked particularly nice that evening. Her brown hair was up in a neat chignon at the top of her head with a few wispy strands framing her face. Her knee length, blue dress hugged her figure in a way that would attract any man's attention if they'd been out in public, but tonight it was for his eyes only.

When Jess had started working for Jack's company she'd immediately caught his eye. She was a pleasure to look at—attractive in a classic film star kind of way—but she knew it too. He honestly never saw himself dating her though. He enjoyed the harmless flirtation from her and would often reciprocate, but he wasn't ready for any kind of relationship, even a casual one. So he was surprised that he'd actually enjoyed her company over the last couple of weeks.

After much repartee, mostly from Jess, he finally asked her out on a date. Jack took her to The Delauney, *a swanky brasserie up town, figuring it would be the kind of place she'd be into even though he didn't much care for the pretentiousness. Afterwards, they went for drinks in a more understated bar down the street. They chatted, they laughed and then Jack dropped Jess off at home with nothing more than a good night kiss. This happened many more times over the coming weeks.*

At Jack's penthouse suite at The Cincinnati on a chilly October evening, Jess reached up and clinked her wine glass against his whiskey glass.

"To us," she said warmly.

Even though he didn't really think there was officially an 'us', he smiled and took a sip from his glass. She took it from him and placed it with hers on top of the fireplace. He noticed a gleam in her eye as she stepped into him. They'd kissed a few times, but even though she'd hinted, they'd gone no further. But maybe that would change tonight. He was a man after all.

Without a word she placed both of her hands on his chest and leaned in to kiss him. He bent his head slightly, meeting her lips with his and slowly sliding his hands around her waist, feeling the curve of her back through the soft material of her dress. Their kiss intensified and he enjoyed it. For the first time, he'd begun to feel aroused by her, imagining her naked in his bed and willing to take things further. He pulled her body closer into his and felt her slight gasp against his lips.

He was just about to move with her over to the sofa, when he began to sway a little, nearly losing his footing. He abruptly broke their kiss and steadied himself by gripping onto the fireplace. He must have gotten carried away, though his head had never spun from kissing a woman before.

"Jack? Are you okay?"

Her voice sounded strangely distant. The room was spinning uncontrollably now, like he'd stepped onto a carousel that was on warp speed, everything rushing past him in a blur of color and light. He struggled to hold himself up and felt himself falling, bringing the ornaments from the fireplace with him as he hit the floor.

What the hell was wrong with him?

He found it hard to speak, but he tried, reaching out to the blurry blue figure that he saw crouched before him.

"Help. . . me. . . " he managed to say, his voice weak.

"I am helping you Jack. It's for your own good. You'll see."

Distant. . . Her voice was so distant. What did she mean? Did she do this?

He blinked his eyes tightly over and over in an attempt to clear his vision but it was no use. He was struggling to hang on to consciousness.

The last thing he saw before he went lights-out was Jess's face right in front of his. . . smiling.

When the events of his final day on earth finished playing out, the pain began to subside and all Michael could do was stare at the woman in front of him.

"We didn't do. . . anything, right?" He didn't know why it was relevant, but felt the need to ask anyway.

"Oh, no. You were far too incoherent for that, unfortunately. The drugs that I slipped into your drink made sure of that. They did make it easier to smother you to death though."

The realization of what had actually happened that evening made his legs weak and he fell to his knees, playing what he'd just been allowed to remember over and over again in his mind. He'd had no recollection of any of it yet now, it was so vivid it was like it had only happened moments ago.

"You killed me? Why? Did someone make you do it?"

Her scornful laugh tugged at his patience. "WHY, JESS?"

Suddenly her face turned serious. "It was our only chance to get you down here without any resistance."

"Our? Who put you up to this?"

"Jack I—"

"Don't call me that!" he snapped, "Jack doesn't exist anymore." The sound of his other name coming from her lips made him angry.

She tipped her head to the side. "Very well. Nobody put me up to this. Killing you was all my idea. It was always part of the plan."

"What plan? You need to explain what the fuck is going on here Jess and fast. And what the hell's wrong with him?"

He looked at Evo before rising back up to his feet. The weakness he'd felt just moments before had now been replaced by rage. His whole body was vibrating with a need to grip the woman in front of him—if that's what she was—around the throat and shake the explanation right out of her. He guessed her guards had sensed it too as they looked visibly anxious and moved closer to her.

Jess threw up her hand to halt them and they responded straight away by retreating back to their posts, clearly showing that she was the one in control right now. She looked down at his friend and then back to him.

"I'm just keeping him quiet. He'll stay that way until I see fit to wake him. It's only you who I am interested in having this conversation with."

"You're keeping him quiet? How?"

She didn't answer, but she had a look on her face that he couldn't quite place.

Michael began to pace back and forth on the rocky ledge; his patience wearing thinner by the minute. He didn't know how much longer he could keep himself under control but was sure if Jess didn't start talking, he was going to do something he probably wouldn't walk away from. Not the way those guards were now looking at him anyway. Things couldn't get any more fucked up. His friend was in some kind of unconscious state on the floor next to him; his ex-girlfriend was standing in front of him in a place that she shouldn't even know existed, and the more angry he was becoming, the stranger his whole body felt, like there was a bomb inside of him ticking down to the moment of detonation. He wasn't sure why he felt that way or what would happen when it reached zero, but it was very close.

"You need to calm him down," one of the guards said to Jess with a voice that was deep enough to vibrate through the very rock they were standing on.

That caused Michael to stop and face them. He saw something in Jess's eyes—uncertainty may be?—and wondered if his own eyes had changed like they normally did when he was angry. Maybe that had thrown her off. Whatever it was, she was definitely showing a little vulnerability, which Michael was happy to see.

"*She* needs to start talking," he shot back at the guard.

She didn't.

Instead, she closed her eyes and inhaled a deep breath. Within an instant her form began to change right in front of his eyes. He watched in disbelief as the woman turned from the pretty, slender brunette, whom he'd had a brief fling with, to a naked, bald, pale skinned creature with pointed ears and long pointed claws at the end of each finger.

Michael couldn't believe what was standing in front of him. "You're a shifter." Not a question; an obvious observation born from encountering one or two during his time as a hunter.

"I can be whatever you want me to be," she said before her form began to change again, but this time, as Michael watched the pale demon's figure wriggle and distort, his breath caught the instant he recognized who was appearing in front of him. "Perhaps you'd like me better like this."

Lacy.

The bitch had turned herself into Lacy. She even mimicked her voice.

He bit down on his teeth to try and keep inside the whirlwind of emotions he was suddenly consumed with; anger winning over the hurt and the guilt he felt for dragging Lacy into this mess. She stalked towards him and for a moment, when she reached up and gently touched his cheek, he allowed himself to imagine that she was real, that all of this had been a crazy dream and he was waking up to her affections and a normal life; the only way he'd allow himself to be with her.

No!

He inhaled sharply and gripped her wrist, pulling her hand away from his face and shoving her back away from him, not allowing himself to think that it was Lacy he'd just been rough with. "Get away from me, now!" he spat.

"Oh, sweetie. . . you were so much more fun when we were dating." She smirked and quickly changed herself back to Jess, much to his chagrin, while returning to her guards. It was getting harder to look at her knowing that he'd been close to her and that her deception had caused his current situation.

He'd never known such loathing.

"That's enough Nhang!" a familiar voice projected across the open space that lay behind the guards. As Michael waited, and the three figures standing in front of him swung their heads around, two more horsemen had appeared from the darkness and were riding towards them. Michael then saw that there was another behind them. He looked at the third horseman in disgust as the familiar demon came into view. All three were now riding in a row. Two guards either side of Varesh. They pulled up next to the cliff face to the left of where Michael was standing and all three demons quickly dismounted. The two guards tied up their horses, then one of them took the reins from Varesh who left them attending the animals.

He walked straight over to Jess. . . or Nhang, whatever the hell her name was. "I think you've already been far too polite with our guest," he told her before walking right past her and stopping a few feet away from Michael. Some of his dark, dishevelled hair fell over his face, but Michael could still see those fiery red eyes that were now almost burning him as the demon looked him straight in the eyes.

"I assume you and Nhang have been formally introduced?" Varesh asked without taking his eyes from him. He seemed taller than Michael remembered. Still, it was hard to judge a creature's size while you were being hurled against a load of scrap metal and almost disembowelled by a burning hand of Hellfire.

"You took your time," the female shapeshifter said with annoyance. "I almost gave up on you."

Varesh looked visibly annoyed at her words. "It was more difficult than you'd imagine getting those vultures to let me out. I ended up having to bribe one or two of them, which was a little insulting. Thanks to that bitch of a friend of his," he raised his chin towards Michael, "I'm minus fifteen of my soldiers."

His soldiers?

Michael continued to stare at Varesh, showing him that he wasn't intimidated even though the demon had to be at least fifty pounds heavier and six to eight inches taller. Michael swept his eyes over him, his black pants were torn in places, like they'd been sliced with a sharp object, and one leg had material bound around the thigh as though a wound had been strapped. His knee-length, leather duster was worn in places and open enough to show thick muscle. The creature in front of him was strong as well as powerful and Michael had felt that power first hand. Still, he wasn't threatened by him in the slightest.

"And the prisoner?" Nhang (because Michael had decided Jess was too nice a name for her anyway) asked.

"Contained." Varesh threw her a quick glance over his shoulder, "and un-cooperative as would be expected from someone whose kingdom has just crumbled around him."

Kingdom? That didn't sound good. "What are you talking about?"

Varesh smirked at him and said, "Let's just say your little meeting with Lucifer has been postponed."

Fuck! He'd taken down Lucifer? Michael was suddenly aware that things weren't going according to plan and that, no matter what, he and Evo had to get out of there. Though how he was going to achieve that remained to be seen. The whole thing had just gotten so much bigger than he'd originally thought. It appeared there was a new king in town and if he was powerful and clever enough to overthrow a legendary ruler, a powerful creature that even the Creator couldn't control, then, in a word, they were all fucked.

He glanced down at his buddy again—still breathing. What had she done to him? And what the hell had they gotten themselves into?

Varesh must have seen him and before Michael could register the demon's movement. . .

"Allow me," was all he said before throwing out a ball of white light from his palm that shot straight at Evo, the force of which threw his body backwards along the rocky ground.

"NO!" Michael bellowed as he watched in horror as his friend hurled towards the cliff edge but he stopped before he got there. To Michael's surprise, Evo groaned and shot to his feet holding his head. He took a couple of steps backwards before looking around and realizing the sheer drop that was behind him. He wobbled for a moment, but, to Michael's relief, immediately rushed away from the edge.

"*Shit!* What the fuck?" He turned his attention to the little crowd in front of him, fixed his eyes on Michael and did exactly what Michael was hoping he'd do: shut the hell up. He joined Michael at his side, eyes widened momentarily as if to ask "What the fuck's going on man?" but Michael didn't answer. Instead, he spoke to Varesh.

"What has all of this got to do with me? Why would I be part of this plan? Why did that bitch kill me?" Michael almost growled that last part as he felt the strange vibration return to his body. At the same time he saw a look of shock that quickly changed to fury in Evo's eyes.

"You have a lot of questions hunter." Varesh began to walk away; turning towards Nhang he walked over and stopped at her side. He faced Michael and Evo with a slight grin on his face. "I'm surprised. Do you know nothing of your heritage?"

"My heritage? What are you talking about?"

Varesh threw a sideways glance at Nhang who spoke quietly. "Looks like he's been kept in the dark about all of it. Better for us that he doesn't know."

It annoyed Michael that his questions were still being ignored. "Why don't you talk *to* me and not *about* me? Doesn't know what? Start talking."

"Your questions are of no concern to me. That is a conversation for you and the Creator. I'm not interested in briefing you about something you clearly know nothing about. Now, tell me why you are here. What is it that you wanted to discuss with my dear cousin?"

Cousin?

"It no longer matters. Evo and I have no argument with you. Whatever it is you think you know about me isn't true. I have nothing to do with this war so just leave me and my friends alone and we will be no bother to you."

Varesh laughed and Nhang looked at him with a malevolent grin, which infuriated Michael to the point where he had to fight to calm himself down before he acted out what he was now imagining doing to the bastard demon in front of him.

"I'm afraid you're wrong about that. And our conversation is over." Varesh waved a hand to the guards behind him then pointed at Michael. "I want him. Dispose of the other one." he ordered, then turned to Nhang and the two of them began a quiet conversation as the guards advanced towards Michael and Evo.

"Okay. What do we do now?" Evo asked quietly out of the side of his mouth.

Before Michael had time to answer two of the guards had disappeared into thin air only to reappear behind him, each one grabbing an arm so that he was unable to move. The other two did the same to Evo.

They towered above him. Michael tried to pull free, but their grip was like an iron vice. He watched as the other two guards began to haul Evo away towards the edge of the cliff.

"Uh, Mike. I'm not sure I like where this is heading." Evo shouted back to him over the howling wind that had suddenly increased in volume and strength.

Neither did Michael. He tried one last time to pull himself free from the iron hands that held him back but it was useless. As he watched his friend being hauled off, he felt his anger rise through his body. Helplessly fighting to free himself, he felt the strange vibration rising up from his legs, through his torso, down his arms to the tips of his fingers. His head and face felt warm and he knew his eyes were probably illuminated now. He closed them and took in a deep breath.

It was hard to register what happened next. In an instant, his head began to sing and he felt a pop as a warm rush of energy appeared to leave his body. When he opened his eyes again, he was surrounded by a thick, white haze and no longer felt the guard's grip around his arms.

He was free.

Michael heard a distant voice, deep and throaty, calling out. "Stop him!" Then, before he knew it, he was moving towards the guards that had Evo. He didn't feel his legs move, nor did he feel he had control over any part of his own body. It was almost like he'd willed himself to go and save his friend and his body was somehow taking him there.

Floating. . . Was he floating?

He was still surrounded by the strange haze as he advanced on the guards who were now standing in front of his friend, crouched and ready for attack. Michael watched as the demons' eyes changed to crimson and immediately felt an invisible force pushing at him. But whatever the guards were trying to do had no effect. He pushed through the invisible shield and felt it weaken, watching the stunned expressions on the skeletal features that stood before him.

He heard a roar behind him, then felt pressure at his back. He slowly turned his head to see that Varesh had hurled a fireball at him, but as Michael watched it approach, it was like time had suddenly slowed down. Before it reached him, Michael inhaled deeply and curved his back until he was hunched over—like somehow he knew how to stop it. The fireball hissed as the flames dissipated on impact.

Michael looked up again to see the guards repeating their earlier reprisal still with little effect.

"Evo!" he heard himself shout through all the commotion before expelling more of the strange energy from his body which sent the two guards flying through the air. Michael just about registered Evo's shocked expression before he grabbed him and they both began to run.

Another fireball headed towards them and Michael pushed Evo in front of him to shield him from the onslaught as two more followed. He knew Varesh wasn't going to let them leave, but he wasn't about to go down without a fight; even though he wasn't sure where his fight was coming from. Michael threw Evo to the ground in front of him and crouched over, protecting him as the three balls of fire hit his back one after the other with little effect.

"Are you okay?" He was still covering Evo who seemed a little perplexed as to what was going on.

"I will be when we get out of here."

Michael pulled Evo to his feet and they continued to run. They headed towards a narrow opening in the cliff face on the other side of the ledge. Michael glanced back and was surprised to see that they weren't being followed. The fact that Varesh hadn't ordered his guards to follow and had just let them run was unsettling. Nonetheless, they continued towards the opening.

Michael ushered Evo through the narrow gap first not wanting to take any chances. If they were being followed, then Michael would be the one to fight not his friend. As soon as Evo was through, Michael followed without hesitation.

When they were out of the way of the immediate threat Evo stopped to catch his breath and grabbed Michael's arm as he went to pass him. "Wait. . . Whoa. Just stop for a minute, okay?" he panted.

"Not a good idea. We need to keep moving."

The tunnel they were in was dark, but short enough so that the light shone through from the other side illuminating Evo's face. He had the oddest look.

"I don't know what went down with you and those demons before my ass woke up. But what the hell was that?"

Michael feigned innocence. "What?"

"Never mind 'what?'. . . What just happened to you back there? How the hell did you manage to fight off four huge demons without even touching them, then go and save our asses from an onslaught of hellfire, all without a hair out of place? And who was the tasty broad?"

Michael chose to ignore the last question. He could just imagine Evo's reaction when he told him he'd dated a shapeshifter, even if it was without him knowing it. He sighed and leaned against the stone wall facing Evo. The sound of dripping water was all that occupied the small space as Michael tried to come up with an answer, but only one thing had entered his mind from the moment the strange power had taken over his body.

"I'm one of them, aren't I?"

He heard Evo's breath catch. "Demon?"

"Yes. It's the only explanation." The only one he could find anyway. He'd suspected it for a while; ever since the first night he'd met Evo, when his eyes had changed. Since then he'd felt the change but just put it down to him getting used to his body. Then there was what happened in Lacy's house when they discovered she'd been taken. He'd felt so much power rushing through him back then and it unnerved him.

But why was he so surprised? After all, he'd escaped Hell. Wasn't it obvious what he was?

Evo surprised him by gripping onto his shoulders hard. "You're not a fucking demon. There's no way." His friend burned him with a look that said "I won't let that be true."

He couldn't blame him for feeling that way. "How could I not be, Evo? There's no other way to explain what's happening to me. I had no control over that back there. It's just like rage consumed me and took over my body. Like I was just telling myself what I wanted to happen and then it happened without any effort.

"It's not the first time I've thought about this. For the last few months I've felt like I was getting stronger. Fighting these creatures has been getting easier. And now, after what just happened out there, I feel stronger than ever."

"But, what about your eyes? Why do yours glow white when theirs are blood red? Surely they would be the same."

Michael shook his head. He had no idea.

Both men were quiet for a moment until Evo dropped his hands from Michael's shoulders and said, "Well, demon or not, I think that was pretty fucking awesome what you did out there." He smiled at him reassuringly.

Michael appreciated it. It didn't make him feel any happier about the situation, but knowing that his friend was trying to make him feel better, he had to smile back. All be it a small one.

"Come on," Michael said. "We have to find some place safe so we can get out of here."

They headed for the tunnel's exit. And as Michael walked on ahead, he tried his best to ignore Evo's next sentence.

"Now, about that female. . . "

CHAPTER TWENTY-TWO

"**I** can't sit here like this anymore. I have to be doing something."

Lacy was feeling far too anxious to be sitting watching the TV. After getting the super to fix Michael's apartment door, she'd sat and analyzed the items spread out on the coffee table. Some of which made her stomach tense. Then she'd figured she'd see if there was anything to watch so she could at least try and take her mind off of Michael.

It hadn't worked.

She couldn't stop her imagination from working overtime as she thought about what both men could be going through right now as she sat and watched trash TV. It wasn't right.

Alethia had spent most of her time in Michael's room in a telepathic conversation with her father and other family members in an attempt to sway them to help but it didn't seem to be working.

The door to the bedroom opened and Alethia walked out shaking her head with a sorrowful look towards Lacy. "They refuse," she growled out of frustration. She explained how her father had told her that they weren't about to get involved in a war they weren't a part of for the sake of two people, one of which was already dead, who had chosen their own path by entering Hell in the first place. Oh, and that Alethia was to stay put. "My father is a stubborn bastard. I'm sorry."

The disappointment hit Lacy hard, but she knew the deity had tried her hardest. If the gods weren't willing to help even when one of their own was asking then things were worse than she'd initially thought.

Lacy started pacing around the room. She stopped at the small window and stared out at the students wandering around the university grounds below with books and files tucked under their arms, completely oblivious to what was happening all around them. She let out an exasperated sigh. "I can't do this. . . stay cooped up in this apartment waiting. I'm concerned for Evo, of course I am, but what if it's Michael that uses the ring? I don't want either of them getting trapped, but Michael. . . " She swallowed the lump that had cut off her words. She wanted to scream; to shout to anyone who could hear.

Alethia walked up to her and placed her hand on her shoulder. "We'll find another way. I don't want anything to happen to them either. Michael is a kind soul and, for your sake, I want to see him return unharmed. Evo. . . Well, I'm kinda fond of the idiot. He reminds me of someone—"

Alethia's face lit up like she'd just remembered the answer for the million dollar question. She began to rush around the apartment, quickly gathering up her things. She put her coat on and passed Lacy hers. "Come on, I know someone who could help us."

Lacy didn't hesitate. She shoved her arms in her coat and had her purse over her shoulder before she'd even finished putting it on properly. "You do? Who?"

"A last resort," she said, her brow furrowed so much that she looked like she could've been in pain. "But it won't be easy."

"What do you mean?"

"I know he'll be hostile towards me. We kind of fell out years ago." Alethia placed her hands on Lacy's elbows indicating what form of transport they would use. Lacy did the same to her.

"Who is he?"

Alethia grinned. "My ex-husband."

After shifting through the air, which Lacy was now beginning to get a little used to, even though it was still weird, the gray mist dispersed from around them to reveal their surroundings. They were standing on a cobbled street in front of a Georgian looking town house that was nestled in the middle of a row of similar looking buildings. Lacy looked around to see that they were in a wide street lit by ornate, black street lamps, that looked like it was in the middle of. . . London?

"Are we in London?" she quickly asked Alethia who simply said, "Yes." As if it was no big deal. All Lacy could do was gawp at her with mouth wide open. It was one thing to shift a few miles away to the other side of town, but to end up on the other side of the Atlantic in just a couple of minutes was completely mind boggling.

"Close your mouth." Alethia smirked. Lacy snapped it shut just as the deity knocked on the front door.

The house had three stories and five bays, and was in pale red brick with a white stone surround around the black panelled door. It was kept well and the size and location of the building suggested that whoever lived inside certainly wasn't short of money.

Alethia knocked again and before she'd removed her hand the door swung open; behind it stood a classically handsome looking man. His dark wavy hair was pushed back from a pale face with a chiselled jaw and prominent cheekbones. He was dressed in a white towelling robe and his feet were bare. Lacy couldn't help but stare at the man's deep hazel eyes that were now pinned widely on Alethia as if the guy had seen a ghost. All of a sudden the door slammed shut, leaving the two women staring at the brass knocker.

Alethia huffed. "I told you. . . hostile."

She knocked again, harder this time. "Jaret! Open the door." And then again, and again until. . .

It swung open again just enough for a head to appear from behind it. "Go! Leave you crazy woman," the man snapped in a strong cockney accent. As he was about to repeat the assault on his own front door, Alethia put her hands up and pushed back to prevent him from shutting them both out again.

"Wait! Jaret, please. I haven't come to cause any trouble."

"Then you won't mind leaving just the same will yer." He pushed harder on the door, but Alethia—who was surprisingly strong and had now wedged her foot in the way—wasn't letting up.

"Jeez! I just need to talk," she said calmly.

Jaret, seeming to admit defeat, pulled back from the door, opened it wide and walked inside without another word.

Lacy looked at Alethia who tipped her head suggesting that she follow her inside.

They walked down a long hallway with a high ceiling edged with decorative moldings. There were paintings hung on the walls, which looked old and expensive: different scenes of valleys and landscapes. At the end of the hallway they turned into a spacious modern kitchen that was bright with pale lemon colored units and dark, granite work tops and lots of stainless steel. Jaret was standing at the counter pouring hot water from the kettle into a mug and stirring it intently—a cigarette hanging from his mouth.

"It's not a friendly hour to be callin' on someone," he mumbled. Of course, Lacy thought, there was a five hour time difference, which meant it would be around one thirty in the morning. "So, talk then."

Alethia flicked her eyes at Lacy then back to Jaret, who had finished making his coffee and had now turned to face her with cup in hand.

"I need your help," she muttered quietly and looked down at the floor. From what Lacy knew of her, the goddess was no introvert so it was strange to witness.

"I'm sorry. What was tha'?"

Alethia raised her head, looked Jaret in the eye, and spoke with more resolve this time. "I. . . *We* need your help."

Jaret laughed so hard he spilled some of his coffee down the front of his crisp, clean robe. "Shit!" He stuck his cigarette in a nearby ashtray, grabbed a towel and began to scrub the material.

"It's not funny." Alethia looked aggravated.

"I disagree," he said and resumed drinking his coffee.

It was clear to Lacy that the exchange that was taking place may take a while, but nevertheless; she was actually a little amused by what was happening.

"I seem to recall you owe me one," Alethia said to her ex-husband who was now stubbing out his cigarette. He looked up at her, his dark eyebrows drawn into a deep frown.

"Oh, no. You ain't pullin' that one on me. You lost that privilege when you burned down me last gaff."

"Your last ga. . . house was *our* house, remember." Alethia corrected.

"Still din't give you the right to burn it daan." He crossed his arms in front of him and leaned against the counter waiting for Alethia's response.

"Look, I know you're upset—"

"Upset?" Jaret interrupted. "Upset is when my 'orse falls at the final fence. . . YOU burned down me 'ome."

She let out a sharp, exasperated exhale. "Look. Can we please not get into this right now?" she asked through almost gritted teeth as she threw a look towards Lacy as if to say "Not in front of present company."

Jaret also looked at Lacy and his mouth set in a line. "Who is this, anyway? And what'ya doin' in London?"

Lacy gave him an uncertain smile.

"This is Lacy Holloway. She's a friend of mine and the main—and *only*—reason I'm here."

"Pleased to meet yer. Sorry about the. . . " He waved his hand between him and Alethia.

"It's okay," Lacy replied. As she watched the two of them across the room, she wondered how long they'd been married.

Jaret was definitely a looker so she could see why he'd grabbed Alethia's attention. She also wondered what had happened that was so bad to make Alethia burn his house down and made a mental note not to piss her off.

"Can I get yer some tea? Coffee?" Jaret offered with a hint of a smile. Lacy was sure she saw a slight dimple in his chin.

"No, Thanks."

"Alethia?" The smile had definitely gone when he asked her.

"Coffee, thanks." She pulled out a chair from the glass dining table at the end of the room. "Can we sit?"

"Go 'head," he said over his shoulder as he began filling up the kettle.

After they'd all sat down and fresh coffee was on the table, Alethia began to explain the situation to Jaret, who, for some reason, seemed to have perked up at the mention of Hell. She explained that if either Michael or Evo used her father's ring they would be trapped in a place that no one would be able to get to. She wasn't even sure where the demons went that got captured by the ring, only that they never returned.

They never returned?

All of a sudden, after the new information that Alethia had casually dropped into their conversation, Lacy felt the air in the room become thicker and she found she was struggling to breathe. She knew it was the beginning of one of her infamous panic attacks and didn't want to embarrass herself in front of the two sat at the table so she made an excuse to use the bathroom. Jaret explained where the one downstairs was. She made it there and managed to lock herself in just in time.

She put the toilet seat down and closed the lid. As soon as she sat down, she bent forward, placing her head between her knees. She tried to usher away the thoughts that she'd so vividly conjured up in her mind of Michael trapped in a dark pit surrounded by feral demons who'd been trapped there for centuries.

The thoughts only added to the lightheadedness she was now experiencing due to over breathing. She tried to slow her breaths down, remembering how Michael had helped her, and after what only felt like a couple of minutes there was a soft knock at the door.

"Lacy. Is everything okay in there?" Alethia's muted voice sounded through the door.

Lacy was still a little shaky, but the worst had passed. She stood and looked at herself in the mirror; smoothed down her hair and made sure she looked okay before unlocking the door.

"Well, you look fine. I thought we lost you for a minute, though, like you'd sneaked out the back door or something."

Lacy found that odd. "I just needed to pee."

"For nearly an hour?"

"What?" No. That couldn't be right.

Alethia smiled at her. "Look, I know that talking about this whole situation is hard for you. You don't have to explain."

She actually couldn't even if she tried.

"I'm glad though. Jaret and I had a much needed talk while you were gone and thankfully things seem to be okay." She cocked an eyebrow. "For now anyway."

Oh, well. Lacy was glad. At least she'd inadvertently helped those two get back to speaking terms.

* * *

After they'd decided to rest up at Jaret's, and they'd both been given a little tour around the house and shown to their separate guest rooms, Lacy was lying in a large, oak, four-poster bed, a small lamp on the sideboard next to her, with the hope of any sleep evading her. Her mind was jumbled with thoughts that weren't welcome, but it seemed they were set in for the evening. She looked around the large room, noticing the many paintings that filled the walls. Jaret definitely loved his art. There was a mix of subjects from old oils of Edwardian females doing household chores to modern abstracts of color and shapes. It was a strange mix, but they brightened the room which had red painted walls and continued the washed wood flooring that had run through the rest of the house.

After tossing and turning some more, she decided to take a trip to the kitchen to see if Jaret had any cocoa. She put her sweats and T-shirt back on, and made her way out of the room.

She was walking along the landing as quietly as she could so as not to disturb anyone when she saw Alethia stepping out of Jaret's room up ahead. She contemplated ducking out of the way, but before she could move Alethia looked up and saw her.

Lacy smiled awkwardly as the deity walked towards her. "It's not what you think. I just gave him something he needed that's all."

Lacy felt a little uncomfortable, and really it wasn't her business, but knew they were about to discuss it anyway. Alethia might as well join her. "I was just going to look for cocoa."

"Sounds good."

When they were both sat at the kitchen table with a hot cup of chocolate each and some cookies that Alethia had found, Alethia looked at Lacy, her face was serious. "Look, I don't know if you've realized, but Jaret isn't human either."

Lacy hadn't, but wondered why she felt so surprised. Alethia didn't look any different to any other humans either and she was getting used to running into otherworldly beings.

"He's a Cambion." She looked at Lacy as if she was supposed to know what that was. After obviously noticing that Lacy hadn't a clue what she was talking about, Alethia began to explain. "A Cambion is a hybrid. Jaret is the offspring of a human and an Incubus."

Oh. So, at least her list of *creatures I've met this week* was getting longer. "Wow. Incubus huh? I've read about those. Of course, I thought they were just a silly myth then. So they really feed on...?"

Alethia's brows raised a little. "Yes. But Jaret is only part Incubus so his need isn't as great as a full breed. He only *has* to have sex once or twice a month.

"Oh," was all Lacy could reply for a moment. "Was that why you..." she tilted her head to the side and Alethia copied the gesture waiting for her to finish her sentence. She didn't.

"Yes. I asked him for a favor, a big one, so it was the least I could do. He's going to need to be at full strength for what he'll be doing shortly, so it's best to make sure. And unless you were going to offer..."

Lacy winced at that. Alethia laughed. "It was just sex. It meant nothing, to him or to me."

Even though it was a strange situation, Lacy kind of understood. "What is it? The favor you've asked of him."

Alethia took a sip from her mug and placed it down on the table in front of her. "Because of what Jaret is—his father being full Incubus—he can enter Hell, however, and whenever, he pleases. No one bats an eyelid down there as long as he doesn't cause any trouble. His father still resides down there somewhere and Jaret's been trying to find him since he was old enough to transport himself there. He once told me how he hated it though. He tried to explain, thankfully without too much detail, how gruesome it is. How some of the macabre things that go on down there would disturb even the strongest of minds. It took some convincing, but he agreed to go and look for Michael and Evo in exchange for something."

Lacy felt a whisper of hope rise from her stomach into her chest. They'd gone from no chance of warning Michael and Evo about using the ring to there being an actual half demon willing to help them. There was still a worry that either of them could have already used it by now, but she hoped and prayed that wasn't the case. She noticed Alethia looking a little perturbed and remembered that there was to be an exchange for Jaret's help.

"What is it that he wants in return, Alethia?"

The goddess rolled her eyes. "He wants to call on me once a month."

"Oh. I see. I'm sorry."

Alethia straightened her shoulders. "Don't be. It could have been worse. I burnt down his house remember. I think I've gotten off lightly. Besides, in no way was sex anything to do with our breakup," she smirked. "He was always very good at that."

Lacy laughed. She got the feeling that Alethia would be using him once a month just as much as he would be using her. "I bet Evo won't be too happy about the two of you."

Alethia frowned. "What's it got to do with him?"

"Well, didn't you two spend some. . . *time* together last night?"

The deity's amber eyes widened. "Yes. He came to my hotel room, but we didn't do *that*."

"Oh. I thought that—"

"You think I'd sleep with that womanizing jerk? Lacy, I do have some morals. I may have just had sex with Jaret, but it's not like we haven't done it before. He *was* my husband after all. And it was for a good cause. But Evo. . ."

Lacy felt terrible, but to be fair, it wasn't exactly her fault. He'd made it seem that way. "I'm sorry it's just that. . . Evo made out that he *seduced* the ring from you."

Alethia nearly choked in her cocoa before pulling the mug away from her mouth. "Oh please. He may think he's *that* good in bed, but let me tell you. . . anyone who says they are, usually aren't. Self praise is no recommendation. No, Evo didn't seduce the ring from me, he damn well stole it. He must have drugged me or spelled me or something, though I've no idea how. I'm a goddess for God's sake." She let out a soft laugh. "I was warned about him, but didn't really take it seriously. That guy knows everything about everything. I'll never underestimate him again, that's for sure. You wait till I see him. . . " The humor disappeared from her face the moment she'd said those words. She looked over the table at Lacy. "Jaret will find them. I'm sure of it."

Lacy didn't speak through fear of breaking down. They had to. And Jaret was the only chance they had.

After an hour chatting about nothing in particular, Lacy realized how much fun Alethia was. This was the first time she'd spoken to her casually and her sense of humor surprised Lacy. She'd been very serious since Lacy had met her, which was understandable given the circumstances. She'd appeared as old as her years—however many that was—but now she seemed a lot younger, more relaxed and playful.

They both looked at each other as they heard the thud of bare footsteps coming down the hall.

"Talk of the demon. . . " Alethia whispered and gave a little wink.

The kitchen door opened and in walked Jaret scrubbing his hand through his dark brown hair until it was a scruffy mess nested on top of his head but it didn't make him any less good looking. He had nothing but pajama bottoms on, hanging low on his hips and Lacy struggled to look away from his bare torso. He was all muscle. Defined in a way only fitness models were. Alethia caught her staring and her face pulled into a teasing smile. Lacy lowered her eyes; feeling a little embarrassed she began to curl the corner of the black, woven place mat that was laid out in front of her. Well, how could she not look? She appreciated beauty just like any other woman. *Stop right now.* She ordered herself.

She sensed him walk right past them. "No point in me tryin'a get any shut eye with you pair is there?" His voice was a little husky.

Alethia answered. "Don't be grumpy. It's not like you need it."

When Lacy brought her eyes back up, she stifled a gasp. Jaret was standing over by the coffee machine facing away from them and a huge tattoo covered his entire back. It was a colorless masterpiece. Like something Michelangelo himself would have produced. She saw Alethia had noticed her awe and she twisted herself around to look at him. "Ah, yes. Jaret likes to show off his art. It's his pride and joy."

He twisted his head around to the pair of them staring at him. "Wha'?"

"Lacy was just admiring your ink."

"Who is that?" Lacy asked of the large female figure dressed in a short toga with armor over her shoulders and knees. She was jumping in the air with a long spear in her hand and was poised as if ready to plunge it straight into the strange looking creature that was cowering on the ground below her. It looked like some kind of battle scene. There were dark thunderous clouds in the background which made the whole thing look eerie somehow. It was beautifully chaotic.

Jaret didn't answer. He just shrugged his shoulder, which suggested he wasn't really interested.

"Jaret's mother was human. She was attacked by a demon that became obsessed with her and eventually raped her after possessing the body of someone she trusted; a man who was her friend and colleague from work. Anyway, long story short, after having Jaret, she spent a lot of her time in and out of psychiatric hospitals because she was never able to deal with what happened. Jaret fought for her. He tried to help her as best he could, but in the end she killed herself."

Lacy's hand pressed over her heart as she gasped a little. "I'm so sorry."

Jaret walked over to the table with his coffee and sat down next to Alethia. He pushed her arm and rolled his eyes at her. "You tryin'a depress the poor girl?" He turned to Lacy. "It was a long time ago. Anyway, she's in a better place than she ever was down 'ere."

Alethia continued as Jaret sipped his coffee. "The female on his back is his mother depicted as an angel, a warrior of the Creator about to kill the demon that raped her."

"One day it will be me." Jaret said with narrowed eyes. He looked like he was imagining that day. He blinked and then looked at Lacy.

"So, what is it that your fella's arfter down there?" he asked.

Her fella? She wasn't sure that he was *hers*. Lacy didn't correct him. "Apparently he and Lucifer have a mutual enemy."

"Why would he be so stupid to even try and talk with that evil barstard? Clearly dying the first time wasn't enough for 'im, eh?"

Lacy winced at that. Alethia slapped his arm.

"Well. . . it's true," he continued. "Lucifer don't just *talk*. He's not someone who takes appointments. He tortures first, talks arfter."

Lacy lowered her gaze. "Yes. I would imagine that's true," she said quietly. That's exactly why she didn't want Michael to go.

"Then you'll know what 'im and 'is friend'll be up against when 'e get's there then."

"Jaret. She doesn't need reminding. None of us do." Alethia's dark brows drew tight. "All we need to know from you is what you intend to do to help them. Because you're going to help them, aren't you?" Not a question by the sound of her gritted teeth. "Or you're going to pay me back for our little rumble in the worst way I can think of."

Jaret laughed. "Oh, Alethia. . . Yer know 'ow sexy I find yer when yer threaten me."

The goddess huffed. "Jaret!"

"Babe, yer know I'm only messin' wiv yer." He put a serious face on "All I can do is go daan there an' look for 'em. . . arsk around. But ya know 'ow received my presence is when I visit that place. Not well."

Alethia nodded her head and looked at Lacy. "Because he's a half breed. He's considered an enemy by most," she explained.

Jaret smiled. "I've never caused any trouble, so most just ignore me."

"Why would you go there at all?" Lacy couldn't help asking. If it was such a horrible place, why would anyone choose to go there? Michael didn't exactly choose. He felt he had no other option. But Jaret. . . surely he wouldn't choose to go there at all. Especially as it was one of Hell's demons that hurt his mother.

"Debt collecting mostly. I've won a few decent 'ands in poker an' those barstard demon's don't like payin' up. And I hope one day I'll find my father daan there." He sank the rest of his coffee and got up from the table, grabbing the other two mugs and walking to the sink.

Lacy mouthed *poker* to Alethia with a questioning glance. Alethia shrugged and rolled her eyes, "don't ask" written all over her face.

Jaret placed the mugs in the basin and began to walk towards the door. "I'm gonna grab a shower then I'll be off."

CHAPTER TWENTY-THREE

It was quiet... Way too quiet.

"I don't like this at all." Michael said as he walked alongside his friend through the dense woodland they now found themselves in. "If we're going to get out of here it needs to be soon."

He'd noticed the screams and bellows that had filled the air around them had died down to almost nothing. It had left him with a feeling of unease that was growing with every second they were left alone. Why hadn't anyone come for them since his fight with the guards? Surely Varesh would be even more pissed now. Surely he wasn't about to let them leave?

They entered a small clearing

"Here's as good a place as any, I guess," Evo said as he began to remove his duster. He placed it on the ground next to him and retrieved what he needed from the pockets. He looked up and his raised eyebrows told Michael what was about to come out of his mouth.

"So, a shifter eh?" He had an annoying grin on his face; the one that he always wore when he was about to make a smart-ass comment. Why Michael had even mentioned that he'd dated that bitch back there he didn't know—would have been better if he'd just kept his mouth shut.

Evo retrieved his knife from his ankle strap and continued. "Well, I think it's pretty cool that you dated a shifter."

"I told you I didn't know she was a shifter at the time"

"Shame." Evo still hadn't wiped that look off his face and Michael wanted to slap it. "Just think how cool that would've been. I mean, if you got bored she could just shift to look like someone else. You could have had a different woman every night."

Michael wondered how long it would take. "Like you'd need to date a shifter. You do that anyway."

"True. But with a shifter you could've had her change into anyone you wanted. Like that Megan Fox chick." He shook his head. "Damn. Why have I never dated one?"

Michael didn't even respond. It was just like Evo to make good out of a bad situation. It didn't surprise him at all that he would be happy dating a shifter even though they were demons. He knew his buddy didn't really have a preference when it came to getting laid.

"We need to hurry. What do I have to do?" Michael knew it was only a matter of time before they were spotted. He didn't trust the place at all.

"We have to cut the shit out," Evo replied as he held out his arm, preparing to slice his own flesh again.

Evo put the wand between his teeth and placed the knife onto the healing flesh of the slice he'd made before. He began to open the wound again, biting down hard on the wand to stifle his grunts of pain. Veins popped out from his neck as he began to remove the lumpy mixture from his arm. After pausing to catch his breath for a second, he took the wand out and seemed to brace himself for the next part. He wiped at his seeping wound and lit the end of the wand with his lighter, before blowing out the flame so that it was just glowing at the end. He inhaled a deep breath and began to cauterize his wound like he had the last time. When he was done, he wiped the sweat from his brow and turned to Michael. "Your turn."

After they were done, Evo had just begun to chant the strange words he'd spoken to get them there, when a piercing screech tore through the air.

They paused to look at each other.

Whatever it was was close.

Another... This time from a different direction. The demons were circling them.

"Shit!" Evo grabbed his coat and quickly put it back on. He shoved the torn shroud and all the rest of the ritual stuff back into his pockets, keeping hold of his knife and holding it out in front of him.

Screech! Screech!

Both men turned so they were back to back, listening to the echoes of demonic cries that were now surrounding them. Michael knew Varesh was never going to let them leave and they were about to face something much bigger than they had before. His spine began to tingle as awareness pricked his senses, bringing his gaze to the thick trees in front of him. He saw shadows moving, lots of them.

What appeared from the black forest sent a bolt of dread soaring through the pits of his stomach.

Black skinned demons, the color of ash, now surrounded the area. Their long bodies curled over—hands with long curling fingers dragged along the floor; their faces were distorted baring sharp, jagged teeth and pointed ears. There were hundreds of them all snarling like rabid dogs ready to pounce.

So that's what Varesh meant by "his soldiers". The bastard was building an army.

"Evo. We can't fight these. There's too many of them."

"You don't say."

Before another word could be said the demons charged.

Evo handed his knife to Michael over his shoulder. "Take this."

Michael paused. "What about you?"

Evo wiggled his finger within eyeshot. "I have this remember."

The ring.

Michael grabbed the knife and faced the onslaught that was now almost upon them.

This was it. He'd guessed there would be a big price to pay for what he'd done in front of Varesh. The demon was never going to deal with being over-thrown by him.

All that was left was to fight, but he feared for his friend.

He threw his arm out and held his only weapon in front of him, hoping that it would at least do some damage before he was outnumbered.

He didn't get a chance to try.

Out of nowhere a hooded figure jumped in front of him. He held his hand out and white hot sparks flew out from his palm while he turned slowly, taking out the whole of the first wave of demons, all of them flying backwards from the force of whatever it was the stranger had thrown at them. They lay on the ground motionless.

Evo spun around, his eyes wide with a similar look of what-the-fuck? as what Michael had. "How did... What... Who the *hell* are you?" he managed.

The hooded figure faced them with a wicked smirk. "I'm the bloke who's about to save your arses," he said in a strange British accent. "Now, can we save the introductions for somewhere a bit safer?"

The stranger began to run. "Come on then!" he called back.

They had no other choice but to follow. Unfortunately, so did those horrific sounds that the demons made.

Michael threw a look over his shoulder. Shit! That blast hadn't killed them and they were now getting pretty close. "They're gaining on us."

Evo was lagging slightly behind. "Hey! Guy with the hood... Can't you fire some of that sparkly shit at them again?" he panted.

"No. That was all I 'ad" the guy shouted back. "Fack!" He halted suddenly and Michael nearly plowed him down.

"Oh shit!"

More demons up ahead.

The three men stood back to back watching the approaching army that had now slowed—taunting them.

Evo began to chant words from a strange language behind Michael, but his voice sounded like it was getting quieter all of a sudden. When Michael turned his head, he saw his friend walking towards the demons, holding out his arm, fist tightly clenched, aimed at the group of demonic predators.

"Uh, you need to stop 'im from doin' that. Now!" The disquiet in the stranger's voice was enough to concern Michael.

"Why? That ring he's got may be our only way out of this."

The hooded man's next words came out in a rush. "Because Alethia said if either one of yer use that ring it'll reverse itself on yer. Now I suggest yer stop 'im."

Alethia? Oh no!

He turned and ran towards his friend. "STOP! Evo. . . Don't use the ring."

"It's okay, Mike. . . Something's happening. I think it's. . ."

"EVO!"

Michael had no way of stopping what happened next. Time seemed to slow, noises faded to distant echoes and as he watched what was happening to his friend, he froze. A bright orange light grew out from the ring and began to form a dome around Evo who had started to shake violently. Michael reached out, but an invisible force pushed him backwards.

He noticed that every single one of the demons was crouched down; cowering away from whatever it was that had surrounded Evo.

"NOOOO!" Michael cried as he hit the ground. The light grew brighter and Evo's body began to glow. It was so bright it hurt Michael to look at him, but he did for as long as he could until he was forced to close his eyes momentarily as everything went intensely white. Then it was gone.

And so was Evo.

He saw the ring hit the floor right at the spot where Evo had been standing and he ran to it. His knees hit the floor and he gripped the ring tightly in his fist.

Those deathly screeches started up again. The demons were ready for another fight and they were about to get one.

"Um, we need to move, mate."

He heard the voice beside him but ignored it and crouched over. Rage was boiling up inside of him, filling his whole body with a heat that vibrated right through to his marrow. He lifted his head and through his eyes, everything looked brighter: the crimson sky, the black forest that surrounded them and when he looked down at himself, his hands, which were now curled into tight fists, began to tremble.

He saw the demons advancing from in front of where he was now on his knees and knew the ones behind him would be doing the same. He twisted his head to look at the stranger who had now removed his hood and was anxiously waiting for some kind of response from Michael. "Get down!" he ordered, but whether the man listened or not was of no concern to him right now. He hunched his shoulders over, feeling the vibrations coursing through him. His head felt as though it would burst and with a final intake of breath, he lifted his head, held his hands out in front of him, opened his mouth and roared.

Through his ears, he heard a deep rumble.

Through his eyes he could see a shield of energy, like a shockwave, rolling outwards from his body. As it hit the demons their bodies burst into flames and disintegrated, every last one of them.

When they were all gone, the shield returned to him as if he was breathing it back inside his body.

Silence.

Only the sound of Michael's heavy breathing could be heard. His energy waned and he fell forwards onto his hands. He saw a movement from the corner of his eye and his head snapped towards it. The stranger pulled himself up from the ground, eyes wide open and scanning the clearing in disbelief. Then he fixed his astonished stare at Michael.

"What the fack are you? How did you just do that?" The stranger was on his feet now, looking around frantically like he couldn't believe his own eyes. "I've only ever been speechless once before in my life and that was when me mum told me I was the offspring of a fackin' demon, but. . . " He swallowed hard and shook his head slowly.

Michael couldn't seem to move for a moment. He closed his eyes tightly.

Evo!

He shot up and charged toward the stranger, grabbing him by his collar. "Alethia? Tell me what she said," he growled, tightening his grip.

"Time to go," was all the dark-haired man managed to choke out before he held onto Michael's arms and their surroundings began to shift into a swirling sea of black and crimson.

"What are you doing?" Michael yelled, still keeping a firm hold on the guy.

No answer.

Michael's hands shifted around the guy's throat and he squeezed. "Whatever you're doing stop!"

The ground fell away, or they'd left the ground, he wasn't sure but as his anger returned and the gray haze that had formed around them began to dissipate, he realized where they were and it was no longer in Hell. He was still hanging on to the stranger's throat when he saw the walls of Lacy's living room appear.

"Take. Me. Back!" He didn't recognize his own voice it was so thick with rage. "Take me back there. . . NOW!" He had to save Evo.

The man choked as he tried to speak. His hands locked on Michael's wrists as he tried to prize him off his throat.

"Michael!" a female voice cried out from somewhere else in the room, but he was too intent on getting that fucker to take him back to Hell to take any notice.

"Michael please! Let go," the female said and he felt small hands wrap around his left arm. "It's me, Lacy. Let go of him, please."

His head snapped towards her and when he saw her face—her beautiful, concerned face—he realized what he was doing and released his grip on the man whose eyes were now a little bloodshot.

Michael heard coughing and spluttering and saw Alethia run to the stranger's aid.

He threw his arms around Lacy.

"Oh, thank God you're back," she said into his chest.

A vision of the horribly charred body that he'd thought was her flashed into his mind. He closed his eyes tightly and willed it away.

Not real.

This is real. This right now.

He inhaled her scent deep into his lungs. The fresh, familiar scent of flowers with a hint of apple from her hair made his whole body relax.

He felt her hitched breaths against his chest and he moved her so that he could see her face. His hands moved up her arms, over her shoulders until they stopped either side of her face. He studied her for a moment, eyes covering every inch of her and stopping at the small red mark at her temple. The healing slice she'd received from the demon that'd held her captive would soon fade to nothing, leaving no trace of what happened, but Michael wouldn't forget. This woman had somehow managed to forge a tangible mark on his heart and there seemed to be very little he could do about it.

He wiped a tear from her cheek with his thumb. "You're real," he breathed.

Her full lips curled up into a sweet, tender smile which made his heart clench. "Yes," she said, "and you're here."

He placed his lips on hers and kissed her gently. "Thank God you're real," he whispered against her mouth before pulling her back into his tight embrace.

For a moment it felt like it was just the two of them, until. . .

Cough! "Shit!" *Cough!*

Then Alethia's voice sounded from behind them. "Okay now?" She was standing over the dark-haired man who Michael had just nearly killed and was rubbing her hand up and down his back.

"Yeah!" he spat out as he crouched over, hands on his thighs. "But what the fack did you send me to get, Alethia?" As he stood up straight, his eyes burned Michael with a hostile stare.

Alethia's eyes narrowed. Keeping them pinned on Michael she asked, "What do you mean, Jaret?"

"I mean what the facking 'ell is 'e?" He nursed his hand over his throat.

Michael didn't react; after all, it wasn't a question he could give an answer to. He stood with Lacy in his arms, but she too had pulled back a little to look at him now. Her brows were pulled tight and she looked concerned.

Alethia walked towards Michael. "What happened? And why are you alone? Where's Evo?"

Michael didn't have to tell her as she must have figured it out from his tortured expression, or pulled it from his mind.

Her face mirrored his. "Oh, no! That stupid son of a bitch!"

* * *

Lacy stood looking through her kitchen window at the man sitting in the moonlight. She'd wondered where Michael had got to. As soon as she'd spotted him sitting on her bench by the willow tree outside, she'd left the light off so as not disturb him.

When he'd appeared in her living room a little over an hour ago with Jaret she was so relieved to see him she hadn't noticed Evo wasn't with them. Michael's rage had surprised her, she'd never seen him like that, and she was glad he'd stopped when he did as she suspected Jaret wouldn't be sitting in her living room, eating the sandwiches she'd made, with Alethia right now.

She'd felt something when she'd placed her hands on his arm as she tried to get him to stop what he was doing to Jaret; a strange sensation, like a buzz of electricity which nearly had her pulling back from him. It felt like his skin was vibrating.

When he'd looked into her eyes just before he'd kissed her, she'd felt something completely different: a connection. She couldn't quite explain it, but it was there as real as he'd been standing before her.

Safe.

Her heart swelled as he'd kissed her and in that moment she knew how far she'd fallen. The time she'd spent without him, wondering if she'd ever see him again, had only confirmed her feelings.

She was in love with him; she knew that for certain now and it scared her to death.

When Michael had explained what had happened before Jaret pulled him out of Hell, Lacy'd sat speechless. She could tell in his voice that he was worried about what was happening to him. And now, more than ever, so was she.

What would become of him?

She grabbed the thick, navy pullover that was on the back of one of the dining chairs and pulled it over her head as she walked out into the garden, closing the door behind her.

"I wondered where you'd got to." She sat down on the small bench seat next to him. The crisp fall air almost burned her lungs, but it was refreshing.

Michael looked at her briefly and attempted a smile. "Just needed to clear my head.' He sighed and tilted his head back to look at the clear night sky. She did the same.

"The world seems so peaceful. I envy them," he said.

Lacy looked back at him with a questioning frown. "Who?"

"All of them. . . The people who are blissfully unaware of the evil that surrounds them. They go about their lives normally, without fear or knowledge of the creatures that hide amongst them." His shoulders slumped. "I wish I could go back to not knowing."

Michael's hand was resting on his thigh and Lacy got an urge to hold it. She wanted to reassure him that he wasn't on his own in this anymore. She reached out and placed hers on top of his. Without saying a word he turned his hand upward and laced his fingers with hers. They both sat quietly, looking up at the dusting of bright stars that shone against the inky black sky, the moon the only source of light.

"I hope he's okay," he said with a broken voice. A voice that was full of pain and guilt. A guilt he had no right to carry.

She knew he was hurting, knew he was blaming himself. "It isn't your fault what happened to him so don't let yourself be burdened that way."

"I have no choice. I should never have let him go with me. I didn't try hard enough to stop him."

Lacy shifted her body so she was turned towards him. "Hey. I haven't known him for long, but even I know Evo wasn't going to let you go down there alone. No matter what you did. It was his choice; just like it was his choice to take the ring from Alethia."

He didn't respond, instead, he heaved a sigh that suggested he wasn't convinced by her words. She hated to see him like this, but until Evo was found, she knew he wouldn't think any differently.

He turned and took both of her hands in his, a desperation in his eyes that made Lacy's stomach tighten. "I want to tell you something," he said and the crease in his brow told her that it wasn't something good.

"When I was down there, I saw something that scared me. You can't begin to know how horrible that place is and it does things to your mind; things that you are convinced are real. I saw you... You'd died in a fire, or so I thought—it felt so... " He closed his eyes for a second and exhaled sharply. "I held you, thinking you were dead and in that moment I'd never felt pain like it." He hesitated, "What I'm trying to say is... It made me realize how much you mean to me."

Oh, God. The breath she'd been holding left her lungs in a rush and she tried to stop her hands from trembling. Her heart sped up as she looked into his eyes, which were illuminated by the soft moonlight. She'd never felt this way about anyone before, never let anyone close to her heart, so how he'd managed to find his way through so quickly she had no idea.

He leaned in and placed his lips on hers. She responded as he placed both arms around her waist and pulled her towards him. She slid along the bench until there was no space between them and she was encapsulated within his strong arms. Her arms went around his neck and as he broke away from his sweet, tender kiss and buried his face in her neck, his warm breath on her skin made her shiver.

They embraced each other tightly. She had no idea what this meant for them, had no idea if any of this was even possible, but right now it felt very real.

She felt his lips move lightly on her neck and realized that he'd begun to kiss her; small, soft kisses which made her flesh tingle. He began to move up towards her ear and she suddenly lost all of the strength she needed to hold her head up, leaving it to flop to the side. He nibbled her lobe, the sound of those tantalizingly wet kisses, combined with the sting of the cold air made her whole body prickle with a need that was overwhelming.

His name left her mouth on a whisper and she ran her fingers through his hair while he continued his soft torment underneath her chin and around the other side. When his mouth finally reached her, she kissed him slowly at first, but then it turned into something more and she was filled with a desperation that she'd never felt before. Mouths wide, tongues frantically duelling with each other, this was nothing like how they'd kissed last night before they'd made love, this was full of smoldering passion and if she didn't keep control of things they'd end up having sex right here under her kitchen window and that was definitely not a good idea.

Somehow, through the fire that had now ignited her whole body, she managed to pull herself away from him.

"Bad idea," she said through panted breaths. Her voice came out in a shaky whisper.

Michael's eyes were heavy as he looked at her. He swallowed hard and leaned his forehead against hers, clearly struggling with the same internal battle as she was. "Thank God one of us was thinking straight." He smiled. "That could have gotten awkward."

They both laughed and Lacy leaned into him as he twisted himself around and tucked her under his arm. He placed a small kiss on top of her head and heaved a sigh.

She knew what that sigh was for and it pained her to think about what was happening.

She was falling hard, for someone who wasn't even human and may not be around for much longer. Right now, she wouldn't allow herself to think of the future and what might happen to him. Right now they were together. So instead, she would embrace what they had for however long they had it.

Like Michael, she didn't know what he was, and was scared to think about that too deeply, but she knew deep down in her heart that whatever he was, he wasn't a monster like those other things. There was no way. Alethia was right: it wasn't evil inside his heart.

"We should get back inside." Michael's voice vibrated in her ear. "Alethia is going to see her father and I should talk with her before she leaves."

After things had calmed down, Michael had hardly spoken after nearly suffocating Jaret. And even though Alethia's ex-husband was still wary of him, he'd said he understood why Michael had reacted the way he had. Jaret had even offered to take him back, but Michael had refused, saying that he needed more information about Alethia's ring and where Evo would have been sent to before attempting to go looking for him.

"Jaret's offer still stands. He wants to help." Lacy sat herself up.

Michael laughed softly. "After I almost killed the guy? Why would he want to help me?"

"Because he's a good guy. And Alethia seems to be good at persuading him to do things." She smiled.

"What's with those two anyway?" He reached up and tucked a stray hair behind her ear.

"He's her ex-husband." She saw his eyebrow rise.

"You're kidding me? Those two?"

She nodded. "They seem to have a bit of a love/hate relationship. I think Jaret still has a thing for her."

"Well, he's a brave man. I can't imagine it's easy being married to someone like—"

"Actually," a voice said from over by the house. Lacy noticed Michael's eyes widen as they flicked passed her shoulder. She whipped her head around to see Alethia stepping out from the back door, "it's more like the other way around. You ever dated an Incubus?"

Michael straightened as Alethia stepped towards them. Lacy flicked her gaze between them both and the awkward look on his face made Lacy smile.

He cleared his throat. "I didn't mean—"

"That's okay," the deity interrupted, "I understand why you would say it and the answer is no, it's not easy being married to me, what with the powerful, all-seeing parents and all. . . But I can assure you, it was no picnic being married to a half man/half demon hybrid with an attitude problem and a severe sex addiction."

Michael laughed. "Fair enough."

"I just came to tell you that I'll be leaving for Asirus as soon as I've helped Jaret find a place to stay."

"He's welcome to stay at my apartment at the university," Michael offered.

Alethia looked at him like he'd grown a second head. "Are you sure?"

He smiled at her. "Consider it my apology. Least I can do."

"I'll tell him. Thank you, Michael."

"No need to thank me. I appreciate what he did. Anyway, I won't be there." He reached for Lacy's hand. "I'm not leaving Lacy here on her own."

Lacy beamed at the thought of Michael wanting to protect her. It meant more to her now that she knew how he felt about her. And she was eager for them to be alone. After everything that had happened today she was pretty exhausted, plus she wanted to help take Michael's mind off things by finishing what they'd started a few moments ago.

"I think that's wise. Look after your woman," Alethia replied with a knowing grin as her eyes flicked between the two of them. *Your woman*, Lacy thought. She liked the sound of that. "I'll let you know as soon as I have any information."

"Appreciate it," Michael said. "And Alethia, thanks for all that you're doing."

"No need to thank me. Evo's my friend too. I feel partly responsible for what happened to him." Her eyes dropped to the floor for a second and then she straightened and turned to leave.

"Oh, and yes. . . Jaret does still want me," she said over her shoulder and glanced back with a smirk before disappearing inside.

CHAPTER TWENTY-FOUR

After Alethia and Jaret had left, Lacy had made food and she and Michael had enjoyed it with a *small* glass of wine. The normality of sitting with him, eating pizza and laughing and joking was nice. It filled her with hope that they'd somehow be okay. She tried not to let him think too much about Evo, talking about her time back in England and telling him how she'd love to go and visit one day, and it seemed to have worked. She'd even had him smiling.

Lacy had finished filling the dishwasher after she'd quickly tidied up the rest of the kitchen, and was wiping around the sink when she glanced up at the window and saw someone standing in her back yard. No, wait! Not in her backyard. . . She turned her head to see the figure of a young man, dressed in casual jeans and a black and white high school jacket, standing in front of the kitchen door. Her breath caught and she blinked a couple of times hoping that it would just go away. He reached one arm out towards her and mouthed something that looked like the word "leave" before dropping his arm again.

Since her experience with the woman at the warehouse, she was glad of the explanation as to why she'd been seeing things, glad she wasn't actually crazy and knew that it was something she was going to have to learn to live with. But they were still going to scare the shit out of her, even though she knew they weren't a threat.

From this moment on, I'm not going to let them faze me. She shivered, straightened her shoulders and whispered, "You leave," before she put her hand right through his body and opened the door.

He disappeared.

She felt a little proud of herself for not freaking out, but decided not to mention it, determined not to let anything disturb their night.

She joined Michael who was sitting on the sofa with his laptop on his knee. Lacy had grabbed the leftover wine on her way out of the kitchen and topped up his glass which was on the sideboard next to where he was sitting and joined him on the sofa.

He glanced up at her. "Thanks."

She leaned back, glass in hand and pulled her legs up next to her. She placed her head on Michael's shoulder and he kissed the top of it through her hair. It was crazy how close they'd become. She felt like she'd known him all her life and was amazed at how comfortable they both were at showing their affections to one another.

If only things were different.

She glanced at the computer screen which had lots of tabs open, the one on the screen now had different pictures of ancient looking rings, all with different types of jewels in them, as Michael scrolled up the page.

"Found anything?" Lacy asked.

"Nothing yet. I've been scrolling through this lot for the past ten minutes and nothing looks the same as the ring Evo had. I honestly don't think it's going to turn up anywhere on the internet. Our only hope is Alethia, but if her father still refuses to talk to her. . . " He huffed, "then I don't know what we'll do."

"I hope she manages to sway him, but he was quite insistent. Alethia told me earlier that he'd ordered her not to get involved because anything she did would reflect on the gods as a whole. But I don't think she's listening." Lacy yawned and then took a sip of wine.

Michael closed the lid on his laptop and placed it on the floor. "You're tired. You should get some rest. I have a feeling that tomorrow is going to be a long day." He lifted his arm to invite her under it and took her glass with his free hand, reaching over and placing it down next to his. She snuggled into him, her arm resting over his stomach. She thought she felt him sniff her hair and the simple gesture seemed to ignite that familiar heat inside her from earlier. There was no way she was going to sleep without spending some much needed time with him first.

"I'm not interested in sleep yet," she said as she sat up a little and brought her face to his.

Michael pierced her with his icy blue gaze. He smiled at her, eyes narrowing as he lowered them to her mouth. She guessed he knew what she meant as he moved towards her and claimed her with his soft lips. This is what she'd been waiting for, and now they were alone there was no time to waste. She kissed him back and before she knew it Michael had scooped her up and was now lowering her down on the sofa. He followed, removing his navy sweater and dropping it to the floor as he continued to caress her mouth with his. He lay his body on top of hers and, once again, she melted into him, losing herself into his fervent kisses.

Hands were everywhere: his stroking down her sides, hers in his hair, then he slid one of his up her top and stroked up her stomach before cupping her breast. He kissed her neck, her ear, every inch of her skin with that same desperate hunger that she'd felt from him outside.

He pushed her top up and she helped him lift it over her head and heard it drop to the floor. Her skin prickled at the feel of his warm body touching hers and she ran her hands all over his hard, muscled back.

Last time they'd made love, she thought it would be their last so right now, she would savor every touch, every kiss, every whisper from him until their troubles temporarily melted away, leaving only the two of them enjoying each other, embracing the moments they had together because who knows what was waiting around the corner.

The demons, the monsters, they could all wait. Right now was only for her and Michael.

* * *

As the hot water ran down her body, Lacy closed her eyes and let out a contented sigh. It was hard to stay away from Michael right now, especially knowing he was lying in her bed naked, but she'd forced herself away from him to grab a quick shower. Somehow, even after everything that had happened over the last few weeks, she felt happy. Though her world had changed drastically and she'd survived a kidnapping from an evil demon, she couldn't stop smiling as she thought about the gorgeous man that was across the hall waiting for her to return.

She rinsed the last of the conditioner from her hair and turned the water off. She leaned over and grabbed the towel from the hook on the wall, wrapped it around her body and tucked the corner in under her arm. She towel dried her hair and picked up her brush from the counter. The mirror had steamed up so she went and opened the small window on the other side of the room. When she stood back in front of the mirror, she leaned across and wiped the condensation away with her hand and began to brush her hair.

She couldn't help thinking about poor Evo and hoped to God he was okay. When Alethia had first mentioned what the ring could do, she didn't really think about it properly because she was too busy worrying about him and Evo using it. But now that she was, she really feared for Evo. And knew that if anything happened to him, Michael would be ruined. She really hoped Alethia could find out where he would have gone, or at least some information that would help lead Michael to him.

She finished with her hair and decided to brush her teeth. She pulled out the drawer from the sideboard next to her and grabbed her toothpaste and brush and as her gaze returned to the mirror, she was shocked to see someone standing behind her in the reflection. She gasped and put her hand over her mouth.

Not again! Honestly... Isn't there some kind of signal you can give me instead of scaring me half to death?

Lacy spun around but there was no one there. She turned back to the mirror where the blond haired woman was still standing behind her.

Then she suddenly remembered the dream she'd had, or was it a dream? This same woman had tried to communicate with her last night while she'd slept.

Lacy didn't panic. Even though her heart was pounding like it was about to leave her chest, she knew the spirit wasn't there to harm her. Just like her encounter earlier in the kitchen, she wasn't scared.

"Who are you?" Lacy asked in a soft voice.

From what she could see the woman was dressed in a long sleeve top with a navy colored neck scarf, both were torn just like in her dream. Her hair was scruffy, her skin pasty with a nasty looking bruise on the side of her mouth. Her head was lowered and her mouth began to move.

She was trying to say something, but Lacy couldn't make it out. "What do you want? What are you trying to tell me?" The woman's mouth was moving, but there was no sound. Lacy stared through the mirror. "I can't understand you. What is it?"

The woman began to look distressed and lifted her arm and pointed at Lacy. She was still trying to say something; it looked like she was mouthing one word over and over. Her hands lifted to her head and she grabbed her hair either side with her fists, her mouth opening wider.

Now Lacy began to feel scared. She started to back away from the mirror, but the woman carried on, desperately trying to communicate with her.

Lacy couldn't believe what happened next. Her own hand began to move on its own. She tried to stop but had no control over what was happening. The more she fought against whatever it was that was moving her hand the harder it became. She watched as she picked up the tube of toothpaste from the side of the sink.

What's happening to me?

Looking at her own arm rising toward the mirror when she wasn't doing it, Lacy held her breath. The woman was still beside her in the reflection, but her mouth was now closed and her stare was wide. She was no longer trying to speak; instead she was using another way to communicate with her.

Lacy's hand squeezed the tube and after swallowing hard in an attempt to lubricate her throat which had dried out through fear, she watched herself write, spelling something out in white toothpaste. But when her hand fell back down as though the ghost had let go of her arm, she was immediately filled with dread as she read the word that she'd unwillingly spelled out:

RUN.

Lacy inhaled sharply and the woman on the other side of the glass disappeared.

Another memory from last night's dream flashed through her mind: *HE'S COMING.*

She saw something move out of the corner of her eye and began to tremble. She didn't want to turn her head to see what it was because she knew, down to the pit of her stomach that something bad was about to happen. She forced herself to move her head and saw a thick black mist coming through the window.

She froze.

The mist flew towards her and she saw some kind of face in it. "Michael!" she shouted.

She grabbed the door handle, but when she went to turn it, it was locked. She hadn't locked the door. How was it locked?

"Michael! HELP ME!" she cried as she continued to frantically twist the door knob, but it was no use. It wasn't budging.

She watched in horror as the mist began to climb up her leg. It twisted around her thigh and slowly crawled up her stomach. *Oh, God!*

What was happening? She went to shout again but her voice was suddenly cut off. She felt pressure around her throat, like someone had their hands around it, choking the air from her lungs.

Her hands went to her throat, feeling for whatever it was that was constricting her airways. There was nothing there. She couldn't breathe. *NO! I'm going to die right here in my own bathroom. And Michael...*

She stumbled backwards, falling against the wall. Her hands still rubbing at her throat as she tried desperately to find what was suffocating her. Her arms began to flail with panic.

She heard Michael's voice on the other side of the door. "Lacy what's wrong?"

The door handle twisted back and forth as Michael tried to open it.

She tried to shout "Help" but it was no use. When she opened her mouth, nothing came out.

Next minute the mist began to crawl inside her mouth and before she could do anything else her vision began to flash and fade like what happened to the reel of tape in a projector when it had reached the end. That was all she remembered before she blacked out.

* * *

"Lacy! Lacy!"

Michael threw his whole weight at the bathroom door, but it didn't budge. Lacy had gone quiet on the other side and he feared that something terrible had happened to her.

Fuck! What the hell was going on?

"LACY!" he called out as he wiggled the handle and pounded the door again.

Nothing.

"Jesus Christ. Lacy! Are you okay?"

That familiar heat began to rise up through his body as he threw his shoulder into the door again. He looked around for something he could use to break it down but couldn't see anything, so he thought taking a run at it might do the trick. He was terrified of what he might find on the other side of the door, but had to get in there somehow.

He was just backing away when the handle moved. He froze. Lacy's voice sounded from the other side.

"Michael! Michael. . . I can't open the door, Michael."

His breath rushed from his lungs with the relief of hearing her voice. *Thank God.*

"Hang on. I'm just going to try and—"

The door opened. Though, how she'd managed it, he had no idea. *What the fuck?* There was no way that door was opening a minute ago, so how in the hell did she just. . . ?

Lacy stepped out from the bathroom. She looked. . . She looked fine.

Michael's brows pulled tight. "Jesus! Lacy. . . are you okay?" He took hold of her shoulders and bent to look at her, checking for any injuries. "I thought something terrible had happened." In fact, he was convinced of it. Her cries for help had made his blood run cold, and yet, here she was, calm as anything.

She blinked and looked at him briefly before her gaze drifted past his shoulder. "I'm fine now. I just panicked because I got locked in."

What?

"You just panicked?" Michael couldn't quite believe what he was hearing. All of that was just her panicking. *Fucking hell.* "I thought you were being attacked or something."

She shook her head ever so slightly. "No. Just panicked. I need to lie down. I'm tired."

He watched in stunned silence as she walked past him towards her bedroom and he followed her inside, still very confused about what had just happened. As he walked behind her, she lowered her towel and let it slide down her body until it hit the floor. She walked naked over to the bed, pulled back the covers and climbed inside. She lay down on her side facing the window, pulled the covers up over her shoulders and closed her eyes.

Michael walked to the other side of the bed and climbed in beside her. "Are you sure you're ok?" he asked again, wondering why she hadn't even dried her hair. She seemed distant. But he'd seen her have a panic attack before and it wasn't pleasant. Perhaps it had taken a lot out of her, or maybe she felt embarrassed. He was sure she'd be fine in the morning.

"Yes. I just want to sleep," she replied softly.

He lay on his side next to her and wrapped his arm around her waist, pulling her close. For a moment he thought he felt her body tense up, but ignored it. He lifted his head and gently kissed her shoulder. "Good night, Lacy."

She didn't answer.

* * *

Michael awoke to bright sun shining on his face. The drapes were open and with his eyes squinted, he saw that the covers were pulled back and there was an empty space where Lacy had been. She must have opened the drapes when she'd gotten up, but he couldn't figure why she would if he was still sleeping.

He stretched his arm above his head and rolled onto his back. He'd just started to yawn when it was cut off as he jumped out of his skin.

"Jesus, Lacy!" She was standing at his side of the bed looking down at him, dressed in her gray sweats and a plain, blue T-shirt. Her eyes looked glazed over. She was still acting strange.

"I was just waiting for you to wake." She sounded strange too, and for a moment he thought she might be sleepwalking.

"Lacy, are you ok?"

"Yes, I'm fine now." She moved away from the bed and left the room.

"Shit!"

Michael jumped out of bed, threw on his camo pants and quickly followed her. By the time he'd gotten into the hall, she was already out of sight, but as he walked towards the front door, he slowed, silencing his bare footsteps and listening intently to the voice that was coming from the living room.

She was singing—well, humming—something he didn't recognize.

He stepped into the room to see that she was sitting on the sofa, with her hands on her knees, staring vacantly at the opposite wall.

Michael's stomach sank. This wasn't right. *What's wrong with her?*

"Lacy?" He kept his voice quiet. But she didn't answer. It was like she hadn't heard him. In fact, she didn't even seem aware that he was standing there.

He heard footsteps walking up the garden path and quickly went to the door. He glanced through the small window.

Jaret.

Michael opened it quietly and put his finger to his own mouth. "Shh," he whispered. "Come in."

After Jaret walked into the hall, Michael closed the door softly after him.

"What's going on?" Jaret asked, keeping his voice low.

"Listen."

After a couple of seconds Jaret's eyebrows rose. "Nice voice."

Michael shook his head. "No. She's acting strange. I woke to find her standing over me, staring. I'm really worried." He pulled Jaret to the living room doorway. "She's been sitting there like that for the past ten minutes."

"What dya think's wrong with 'er?" Jaret went to walk in but Michael caught hold of his arm.

"Wait!"

Michael slowly walked over to where she was sitting; being careful not to startle her just in case she *was* sleepwalking. He knew that you weren't supposed to let the person wake too suddenly because it could scare them, so he gently knelt down in front of her.

"Lacy?" he whispered while taking hold of her arms. "Wake up, Lacy. Look at me."

Still nothing.

Michael ran his hands up her arms and was surprised at how rigid she was. He swallowed hard and shook her gently. "Lacy, baby. . . is everything okay?"

She went silent. Michael paused. The eerie way her eyes were staring out was unsettling. He had a very bad feeling and was growing more anxious every minute she remained in that state.

"La–"

Her head jerked and her eyes pinned him with a fierce stare. "NOOOOOO!" she shrieked, startling Michael and making him jump up on instinct. "Fuck!" he gasped. But went straight back to her, pulling her up by her arms. "Lacy! What the fuck's wrong with you?"

"GET. OFF. ME!" she screamed at him, her eyes were vicious like she was looking at someone who was trying to hurt her. He would never hurt her. His spine went icy cold. Her arms began to flail around and he had a hard time keeping hold of her. She broke away and began punching his chest. "GO!"

Michael backed away from her, completely shocked by what was happening. Jaret immediately took his place.

She was breathing heavily, her chest pumping up and down violently. His hand went to his mouth and he watched with despair as, somehow, Jaret managed to calm her.

What the hell? Why was she okay with Jaret?

Something had gone very wrong between last night when they'd made love and now. He scrubbed his hand through his hair and thought back to what had happened last night in the bathroom.

"Michael! Help me!"

He remembered how scared she'd sounded behind that door. That wasn't just a panic attack.

"Michael! Help me!"

Fuck that. She'd sounded terrified.

His whole body buzzed with a heavy feeling of dread as his mind replayed what had happened. Then he was out of the door and flying up the hallway. He threw the door to the bathroom open and... *What is that smell?* His hand covered his nose and he heard Jaret call his name from down the hall.

What he saw when he turned around made him gasp. He stepped back.

The word RUN was spelt out in—what was that?—toothpaste?

Jaret appeared at the door. He must have seen the look on Michael's face. "What's wrong?" His eyes followed Michael's and when he saw the mirror he cursed.

"Something tried to warn her," Michael told him, closing his eyes and dropping his head. He thought back to what Lacy had said about the spirit that had helped her in the warehouse.

"What dya mean?" Jaret asked.

"Lacy has some kind of ESP," he explained. "It seems that spirits can communicate with her. I don't really know much about it, but something has helped her before. When she was kidnapped." Michael's eyes darted to Jaret. "Where is she?"

"I left her in exactly the same position she was in when we first went in there. She's just sitting quietly staring again."

"She called for help last night. She was trapped in the bathroom and it sounded like she was being attacked or something. But when she came out she said she'd just panicked because she was locked in. After that she seemed distant. I should have known something wasn't right. I. . . "

The thought of anything hurting her made his body hum, that same sensation he was now so used to feeling when he was angry. He remembered it happening last night, but had managed to calm himself. If only he'd let it happen then maybe he'd have caught whatever it was that had hurt Lacy. Heat began to rise through his body. He was going to lose it. . . He had to get a grip of himself and focus.

Michael inhaled deeply through the anguish that was almost suffocating him. "Something was in here with her last night, Jaret." It killed him to think that he was right, but it was the only explanation for what had happened. "I think there's something inside of her."

CHAPTER TWENTY-FIVE

The burning was excruciating.

Her whole body was on fire.

Lacy had tried to get Michael away from her—tried her hardest to fight what was now controlling her body so that she could get him away from the evil that was inside her. And for a moment she'd found the strength, but the evil had fought harder.

To see the pain on Michael's face when she'd screamed at him had almost killed her. He didn't know. He couldn't know. But she had to try and make him get away from her.

She was trapped.

Her body, her actions, they were no longer her own.

It didn't matter how hard she tried to fight now. The evil had locked her down.

She thought she'd died last night. The suffocation, the burning, she thought she'd reached the end of her life. But that would have been too kind. The bastard that had latched itself onto her body was keeping her awake so she could feel and witness everything.

Dying would have been easier.

Her rapid breaths echoed inside her ears. She was confused, scared, hurting in ways she'd never experienced before and there was nothing she could do.

Quiet laughter rumbled through her ears. The demon. . . it was laughing at her. It knew what it was doing: torturing her, making her feel and see everything, and the pain. . . the pain was extreme. She had no choice but to bear it; the demon wouldn't let it be any other way.

And Michael. . .

He'd been completely unaware of her body standing over him as he'd slept peacefully. She'd feared the demon was about to hurt him, so she'd screamed as loud as she could but her cries had gone unheard. When he'd awoken to see her standing there, she'd called out to him again, trying desperately to warn him but he'd heard nothing. Then she'd watched herself leave the bedroom and walk down the hallway. It hadn't been her making her body move, just like it wasn't her choosing to sit on the sofa now.

Michael had left the room. *Thank God he's left the room.*

She needed him to leave—couldn't bear to see his pain when he eventually realized what had happened... Because he would—if he hadn't already.

Oh, no! He's coming back!

"NOOOO! LEAVE!" she cried out so loudly she heard her voice distort, but her desperation wasn't enough. Michael couldn't hear her plea. Nobody heard her.

Not true. The demon heard her.

Outside, her body was still, but inside she was frantic.

She looked at Michael as he approached her. He gripped her arms—she felt it, oh, thank God she could feel him—and his voice was a distant echo that she could only just make out.

"I know you're not Lacy! What do you want?" She heard him shout.

He knew. Of course he did.

All she could do was observe his agony as though she was looking through the eyes of a mask. Her body wasn't her own anymore and it pained her to not be able to reach out to him.

She wept uncontrollably.

The deep laughter started again.

"You BASTARD!" she cried, but then noticed Michael's face. He looked alarmed as he stared at her now. His beautiful pale blue eyes were locked onto hers and she swore she could see slight, unshed tears in them.

She soon realized why he looked the way he did. The demon was laughing at Michael not her; not just in her head. She heard it, but it was much louder this time and sounded like her voice. *It was.* The demon was using her own voice to communicate with Michael and Jaret—to mock them.

She still felt the sting of agony rushing through her body, so much worse now, but being able to see and hear Michael, and not be able to speak to him—to reach out to him—was worse than the physical pain.

"Let her go." She heard Michael's demand. "I'll fucking make you suffer for this."

She felt his grip tighten on her arms.

No Michael. Don't make it angry.

She saw Jaret reach out and place his hand on Michael's arm and she heard his muffled voice, like she was listening under water. "Don't," he told him. "She'll feel that."

Michael's eyes widened and he immediately let go of her, pulling his own arms away in a panic.

NO! Please, don't let go. I'd rather you hurt me than let go.

Knowing that she could feel Michael's touch, Lacy tried to move her arms so she could reach out to him. She used all the strength she could muster, but the bastard was too strong.

More laughter.

"Seems your woman here has more determination than previously thought," she heard the demon say. Michael stared at her with such fierce hatred that for a moment she had to look away. Even though she knew his anger wasn't directed towards her, it was still *her* that his eyes seemed to burn with great hostility.

It was hard to witness.

"She's a feisty thing. I'm using a lot of my strength to keep her restrained in here."

Michael made a move towards her, but Jaret held him back. "Ignore it," Jaret almost growled as he appeared to use all of his strength to hold Michael's arms. "It wants you to react this way. That demon would enjoy nuffin' more than for you to strike out."

Michael!

She hated seeing him suffer like he was. She imagined he was used to being in control whenever he was faced with a possession, so to have to hold back like he was, so as not to hurt her, must be hard for him.

"What do you want from me?" Michael asked through gritted teeth. She noticed a slight change in his irises where a white glow had begun to replace the blue.

She dropped her gaze, refusing to look at him while he was hurting so much. She felt she was to blame for all of this. It was her stupid fault that she was now a prisoner inside her own skin. If she'd have just paid more attention to the warning signs she'd been so blatantly given instead of trying to ignore her *ability*—she refused to call it a *gift*—or if she'd have mentioned it to Michael then perhaps she could have prevented it.

Her train of thought was interrupted by the demon that was now laughing tauntingly at Michael again. "You misunderstand the situation," her own voice echoed. "We don't want anything *from* you. We just want *you*."

Lacy gasped.

NO!

CHAPTER TWENTY-SIX

Michael was silent.

His mouth felt dry. His head was ringing. And his body buzzed with the rage that he was fighting to keep under control through fear of hurting Lacy. The last thing he needed was to let loose on the bastard demon that possessed her body. He had to keep a lid on things.

He knew Varesh would retaliate after what had happened in the pit so he should have kept a closer eye on Lacy. He mentally tore himself to shreds for not keeping her safe. He shouldn't have let her out of his sight for a moment. But that was all it had been: a moment. Now she was suffering and it was all because of him. He'd foolishly dragged her into a war between creatures she never even knew existed a few weeks ago.

He had to make it right.

His mind went to his friend. If Evo was here he'd be calm, composed. He'd know what to do. But he wasn't was he? Instead, he was somewhere dealing with his own hell.

Man, he had royally fucked up.

He stared into Lacy's pale green eyes, eyes that he'd been lost in and had gazed back at him adoringly as they'd lain in each other's arms only a few hours ago. But now they looked at him with repulsion so palpable it turned his stomach.

He closed his eyes. *Lacy.*

A hand on his shoulder made him open them again to see Jaret leaning towards him. He spoke quietly into his ear.

"Alethia will be 'ere any minute. I messaged 'er to let 'er know what's goin' on."

Michael nodded. He doubted she could do anything to help. There was no way they could exorcise the demon out of

Lacy because humans didn't usually survive the process, and if they did they were a mess. The only way she would live through what had happened was if the demon left of its own accord and that wasn't going to happen.

Unless he let them take him.

"What if I agree to go with you? What then? Will you let her go?" Michael saw Jaret's head whip around in surprise.

"You're not serious—?"

"What else do you suggest?" Michael snapped. Jaret remained silent, his brows pulled tight. No. There wasn't any other solution was there? Varesh knew how Michael felt about Lacy and was using it to get what he wanted. The bastard knew he wouldn't let her die and that this was the only way it could win: to trade her life, for his death.

A whirring sound came from by the living room door as a cold draft swept through the room. When Michael looked up, a dark shadow had begun to form over by the fireplace.

Alethia.

When she appeared she looked straight over at Lacy and paused, her eyes full of sorrow. Then she looked at Michael and flicked her head, calling him over. "Jaret, watch her?" she said before walking out of the room.

When Michael joined her, he noticed she looked troubled. Her eyes dropped to the floor and she exhaled sharply.

"What is it?" Michael wasn't sure he wanted to know.

"I know you won't want to hear this right now, but I have some news about Evo."

Michael swallowed hard. "What Alethia? Just tell me." He hadn't meant to snap at her, but, thankfully, she didn't seem too bothered by it.

"After I'd managed to convince my father to talk to me, I found out more information about the ring. I wanted to come and tell you straight away but my father wouldn't allow me to leave. He's pretty determined to stop me from getting further involved in whatever this thing is between you and Varesh."

Michael began to feel impatient. "Evo. What about Evo?"

"I'm getting to that," she said in a harsh tone.

Michael took a deep breath. Biting Alethia's head off would achieve nothing. He needed to remember what she'd already done for them and all by her own choice too. "I'm sorry. Go on."

She nodded her head in acceptance of his apology before she went on to explain. "There is a prison, a dungeon deep in the underworld, called Tartarus. It's a place where the supernatural version of the criminally insane go: demons, monsters, even gods who have committed horrific crimes. Tartarus houses every single creature you can think of and more.

"But that's not all. There is another part of the prison, a dungeon that houses the most malevolent sinners. The ones that are so evil that even the devil himself wants them locked further away than anything else to rot for all eternity."

Her brows twisted together until her face only displayed pure anguish. "That place is called Mathrah. And that's where Evo is."

Suddenly, Michael felt like he'd been hit around the head with a lump hammer; unable to move or speak. He stepped back until his back hit the wall and he could go no further.

His buddy, his pal, was in the worst place imaginable. Worse than anything Michael could have thought of. He nearly went down, bowled over by the burning fear that he would never see his best friend again. "Jesus Christ," he managed to say, his voice more a whisper.

"I hope *he* can help us," Alethia said as she walked towards him and placed her hand gently on his shoulder, squeezing it a little in acknowledgement of his grief. "Because right now. . . I don't know who else can."

Michael could tell she was hurting too. Evo had become a friend to her as well and she wanted to find him as much as he did.

His head began to spin. How would he find him? And even if he did, how would he free him. Assuming there was enough of his soul left to free.

This new information, on top of what was happening to Lacy in the room on the other side of the wall that was now holding him up, was too much to handle. He had to do something. He had to make it right.

He looked into Alethia's unusual golden eyes. She was strong, more powerful than he'd ever seen a woman. Yet she couldn't help them out of this. With her father refusing to help, he was all on his own.

He knew what he had to do. He couldn't allow Lacy to suffer any more than she already had. He'd nearly lost her once when Varesh had abducted her, he wasn't about to lose her now.

Alethia's despair over Evo quickly turned to concern. She knew what he'd decided. He hadn't needed to say the words as she'd seen them in his mind. She began to shake her head. "No. I won't let you destroy yourself like that. Lacy and Evo need you."

"That's why I have to do this." He took both of her hands in his. "Don't you see? If we exorcise that demon from Lacy she'll almost certainly die. I won't allow that to happen, Alethia. She means too much to me." He inhaled deeply, then blew out his breath on a shaky exhale. The thought of Lacy dying was too hard to even allow it to enter his mind. "Nothing they do to me down there can kill me because I'm already dead."

"And Evo?"

"If there's a chance of me finding him at all then it has to be while I'm in Hell." He'd already thought about how being down there would mean he had a better chance at finding this place, Mathrah. Knowing the name of the place where Evo was being held was a start. Plus, Varesh had wanted him to join them, whoever *they* were. He didn't know what that demon was up to but he seemed to have plans for Michael. He doubted he would spend his time being tortured like the last time.

This was his only chance to save both of the people he... *loved?*

Oh, shit! Do I love her?

He wasn't sure he was even capable of such a thing. But it sure felt like it.

Michael felt Alethia's hands tighten around his. "You are," she said softly.

"Are you in my head again?"

"I'm sorry." She smiled at him. "But I'm right. You *are* capable of love. I can feel that that's what's in your heart. Look, I don't know what's going on with you, but I do know that you returned to earth for a reason. I believe that. I sensed something good in you the moment we met at the airport.

"Fate, Michael, that's what brought you back. You do believe in fate don't you?"

He thought back to the conversation he and Lacy'd had not so long ago and smiled a little. He nodded his head.

"Good, because I know of three very powerful females who would be hard to convince otherwise."

Michael raised his eyebrow in a questioning glance.

"My great-great aunts, The Fates," she explained casually, like it was perfectly normal to have powerful goddess' for relatives. Well, he supposed it was for her.

"I want to love her." He felt his chest tighten around his heart, or was it that his heart had swelled to twice its size? Either way he knew what he felt for Lacy was deeper than anything he'd ever felt before, in this existence or his last. Whether or not it was actually love, he didn't really care.

"Then isn't that your answer?"

They both stood in silence for a few moments until Jaret's head popped around the door. "Uh, she's making some strange noises in 'ere. I think you should come back in."

Michael rushed away from Alethia but before he went back into the living room he turned to her. "I need you to promise me something." There was no more time. He had to make the deal and he had to do it now. "Will you make sure she's doing okay? I mean, after I've gone? Check on her from time to time for me?"

Alethia didn't say a word, but it was clear from her face that she wasn't totally on board with the idea of him making the trade. After a moment of silence, she nodded.

He let out a sigh and grabbed her hand. "Thank you." Knowing Lacy had someone to look out for her would appease him a little. He had no idea what his *fate* was, or where—even *if*—his future would lie, as long as she was safe, that was all that mattered to him now.

"Michael! You need to get in 'ere mate."

Michael didn't like the concern in Jaret's voice and rushed into the room. What he saw made his stomach turn. Jaret was battling with Lacy to try and stop her from clawing at her arms, but he was losing the fight. She had blood and open scratches trailing down her forearms.

"Shit!" Michael knelt down in front of her and while Jaret grabbed one arm, he grabbed the other and together they managed to stop her. "Stop it you fucking asshole. Just STOP!"

When her eyes met his, he gasped. Crimson had begun to replace the green of her irises and she looked at him with such ferocity that it caused him to step back a little.

"Oh, by the way, don't worry that your girlfriend is unconscious in here. She's aware of everything that's going on. Wouldn't want her missing all the fun now would we?"

No! "You bastard! I'm gonna fucking kill you," Michael growled

Lacy fought against both men, but they managed to keep her arms spread enough so she couldn't do any more damage. "Alethia, I need something to restrain her with." No sooner had he said the words than she'd disappeared into thin air.

"Bloody 'ell, she's strong. . . Whoa!" Lacy tried to bite Jaret while he wrestled with her arm. He struggled to push her snapping mouth back away from him. "Shit!"

Alethia appeared with a pair of silver handcuffs and a piece of rope. She rushed towards them and climbed behind Lacy on the couch.

Michael saw Jaret eye her with one of his brows raised. "Should I arsk?" The guy nodded towards the cuffs.

"Do you really need to?" She rolled her eyes. "The sheriff's office, where else?" She helped them to pull Lacy's arms around her back.

After Alethia had secured the cuffs around Lacy's wrists, Michael tied the rope around her arms just to make sure it held, and also to stop the cuffs from cutting into her skin. She still thrashed her body and was now spitting at him.

"Stop hurting her asshole! I'll do the fucking deal. I'll go with you!"

Lacy stilled immediately.

She sat panting along with the rest of them; her eyes—well, the demon's eyes—lifted to meet Michael's. They were full-on crimson now, as red as blood, and his stomach tightened to see her that way.

Alethia and Jaret stood either side of him while he remained crouched in front of her.

"I'll trade. Me for her. But you leave her alive and unharmed."

He felt a hand on his shoulder and looked up to see Alethia looking at him with unshed tears.

The tension was thick in the room as he waited for the bastard to speak.

"Deal," was the demon's only response before Lacy closed her eyes and tilted her head back.

"Wait!" He couldn't leave like this. Not without saying good bye.

Lacy's neck straightened and her crimson eyes returned to his while the demon sat waiting for Michael to speak.

He felt his heart racing. It was a strange feeling. Not like anything he'd ever felt before. "Before you take me, I want to speak to her."

That same sadistic laughter that made his skin crawl started up again from deep in Lacy's throat.

Michael was done playing games with this asshole. "I'm not going anywhere with you until I speak to her." He turned his head to look at Alethia and Jaret. "Alone."

They immediately left the room and closed the door behind them. Michael turned to Lacy. "NOW! Asshole."

The demon leered at him. "Five minutes. That's all you get."

Before Michael could argue, Lacy closed her eyes and remained still for a couple of seconds. Michael leaned into her and placed his hand on her knee. In the next instant her eyes flew open and she dragged air deep into her lungs as though she'd been struggling to breathe underwater and had just reached the surface. It startled him, but his hands flew to each side of her face. He held her head and looked into her eyes.

"Lacy?" The crimson was gone, replaced by her own wonderfully green colored irises.

"NO! Michael!" she gasped.

His arms flew around her back and he quickly freed her from the rope and then the cuffs with the key Alethia had given him. She flung her arms around him and sobbed into his shoulder. He held her tightly, dragging her scent deep down into his lungs where he planned to keep it for as long as possible.

"Don't do it. Please. . . Michael, don't do this," she begged. Her breath on his neck was like soft kisses on his bare skin. He fought back his anguish, locking his teeth together so hard he was in fear of them crumbling under the weight of his bite. "Please," she repeated.

He kissed her on the mouth, her chin, her cheeks, holding her face in his hands and tasting her salty tears. How could he do this? How could he find the strength to leave her?

When he pulled back and saw the tears that he'd just tasted trailing down her cheeks, his heart shattered into pieces. He wiped them with his thumbs and bit down on his jaw in an attempt to keep his own at bay.

"We both knew this would happen. We knew that we'd be parted from each other. It's just happened a lot sooner than I'm ready for."

"I'm not ready either." Her voice trembled. Her eyes closed tightly.

"Lacy, look at me." When her eyes met his again he swallowed the lump that had formed in his throat. His face was close enough to hers that he could feel her warm breath. "I will find you, in this life or the next. I promise you that one day we'll be together again."

He leaned in and kissed her on the lips—her warm, soft lips. The lips he would crave for the rest of his days, however he would spend them. He pressed his forehead to hers and closed his eyes. The pain in his chest was too intense to handle, a fire that burned deep into his very soul. The only solace he had through all of this would be the knowledge that she was safe. This was his way to make things right and even though she would hurt from losing him—grieve for him, as he would for her—in time she would heal. Then she would get to live the rest of her life. That was all that mattered.

As for him, he knew where he was going. He'd been there before and survived it. This time it would probably be for eternity, but he knew his sacrifice wouldn't be in vain: he was doing it to keep Lacy safe and at the same time he would find a way to free Evo. Then his best friend would continue on with his life too.

Evo and Michael had fought together, saved each other numerous times. He owed a lot to his buddy. For the short time in which he'd known him, Evo had proved himself to be a true warrior, passionate in his beliefs, and though he worked for the enemy sometimes, he was honorable to his very core. But most of all he was a true friend. If. . . no, *when* Michael freed him, he would ask him to check in on Lacy from time to time. Then, at the very least, Michael could go to his grave—if ever he did—knowing that Evo would keep his word.

The time for stalling was over.

"I want you to promise me something," he said to Lacy as he took both of her hands in his—cringing when he saw the scratches and dried blood on her forearms—while trying to stop the onslaught of emotions that were almost breaking him apart. His voice broke. "Promise me you won't try to find me—to save me. Please."

She inhaled sharply, about to speak, but he placed his finger over her mouth to stop her. "Shhh. Just. . . give me that. I won't survive down there if I thought there'd be a chance of you putting yourself at risk for me. Knowing you are safe is the only thing I need."

He placed his hand on her racing heart. "The pleasure of knowing your heart, no matter how brief, is what will make my memories of our time together stronger. I love you, Lacy, and until we are together," he took a deep, shaky breath, "I will always be here."

She choked back a sob and he felt her pain as his own, like acid stinging through his veins.

"I love you too," she whispered and the last tears fell down her cheeks before her eyes widened and panic overtook her. "NO! Michae—" Her words were cut off and her eyes glazed over before closing. When they flicked back open he knew she was gone, replaced by the blood-red eyes of the cock-sucking demon that would one day pay for putting her through this.

They'd all pay.

He would do whatever it took to exert revenge on Varesh. Whatever the demon had planned for him, he would not make it easy. Knowing the power that Michael seemed to possess now, he would use it against Varesh, and his minions, again and again. And when he was through with them, and after he'd found Evo, he would return to Lacy. It was a promise that he intended to keep.

A sinister laugh crept out of Lacy's mouth in a voice much deeper than her own. Michael shot to his feet. His fists were clenched at his sides as he fought to keep his ever present rage under control. It was something he'd gotten quite used to doing over the last hour.

The door opened and he saw Alethia's head pop around for a minute, he assumed, to check that everything was okay.

"She's gone. Come in. Both of you."

Alethia must have sensed the dejection in his voice because her brows pulled down and she looked upset as she walked over to him. Jaret followed.

"I don't like this at all. Surely there's another way." She looked at Lacy and then back at Michael.

"No," he shook his head. "It has to be like this."

Michael turned to her and placed his hand on her shoulder. It was time for his final goodbyes. He knew the demon would be getting impatient and he didn't want to risk anymore hurt for Lacy.

"Thank you, Alethia. I hope you know how grateful I am that you saved Lacy and me when you did. I'll never forget that." He saw her eyes begin to water and she threw her arms around his neck. He hugged her back and then she pulled away.

Looking down at the floor, she said, "Ahh," then shrugged her shoulder, "It was nothing." She looked at him with a hint of a smile. "I'm glad we met, Michael. And I know I'll see you again soon."

Michael hoped so.

Alethia stepped back. "Oh, hey. . . one more thing," she said as she stood twisting her fingers together, "Give Evo a nice kick in the balls for me when you see him, yeah?"

She was smiling, but Michael knew she was putting it on to try and lighten the mood.

He nodded his head. "Sure."

Michael turned towards Jaret, who stuck out his hand.

He felt sorry that he'd almost killed the guy, but was impressed that Jaret hadn't held it against him. Michael took hold of Jaret's hand and they shook a firm, meaningful shake. "Thank you."

Jaret smiled. "No worries mate. An' if you need anythin'. . ."

"Yeah." Michael smiled back. He would hold him to that. The fact that Jaret could enter Hell whenever he liked might come in handy one day.

Finally, he walked over to Lacy and knelt down in front of her. The demon's eyes looked at him with distaste and it was all he could do not to slap the thing. But instead, he leaned in and placed a kiss on Lacy's cheek. He heard a low growl come from the demon, but ignored it. He knew she was in there. Knew she could probably feel him.

His chest ached at the thought that this might be the last time he'd ever see her. He tried to ignore those blood-red eyes.

He reached up and ran the back of his fingers down the side of her face, then softly whispered, "I love you. . . " only for her to hear as a single tear ran down his cheek.

"Time to go," the demon said. Then all he heard was Lacy's screaming voice before he blacked out.

CHAPTER TWENTY-SEVEN

Michael's eyes opened slowly. His head pounded like he'd overdone it with the liquor the night before. Through his blurry vision he saw an orange glow and followed the light to the far corner of the room. He blinked a couple of times, trying to focus, and when his sight began to clear he noticed there was a silhouette of a man sat in an armchair across the way.

"Finally, you're awake. Thought I was gonna have to come and shake you," a rich, husky voice said.

Michael sat up abruptly, realizing he was in a. . . motel room? He tried to focus his groggy eyes on the large figure.

"Who the hell are you?" he managed to say even though his throat was as dry as a bone. "And where am I?"

"Now. . . is that any way to talk to someone whose just saved your ass? And not for the first time may I add."

"What. . ?" Michael cleared his throat, "what are you talking about?" As he moved to sit up, he gripped his head in his hands as it pounded. *Jeez!* He felt like he'd been hit round the head a few times.

All of a sudden the room came into view as a few candles that were mounted on the walls flared of their own accord, lighting up the stranger and making it easier for his eyes to focus. Thick, blond, wavy hair was slicked back from a rugged face that had a strong, chiselled jaw shaded with stubble. He was dressed in leather trousers and a black turtleneck sweater that showed off the size of his wide shoulders. He looked huge from Michael's vantage point, which he soon realized, was on the floor. The guy had his ankle propped on top of his knee; one arm hooked on the back of the chair and was staring down at him.

He waved his hand casually in Michael's direction. "Uh, Yeah. . . the head thing. That's just temporary. It'll clear soon enough."

Michael shuffled himself back to sit against the wall. With a huff, he said, "Never mind my damned headache. What the fuck's going on?"

The stranger shifted himself forward and propped his arms on his knees. "Relax buddy. And take a look around you before you fly off at me. You might just realize you're not where you should be."

Shit! That's right. This wasn't Hell. His eyes scanned the room, which could have been a motel room but, no. . . the beige carpet was far too clean, and so was the rest of the room by the looks of things. There were a few sconces on the walls, which made Michael wonder about the candles, and dark framed pictures hung randomly from a picture rail. Next to him was a dark wood vanity and across from that was a double bed, also made from heavy dark wood. Now that he thought about it, the furniture looked expensive, antique even.

"I knew the lights would be too bright for you when you finally came to."

Michael looked over at the stranger who used his finger to tap his temple.

"Your head." He used the same finger to point around the room. "That's why the candles," he explained.

Michael lifted his chin in acknowledgement. "Well, what is this place? It doesn't look like Hell, but this could just be one of those damn hallucinations. Yeah. . . that's exactly what this is, isn't it? I'm imagining all of this, aren't I?"

"Nope. All real."

"Right." Michael wasn't convinced. He'd seen how real things could appear in that shit hole of a place so why couldn't this just be the same thing. "Okay. And you are?"

"Here to help," was all he got for a reply from the guy.

"Wait... Okay, I get it... I *am* hallucinating. I'm in some freaky game show where I have to guess the answers to what happens to me next. Right? 'Cos why else would I be sitting here still waiting for answers?" Michael said sarcastically. "Are you gonna start talking?"

The candles flared brighter all of a sudden and Michael looked around the place again. *Definitely not a motel room.* The walls were painted in deep yellow and a small, glass chandelier, which matched the sconces, hung from the ceiling in the middle of the room. Okay, so the candle trick meant that this guy was clearly not human.

"You're still in Garrett, and this house belongs to a friend of mine."

Okay, not quite what Michael meant. "About what the hell's going on here not whose goddamn house this is?"

The stranger sat back in his chair. "I am Raziel, and this is the second time I've pulled you from damnation." He must have seen Michael's surprised expression because he quickly continued. "Yes. I'm the reason you got out the first time, only I wasn't expecting you'd liked it so much to go straight back in there of your own accord."

Michael's eyes widened with shock and confusion. Why did he have no idea? "What *are* you?"

"I suppose you could say I'm your guardian angel."

Silence.

There were times when Michael questioned his own sanity; questioned whether or not his recent experiences had been some sort of distorted reality that only existed inside a troubled mind of a version of himself that was locked up in a padded room. It was easy to think that, given how he'd spent his past year. The many unexplainable things he'd witnessed could all be put down to a misinterpreted reality.

He'd fought demons a plenty, encountered spirits, wraiths—both good and evil, had been to Hell and back.

Literally. But this was the first time he'd ever encountered an angel.

Angel. He repeated it to himself, as if that would somehow make it easier to swallow.

Even after everything he'd been through, he was having a hard time processing the fact that the guy sitting across the room from him, a guy who looked like he was out of some TV show about renegades who ride around on souped up, classic motorcycles, was an actual angel.

All of a sudden an uncontrollable roar of laughter erupted from Michael; the kind of laughter that had you gripping hold of your stomach and wiping tears from your eyes. He noticed a bemused look on the face of the stranger who seemed to be waiting patiently for Michael to compose himself.

"Care to share what you find so funny?"

He finally managed to swallow his amusement and explain his sudden outburst. "It's. . . of all the ways I expected an angel would look, you are not one of them."

The angel huffed. "Glad I amuse you."

"I'm sorry. I mean nothing by it. It's just," Michael shook his head, "if someone had said to me that I would meet a real life angel one day, I'd be expecting long, flowing, white gowns and fluffy wings or something, not a celestial version of Jax Teller."

"Who?"

Michael shook his head. "Never mind."

Raziel seemed to relax a little. "I think I would honestly end things for myself if that was required attire."

Both men, for want of a better word, sat in silence for a few moments. Thankfully Michael's headache had started to ease a little and he was feeling much better. But he needed answers. Why had this angel saved him? Twice?

"You saved me? Why?"

"Because I was ordered to," Raziel replied without hesitation.

"Ordered by whom?"

Raziel just looked at Michael without saying a word. He let out a long sigh and shifted forward in his chair.

"You might want to brace yourself for what I'm about to tell you."

Michael stood up; his head still throbbed a little, but it was almost back to normal. He walked over to the side of the bed near the angel and sat down, feeling a little apprehensive at Raziel's words. "Go on."

What the angel said next, he could never have been prepared for.

"You've never been fully human, Michael." Raziel looked up when he heard Michael's gasp. "Your father was one of us, a warrior of the Creator, or an *angel*. You are a Nephilim: half human/half angel."

Well, that was enough to make a guy want to lose his stomach right here on the nice beige carpet. Michael sat stock still as though someone had hit pause on his remote control. He had no choice but to listen to Raziel as the guy continued.

"There was a war, a long time ago, between Heaven and Hell and some decisions were made by the Creator—the one you call God—that some of my fellow warriors didn't agree with. It caused a division amongst us, eventually leading to a rebellion. Those rebels were due to be cast out for their behavior, but before the Creator could do it, the rebel warriors came to earth and decided to punish him in the worst way possible: by hurting his humans. They raped and murdered, and all because they'd been *branded*. When one of us is about to be punished, and in most cases cast out, we are *branded*, stripped of our powers, though not our strength, before being put on trial before a jury of our leaders.

"A team of elite warriors were sent to retrieve the rebels from here on earth and return them to the Creator who would make them *fall* for their crimes. One of these elite warriors was your father, Samael."

"Shit!" Michael managed to say before swallowing the saliva that was quickly filling his mouth. The news should have been implausible, so why was he not finding it harder to accept what Raziel was saying? "Was my mother raped?"

Raziel shook his head. "No. Your mother helped Samael and he fell in love with her. Some of the women who *were* raped went on to have children. Those Nephilim had defects: they grew to be monsters. Some raped, some murdered and some just simply went insane, but all are dead now.

"But you, Michael. . . you were born out of love. Because of that, your heart is pure."

Michael was stunned beyond all comprehension. Not sure how to process the atomic bombshell that had just been dropped on him. How could this be true? An angel? He was half angel? How is that even possible?

For some strange reason his thoughts went back to that day in the hospital when Jake had shown his face. After he'd gone to get coffee and he'd stopped to check if the lady was okay.

"Are you here for him?" she'd said. *"Please, take good care of him. Look after him until I get there."*

Suddenly, the penny dropped. Her son. . . He'd been close to death. She'd thought Michael had come to take him. He scrubbed his hand over his stubble. Jesus. Had she really thought he was an angel? And how did she know that he—?

"Some people can just sense these things." Raziel answered the question that Michael had only asked in his mind.

Michael straightened. "Can you—?"

"See what's in your mind? Yes."

"Good to know." A pain shot through Michael's left temple and he winced. "Damn. I thought you said this would ease?"

"It will."

Michael pinched the skin at the top of his nose in the hope that it would help. It did a little. Well, it helped with the head pain. He still had that horrible tightness in his chest which seemed to be getting worse.

He thought about his parents. "What happened to them?"

Raziel sat back in his chair and ran his hand through his wavy hair, keeping it off his face. "Your father was punished for his crime, cast out, made to fall. I don't know what happened to him after that, no one does. Your mother never got over losing Samael, and after giving birth to you she killed herself."

Even though he never knew his real parents, Michael couldn't help but feel the loss of them. Growing up, he was always led to believe that he wasn't wanted, and made to live with more people that hadn't wanted him. But he couldn't be too angry about it. After all, he'd lived a life to be proud of. That was until. . .

"So, if I'm half angel, how did I end up like this?" It didn't make any sense.

"After you were born you were protected. We knew, as the only surviving Nephilim and one of pure heart, that you would be hunted," Raziel explained.

"Hunted, why?"

"It has always been said that if you create a life by mixing the DNA of a human with that of an angel then that child, or *Nephilim*, would grow to be extremely powerful. So we took steps to ensure your safety. Your mother named you Gazriel, which is the name your father wanted to give you, but we changed your identity and let you live on earth as a normal human with protection from us. We watched over you."

"And Varesh? Where does he come into this? And do you know he's building an army?"

"Yes. All we know is that he's up to something. We're watching him. Closely."

Michael stood up from the bed and began to pace the length of the room. "Then how did that bitch kill me?" he snapped. It was because of her that he was in this mess; that Lacy and Evo were... *Oh shit!* Evo. How was he supposed to find Evo?

Raziel waited for Michael to calm down before he answered. "*That* we didn't see coming. But once that demon had killed you, your protection didn't work anymore. That meant that every creature, every being that knew about you would be able to find you."

They both sat in silence.

Gazriel.

That was his real birth name. Another memory shot into his mind, this one from further back than the last. The night he'd first met Evo in the alley when he'd saved him from that demon. "*Gazriel!*" it had said before vanishing. That demon had recognized him back then.

Amongst Michael's memories an idea surfaced. If Raziel had saved him twice from Hell, then surely he could save his friend. "What about Evo? Can you..." Michael didn't need to finish his question because when he looked over at the angel, he was already shaking his head. Oh yeah, the mind reading thing.

"It's forbidden for an angel to enter Hell without *falling*. The first time I saved you was an exception: I had help from my superiors, which is rare. The second... I didn't need to go into Hell. I just grabbed you before you got there." Raziel looked at Michael, his gaze sympathetic.

Michael walked back over to the bed and plunked himself down, the temporary hope he'd just felt leaving him as quickly as the air from a deflating balloon.

"Sorry," Raziel said as Michael looked down at the floor. "Besides, where he is, is not an easy place to get to."

Michael's eyes shot back up to his. "You know where he is?"

"Yes. And it's damned unfortunate."

Yes, it was. But not impossible.

He had to get going.

Michael got up from the bed and began to walk towards the door. He paused as he looked at the angel. He at least needed to thank him for saving him twice. He had a feeling this wouldn't be the last time he saw Raziel, but for now he had to leave.

"Thanks," Michael said. He sincerely appreciated what the angel had done. Without him, he'd have never gotten out of the pit the first time, and he'd have never met Evo or Lacy.

Now it was time for *him* to save someone.

The angel cocked a brow at Michael and simply said, "No need. Where will you go?"

Michael smiled. "I'm going to find a way to save my buddy."

EPILOGUE

A biting wind whistled through the tall trees behind Michael as he stood across the dimly lit parking lot of Albert's Grocery Mart watching Lacy pack her shopping bags into the trunk of her car. Nina was about to put the bag that she'd been carrying in there too, until the handle snapped, spilling the contents all over the floor. Both women laughed as they bent to retrieve the scattered shopping as Michael watched from the shadows with a yearning deep in his heart that was inconceivable.

It had been seven days since Raziel, the angel, had pulled him back from the pit, and for every single one of those days Michael had tortured himself over what to do. He'd wanted to go running straight to Lacy, to tell her everything was okay, and that he wasn't in Hell, but something had stopped him.

Finding that he couldn't risk everything he'd fought for, Michael had refrained from contacting her and it had damn near ended him.

Instead, he'd called Alethia.

The deity agreed that what he was doing was right and wanted to help him. He needed to find his friend and to make sure he destroyed Varesh and his minions so they could never hurt Lacy again.

Only then could he return to her.

He had to know she was safe.

As Lacy looked up from her crouch on the floor, he saw a distance in her eyes that hadn't been there before. Behind her smiles was a vacant space that he knew he was responsible for.

But this was how it had to be.

She couldn't know he was back.

"We really should leave," a voice said from behind him, pulling him from his thoughts. Alethia had been patient while he'd observed the woman he now knew he loved. But she was right: the longer he was around Lacy, the more at risk she was.

The deity was taking him to the airport where he would be catching a flight to Cincinnati to meet with an acquaintance of hers. Alethia had found out that there was another hunter in Kentucky, who'd also had a run in with Varesh, and Michael had arranged to speak to him. He knew he couldn't deal with Evo's situation alone with what little information he had, so he needed to cover every angle. Hopefully the guy in Newport would be able to help.

He nodded his head and forced himself to break the intense magnetic force that was holding him to her. Leaving her was the hardest thing he'd ever had to do, but the knowledge of someday returning to her, without any of the danger that would surely follow him now, was the only thing keeping him strong enough to walk away.

He walked towards Alethia's BMW but before he opened the door, he turned to look at Lacy once more.

She was just about to get into her car when her head lifted and she looked over in his direction.

He froze. His heart sank as his eyes met hers. But she wouldn't know it was him under the dark hood he wore. She got in the car and shut the door.

All he could do was watch with tortured anguish as the woman he loved drove away from him.

"I'll be with you soon, Lacy," he whispered.

And vowed to keep the promise that he'd made.

THE END... For now...

ABOUT THE AUTHOR

L.J. Sealey was born and raised in a little Welsh town by the sea. It rains a lot, so she often has a great excuse to sit at her writing desk and while away the hours at her laptop.
She still lives in N.Wales and when she's not travelling around the country working with her husband – who is a professional singer – or singing backup vocals herself, she likes to read and watch her favourite TV shows which normally includes plenty of CSI, The Vampire Diaries and endless amounts of sitcoms.
Being addicted to reading about vampires, demons, shifters and angels, she has always had a thing for all things paranormal and is a big sucker for impossible love stories. So it was inevitable that when she started writing herself, she would mix the two together.

Awaken
is the first book in her new paranormal romance series
Divine Hunter.

Connect with L.J. Sealey

Website: www.ljsealey.com
Facebook: www.facebook.com/authorljsealey
Twitter: www.twitter.com/lj_sealey
Goodreads: www.goodreads.com/ljsealey

Please help us to promote this book by leaving a review on the site of the retailer where you purchased it.

A FIRST LOOK AT
DARK DELIVERANCE: Divine Hunter Book Two
Coming in 2014

PROLOGUE

Denver, Colorado.
January 27th, 1980.

Dawn was near breaking. . .

A woman crouched down behind the lectern at the sanctuary of St Barnabus' church of Latter Day Saints, trembling with fear as the battle continued to rage outside the heavy, wooden front doors. She wrapped one arm around the small swell of her pregnant stomach and prayed like she'd never prayed before.

Just then, the panicked voice she heard, the one that bellowed through the ancient building she'd taken refuge in, made her chest tighten and a strange sense of relief pushed its way through her fear.

"Larissa? Larissa, where are you?" the familiar voice shouted and she heard the heavy footsteps of her Saviour quicken down the aisle.

She rushed to her feet and when she saw him, she couldn't hold back her tears. "I'm here, Samael."

"Larissa!"

She stepped around the lectern and began to rush towards him.

"No!" he shouted. "Stay where you are. I'll come to you."

When he reached her, she gasped at the blood on his face—some by his left temple and some around the right side of his mouth. It was deeper in color than a human's, so deep it was almost black, and it made her legs feel weak to see him in that state.

Her angel.

He crouched down, pulling her with him so they were both now hidden behind the wide, wooden stand. He flung his arms around her, pulling her into his hard body. "Thank the heavens you are safe," he said as he kissed the top of her head.

She closed her eyes as she sank into his embrace. She was still overwhelmed by him, even now. It was hard to believe she'd fallen in love with a beautiful angel, one who loved her back equally, even though their time together had only been brief.

And now she was scared to death; scared for the two of them, and for their unborn child. She knew that she was going to lose Samael. There was nothing they could do to stop it. He'd broken the rules. No angel was allowed to mate with a human. It didn't matter if that angel loved with all his heart as she knew Samael loved her.

The war had started almost three months ago when the angels had come to earth to collect the rebels who were causing mayhem, raping and murdering innocents in a bid to get revenge on the Creator for tightening the rules of how they existed.

Those rebels, when the warriors finally caught up to them, were stabbed with a celestial, iron sword which sent them back to the Creator where they would then be tried and punished for their crimes.

The human race had no idea that the war amongst these divine beings was happening all around them: Angels could not be seen unless they decided to show themselves and that would usually only happen with the rebels while they attacked their prey. They were angry, strong and virile and there was no escaping them, unless, of course you had an angel to look out for you.

Samael had been one of those warriors sent down to clean up the mess and rid the earth of such hostility. He'd kept himself hidden, just like he was supposed to, until he'd seen Larissa being dragged down a dark alleyway. She winced at the memory of that night and how strong her attacker had been. If Samael hadn't appeared from thin air to save her, she'd have been one of those poor victims of the rebels. Samael had stabbed her attacker before the violent male had even realized anyone was there, causing him to disappear in a cloud of white smoke before her very eyes.

Later, Samael had told Larissa things that she couldn't bring herself to believe at first. Angels didn't rape and murder people. Not that she'd really believed that they existed at all, but no bible, no stories had told of such a thing.

After that night, she'd seen the impossibly beautiful angel again when he'd checked in on her to make sure she was still safe. Then again the next night, and the night after that, until two whole weeks had passed and during their time in each other's company, something began to stir between the both of them. After they'd fought hard to keep their feelings for one another in check, one night, in a moment of weakness, they ended up sleeping together. The only night she'd lay with him and it had been the best night of her life, perfect in every way.

Heaven.

Of course, the fact that she'd gotten pregnant didn't help to hide what they had done. From then on the angel, the hunter who had been sent to collect the rebels, had become the hunted.

For the last two months Larissa and her angel had been fugitives. And every day the pull was getting harder for Samael to fight. The Creator was summoning him to return and admit his fate, but he wouldn't and he hid from the warriors that had come to send him back.

Now, they were at the end of the line. Larissa knew she was about to lose him.

My angel.

They both huddled together, and she closed her eyes as he whispered tender words into her ear. Words that made her heart feel as though it were being crushed by an invisible hand.

"I love you, Samael" she whispered.

He pulled back, grabbed her face in his hands and kissed her with such fervor the chaos that ensued around them momentarily disappeared. She allowed herself to imagine that they were safe; that while his lips caressed hers, they were somewhere else, somewhere they could be together in each other's arms forever.

But then the nightmare returned.

The doors to the church slammed open with an almighty thud and Larissa jumped. Samael held her close and she gripped onto him tightly, crying silently into his chest and trembling with the fear of what she knew was about to happen. He'd always said if his brethren ever caught up with him he wouldn't give them the satisfaction of stabbing him. He would leave on his own, and she knew that when she let go, it would be for the very last time.

He knew they'd come for him, knew there was no escaping his fate. They both did.

Samael held her arms, pushing her away a little so that he could look into her eyes. His pale irises were softly glowing, reminding her of when she'd first seen them on their first night together. "I love you too, Larissa. I always will." He placed one hand on her stomach and gently stroked it. "Take care of our child."

She couldn't speak, just nodded as tears streamed down her face and she took his hands in hers.

The heavy footsteps indicated the angels were closing in on them. Samael held Larissa's gaze for one last moment before he rose, bringing her with him and tucking her under his arm.

They stood facing the warriors who were now pacing towards them showing graceful strength. One walked in front of all the others, his wavy, blond hair slicked back from his face. His stare was unwavering as he stood before Samael. "My brother. It is time."

There was no malice in the warrior's voice. In fact, Larissa was sure she saw sorrow in the Angel's eyes.

"Raziel. You know I won't allow you or anyone else to take me." She felt him tighten his hold on her.

"I know Samael. We are just here to see that it's done. I'm so sorry this has happened, my good friend." Raziel slid his gaze to Larissa for a second then back to her angel again.

Samael looked at her; his eyes glistened with what looked like unshed tears. They were glowing brighter now than before. "I am not." He bent his head and met her lips for one last lingering kiss before he stepped away from her and held his arms out to the side. Larissa's heart broke into pieces as she and the other warriors watched Samael become engulfed in bright, white light. Beams shot out from his body, lighting up the whole space.

Then suddenly it was gone.

And so was her angel.

Playlist

Music has a huge influence over my thought process sometimes. I drive for many hours at the weekends, so listening to my favourite playlists while on the road really helps to inspire me with my writing. Here are some of my favourite songs that I listened to a lot while writing *Awaken*:

Sing – Sounds Under Radio
All I Wanted – Sounds Under Radio
Glorious – Muse
When A Heart Breaks – S.O. Stereo
Beauty of The Dark – Mads Langer
93 Million Miles – Jason Mraz
Unintended – Muse
Tighten Up – The Black Keys
Clown – Emile Sandé
All This Time – One Republic
I Was Wrong – Sleeperstar
Distance – Christina Perri
I Know What I Am – Band of Skulls
Unintended – Muse
Down – Jason Walker

Please pay all of these artists a visit and check out their awesome music.

Printed in Great Britain
by Amazon.co.uk, Ltd.,
Marston Gate.